I0672462

Goddess, Awakened

Cate Masters

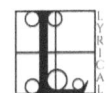

LYRICAL PRESS
Kensington Publishing Corp.
www.kensingtonbooks.com

Lyrical Press books are published by
Kensington Publishing Corp. 119 West 40th Street New York, NY 10018

All Kensington titles, imprints, and distributed lines are available at special quantity discounts for bulk purchases for sales promotion, premiums, fund-raising, and educational or institutional use.

Special book excerpts or customized printings can also be created to fit specific needs. For details, write or phone the office of the Kensington Special Sales Manager:
Kensington Publishing Corp.
119 West 40th Street
New York, NY 10018
Attn. Special Sales Department. Phone: 1-800-221-2647.

First Electronic Edition: July 2014
eISBN-13: 978-1-61650-630-8
eISBN-10: 1-61650-630-X

First Print Edition: July 2014
ISBN-13: 978-1-61650-631-5
ISBN-10: 1-61650-631-8

Printed in the United States of America

With a little help from a goddess, battling evil is a piece of cake for Jocelyn Gibson.

A descendant of the goddess Iris, Jocelyn Gibson may have forgotten about the realm of magic, but it hasn't forgotten her. When Eric Hendricks is targeted by a demon, Joss must step in to battle the evil and save the town's awkward, but endearing, vet...who also happens to be the man she loves.

Joss's new inn, a culinary career specializing in cooking with lavender and a new love all make for a fine recipe of disaster. She needs to embrace her inner goddess and harness the powers she never knew she had before it's too late.

Books by Cate Masters

Rock Bottom
Goddess, Awakened

Published by Kensington Publishing Corporation

To Gary, who always made me feel like a goddess.
Every woman should be so lucky, and demand nothing less.

Chapter 1

In starting her life over, Joss had expected some resistance, even some trouble, but not this. The bedroom floor boards trembled beneath her golden-slippered feet. Tendrils of an unseen power curled upward from deep within the ground, tingling through her toes. She paused to steady herself, then continued to put the finishing touches on her costume. The tremors grew into rumbles and their hum seeped beneath her skin. When their tiny wisps twined through her mind, she clenched her hands. Enough. Go away.

Thick as starlight on a clear summer's eve, sweet as the lavender blossoms she had yet to plant, energy whooshed up through the cracks of the worn wood and out into the October night.

She gripped the bureau until it passed, the vibrations rolling over her in lessening waves. Bubbly, effervescent waves. "Third time tonight, Taz." Each departure took longer, and more of the essence remained.

When the dog whined, she stroked his fur. "Don't worry, it won't hurt you."

Even if tonight the waves were palpable enough to make her hairs stand on end. *Oh, no, please.*

Nothing could ruin tonight. More than a party, this event would determine her future. And after three years of grief, she'd never allow anything to trap her in its clutches again.

Joss adjusted the golden leaves in her honey-colored hair. Amazingly still in place, her boring shoulder-length locks swept into a passable French twist. Relief escaped in a laugh. "Good thing. I can't spend another hour transforming myself."

On a tight budget, the cream top and skirt cinched with a golden scarf, and bronze eye shadow and lipstick sufficed to complete her outfit.

Her new neighbors would start arriving soon. Or so she hoped, if they'd accepted her invitation to the Halloween party.

Taz tilted his head, and she patted it. "I know. Some golden goddess, huh?" *Way to make a first impression.* No goddesses in mythology books were middle-aged. At least, none she remembered anyway. Maybe a few widows among them, the status adding to their power. But not her. After John died, she'd struggled for three years to gather herself together, move her life forward, sell her home, and buy this old bed and breakfast to renovate into an inn. A chance to surround herself with people, make herself useful. Needed.

The dog whipped his head toward the window, then ran and stood against the sill to yip.

Drawn by what appeared in the fields beyond, Joss followed. "Shh," she whispered, half afraid to disturb them. Or call attention to herself.

Tiny flickering lights bobbed and weaved in the darkness. Too late in the year for fireflies, but if anyone mentioned the unusual activity, she might pawn that off as the excuse, though she knew better. Had known the truth her entire life.

"They must feel the energy too." As usual, they probably discerned her presence as deeply as she did theirs. Awed by the sheer number of them, she watched in silence. What had gotten into her, planning a Halloween party? On All Hallow's Eve, the one night when spirits stirred from beyond. When invisible doors between realms opened and allowed normally dormant beings, both light and dark, to return to this world. The very sort of weirdness she'd spent the last two decades trying to keep out of her life.

Headlights flashed across the back field as a car swung down the long driveway, erasing the flickering glow.

Joss squared her shoulders. "Too late now. It's already begun."

The foreboding words chilled Joss, though it began long before tonight. She'd known the first day she'd set eyes on the property in September by the still-vibrant gardens, filled with flowers that should have gone to seed by then. More importantly, it resonated in her bones. Beneath this ground. And *they* visited nearly every night.

She shook off her wariness. "Let's go. It's probably Annie." Her friend had already spent all day preparing the tempting treats for the party.

With a *woof,* Taz led the way down the hall, Joss close behind his long, fringed tail. He nosed open the swinging door to the kitchen. By the time she peered out the back door, the car's trunk had popped open. Annie climbed out, flew to the back, and loaded containers into her arms.

Joss hurried outside. "Hey Annie, let me help."

"Great." Annie stacked trays in her arms and smiled at the dog trotting past toward the field. "Hello to you, too, Mr. Taz."

"He's on a mission." For the second time, her own words hit hard. Did her dog commune with them? He seemed drawn to the fields whenever they appeared.

"So am I." Annie cackled with a definite witchy air.

At the sight of the myriad of food containers and aluminum warmers, Joss halted, uncertain where to start. "You've outdone yourself. We'll have enough to feed the entire town."

Her friend worked efficiently, lining up everything on the counter, then lighting the sterno beneath the warming trays. Joss could almost believe Annie's witch outfit wasn't a costume, but instead revealed her true magic as a chef.

"That's the idea." Annie kept working as she spoke. "Reel 'em in tonight and dazzle their taste buds so they'll fill up our dinner calendar for the rest of the year."

Her friend nailed it. The inn—and Joss—depended on tonight's success. "Tell me what I can do."

"Besides charming our guests?" Annie gave her a quick once-over. "Love the costume, by the way."

A humorless laugh burst out. Hopefully, she could contribute more than charm, otherwise the inn was doomed. "Yours, too. I'll do my best to be a hostess goddess, but before anyone arrives, I'm going to make myself useful. Put me to work."

Pausing, Annie aimed her steadfast grin at Joss. "We're going to make this work, you know."

A sudden lump in her throat prevented Joss from answering. Instead, she nodded.

In three steps, Annie stood in front of her, hands clasping her shoulders. "We will."

"I know. At least the kitchen's in good shape." Unlike the rest of the house. Joss couldn't help thinking of the mountain of work ahead.

"Okay, so the inn's a fixer-upper." Annie shrugged. "You knew that going in. We'll remake this old Victorian into the gem of Boiling Springs. Right?"

She drew Annie into a quick embrace. "I love you."

"I love you too, hon. Now, grab a pair of oven mitts and carry those servers into the dining room. People will be arriving soon."

Shaking off the gloomy mood, she set to work. After relocating the third tray of food, Joss returned to the kitchen.

"I almost forgot." Annie rummaged in her handbag and drew out a disc. "Pop this CD in the player. Not exactly "Monster Mash," but it'll set a spooky mood."

"Great. I tried to find some suitable music, but wasted too much time searching through boxes. I have to finish unpacking." Joss hurried to the front parlor and inserted it into the stereo. Strains of a crisp violin solo filled the room, a haunting melody she could easily imagine hearing through the misty forests of Transylvania. Right before the vampire attack. *Perfect.*

Humming along, she double-checked the beverage setup. She didn't mind the peeling wallpaper or the cobwebs in the corner so much anymore. They set a great atmosphere. And like tonight, would soon be a memory. Starting her life over might present a challenge, but Joss intended to give it a hell of a try.

The first chime of the doorbell caused her stomach to flutter. "Oh, dear."

A *squee* echoed from the kitchen and grew louder as Annie flew to her side in such a rush, the resulting breeze twirled the paper bats strung along the ceiling. Flashing two thumbs up, she jerked her head toward the front door. "Let them in. We're ready."

Ready as Joss would ever be. She mustered a smile and froze it there, then marched to the foyer. A quick check in the mirror, a primp of the scarlet and black flowers on the table below it, and she inhaled deeply, set a smile on her face and opened the door. "Happy Halloween."

For three years, her dog Taz had been her main companion, but now strangers arrived in waves. Costumed as witches and vampires, cowboys and clowns, guests meandered through the front room as more entered.

Remember, be the goddess hostess. She widened her smile. "Welcome to Lavender Hill Inn. Please help yourself to refreshments in the dining room."

Passing with a nodded hello, they formed a polite line to the food table. Some wandered across the foyer to the front room again, clutching their drinks, eyeing the door as if ready to bolt. That is, when they weren't eyeballing the worn carpeting or the dim light fixtures straining to eke out a glow. Or scrutinizing her. Most of them probably came to ogle the woman foolish enough to buy the broken-down B and B.

She forced herself to the center of the parlor. "I'm Jocelyn Gibson. I'm so happy you've joined our celebration tonight. Please let me know if you need anything."

No response, not even the chirp of crickets. *That reminds me.* She needed a brass one for the hearth. For luck. Too bad she hadn't bought one in time for the party. The silence of two dozen guests grew unnerving. "Isn't the food delicious? Annie Wilkens is a magician in the kitchen." Nods. *Whew, an ice breaker. Well, maybe an ice cube.* Everyone in town knew Annie, a lifelong Boiling Springs resident. Joss counted herself lucky the day they'd met at middle school summer camp, a friendship more solid than any she'd known despite attending different schools in neighboring towns.

Crumbs lined an older man's lips as he chewed. "Is she your cook now?"

"Yes, Annie's the chef for Lavender Hill Inn."

Sitting on the wingback chair, he grunted. "I like the pulled pork she makes for our summer festival."

Joss clasped her hands. "She has some fantastic menus planned."

Hushed *ohs* rippled through the room.

"I can't wait for you to try them. After we finish renovating, of course." She wondered if her facial muscles would give out trying to maintain a cheery expression.

Conversations began in muted tones, then grew louder. Joss strolled around the room, offering to refill drinks, fetch more food. Anything to keep busy.

The doorbell chimed, and Joss excused herself from her guests. She pulled open the door and slumped in relief. "Aunt Lydia. Thank goodness." If anyone could enliven the party, it was her.

Her aunt entered with a flourish. A silken orange and red skirt and shawl set off her auburn hair. She swept past Joss, then halted abruptly, palms open to the air, eyes wide as she circled the foyer. She stopped long enough at the entryway to the front room, then the dining room, to scan inside with a look of concentration and awe.

Joss braced herself. Lydia must sense it too. The undeniable vibrations sizzling up from the earth.

As if she hadn't noticed Joss before, her aunt's loud greeting carried across the foyer. "Jocelyn, my dear." Lydia rushed toward her with open arms and crushed her against her ample bosom, then held her at arm's length. "I'm not late, am I?" Her aunt relived her theater days in any crowd.

"No, you're right on time." To save this party from an early death. Her aunt had offered to give readings, certain to entertain some people.

Lydia's hands went to her heart when she noticed the grandfather clock. "You kept it. I'm so glad."

"I'll never part with it." How could she? Hand carved by her grandfather for Gram, it displayed the correct time, but never chimed the right hour. Not since… The realization struck. *Since I married John and turned my back on them.* And, her family had accused, real love.

"Darling, when you first told me about your purchase, I thought you'd gone mad. Buy a ramshackle bed and breakfast? But oh"—Lydia clasped her hands, her smile self-assured—"now that I'm here, I know."

"It doesn't look like much now, but some refinishing will make the inn good as new." Glimpsing the sagging wallpaper, Joss withheld a wince. "Well, almost."

Leaning close, her aunt murmured, "The energy drew you here. It's palpable. You must be careful. Others will be drawn here seeking to tap into its force too."

A curious warning. "What do you mean?"

Trembling, Lydia grabbed Joss's arm tight.

This was no act. "What's wrong?"

Closing her eyes, Lydia moaned. "Oh, it's…overwhelming."

"What is?" In alarm, Joss squeezed her aunt's quaking hand. "Aunt Lydia? Is something wrong?"

As the door opened, Lydia opened her eyes. Gusts of warm wind blew inside, gaining in intensity. They riffled through the black and scarlet flowers on the foyer table, danced with the candlelight until it flickered, and whirled the paper decorations.

The grandfather clock began to chime, echoing like gongs through the entryway. Shimmering white lights swarmed inside and filled the room. They played across the walls and ceiling as if reflecting a thousand tiny mirrors.

Or like a flock of glowing wild creatures breaking in to wreak havoc.

The fae. It took Joss's breath away to see them enter her home. Only once before had she witnessed such an event. The grandfather clock struck again and again. Was she imagining it, or did the chimes grow louder?

The shining figures flew everywhere, though no one else appeared to notice. Except for Taz, who pricked his ears and trotted along with the shining display, barking happily.

From the dark porch, a man in black emerged and stood in the foyer. Behind the matching eye mask, his gaze darted to follow the lights. He pushed the door shut and the air stilled. The shimmering figures flocked to the windows in the front room and disappeared.

On the last strike of the clock, everything returned to normal.

"Seven o'clock," Joss murmured. The right time.

"Him." Lydia's husky voice ground out the word.

Joss didn't need her aunt to tell her this man was different than most. Since moving into the B and B two weeks ago, she'd found herself repeatedly drawn to the window for another reason besides the fae—the veterinary practice across the road. A cloud of emotions roiled above his house like a summer storm, a confusing swirl of auras: grief and longing, anger and loneliness. All emanating from the man who owned the property.

Eric Hendricks. A widower, Annie had told her. Handsome enough to be a movie star, but ruined, she'd warned, by his wife's tragic loss. He never socialized. People said his curt manner was an unfortunate side effect of grieving.

Annie was dead-on about his looks. Through the black eye mask, Eric's steely glance pierced Joss's, his brow furrowed beneath a tangle of dark hair. His intense assessment shocked her to a halt, electrifying as a Taser to her nervous system. He walked toward Joss in what seemed like altered time. Capturing her gaze, his gait slowed. Heat twined through her like a wisp of smoke above smoldering embers, crackling to life.

She wasn't ready for that type of burn yet.

* * * *

Such a fool. Eric should have dressed the part—clown, jester, harlequin. In the plain black outfit, he probably appeared more conspicuous rather than less. He was clueless about how to assemble a costume. The cheap face mask had caught his eye on a quick stop to the pharmacy for vitamins, and he'd tossed it in with the other items without thinking.

Everything leading up to this moment, in fact, he'd done without thought. He'd simply gotten dressed and driven here as if he'd planned to, when he had no intention of attending. Costume parties made him uncomfortable. Even at regular parties without a disguise, his throat grew dry, his brain function slowed, and appropriate replies occurred to him long after the conversation ended. Yet here he was, standing in the foyer of the bed and breakfast, awkward as a teenager at the prom.

In utter contrast, there stood his new neighbor Jocelyn Gibson, angelic in creamy white and gold. Looking at him with wonder and surprise. Probably thinking him a lunatic. He'd glimpsed her a few times in passing the old place. What would make a single woman want such a Victorian horror? Perfect for Halloween, at least.

Inhaling a reinforcing breath, Eric moved stiffly in her direction. A few minutes, he'd stay. No longer. Then he'd slip out, he hoped with less fanfare than he'd arrived.

Strange. The gust of wind had come on unexpectedly. Swept up the fireflies from outside and carried them into the house, swarming in front of him like a glimmering cloud. Everywhere else in the area, fireflies died out weeks ago. Around the inn, they concentrated every night. Funny, no one but Jocelyn Gibson and the woman standing beside her seemed to notice. And the border collie mix.

To his dismay, she glided toward him. Paralyzed by nerves, he could only stare as she approached. Candlelight caught the gilded leaves woven through her hair, the golden chains at her wrists. Her white tunic, leggings and split skirt revealed enough of her curves to tantalize him to distraction.

A few steps away, she halted. "You're here."

Even in the dim light, she had a glow about her.

"You're luminous." He snapped his mouth shut to stem the flow of any more errant thoughts.

Rose tinged her golden face. "It's the glitter makeup. You're Dr. Hendricks, aren't you?"

"Right. Eric." Tonight, he wished he were someone else. A man with no history who could start fresh, not mired in the past.

"It's good to meet you. I'm Joss Gibson."

He searched for something witty to say, something to ease the awkwardness. In the five years since his wife's accident, the most he'd said to a woman was hello. They'd already covered that.

"Everything looks great." Except for the woman in the short white dress covered with bright red hearts. Staring at him. Wait, wasn't she the diner waitress, Sheree? What the hell was she supposed to be, a clown?

Lifting her chin, Joss smiled. "Tonight's party is kind of a last hurrah for the old girl before we start renovations."

"Oh." He'd never been one for small talk, and never was the fact more painfully obvious to him than now.

Joss's smile wavered. "You don't approve?"

"It's not that." Right now, he approved of most everything about her.

Before he could explain, the tall, older woman reappeared next to Joss. Her auburn hair fought the red of her lips, pursed as her gaze cut into him with sharp assessment. She gave a *tsk*, and in a throaty voice, said, "Oh, my."

Joss shot her a warning glance. "Aunt Lydia, this is Dr. Eric Hendricks."

"Doctor." Her aunt's tone caressed the word like a favorite pet.

He extended his hand. "A veterinarian. Nice to meet you."

Encasing his hand in hers, she turned it over and traced a finger across the center of his palm. "Oh, yes. Come with me." Turning, she tugged him through the crowd.

With Frankenstein steps, he rigidly followed. Glancing back at Joss gave him no reassurance. Frowning, she might have been irritated with him or her aunt, he couldn't tell.

They passed underneath paper bats fluttering from the hallway ceiling. Small carved pumpkins leered at him with crooked fiery smiles from atop book shelves.

Sheree turned as he passed. "Eric? Where are you going?"

Good question. It seemed futile, but he had to ask. "Where *are* we going?"

"The future awaits those who dare to seek it," Lydia said over her shoulder.

Future? His life had ground to a halt five years ago.

Near a small wooden table holding cards and a candle, she dropped his hand and plopped onto the chair. "Please sit." She waved toward the chair opposite, scooped up the cards and handed them to him.

A sigh and he sat. Might as well. Cooperating would at least hurry this along so he could disappear into the crowd again. Or out the door.

"Clear your mind and shuffle the cards." She gestured toward the deck.

He did as she asked and set them on the table.

"Fan them out," she said, "and then select five cards."

Surely, she didn't intend for him to take this seriously. He slipped five from the rest. "I don't—"

"Shhh." Concentrating on the cards as she laid them out, her eyes widened.

At her audible gasp, he leaned closer. "Something wrong?" He tilted his head to read their titles: The Tower. Judgment. The Fool. The Lovers. The Moon.

Lydia nodded like a statue of a coin-fed fortune-teller. "Oh." She leaned closer. "Oh, my. Most unusual."

He tensed. "What?" What sort of trickery was she up to?

Her voice softened. "You've been through an ordeal. Rest assured your loneliness will soon end. Great happiness awaits after a terrible trial."

His gut churned. "You don't know what you're saying." The accident ripped his happiness away when it took Karen. Nothing could be worse than that.

Cate Masters

"Of course, I do. I'm never wrong." Lydia's gaze slid to the room's entrance.

Joss spoke with Charlie Fulton dressed in painter's overalls. Some costume. But then, next to her, anyone would appear silly.

Lydia rested her palms against the table. "Tonight is a fateful night."

The ominous statement settled over him like a mist. Fate had never been kind to him before. "Why?"

She leaned forward, candlelight sparking in her brown eyes. "Your life is on the verge of great change toward a destiny you cannot avoid. Finding your true soul mate." She spoke as if revealing a great secret.

The words pierced his heart. "No."

"Oh, yes. The cards indicate it here." She splayed her hands across the cards.

A parlor trick, nothing more. A reminder he didn't need. "I have to go."

Pushing away from the table, he strode to Joss, who poured green liquid into the punch bowl. He'd approached her with the intention of bidding her good night and getting the hell out of there. Instead, he asked, "What is that?"

After ladling some into a glass, she held it up. Wisps of smoke curled up from the drink. "Taste it and find out."

More than the drink tempted him. "It looks dangerous." But its citrus scent enticed him. His fingers closed around hers, and the tiniest jolt sparked through his hand, like deadened tissue reanimated.

Alarm crossed her face as she slipped her hand away. "Appearances can be deceiving."

Did she know his costume hid a damaged man? Wincing, he sipped. His taste buds danced in delight at the refreshing fizzy liquid.

Her focus concentrated on his mouth and her smile returned. "Good, isn't it?"

Unlike his evening. The way she watched him drink unsettled him. Awakened parts of him that, for the last five years, languished in a numbing, deep freeze. The shock of returning to life overwhelmed him. "Your aunt shouldn't play at things she doesn't know." Neither should he. This woman was obviously out of his league.

Her shoulders stiffened. "My aunt does know. She's been reading tarot and palms since I was a girl." She turned the corner and disappeared down the hall.

Now he'd insulted her family. He had to make her understand. Following, he caught her arm. "She shouldn't meddle. Not where people's private lives are concerned." Her silky softness invited his touch. He became sharply aware of every detail about her. A loose strand of hair flowing against the graceful curve of her neck. Hazel eyes ablaze with a fire he couldn't fathom, but ignited sparks, surging along his veins like a lit fuse. Every impulse urged him to press her against the wall and taste her golden skin. Explore her curves.

Her lips parted and hovered open for blissful seconds. "I'm sorry."

Her whisper hit him like a gale-force wind. It broke whatever spell he was under, and he stepped back. "No. I am." *For coming here.* Jesus, what the hell was wrong with him, grabbing her like that?

A glance to the other room revealed her aunt staring with an odd expression. Pity? Self-satisfaction?

He couldn't get away fast enough.

Outside, he ripped away the mask and let it fall to the ground as he climbed in his truck. A fateful night, the aunt said. The only thing tonight portended was more social disaster. A destiny he seemed doomed to relive over and over.

Chapter 2

The sting remained with Joss long after Eric fled the inn. Deep-rooted pain emanated from him when he'd first entered, and his palm against her arm sent an electric shock straight to her bones. The poor man. Grief kept him its prisoner. Joss understood how easy it was to fall into that dark trap. The way he'd held her, he sought escape. Comfort.

He awakened deep-seated sensations in her. In the few moments with him, she'd felt more alive than she had in three years.

So strange. Normally, one look allowed her to see the person inside. With Eric Hendricks, her receptivity went into overload. His soul, pent up for years, stirred to life and churned up love, fear, joy, hopelessness, yearning, jumbled and shifting faster than light. He displayed great strength in his firm stance and gentle touch. Beneath a hard veneer of sheer pain, one other trait came through clearly—purity of spirit, and integrity enough for many men.

The arrival of more guests drew Joss to the foyer again. Another matronly witch and an older man wearing a checked flannel shirt, jeans, and boots stepped inside, followed by a princess and a boy in a fabric turtle shell.

Joss recognized the girl as one of the riders whose horse was boarded at the inn's stable. After greeting them and pointing them toward refreshments, she returned to Lydia. "Sorry about Dr. Hendricks."

"Don't apologize. It's wonderful you have so many guests." Lydia fingered the flowers in the vase on the table.

One woman stood in the archway to the front room, her bright-eyed glare directed at Joss. Wearing a short white shift adorned with large red hearts, the woman held a wand topped with a glittering red heart.

Confused by the woman's malevolence, Joss approached and fought to overcome the negativity oozing from her. "Did you try some of the booscotti?"

The woman tilted up her chin. "I'm not hungry, Mrs. Gibson," came her familiar nasal reply.

Recognition finally hit. Of course—the girl who worked at the diner in town. "Sheree?"

At her curt nod, Joss forced a smile. "I love your costume."

Sheree's gaze darted her length. "Likewise."

What could be her problem? The woman wielded her wand like a weapon, ready to strike. "Please have a drink and make yourself at home."

"Thank you." Her narrowed eyes swept the room as if suspecting an ambush, and then she moved stiffly away.

Joss crossed the room to Lydia. "That was weird."

Lydia whispered, "Be careful of her."

"Sheree? I can't imagine why." Could she be nervous the inn would take away some of the diner's business? Though Joss would have liked to think it was the cause of her strange behavior, Sheree's vibes told Joss otherwise. Business had nothing to do with it. The waitress directed her bad juju at Joss personally. Had Joss unintentionally insulted Sheree? She'd barely met the woman.

Leaning close, her aunt spoke sternly, "I warned you to watch for others who seek the power of this place."

Sheree? Her aunt must be mistaken. The woman's terrible attitude resulted from something. Maybe an imagined slight? Joss would find a way to put Sheree at ease.

More guests entered, and Joss excused herself. She left Lydia deeply inhaling the air. Joss couldn't deny the charged atmosphere was one of the reasons she'd bought the place. Not to tap into any lines of power for herself, but maybe to enhance the lavender field she planned. Joss needed the garden to thrive so the inn would as well.

Waving to the costumed guests arriving, she recognized Tom Larsen in his jodhpurs and riding jacket. The stable manager set her nerves on edge. He spoke too harshly to the horses, and they rebelled at his touch by tossing their heads and pinning their ears. Unfortunately, her opinion about Tom held no weight. The boarders chose their trainer based on their personal needs.

"Welcome." Joss extended her hand. "I'm glad you could come."

He grunted. "Where's the bar? Drinks are free, right?"

She pointed him toward the refreshments table. "Of course." Tonight they wouldn't make any money to cover their expenses. The value would be in gaining recognition for the great food. Already, Annie's werewolf cupcakes, booscotti and goblin cheese balls had practically vanished.

To her relief, the arrival of a cowboy and cowgirl nudged Tom ahead. Following, Joss welcomed a princess and prince, a jester and wench, and two clowns.

"Jocelyn." Down the hall, Aunt Lydia waved furiously.

"What is it? Shh, Taz." The fur on his neck stood up, and the dog growled beside her. What had gotten into him tonight? Maybe the same thing that had bothered Eric Hendricks. She sent a rueful glance toward the door the veterinarian had slammed on his way out earlier.

"The question is who," Lydia said. "The man standing with the Queen of Hearts. Or princess, whatever she is."

Following her aunt's gaze, Joss froze in skin-crawling fear. "I don't know who he is. And I don't want to."

He moved like a shadow, furtive and with the dizzying illusion he was underwater. Beneath his black face mask, red flashed in his eyes. When his gaze passed over her, so did a wave of nausea. Her heart flipped, and her stomach churned as if she rode a roller coaster through the dark, not knowing where the turns lay ahead.

The dog growled more fiercely. Grabbing hold of his collar, Joss gasped. "I wish that...*person* would just leave." Maybe not a person at all, but something much darker.

She reached deep inside for the force of her heart. *Go!*

A deep rumble shook the ground. The windows rattled in their frames. Guests cried *oh!* and clutched at their chairs or one another.

"Not again." Joss wished the disturbance would stop, and it faded away.

Lydia rushed toward Sheree, now standing alone. "Where did he go?"

Hot on her aunt's heels, Joss wondered the same thing.

"I have no idea." Sheree held a hand to her head. "I don't feel well."

Taz sniffed at the waitress tentatively, cringing as if she might strike him.

Arching a brow, Lydia said, "I imagine you wouldn't. You should not dabble in darkness until you understand the risk. What did it say to you?"

"It?" Joss asked in alarm, and searched the crowd to be sure the man didn't linger there.

Sheree held a hand to her stomach. "I think I'm going to be sick."

"You should leave." Lydia pointed to the door. "Now."

"Yes. I need to go home." Sheree headed for the foyer.

"Please Lydia, she was a guest." Joss knew the man with her wasn't. Her aunt had confirmed he wasn't a town resident, nor even of this world. "What's going on?"

Tugging her to the end of the hall, Lydia said, "You could be in danger, my dear."

"I don't understand." Yet somehow, she knew it was true.

Lydia's shoulders slumped. "I must call your grandmother. It's time you knew."

"Knew what?" What was her aunt going on about?

"Your family heritage." Taking out her cell, Lydia's nails clicked the screen.

* * * *

Driving down Yellow Breeches Road, Sheree cursed. *I hate this town. Why don't they put street lights on these back roads?* Her head still spun, and so did her stomach. The gusty wind blew so many leaves against her windshield, she switched on the wipers. "I want to move someplace warm."

A man's deep chuckle echoed. "We can arrange it." The voice came clear and distinct, but who the heck had spoken?

Screeching, Sheree hit the brakes and skidded to a stop. "Who's there?" Pain pulsed through her head. Had she imagined the whole thing?

A black figure materialized outside the car, barely discernible in the darkness.

The man she'd spoken to earlier slipped inside. "*Tsk.* Forgot me already?"

She'd like to. Tiny pinpricks crawled across her skin, and she shuddered. She'd never seen a costume make a person appear to shift through the shadows. He probably wasted a fortune on the thing.

"Hold on there, bud. Do you think you can just invade someone's car?" Sheesh. Talk to a guy for one minute at a party, and he assumed he could take liberties.

As if bored, he sighed. "The question is, how badly do you want your veterinarian friend?"

She should demand this guy vamoose. He seriously gave her the creeps. "What do you care?" How did he know anyway?

He hooked an elbow behind the seat. "I don't. Except I might be able to help you. If you help me."

Sure, there was always a catch. She could never get a break, not unless she forced one. "Help how?"

"Which? Help you or help me?" he prodded.

"Both." Her patience waned. Tired and queasy, she wanted to go to bed. This guy frightened her, but if he could help her get Eric, she'd at least hear him out.

"The gentleman for whom I work is interested in the property we visited. If you could distract Dr. Hendricks, my employer would have a better chance at gaining control."

Would Mrs. Gibson sell so soon? Oh…she might, if the situation grew too uncomfortable. Sheree had noticed the gleam in Joss's eyes when she looked at Eric. A gleam Sheree wanted to turn to ice. "Control? You mean buy the inn?"

With a smug smile, the man said, "Something like that."

Get to the fine print. "So what would I need to do?"

He spoke with a casual air. "Become our ally. Report to us on the goings-on of the town. Especially the inn and its proprietress."

No harm in spying on her, right? Somehow it sounded too easy. "What's it have to do with me and Eric?"

When the man smiled, the air in the car grew hot. And smelled like something burning. Something awful, like rotten eggs.

"Let's leave that to my employer and me, shall we?" he sneered, easing closer.

Sheree's vision blurred. She fought to murmur, "I don't know."

Red flashed in his eyes like flames. "Of course you do. You want Eric so badly, you'll do anything. Won't you?"

An urge came over her, compelling her to answer. "Anything."

"I thought so." His voice trailed into a hiss.

Gripping the steering wheel, Sheree touched her forehead to it. "Anything."

"Excellent. One note of caution. If anyone asks, never mention me or my employer or this agreement."

She snapped her head up. "Who'd care? Other than Mrs. Gibson?"

"If the need for you to know arises, you will."

Sheree didn't even care. She just wanted this guy out of her car sooner rather than later. She imagined walking hand-in-hand with Eric, him stopping to pull her close, bending to touch his lips to hers.

A knock on the window startled her.

A state trooper stood outside.

"Great." She opened the window, her mind racing with possible excuses.

His grimace filled with suspicion. "Everything all right, miss?"

"Yes, officer. I'm a bit dizzy. Nothing serious." *Stupid!* Now he'd think she was drunk.

Straightening, he sighed. "Right. Step out of the car please."

"Both of us?" How would she explain this guy to a policeman? Her passenger's appearance went way beyond any Halloween costume. She didn't even know his name, for crying out loud.

The officer crouched again and scanned the interior. "Pardon?"

"Do you want us both to get out?" She gestured to the passenger side and froze.

The seat was empty.

* * * *

A knock echoed through the hall. Joss rushed to the front door. Another great gust of wind ruffled the scarf of the woman standing on the threshold. Diminutive, yet she projected a force to reckon with, her sapphire eyes sparkling as she assessed Joss with a loving smile. Short hair framed her face in layers, mostly gray but still a hint of blond.

"Gram. How did you get here so quickly?" Delighted, Joss hugged her.

The last party guest departed minutes earlier, followed by Annie. Her grandmother must have left her Solebury home immediately after speaking to Lydia. A two and a half hour drive, and one she'd rarely endeavored during Joss's marriage due to John's disapproval of the family's magical practices.

Now Gram stepped inside without hesitation. "I needed to see for myself if Lydia exaggerated about this wonderful inn." Her authoritative tone clipped the air.

"And? What do you think?" Expectation hung thick as Joss waited.

"Her description didn't quite capture its splendor." A gleam lit Gram's eyes. "Or its intenslty. I've never experienced such powerful vibrations."

"Neither have I." Every day, its undercurrent infused her consciousness more. Life had grown dark after her husband John died three years ago. Every day, the sunlight had dimmed, and every night, the shadows blacker. Their silky depths had beckoned. Bits of her soul had wanted to follow John, to pass through the dark curtain and into his arms again. If not for Taz, Joss might have allowed herself to melt into those murky shadows.

After moving to the inn, her haze of grief dissipated to unveil colors more vivid than she'd remembered. Their brilliance breathed new life into her too. Gram would call it a good sign. Before coming here, her life ran short of those. Joss finally had turned that around.

Removing her coat, Gram said, "Certainly explains your uninvited guests tonight."

"Yes, the biggest surprise of the evening." She caught Lydia's wide-eyed glance at Gram. "Lydia says you have more to tell me."

Gram came to her side, her hazel eyes clear. "Are you sure you're ready?"

Probably not, but putting things off never helped. "Yes."

Gram winked at Lydia. "I think we need margaritas."

"I sure do." Lydia headed for the kitchen.

"That must be why I bought fresh limes today." At the farmer's market earlier, Joss had picked some up automatically, as she sometimes did when intuition kicked in.

"Excellent." Linking her arm through Joss's, Gram led her on.

Not that Joss needed further encouragement. "Please, Gram. I can't bear to wait."

Her grandmother patted Joss's arm. "Do you remember when you were seven?"

"Vaguely." Her childhood came back in a blur, fantasy mixed with reality. Her dolls had been fairy princesses riding unicorns. Dogs and cats weren't mere family pets but dignified servants of fae royalty.

Gram smiled. "You were a special girl. You still are exceptional, of course, but as a child, your innocence was pure, and you believed without questioning."

Believing. Joss knew where this was headed. "Yes, I had quite the imagination."

"Call it what you will. You were favored, and still are. Because of your heritage."

Casting a skeptical glance, Joss sat on the kitchen stool. "Oh, Gram."

With a wicked grin, Lydia dropped the last of the ice cubes into the blender. "It's high time you acknowledged it, Jocelyn." Pressing the machine's button eliminated the opportunity to argue over the loud whir. Once the mixer reduced the ice to shards, Lydia added the triple sec and tequila.

"What does it mean, exactly?" Joss asked. "I'm some sort of fairy princess?"

Rimming a glass with salt, Lydia tilted her head. "Not a princess."

"Not even a half-blood." Gram filled the glass and handed it to Joss.

For fortitude, she sipped. "All right. Let's have it."

Gram clinked her glass to Joss's. "Do you remember the stories about Iris?"

"Yes, those were always my favorites." Strange, Iris featured so prominently in the family history even though she lived centuries ago. "I thought she died in her mid-thirties." Younger than Joss by almost a decade.

Lydia settled on the bar stool beside her. "The family fudged her story to cover up the truth."

After sipping, Gram said, "Iris left the mortal world to fulfill her duty." The *mortal* world? It sounded more like a fairy tale. "Which was?"

Gram and Lydia exchanged a serious look before Gram said, "To act as a bridge between earth and the other realm."

"What about her mortal marriage?" Joss couldn't believe the ease with which the strange words slipped from her mouth.

Lydia sighed. "Her family never recognized the union."

"Didn't Iris love her husband?" She couldn't recall his name. Must be the tequila kicking in. Not enough, so she sipped more.

"Very much," Gram said. "She was bound by duty and left him to raise their daughter alone."

"She left her child?" The thought astounded her. How tragic. She could relate, having only been nineteen years old when Mom left. Joss had married the year before at the tender age of eighteen, but still felt abandoned. Especially since her dad had died soon after.

"Because of Iris's lineage," Gram continued, "her descendants rightfully deserved certain privileges. Protection, for one."

Lydia tapped a nail on the counter. "Their protection has carried down through generations."

"To me?" Joss couldn't quite grasp the concept.

Gram swept her hand in the air. "To every member of our family."

"What about Mom?" Joss gasped. "Where did she disappear to?"

"She didn't want to leave you," Gram said. "I assured her we would look after you." She leveled a serious look at Joss. "You understand she had no other option. They'd already killed your father."

Joss's breath escaped her. "What? No. Dad died after a massive heart attack. Everyone said so. Every one of you." They'd lied. Betrayed her.

"We couldn't tell you then." Gram's voice strained with emotion.

Lydia grew more somber. "Your mother left this world to draw focus away from you. She hoped your mundane, non-magical lifestyle would deter any would-be assassin from The Underworld."

She couldn't have heard right. Anger welled up. "Who murdered Dad?" What gave them the right to tear her family's lives apart? "And why?" The last word came out as a whisper.

"A certain group of demons bears a grudge against us. We'd hoped they'd satisfied their need for revenge, but unfortunately not."

The Underworld. Demons. Dread crept over her like footsteps across a grave. "Do you mean John? They killed him too?" It couldn't be.

"We couldn't stop them." Sorrow filled Gram's face. "I'm sorry, Jocelyn." Gram laid her hand atop Joss's and squeezed. "I came tonight to warn you. You may be in terrible danger."

She gulped her drink. It would take awhile to process all this.

"I can't believe it." An ironic laugh escaped Joss. "Guess I chose the right costume." A golden goddess. What a joke. Too bad the joke was on her. What if she were to fall in love again? Now that the demons who'd murdered her family had set sights on her, would they target him too? Her head swam, drowning in what-ifs and fear.

Leaning forward, Gram set her gaze on Joss. "Do you recall the night you stole away from home at midnight? To dance with your imaginary friends?"

The memory, repressed for so many years, returned with clarity. The glowing figures flitting in orchestrated sequence, too beautiful to be real.

"I remember it as a dream. A nightmare, honestly." After the stray coyotes crept out of the shadows, snarling with fangs bared.

"Certainly for your parents, it was a nightmare. They found you in the morning, sleeping safe and sound."

"Inside the fairy ring." Joss remembered distinctly now. The glimmering lights guided her inside the circle, and the wild creatures couldn't follow. Neither could she leave the protection of the ring, and so had fallen asleep. "Because I'm part of their family?" Saying it sounded ridiculous, though she'd always secretly suspected it.

"In the truest meaning of the word."

"I can't be related to a goddess." Yet it would explain why Joss had always seemed different than others. Separate. And had been aware of the fae, even if none of her friends had seen them.

"You are." Lydia raised her glass. "We all are, sweetie."

"And the fae are protecting us?" At Gram and Lydia's nods, Joss went on. "Is that why beings from The Underworld are surfacing? The man, or whatever he is, from the party is a demon, isn't he? Why Boiling Springs? Why my house?" She suspected she already knew—the energy here. They wanted to tap into its power.

"You already know this place is special. The moment I arrived, it excited me. My perception tingled with possibility. They'd targeted the town several times before. With the economy's downturn, people became more desperate and vulnerable to them. The juxtaposition of the ley line made this an almost perfect spot to rise."

"A ley line?" Joss had heard of those. "Like at Stonehenge?"

Lydia nodded. "And Sedona, Arizona, or the Great Pyramid at Giza, at Nazca in Peru and more sites across the world."

A chill passed through Joss. Incredible. She'd never have guessed the energies meant such power coursed regularly below the inn like a river. Or maybe hadn't wanted to acknowledge it. "So, what now?"

Aunt Lydia glanced at Gram, who pressed her lips together. "It depends."

Meaning, even Gram had no clue. Great. "Wait and see?"

"For now. Promise you will be ever vigilant."

No need to tell Joss twice. She'd need more than margaritas to fortify her if she ever saw that dark creature again.

Chapter 3

Main Street in Boiling Springs saw a few more pedestrians and slightly fewer parking spaces than normal as locals gathered for Sunday breakfast at Kara's Kafe. Eric cringed at the kitschy spelling, but the place offered great cuisine. More than the usual diner fare, it provided the closest to a home-cooked meal he could hope for, along with the company of other people.

A lime green Beetle sat in the prized space directly out front. A jolt shot through his chest as he slid his truck a few spots behind and got out. The Bug was hers. Jocelyn's. Hard to miss the neon car when it passed his practice, and sometimes he shut his blinds so it wouldn't distract him. Since the Halloween party two days ago, he couldn't stop his mind from stripping away her gold and cream outfit to explore her golden skin. First, he'd better apologize for his behavior the other night. He hated for her to think he always acted so awkward, even if it were true.

In the Beetle's front seat, the border collie edged its nose out the window, open nearly halfway. Eric stopped beside the car and the dog wagged its tail. "Hey, boy."

Jocelyn Gibson. Her name rolled through his mind. What was she doing here so early? He'd noticed lights on inside the B and B as he jogged past every morning. Local farmers rose that early, of course. He hadn't expected her to.

Most clients at his veterinary practice pressed him about her. Was she as nice as she was pretty? What were her plans for the place? Did he know she was a widow too? The last question ended every conversation fast.

Occasionally, he considered dating, but he couldn't get past the numbness inside. The first year after his wife Karen's sudden death, he'd fought to maintain enough interest in just getting out of bed every morning. If it hadn't been for his practice, he might not have.

Through the glass front of the diner, he saw her. In jeans, a T-shirt, and denim blazer, her honey blond hair and petite form caught his full attention.

The bell over the door jingled as he entered. Behind the counter, Sheree flashed her usual smile and waved. "Be right with you."

Jocelyn glanced behind her, directly at him, and smiled. "Hello, Dr. Hendricks."

Her warmth washed over him, and like waves frothing over the sand, soothed him.

Turning, she pressed closer to the counter. "So you don't mind if I hang a sign in your window?"

"Sign for what?" He hadn't intended to move beside her. Usually he minded his own business.

She held up a handmade poster. "I'm looking for a handyman or two." Her creamy skin still had a glow. Must be some special type of makeup. No one looked that good under the harsh diner lights. "Oh right. You're fixing up the bed and breakfast." Stupid thing to say. He already knew she was.

Pointedly, she said, "Lavender Hill Inn."

"Lavender Hill?" The hill's sparse grass added to the rundown appearance of the old place. He'd always believed the B and B held much more potential.

"Yes. Lavender will be our specialty."

"What sort of specialty?" An image came to mind of Jocelyn lying atop gauzy, lavender-colored sheets. Naked. At a sudden rush of heat, he edged away from her, embarrassed. What the hell had gotten into him?

"Old family recipes with culinary lavender." A gleam lit her eyes, blue and clear as a spring sky after a rain storm. To the waitress, she said, "Thank you, Sheree. Could I get a cranberry orange muffin to go? They're too tempting to pass up."

"Don't you make your own at the…*inn*?" Christ, he wished he would shut up. He must sound like an idiot. Even the waitress shot him a disdainful look.

Her petal-pink lips open, Joss stared. "Annie will make a wonderful assortment of dishes, once we're fully up and running. I still like to support other local businesses." Taking the small white bag Sheree offered, Joss paid, then went to the door and taped the poster on the window beside it.

He stood watching like a village idiot.

Charlie Fulton approached from the back of the diner to sit at the counter, then ducked his head with sudden interest in his cup. Probably because he never paid for the last vet visit. Laid off, he likely owed more than a few others around town.

Taking the empty stool next to Charlie, Eric nodded in greeting. "How's it going?"

"Slower than I'd like." Charlie's features hardened.

"No work yet?" Seemed like half the town had been pink-slipped or forced into early retirement.

Charlie grimaced. "I'm looking, believe me. Full time jobs are few and far between. I'm paying what I can as I get occasional work."

Joss smoothed the last piece of tape across the glass behind them. "What sort of work do you do?"

Angling to face her, Charlie shrugged. "Whatever needs to be done."

"I have plenty of that." Her face lit in a smile and she extended her hand. "Hi, I'm Joss Gibson. I bought the Suttons' old place on Yellow Breeches Road. Can I give you my number?"

"Sure," Charlie said.

Pulling a scrap of paper out of her handbag, she scribbled and tore it off. "I can keep you plenty busy. How about if we talk specifics later? Sorry to have interrupted. Bye."

Her gaze caught Eric's and held for several thudding heartbeats. His stomach tightened. The overhead lights gave sheen to her hair and her eyes shone with warmth and intelligence, like she could see inside him and understood the turmoil beneath the hard exterior.

The world slowed around them. Background chatter, the clank of silver against dishes, faded with a roar of white noise in his head. When she turned away, an unnamable ache surged through him. An aura of light swirled in her wake.

The jingle of the bell riveted him until the door closed behind her. Like an antique record player cranked to life, the air crackled again with talk, forks on scraping plates, newspapers folding.

"Doc? Can I get you something?" a woman asked.

As if awakening from a dream, he blinked to focus. "Pardon?"

Sheree waited on the other side of the counter, concern evident in her pursed red lips and furrowed, overly tweezed brow.

"What?" He stood, his appetite gone. "Yes, give me a cranberry-orange muffin to go too, please."

The waitress frowned and dropped a muffin into a bag. "I hope she doesn't change the B and B into one of those garish commercial inns with a yucky blinking sign."

An older woman at the end of the counter spoke up. "We don't need that. Next thing you know, there'd be fast food joints on every street corner."

Charlie grumbled into his coffee. "Boiling Springs would become another tourist trap town."

Sheree gave a proud smirk. "We like it the way it is."

Not likely to happen in this sleepy Pennsylvania hamlet. Glancing warily around, Eric paid for the muffin. Why the absurd conspiracy theories? Had mass hysteria taken hold? Nothing ever happened here. Everyone knew it. What the hell had gotten into them?

Making his way to the door was like fighting an upstream current. By the time he stepped outside, the lime green Beetle was gone.

* * * *

Sheree dug her glossy red nails into the countertop. What the frack just happened? Like some teenage boy, Eric stood on the sidewalk, looking down the street. After *her* car.

Jocelyn Gibson. If that woman thought she was going to steal Eric from her, she had another thing coming. Sheree had waited years for him to get the hint. He'd finally been warming up, smiling when he talked to her. She'd been patient as a saint, and it was wearing her out. The man could only grieve so long. She'd waited five years, for goodness sake.

When he was ready to open his heart again, he would open it to her. Sheree. No one else.

The sign in the window caught her eye. A handyman or two, indeed. The man in black was exactly right. Jocelyn Gibson had to go.

* * * *

Standing in the foyer, Joss surveyed the expansive front parlor. The inn needed renovations. Now. She wasn't about to let a little thing like demons stop her.

Her mother had always said every house had its own personality, and just needed the right touch to bring it out. This place held such promise. When the realtor had called the rambling Second Empire-style Victorian a gem in the rough, Joss had agreed. She loved its woodwork details, not fussy like the gingerbread of other Victorians. No one else seemed to share her clear vision of the inn standing out on the hill like a shining jewel. Instead of its cracked gray-green paint, Joss pictured a magnificent Painted Lady of violet and lavender hues.

It would take a lot more than visions to make it happen. First things first. After dragging the step stool to the window, Joss unfastened the heavy drapes. Their faded burgundy accented the hues of the worn Chinese carpet, but that musty old thing was going too.

Overcast as the day was, light filled the room as the curtains dropped atop a plastic bag. Stepping back, her excitement grew. The three floor-to-ceiling windows provided a wonderful view of the field leading to the road. "What a huge difference." The next curtains would be sheer to let in the sunshine.

Behind her, Aunt Lydia said, "Oh, my, yes."

"Good morning. Did you sleep well?"

"You know me. I never sleep well. Too sensitive to atmospheric disturbances." Her slippers scuffed across the rug to the tufted sofa where Lydia draped herself. "Except for the stale odor, this is rather comfy."

"Isn't it? I'm having it cleaned and reupholstered." When her grandmother entered, fully dressed, Joss went to her. "Morning. Coffee's on in the kitchen."

Gram hugged her. "Jocelyn, you had an eventful evening."

To say the least. Gathering the votive candles, she spoke as if distracted by her work. "More guests than I expected."

Standing slowly, Lydia's blood-red nails clenched the air as if pulling herself up. "I've never seen so many fae invade a home at once."

Neither had Joss. When she was a girl, swarms of glowing beings would flicker in the blades of grass, or leaves of trees. Sometimes flit to her window. But come inside? Only on occasions of rare importance, according to Gram. "Aunt Lydia—"

Her aunt came toward her. "The sign was very clear."

Evading the interrogation, Joss wrestled a wing-back chair to the center of the carpet. "I can't let myself believe in bad luck." Safer to make her own luck through hard work than rely on luck bestowed by mythological creatures.

Gram stepped closer. "They've come back, Jocelyn. I'm not surprised you found their favor again, given our family history."

Lydia added, "You must treat them with respect."

How could she admit she'd hoped they'd return? That in planting a field of lavender in the spring, she'd hoped to encourage them to stay? Nor could she admit last night's dream to her aunt. Like the fae lights, it had happened before. She had the same fantasy every night.

Long after saying goodnight to Gram and Lydia, Joss had stood at her bedroom window and had imagined a field of purple waltzing with the breeze beneath the stars. The image stayed with her as she settled into bed, coaxing her to sleep. Rather than fading, the dream had grown more vivid with the lights out.

The evening star shone more brightly than usual and led her to the stone bridge connecting the yard to the field. The silhouette of a man beckoned from beyond it. She crossed the bridge into the lavender, and its blooms caressed her legs as she walked. Instead of its scented oils soothing her skin, it stimulated her. The thought of meeting him excited her too. Dusk deepened quickly, and even though she stood in front of him, she couldn't see his face. He leaned down to kiss her. Pressing against him, her body fit snugly against his curves. He took her down into the lavender, then filled her, body and soul. The stars glimmered so bright and low, they mingled with the violet blooms. He was so tender, yet strong. His caresses so loving, he brought her to heights she never imagined, and only after she was fulfilled did he allow himself release. Afterward, he rolled onto his back and pulled her close, his skin warm against hers. His voice rumbled through his chest. "Who needs fireworks with so many fireflies?" Her fingers trembled with the reverberations and she closed her eyes to listen to him breathing.

She'd awakened in a luscious afterglow, yet bothered because she had no clue who he was or when she'd find him. Or what he'd meant about fireworks. In the dream, she'd understood his words clearly, but in the light of day, the meaning evaded her.

A knock at the door provided a welcome distraction. Joss crossed the foyer to open it. "Should be Mr. Fulton. I've hired him to help with restoration work. You might want to get dressed, Aunt Lydia." Providing Charlie with a paycheck gave her the warm and fuzzies, but she'd have to be careful with her limited funds.

Lydia finger-combed her hair. "Oh, I don't know. He might be a fellow in need of some womanly charms."

Clucking her tongue, Joss couldn't hold back a smile. She waited for Gram to lead her aunt through the dining room before opening the door. "Good morning."

Mr. Fulton's greeting faded away as his gaze followed Lydia, who threw an inviting glance over her shoulder and sashayed into the kitchen. He snapped shut his mouth. "Mrs. Gibson. Hello."

"Please call me Joss. Ready to get to work?"

Stepping inside, he scanned the foyer. "Call me Charlie. And just tell me where to start."

"Good question. Probably stripping the wallpaper, don't you think?" With a nervous shrug, he chuckled. "Sounds good to me."

Poor man, so anxious to make an impression. Or maybe he wasn't used to owners pitching in to help. Time was of the essence. She needed the work done quickly.

Outside, Annie's car pulled alongside Charlie's truck.

To Charlie, Joss said, "I'll whip up the wallpaper removing solution and be back in a second. Would you move the rest of the furniture away from the walls?"

"Sure," he said. "I brought some tarps along too."

"Great. Be back in a minute."

She entered the kitchen as Annie plunked her purse on the counter. "Morning, everyone. I'm not late, am I?"

"Right on time."

After sipping the last of her coffee, Lydia washed the cup. "I should get out of your way." She sidestepped Joss, waiting with the bucket.

"Will you be staying today?" Joss directed the question at both Gram and Lydia.

Lydia tightened the belt of her robe. "I have an appointment this afternoon. I need to get dressed and vamoose." She sauntered into the dining room.

Mouth agape, Annie watched. "She's a wonder."

Gram sighed. "Exactly. We won't define what sort."

Joss gave a wry smile and filled the bucket with hot water mixed with dishwashing detergent.

Pouring coffee, Annie chuckled. "It's a shame she couldn't stay to help."

"She's better at existential projects. But I appreciate you coming."

"I wouldn't miss it." Annie grabbed the three sponges off the counter. "I'll go say hi to Charlie."

Joss carried the bucket to the front room where Charlie finished tugging the last tarp along the floor, the clustered furniture in the center already covered. They set to work in easy camaraderie.

When Lydia and Gram said their farewells, Joss took a short break to see them outside. On the porch, Taz barked once when Lydia tooted the horn.

By noon, a pile of shredded wallpaper sat atop the tarps. Joss ran her hand along the wall. "Some parts are still tacky. Diluted fabric softener should take care of it."

Charlie stood back to assess their handiwork. "In a way, you're lucky the paper was so old. Newer types can be tough to remove."

Giving her shoulder a squeeze, Annie brightened. "I'm starving."

Joss's stomach grumbled in reply. "Yes, let's eat."

Annie drew her to the kitchen and unpacked the cooler. The chicken salad pita pockets lined with lettuce revived them, and they worked past six.

Before leaving, Charlie hesitated at the door. "Same time tomorrow?"

"Absolutely." An uneasy vibe emanated from him and Joss suspected the trouble. "I forgot to ask earlier. Would you like to be paid at the end? Or every week?"

His face relaxed. "Weekly would be a big help."

She gave a reassuring smile. "I'll have a check ready for you Friday."

Charlie nodded. "I appreciate it. See you in the morning." With a wave, he left.

Joss ran her hand across the smooth bare wall. "I'm so glad we found Charlie to help."

"I know. I'm pooped. I'm going home too."

Stripping the wallpaper sapped Joss's strength for the day. Gratefully, she crawled into bed after showering. "It's going to be great once it's done, Taz."

The dog leapt up and nestled against her legs with a sigh, and Joss fell into a deep sleep.

* * * *

The next morning, freezing rain pelted the windows. Her muscles aching, Joss pulled the covers over her head. *No,* she reminded herself. *Today I want to finish priming the front room.* And Annie and Charlie would be arriving soon.

Forcing herself out of bed was no easy task, especially when Taz burrowed deeper into the covers. "Traitor." Grinning, she tousled his fur.

Shaking off the early November chill, she told herself the work ahead would make her forget the bad weather. After a quick shower, she threw on old sweats and sneakers and clipped back her hair on both sides. Fortified with fresh coffee, she began.

She had already primed one wall when Charlie arrived, and Annie soon after. About mid-morning, she caught the movement of a vehicle down the driveway. "Who's here?"

A quick glance hardly interrupted Charlie's roller stroke. "Looks like Doc Hendricks."

The name sent a buzz through her.

The dark blue SUV stopped outside the stable, and the vet jogged to its doors, hunched against the elements.

"The barn must be cold." She hadn't meant to say it aloud.

"Invite him in." Annie nudged her.

"No, he's busy." But it's such a raw day. He could use a hot drink.

He needed something all right, but nothing she could give him. An internal battle raged within the veterinarian. Their initial brief encounter left her reeling for days, unable to negotiate the tsunami of emotion beneath his hard exterior.

Taz finally lumbered down the hall, sat down and yawned.

"Good morning, sleepy head. Do you need to go outside?"

The dog sneezed and looked disdainfully toward the wet window. At times, Taz's other half—Labrador—seemed to take over his brain. Joss joked he had the brain of a lab and the nervous system of a border collie. Still, when grief snuck up on her—and it still did—he'd snuggle against her and gaze up at her with soulful eyes. She treasured Taz because John had given him to her. To keep her company when he was no longer there, he'd said. To guide her. It had struck her as odd, since he'd been so opposed to any talk of magic or the fae.

The memory stung her grief to life. To quell the raw ache, she did what she always did—spun into motion. "Come on. A little rain won't hurt you." Pulling open the door, her heart leapt to her throat, and Taz rose, barking.

The vet stood on the threshold. "I was about to knock."

His strong presence overwhelmed her. She could only stand there, bracing herself.

* * * *

The sight of her mesmerized him. Eric purposely ignored the inn, changing his jogging route to avoid passing. To avoid seeing her. Like a school boy, he dreamed of her at night. During the day, she popped into his mind unbidden.

Dr. Avery, the large-animal vet, had asked Eric to fill in during his vacation. Unfortunately, one of the horses needed immediate attention, according to the owner. He couldn't put an animal's welfare above his own comfort. Or lack thereof.

No less luminous than the last time he'd seen her, Joss stood before him, her lips slightly parted, blinking in surprise.

The dog's tail wagged even though he still barked.

"Morning." *Idiot, saying good morning to the dog in front of them.* A hazard of the veterinary profession, one he normally didn't allow others to view.

Taz's wagging tail swept the floor.

With a downward thrust of her hand, she commanded, "Go outside, boy."

In passing, the dog nudged Eric's hand, so he patted his head.

Straightening, she stared after Taz in surprise. "Can I help you?"

His throat dried and his voice withered like a November leaf. "My cell's dead. Any chance I could use your phone?"

She stepped back. "Sure, come on in."

Apologetically, he glanced at his wet coat. "I'm soaked. I could go around to the kitchen."

His humility might have touched a soft spot because she inclined her head toward the desk. "No, you can use this phone."

After wiping his feet, he sloughed water off his coat and stepped inside. Tension subsided when Annie and Charlie both said, "Hi."

Before Joss could close the door, the dog ran in and shook, droplets flying from his fur.

"Wait, Taz. Sit and don't move." Joss hurried to the hallway closet and returned with an old towel. "Everything all right?" She knelt to rub down the dog.

Work, he had no trouble talking about. He relaxed. "No, actually. I have to speak with Tom." He strode to the desk. "He was supposed to apply ointment every day to Triple Power's eye. It's still swollen, so I suspect he's missed a few applications. Have you noticed, by any chance, if he's been out here?" He lifted the receiver from the charger.

"Two nights ago, yes. We've been so busy these past few days…he may have slipped in unnoticed."

After pressing the numbers, he scanned the rooms. "You did this much work in a few days?"

Pride lit her face as she stood, admiring their handiwork. "Yes. We have a lot more to do though."

With a wince, he held the phone to his ear. "More?" He couldn't imagine where she got the energy. Glancing around, he noted that with the curtains down and the faded wallpaper gone, the rooms appeared much more inviting.

She smirked. "I may keep the stair railing as it is."

He stifled a smile. *Touché.* He held her gaze as the call rang through. Even the small connection charged the air between them.

A man picked up. Eric tilted the receiver to his mouth. "Hello, Tom? This is Doc Hendricks. I'm out at the old bed and breakfast on Yellow Breeches Road."

The old bed and breakfast. Probably shouldn't have called it that either.

Joss drifted into the front room with ethereal grace. She'd have fit easily into the home's setting in the nineteenth century. The house must have been magnificent when its original owners built it in the late 1800s. Even as he argued with Tom about the horse's proper care, Eric envisioned her in a lacy gown. Imagined the two of them riding in a horse-drawn wooden sleigh, its runners gliding across snow-covered roads.

The stable manager denied ignoring the horse's needs. Eric knew better. Hanging up, he muttered, "Incompetent ass."

Joss turned. "Will the horse be all right?"

Eric trudged to the hallway. "No thanks to Larsen. I'd like to take a crop to him."

Annie frowned. "Shouldn't the owners have looked after their horse?"

"Yes. Unfortunately they lavish their attentions on their prize Saddlebred, who brings home the pretty blue ribbons. And put too much trust in Tom to follow through with his responsibilities as stable manager." He stared at the face of the grandfather clock when it chimed eleven. "Is that the correct time?"

Joss set the paint roller in the pan. "Sorry, it's never right."

Glancing at her watch, Annie frowned. "It is now."

With a breathy laugh, Joss's body went rigid. "What?"

"Eleven o'clock." Confusion crossed Annie's face.

"It can't be." From Joss's reaction she might have said a bomb was about to explode.

"Why not?" Had he missed something?

Blinking hard, Joss glanced at the old clock, then at him. "This clock never tells…the right time." Her voice faded as she spoke the last words. Her narrowed gaze swept over him, leaving a trail of heated pinpricks.

Blood coursed like gasoline through his veins, cold but ready to ignite. Every sense snapped to attention, focused on her. Something very odd was going on. Their conversation seemed to be on two levels; the words they spoke corresponded to a deeper meaning, and he had no clue what it meant. Only Joss understood, and Annie, who looked on in surprise. Charlie, however, kept painting.

Unsure how to respond, Eric flashed a tight grin. "Well. Glad it's working again. Thanks." He pulled up his collar and opened the door.

Joss called, "You're welcome."

Something in her voice halted him. A husky tone caught in his throat as he croaked a goodbye. He blinked hard and turned away without another word.

The wind drove the freezing rain into his face. Glad for its cleansing chill, he tilted his head up and strode to his truck, hoping it would clear the fog from his brain. Being around her gave him a dizzy sensation, as if she were a whirlwind enveloping him. Paralyzing him. Turned him into a mute, and deaf to anyone except her. He'd never experienced anything quite like it. Fumbling the keys into the ignition, his hands shook, though the cold temperature didn't register.

Edging the truck down the driveway, he couldn't stop searching for her. One last look. Stalling rewarded him with a glimpse. Joss glided past the window, then edged back, half-hidden. She was looking for him too. Impulsively, he jammed his foot against the accelerator and the tires kicked up gravel behind him.

Maybe the crazy aunt's a witch. She's cast a spell over me.

Now he sounded like the gossipers at the diner. The fact that he entertained such a notion proved something was amiss. Or why he reacted to her so strangely. No, overreacted. Her presence threw off his internal compass, sent the needle spinning. He had no idea which direction was up. Knew only that whatever force was at work, it drew him back, uncontrollably, to her.

He found himself outside his practice without any memory of driving there.

Glancing back, the Victorian atop the hill gleamed like a beacon in fog. Light poured out the windows with a vibrancy reflecting the life of those within. Again, the distinct impression of being an outsider struck him. Normally, he didn't mind spending his spare time alone, or at least, he never had until he met Joss.

For the first time, memories of Karen appeared to him in an abstract way, as if from a distance, instead of hitting him like a freight train. Strange. Before, he'd been vaguely aware of his wife's presence. Of course, he didn't believe in ghosts, but sometimes his ache for her would ease, and Karen's warmth would wrap around him like an invisible embrace. In the past year or so, even those brief encounters with her had abandoned him, leaving a gaping void. He finally shook off the sensation of being suspended in nothingness, of seeing life happening around him yet not immersed in it.

Being with Joss brought his solitary lifestyle into sharper relief, revealing a deep loneliness that he hadn't acknowledged. He had his work. The practice. Memories of Karen. No need for anything else.

Though lately, the waitress at Kara's Kafe had popped into his head uninvited. And unwanted. He'd awaken and imagine her beside him. He'd jump out of bed to put distance between them, though he knew she wasn't actually there. Or when he drove, he sometimes imagined her cuddling into his side. It wrenched his stomach. Worse, it interrupted musings of Joss, almost as if on purpose. Sheree didn't interest him. Why did she appear in his head?

Only when he was near Joss did the unease about the waitress subside.

* * * *

After the door closed, Joss let out a ragged breath. She waited, listening to his footsteps recede. Waiting for them to return. *What am I doing?* Apparently getting caught up in the poor man's need for comfort. Then why did she wish he'd stayed longer?

He didn't talk to her, so much as at her. Maybe he didn't know how to relate to humans. What a shame, for such a ruggedly handsome, virile man to close himself off to others. To happiness. Maybe his vet practice provided enough for him, and filled any void of loneliness.

Concern in his eyes, Taz tilted his head, as if reading her thoughts.

Seemingly oblivious, Charlie faced the wall, painting intently. Annie, on the other hand, moved the roller slowly up and down. With frequent, furtive glances, she watched Joss.

Joss forced a smile. "We're making good progress. The inn will be ready for Thanksgiving after all."

In an unintentional imitation of Taz, Annie's shoulders slumped when she tilted her head, her face filled with yearning. A silent beg for inside information. The effect was comical, but Joss couldn't talk about what had happened.

Joss shot her a silent warning. Strange the old clock struck the correct hour. To mention it would open an avenue of discussion for Annie, so Joss bent to retrieve her paint roller. "Let's see how far we can get before lunch."

"What's for lunch today, Annie?" Charlie asked.

Annie answered, "Chili and corn bread. It'll warm us up."

"Sounds perfect." Even if Joss was plenty heated by Eric's visit. His essence still permeated the room, emanating heat like a hearth fire.

Charlie agreed, and engaged Annie in a discussion of recipes.

The ping of hard rain against the window captured Joss's attention. Beyond the spattered glass, the dark blue SUV swung away from the barn and down the long drive. A plume of exhaust trailed from his vehicle. She could have sworn he watched from within.

I don't need any trouble. I don't care how handsome he is. More than handsome. Now she knew why younger people referred to the opposite sex as hot. When near him, a side of her she'd locked away returned, hungry for more. The hair on her skin shot up with electricity when he stood close.

No, she should leave him alone. And every other man, after what Gram revealed.

Chapter 4

The dream again. The same man, mysterious, yet her soul mate. Joss awoke damp with sweat. Light edged the horizon and gradually diffused the shadows from her room. Taz jumped atop the bed and nudged her hand with his snout.

Sitting up, she hugged him, stroking his long black and white fur. "Oh, Taz."

When John's friend had first brought the border collie, Joss balked. The last thing she needed was another life to depend on her. John had told her the herding dog would guide her. Taz had turned his brown eyes toward her, a connection beyond love. Somehow the dog had shared her sadness and promised better times lie ahead.

The dog's soft tongue licked her cheek. "I know. We have a lot of work to finish." Enough dreaming, for now.

After a quick shower, she threw on jeans and a sweatshirt.

Taz woofed at the window, tail wagging.

"Someone coming?" Joss ruffled his fur and peered outside. "It's Annie."

Bounding ahead as she opened the door, the dog reached Annie before Joss, who rushed down the porch steps. "You're here early."

Annie smiled. "I brought breakfast. I know you've been working before Charlie and I arrive and after we leave. You're going to exhaust yourself."

"Not a chance. I'm in love."

Annie's jaw dropped. "What?"

"I fall in love with the house every time I look at it." Joss delighted in every detail. Arched wooden frames protruded around the third floor windows. From its near-flat mansard rooftop, shingles curved delicately down to the second floor, rimmed in dark wooden molding set with evenly spaced carved brackets beneath the eaves. Like the first floor, the second floor boasted narrow floor-to-ceiling windows in pairs. Topped by an aged copper roof, the main rectangular tower jutted past the front door, its three windows angled hexagonally. Columns sat at the front of the roofed porch, extending past the dining room windows.

"Yep, the inn's beautiful." Annie chuckled. "Or will be."

"It's a Second Empire Victorian. Did I tell you already?"

Annie's lips twisted to the side. "You might have mentioned the fact a few times."

"Doesn't its name seem perfect? For both the inn and my life. A second empire."

"You will rule in both," Annie joked, following her to the back door. "I have to admit, I was afraid I'd be cooking over a hearth."

"Not quite." The previous owners had updated the kitchen beautifully. In the morning sun, the room gleamed in ceramic and steel perfection. Graced with four large arched windows, light blazed through.

After setting down her bags, Annie ran her hand across the large, shiny stove, then the huge refrigerator. "I still can't believe how gorgeous it is."

Joss leaned against the large central island. "I'm glad the one room they updated was this one."

"Ah, my dream workspace." Annie caressed the light gray granite countertops. "I want to live here."

"Once we're up and running, you practically will." Joss moved to the back door. "And the outdoor summer kitchen's only a few steps down the walk."

Stepping beside her, Annie said, "Where you'll make the specialty of the house."

"A few specialties, actually." Joss planned to create delectable concoctions using her grandmother's potent ingredient—lavender. She'd stir it in lemonade for hot summer days, mix it with sugar to dust on cakes, and adorn rooms with its blooms.

"The entire field will be filled with a sea of purple flowers." She couldn't wait until the view transformed her vision into reality. "Gram used to tell me lavender keeps away everything from insects to bad luck, if you believe in superstition."

Rapping her knuckles on the wooden door jamb, Annie chuckled. "Don't knock it. We could use some luck."

"I don't believe in luck, Annie. I believe in working hard, and making my own luck." Joss had ignored her grandmother's advice to entwine the perennial in her hair for her wedding to John. Gram had told her the sacred rite would ensure she retained her female power and bring good fortune. Joss hadn't needed a flower for that.

"We're going to make this work, Annie."

"You betcha." Annie slung an arm around her shoulder. "I'm so happy to see you moving on, honey. I was worried about you."

"I was fine." Joss couldn't admit to Annie she had reason to worry. "You're right, buying this place was the right decision. Running the inn will keep me busy, if nothing else, and Taz has the run of the property's seven acres." She reached down to pat his head, and he looked up at her with his warm brown eyes, mouth open in a doggy smile.

Annie's careful scrutiny crawled over her. "Nope, something more. You look more like you. Even more like you than when John was alive." She waved. "I can't explain it."

"I know what you mean. It's true." Since moving in, Joss was more herself than she had been in years. Stronger, more vibrant. "I'm looking forward to the future again, instead of dreading it. I can't wait to plant the first crop of lavender next spring." It would bring happy childhood memories, and hopefully happy customers who loved her lavender-based recipes. If the blooms brought a bit of luck, all the better.

* * * *

Lavender Hill Inn's flow of guests grew steadily. Her full days gave Joss no time to think about anything besides work, or so she told herself. Despite her resolve, Eric barely left Joss's thoughts for the next few weeks. In the mornings, she pointedly avoided him, waiting to walk Taz until after his early run.

Until the morning Taz broke from their early morning walk to run to the barn.

"Where are you going?" Rounding the back of the house, she slowed at the sight of Eric's truck.

Tail wagging, Taz stood beside it. Eric climbed out and bent to pat the dog's head.

"Oh, no." She'd planned for this eventual visit—and had planned to be away, out of sight, where she wouldn't have to speak to him. If she hurried into the summer kitchen, she could avoid him. Her pace quickened. As she reached for the door, Taz barked.

Glancing back, she shushed the dog. Too late. The vet stood, hand on hip, watching.

"Hello." She waved and grabbed the door knob.

"Morning." He strolled closer.

"How are the horses?"

GODDESS, AWAKENED

45

"Good. I'm giving shots today."

Was the regular vet still on vacation? "Poor things."

"They don't feel much."

"All animals experience pain." How could he claim otherwise?

"Horses have such thick skins. Nothing like humans." He winced and turned away.

She wished she had such a protective barrier. One would come in handy right now. "Good. Well…" Stepping back, she beat a hasty retreat and entered the house through the back door.

In the kitchen, Joss rubbed the sudden gooseflesh on her arms. Turning toward Annie didn't erase the pull from the barn. "So what else do we need for the Thanksgiving dinner?"

Thankfully, Annie said nothing about the vet's presence, though her gaze returned to the blue SUV several times. "I'm finished shopping. Will Kyle come?" The hope in Annie's voice shone through, though she seemed to struggle to remain casual.

"Overnight, yes." Her son hadn't missed a holiday yet. "Lydia too."

Annie brightened. "Oh, good. I like her."

"Thanksgiving wouldn't be the same without family." Not necessarily a bad thing when your family's certifiable.

Since Halloween, everything had remained calm. Normal. If only she could say the same for her family.

Wiping her hands, Annie asked, "How are reservations?"

"Five more booked for dinner, so we'll have thirty." More than she'd expected.

"Great. Any staying overnight?" As always, Annie's enthusiasm made even small news seem huge.

"Seven, including Kyle and Lydia." She'd hoped for more, with people's relatives coming into town for the holiday, but the inn needed time to build its reputation.

"Once people see how beautiful the inn is, word will get out, and we'll be turning people away."

Nice to dream big, anyway. Joss wouldn't dampen Annie's hopes. "It does look wonderful, doesn't it?" The walls in the front room were light sage, the trim painted in cream, carried into the foyer. "Better than I'd imagined."

"When will the new sign arrive?"

"Not until after Christmas, because it's a special order." Joss sighed. "I can't wait until spring, when we can paint the outside."

"And plant the lavender." After a slight *squee*, Annie said, "Your dreams are coming true. By next summer, they'll bloom into reality."

Something about the words struck Joss hard. The dream. Every night, it recurred: the man in the lavender field. Her soul mate. Who was he? Where was he right now?

Joss didn't realize Annie stood beside her until her friend touched her arm.

"Are you all right, hon?"

Shaking off the odd sensation, Joss smiled. "Fine. I can't stop worrying about the enormous amount of work ahead. Especially the barn. I hope the boarders will understand why we need to make the changes." Moving the pasture to the other side of the stable, for starters. Building a new tack room so Joss could make use of the old summer kitchen.

"Don't forget the patio." Dreaminess filled Annie's voice. "It will give us a lot more options. Just think, people will book birthday parties there, graduation parties, anniversary parties…and weddings! How perfect will that space be for weddings?"

At the word, Joss's stomach twisted. "Absolutely perfect."

The kitchen echoed the click of Taz's nails across the floor as he went to the door, then glanced back at Joss.

"You want to go out?" She hesitated before opening the door. "Don't bother the doctor."

To her horror, Taz beelined for the stable and squeezed inside the barely-open entrance. "Oh, no."

Annie chuckled. "He likes to keep an eye on everyone and everything."

Sometimes the wrong things. With growing caution, she found herself riveted to the scene outside. She opened the door to listen.

"You're not worried, are you?" Annie's voice sounded far away.

More vividly, a horse's snort came from inside the barn. Shuffling hooves stamping the ground. A dog's yelp sounded.

Red flashed through Joss's mind and her blood chilled. "Taz!" She ran with only one thought in mind, *please let him be safe*.

Eric's loud commands sounded across the yard. "Settle down. Whoa."

She scrambled to push the barn door wider and halted, her throat constricted.

Eric crouched over Taz, lying on the ground. With calculating precision, Eric ran his hands across the dog's rump and back legs.

Heart pounding, she halted. "What happened?"

"A small kick. He got between Triple Power and me in the stall." Eric stood. "He's fine."

As if to prove it, Taz scrabbled to his feet, tail wagging.

Joss released a long shuddering breath. "Thank goodness." She went to him. Instinctively, she ran her hands along the same path the vet's had taken. Everything appeared to be in place, and Taz gave no protest.

She turned to Eric. He stiffened. His gaze lit with an intense fire. One that ignited within her. She nearly forgot to say, "Thank you."

Eric lurched to a stand. "No problem."

Lost in the whirl of his emotions, she steeled herself against reaching for him. "I'll take Taz inside."

He stepped closer. "He's no bother."

At first surprised, Joss reasoned, *Of course. Animals, he's comfortable with. It's people he doesn't like.* The storm brewing beneath the man's skin unnerved her.

Sensing his deep discomfort, she blurted, "We're open for Thanksgiving dinner. If you have nowhere else to go." Not a very gracious invitation, but it hid the hope he'd accept.

Darkness crossed his face, hardened his features. "I'm not sure yet."

Three days away and he hadn't firmed up plans? "Annie's turkey dinner is legendary."

He jerked his head, not quite a nod so much as a dismissal.

With no other reason to stay, she strolled to the door. "I should get back." A final glance at Taz revealed the dog wouldn't follow. Taz sat watching, unmoving except for his tail swishing against the ground, mouth open in a pant, uncannily resembling a smile.

* * * *

Sheree closed the door of her apartment harder than she intended. Another night alone. She'd grown tired of waiting. When would the shadowy guy fulfill his end of the bargain? She'd told him everything she'd learned. Sure, it wasn't much, but could she help it if Mrs. Gibson was about as boring as could be? She worked throughout the day and stayed in at night. So far as Sheree could tell, so did Eric.

Lately, though, when he came to the diner for lunch, Eric looked at her funny. Like she was up to something.

He wasn't supposed to know. They must have messed up somehow.

"I'll give you an earful this time." Grumbling, she hung her coat in the hall closet, closed the door, and gasped, heart suddenly in overdrive. "When did you get here?"

Leaning against the wall, the dark man chuckled. Not the kind that inspired her to laugh along, either. "This instant. What juicy tidbits have you gathered this week?"

Sheree gulped. "Mrs. Gibson's having Thanksgiving dinner." Not exactly earth-shattering.

His smile faded. "You're joking."

"No, she's been renovating the inn." Wasting tons of money on the old rundown place.

He stood straight. "Come now," he hissed. "Is that the best you can come up with?"

What the hell did he want? Lies? "Yes."

He clucked his tongue. "How unfortunate. For you." He glared, his eyes flashing red.

Piss on those special effects, bud. He could save them for a newbie who cowered easily. "It's not my fault she hasn't done anything wrong. If you'd tell me what, specifically, you want to know, I could watch for it." Hiding in the bushes grew old the first night she spied on Joss. It was damn cold outside.

Looming closer, his nostrils flared. "Everything. How much plainer can I state the objective?"

Two could play this game. She had her own agenda and nothing would stand between her and Eric. She mustered her bitchiness, never very far below the surface. "You're not giving me anything either. Eric hardly pays attention to me. And I think he knows."

Drawing back, the man's eyes darted to her. "What do you mean, he knows?"

"Ever since Halloween, he looks at me funny." Hopefully, Eric hadn't spied her sneaking around the inn. If only he didn't live across the damn street from her.

The man ran his gaze up and down her. "So?"

"You're keeping too much from me." Like Eric. "What the hell are those crazy lighted buggy things outside the inn? They kept dive-bombing me until I couldn't stand it anymore."

He waved her off. "Oh, the fae. They're harmless, mostly."

Freaking fairies? Well, why not, if she stood here chit-chatting with a demon. One who owed her big-time. Apparently he'd forgotten that little tidbit. "When are you going to make him fall in love with me?"

He huffed. "I never said such a thing."

She fumed. No way would he back out on her. "Yes you did. In the car the night we met."

In contrast to his casual tone, his eyes flashed. "I said you'd have him. I never promised he'd love you."

Talk about a piercing gaze. His stare drilled into her brain. Her head swam. "I don't understand."

His deep voice echoed as if through a canyon. "Understand this. If you fail, you will suffer for eternity." He sank into the wall and was gone.

What the... "Hello?" What kind of screwed-up mess had she tangled herself in this time? *Not a mess. An objective.* For once in her pitiful life, she had a goal to reach, and boy howdy, did she intend to win.

Then his words sunk in.

Eternity? Hey, screw that. And what good was having Eric if he didn't love her? Strolling to the bedroom, she stopped short at seeing Eric reclining across her bed, the sheet covering half his bare rear. Smiling, he patted the space next to him.

Her heart flip-flopped.

Oh, yeah. Finally.

Ripping the band out of her hair, she shook it loose around her shoulders. "Here I come, baby, ready or not." She squeaked the last word.

Like a video game gone bad, Eric pixilated into static.

"No." She dove for the bed, landing on nothing but rumpled covers.

Rolling atop them, she groaned and clutched them to her chest. Where Eric should have been.

Okay. She wasn't completely thick. This was a message. Having Eric, even if he didn't love her, had its perks.

She could deal with it.

Chapter 5

The gold and silver painted pumpkins decorated the foyer hardwood floor, its soft sheen testament to the recent refinishing. The ceramic pheasant her grandmother had given her sat beside the vase of sunflowers on the table below the mirror. Edging the door frame, the garland of yellow and orange fabric leaves twined with white lights provided a welcoming entry for Thanksgiving guests.

After surveying the guest list, Joss walked to the dining room for a last-minute check of tables for correct silverware. As soon as they arrived, she'd light the candles and dim the lights. Everything appeared ready, so why did she have the nagging notion of something left undone?

Needing to busy herself, she went to the kitchen. "What can I do to help?"

"Not a thing. We have it covered." Annie smiled at her cousin Tammy, hired for the day as a server.

"I don't know why I'm so nervous." Her nerves tightened by the minute.

Having finished squirting decorative frosting on a cake, Annie stepped back to admire her work. "It will be great. See? People are arriving right now."

Outside, three cars queued up beside one another. People exited and approached the inn. Joss untied her apron. "Show time." Although excited by her expected guests, something else lingered in the air, hidden by their smiling faces and chatter as they approached the house. Larger and more powerful than their pleasantries, yet mingled with them. She couldn't quite put her finger on it, and her apprehension grew.

Distractedly, Joss asked, "You didn't take any more reservations, did you?"

"No," Annie said. "Why?"

"No reason." Except she'd been so sure Eric would accept the invitation, despite his reluctance. No time to worry about it now.

The silver sedan pulling in caught her attention. "Aunt Lydia." Standing on tiptoe, Annie strained to see. "Oh, good. Will she be telling fortunes again?"

Tammy gasped in delight. "She's a fortune teller?"

Joss shot her a sardonic glance. "Not today if I can help it." Ignoring their disappointed whines, she hurried to the lobby to greet an entering couple, whom she didn't recognize. Seeing their overnight bags, she checked them in.

Another couple arrived as she directed the first to their rooms. After taking their coats and hanging them on the coat rack, she ushered them to the front room. "Make yourself at home. Dinner will be ready soon."

When she returned to the foyer, Lydia was stamping her heeled shoes on the carpet. "It's so cold." Turning back, her aunt held open the door for the person behind her. "Come sit by the fire."

The powerful presence hit Joss before she spied her grandmother, who followed Lydia. Her mouth fell open in delight. "Gram."

"Happy Thanksgiving, dear." Her grandmother opened her arms.

Joss went to her embrace. "What a lovely surprise. I had no idea you were coming."

The love in her grandmother's voice warmed Joss as much as the hug. "The inn looks lovely."

"Wait till you see the house next year after we paint the outside. And after the lavender's planted."

Gram's eyes crinkled in a smile. "How lovely you'll carry on the family traditions."

Not the way her grandmother hoped. "Only your recipes."

"I'm still pleased." Gram squeezed her hand. "Your special visitors will be too."

Her aunt primped in front of the mirror.

Joss moved behind Lydia. "Let's not mention such things tonight, please. Or anything else out of the ordinary."

Lydia pecked her cheek. "We wouldn't dream of it, darling." Halting outside the front room, her aunt gasped. "Oh, my. How gorgeous! The color's extraordinary."

Joss had to admit, it would complement the outside colors nicely. Linking her arm through Gram's, she led her inside. "Come in and get warm." After settling her on the loveseat nearest the fireplace, she excused herself when the door opened.

The sight of Eric in the foyer holding a potted flower stopped her.

A wan smile crossed his face. "Happy Thanksgiving."

"Thank you. I didn't realize you were coming."

His nervousness plain, he peered into the dining room. "I neglected to make a dinner reservation. If you don't have room—"

"We do." A bit too forceful, she admonished herself.

"Great." Stiffly, he held out the mums, decorated to look like a turkey. "These are for you."

"How sweet. You didn't need to."

"I wanted to."

She hadn't intended to insult him. "They're lovely." Her fingers grazed his in accepting them. The small contact zapped his energy through her, sizzling along her nerve endings.

As if aware of it too, he tensed, and somehow loomed taller beside her. His presence seemed to fill the foyer. Her feet anchored in place, concentrating her focus on him. When his gaze dropped to her lips and he eased closer, her grasp on the flowers loosened.

The rattle of the door opening caused him to glance away to the couple entering with overnight bags.

To clear her head, Joss stepped toward them. "Welcome."

She remembered to tell Eric, "Why don't you hang up your coat and join the others?"

"Of course." He stepped into the front room and halted. His fists clenched when Lydia looked up.

Her aunt brightened. "Doctor Hendricks. How wonderful. Come sit beside us. Tell us how you've been."

He shot a tentative glance at Joss.

She cradled the flowers. "Go ahead. It's safe. My aunt won't be doing any readings tonight."

He released a breath, seeming to steel himself before going in.

Maybe it was time to open a bottle of wine. First, she greeted the newcomers. After setting the flowers on the reservation desk, she engaged in small talk with a couple registering for a room, nerves rattling from her encounter with Eric. Would he have kissed her if the visitors hadn't arrived when they did?

At the foot of the stairs, she directed the people to the second floor. Instinctively, she turned to the front room and immediately met Eric's gaze. Electricity shocked her, concentrating in her lower belly. Hoping it would subside, she hurried to the kitchen.

The vibration remained steady. "I think I'll open the wine now. Lydia's latched onto Doctor Hendricks already." Joss rummaged in the drawer for the bottle opener.

"Doc Hendricks is here?" Tammy strained to look past her.

"Yes. He brought flowers," she blurted, then regretted it. Unsure why she mentioned it, Joss's cheeks burned.

Annie's brows flew upward. In a knowing tone, she said, "Oh," and exchanged a sly glance with Tammy.

She should never have said a thing. "It's a formal gesture from a guest to a host."

All innocence, Tammy said, "Sure." She busied herself arranging stuffed mushroom caps on a platter.

Despite the buzz still singing along her veins, Joss kept her voice airy. "They're cute. Mums shaped like a turkey."

Too enthusiastically, Annie nodded. "I've seen those. They are cute."

At her placating tone, Joss worked the corkscrew faster. The blessed pop of the cork's release was a wonderful sound. She poured a glass of Riesling and gulped.

At Annie's quizzical glance, she swirled the last in her glass. "Had to test it. It's a new brand. Very good." She downed the last of it. The tingle working through her subsided, and her muscles relaxed.

Grabbing napkins, Tammy shouldered the tray. "I'll take these out front."

Annie opened the oven door. "Twenty minutes, tops, before dinner."

"Perfect. Hopefully everyone will be here by then." If only Kyle had the courtesy to arrive early. Joss suspected he'd make a late entrance and an early departure. At least her family would spend the holiday together.

* * * *

The crackling fire and mellow wine eased Eric's tension. Another last-minute decision, coming here. Because of an emergency call, he'd missed the flight to Denver. Profuse apologies to his sister failed to ease her concern about him spending Thanksgiving alone, eating a microwaved turkey dinner.

"I won't be. There's a new inn down the street. I'll eat there with neighbors." That placated her, and the idea gained appeal. Why not? He'd hate to miss an old-fashioned turkey dinner. A legendary one. He had almost smiled.

By the time he'd parked outside the inn, his grin had disappeared along with his confidence, and he'd wondered why the hell he'd come. The urge to flee had momentarily overtaken him. He'd slipped the keys back into the ignition. An image in his head had stopped him. Sheree, opening her apartment door, pulling him inside.

Another vehicle parked beside him. He forced himself out of the truck and followed the couple inside.

Luckily, Charlie Fulton's arrival shifted everyone's focus to him. He described at length the renovation process, praising Joss and Annie for their hard work. "Especially Mrs. Gibson. She's a dynamo, always on the move. You know?"

Eric knew too well. Anytime he was near her, his head spun. She was always in motion, always changing things. A whirlwind of energy.

When Joss announced dinner, Eric followed everyone into the dining room. He evaded Lydia and sat near Charlie. Joss, Annie, and Tammy rotated from dining room to kitchen, kitchen to dining room, carrying trays of food.

The buffet style reminded Eric of home, jostling for first place with his sister. It lent a casual atmosphere to the evening. The food itself was another matter. A turkey at his parents' home seemed bland as flour paste in comparison. Whatever herbs mingled with ingredients in each dish tantalized his taste buds, and his senses. His awareness of the room around him heightened. He was especially sensitive to Joss's presence. Throughout dinner, he glanced frequently at her whenever she entered the room. Stupidly, he'd imagined her sitting beside him during the meal. She didn't sit anywhere, unless she'd eaten in the kitchen.

Charlie dominated the conversation, so there was little pressure to contribute much unless asked. Eric wondered whether Charlie's interest extended beyond the inn. The handyman perked up whenever Joss came by, and went out of his way to speak to her. She graciously stopped at their table, her easy laughter a reminder to Eric of the many hours she'd spent with Charlie. Her glance strayed to Eric many times, each time riveting him further. A curiosity lingered in her gaze. An invitation so compelling, when she stopped to ask if he wanted coffee, he rose from the table.

"You're not leaving, are you?" she asked.

"No," he blurted. He couldn't leave. Embarrassed at his inexplicable reaction, he covered by asking where the rest room was. The warmth—and relief—in her face told him he hadn't imagined it. Something was happening between them. He had no idea what, yet it overwhelmed him. He found himself in the downstairs bathroom with no recollection of having walked there.

Splashing cold water on his face, he told his mirror image, "Get a grip."

A long-forgotten urge twisted through him, making his hands fumble the towel onto the rack. *You're getting carried away.* Yet he couldn't deny, something about her beckoned to him on the deepest level, and he didn't want to stop. He returned to his seat and stared at the apple cranberry cake on the plate. Unadorned of whipped cream, it needed no embellishment. It smelled delicious.

Mr. Appleton inquired about his practice, and, as Eric suspected, wanted free advice on his cat's condition.

"I couldn't be sure without taking a look. If you'd like, bring him by tomorrow." He had nowhere else to be. The thought of spending the day alone used to appeal to him. No harried travel. No inquisitive relatives. Suddenly, his immediate future seemed bleak and pathetic. Nothing like when he visited the inn, always too short a stay.

As he spooned the last of the cake into his mouth, he met the scintillating gaze of the aunt, a knowing smile curling her lips. Surely as she'd emptied a bucket of cold water atop his head, a blast of cool passed over him. The woman gave him the heebie-jeebies. He hoped she'd left her damn tarot cards at home. He flashed a polite smile.

When Charlie announced his interest in going to the front room, Eric quickly said, "Good idea."

Lydia and the grandmother followed like wraiths, inspecting him with weighty stares.

Most of the others left soon after finishing their desserts. The few overnight guests retired to their rooms, leaving Eric with the aunt, the grandmother, and Charlie.

Lydia stood at the front window. "I don't believe it. Snow."

"Snow?" Charlie lumbered to his feet. "The forecasters didn't call for any."

"Whether they called for it or not, it's here. Quite a bit too."

Strange. The forecast predicted clear skies, yet a layer of white already covered the ground. An odd shiver of awareness passed over Eric when Joss emerged from the kitchen and a smug glance passed between the grandmother and aunt.

Gram sipped her tea like the queen regent. "You did a wonderful job with the renovations. As large as it is, this room has a cozy, inviting atmosphere."

Leaning against the back of her grandmother's chair, Joss smiled. "All it needs is a brass cricket for the hearth."

"A brass cricket?" Eric asked.

Lydia batted her lashes. "For luck, of course."

Slapping his hands against his knees, Charlie pushed to a stand. "I better be going. I'll be back soon enough tomorrow. Still have some rooms to paint upstairs."

A hint of encouragement edged Lydia's voice when she said, "Good night." She turned to the older woman. "Shall we get settled in our rooms?"

Gram sighed. "Yes, even a few hours of travel tire me out."

Annie burst from the kitchen. "Honey, I'm sorry. I have to take Tammy home. She's sick to her stomach."

Joss hurried to Annie's side. "Go, don't worry about a thing. I'll finish up."

Annie hesitated. "If this snow keeps up, I may not be able to come back."

She gestured her away. "Don't even try. I can handle it. Go, before the roads get worse."

Her friend scrambled back to the kitchen. The others scattered in every direction, upstairs and into the kitchen and outside, leaving Eric the sole remaining person. Besides Joss.

For a moment, they stood there uncertainly, the air between them crackling with tension. At a door slamming upstairs, she broke away her gaze. "Excuse me. I have to…" Jerking a thumb backward, she frowned and then hurried to the kitchen.

To appear busy, he poked at the logs in the fireplace. The flames leapt higher, and he crouched to stare into the fire. He should be used to it by now—everyone else had a family to share the holidays with. Everyone except him. And Joss. His awareness of her heightened. Each time he tried to dredge up a memory of Karen, the vivid image of Joss in the kitchen blotted it out. He shouldn't sit here. He should go home, but if he did, Joss would be left to clean up by herself.

As if in a dream, he moved to the kitchen doorway. "Need any help?"

Dishes and food warmers crowded the counters. She flashed a humorless smile. "No, I'm fine."

Then why didn't she sound fine? She sounded upset. He moved closer, needing to do something, anything, to soothe whatever pained her.

She fumbled containers into the fridge. "Why don't you go relax? You're welcome to put on a CD, maybe sit by the fire. Before you go home."

He didn't want to do any of those things. He stood dangerously close, fighting the urge to touch her hair, run his hands down her back.

With wide eyes, she averted her gaze, her body tense as she moved to the sink, picked up the towel and dried a glass. "It's supposed to dip into the twenties tonight, so if you need to get going now, then—"

He slipped the towel from her hand. "I live three minutes away."

"Oh. Right." She turned toward him, opening to him. To the possibility of him. "The snow…"

Only inches away, the heat from her body cleaned the slate of his mind. He operated on impulse. On need.

In a breathless rush, she asked, "Did you enjoy your meal?"

"Mm hmm." Every course of the meal brought his taste buds to life as never before. He traced her collar bone with one finger.

"Eric…" She inclined her head toward his hand.

The motion, slight as it was, spurred his pulse faster. At hearing her murmur his name, his heart revved in his chest like a race car engine ready to explode at the starting line. "Don't send me away. Please." He touched his lips to her forehead, then her nose.

Her breath smelled of coffee and cranberries, and a hint of lavender. "You're making it difficult to…"

His mouth hovered near hers, just out of reach. "Don't say no," he whispered.

The honey gold of her hair caught the light, and she appeared illuminated from within. Parting her lips enticingly, she searched his face.

It wasn't a no. It was enough of a maybe that he closed the space between them. He shuddered with tantalizing release as her soft lips and sweet-tasting tongue moved against his. She pressed against him, driving him wild. Years of pent-up need rushed through him, and he crushed her to him, his hands in her hair, then along her waist and thigh, wanting to know every curve, every inch of skin.

At a banging on the door, she jerked away, breathless.

"Mrs. Gibson?" A man stood outside.

Whoever it was, Eric hated him for interrupting.

Extracting herself from his embrace, she smoothed her hair and opened the door. "Yes?"

A strange kind of happiness filled Eric when her voice shook.

The man shifted on the step. "I'm here to pick up the food."

"The food?" She held a hand to her head.

"Yes. For Second Harvest."

"In the snow?" She leaned out the door in amazement. "Oh, it's stopped."

He frowned. "Flurries never bothered me. Now, the food?"

Flurries? Eric peered out the window. The snow had stopped as mysteriously as it had begun.

"Yes. Sorry, I'll get them for you." Joss rushed to the counter, where the half-full aluminum containers sat. "Give me one minute."

"It's not ready?" the man whined.

"I'm sorry, dinner ran late and…" Her breath strangled. "Oh, never mind." She whirled into action.

"I'll help." Eric scraped the stuffing into the tin. He maneuvered around her, anticipating her needs by handing her bowls, taking away empty ones. Together, they topped the tin containers with a foil lid and stacked them in a box.

The man grumbled a thank you and left.

With a sigh, she leaned against the counter. "Next year, I'll know to be ready for him."

"I hope he doesn't serve it to the homeless with the same scowl." He wanted to move closer, back into her arms, but wasn't sure how to span the distance. "It's generous of you to donate leftovers."

Her eyes bright, she sounded breathless. "We'd have been eating turkey sandwiches for weeks otherwise."

"It's very nice." Already said that. *Hell.*

She turned. "I should finish cleaning up."

He caught her arm and twirled her, pinning her against him. "Can't it wait?" He wasn't sure he could. Once he'd tasted her, his appetite grew ravenous. Maybe he'd never get enough of her. He had to find out.

* * * *

Joss's arguments fell away. He radiated heat and need, crackling along his skin like an electric storm that sent vibrations to her core.

"Joss."

His low voice rumbled over her like thunder. The whisper burned along her nerve endings like tequila, at once loosening her inhibitions and tightening her insides. She ran her hand up his neck and into his hair. A dangerous motion, possibly self-destructive, like throwing herself into the fires of Hell. At the moment, she wanted to risk the burn of his fire. The intensity shone in his eyes. Penetrated her skin wherever he touched. Rather than the scorching she expected, his warmth proved surprisingly pleasant, and she wanted to burrow deeper.

She clung with the desperation of one drowning. She gave herself over to the cresting wave crashing over her head. Risky as it was—anyone could have walked downstairs, come through the back door, or seen them through the window—she didn't protest when he reached beneath her skirt and scooped her up to the counter. In clumsy haste, she unzipped his trousers and wrapped her legs tightly around his thighs, urging his upward thrusts from his tiptoe stance. His urgent whispers, constant murmurs of her name, brought her to a quick climax. Soon after, he clutched her tighter yet, and his body shuddered against hers. Through his dampened shirt, his heart pounded against her chest.

His breaths deepened and slowed. "Are you all right?"

The question—his concern—surprised her. Touched her. "Yes."

With a shy smile, he caressed her cheek with his thumb. "It was uh, quicker than I would have liked."

"For me too."

"We could go to your room." He eased away to meet her gaze, his intensity concentrated on her. "I'll try to make it last longer next time."

Her stomach clenched. Next time. There couldn't be a next time. There shouldn't have been a first time. "No, I can't." What if *they* found out? Her head still reeled from trying to absorb all the family history. She couldn't chance becoming involved with anyone right now.

His hand stilled at her waist, and he drew further back. "Right. You're probably exhausted."

"Yes," she lied. She wouldn't sleep a wink.

"I could help you finish up."

Sending him away would be easier if only he would stop acting so nice. One hint at all the strange goings on in her life, and he'd disappear in a hurry. "It's better if I do it myself." Less dangerous for him should an Underworld spy lurk outside. And the sooner he left, the less chance her family might spot him too.

When she heaved a strangled breath, his smile faded.

Easing away, he said, "Right, I'll go."

She opened her mouth, then closed it. Much as she wanted him to stay, he was safer to leave. With his vibes still so unsettled and chaotic, she doubted he could handle much more. Yet, anyway. Better to take it slow.

He kissed her, brief, warm, and all-enveloping. "I'll see you."

Unable to bring herself to repeat the words, she nodded. "Good night." She fought the urge to call him back when he hesitated at the back door.

Time. She needed time to think. It had happened so quickly, sweeping away her reason. Her sanity, apparently.

With his hands on her skin still vivid in her mind, she went to bed.

* * * *

Driving the short distance to his place, Eric couldn't stop smiling. He hadn't planned to make love to Joss. It simply had happened, as naturally as if they'd done it thousands of times before.

In his imagination, they had. He'd never expected to be so lucky as to experience it for real.

Pulling his truck to a stop outside the door, he sat for a moment. Heat washed over him, reliving her touch. He'd never dreamed it would be so amazing. Desire so intense, it burned away any thought except to have her, every bit of her. He couldn't hold her close enough, get deep enough inside her.

So why had she pushed him away?

Stepping out of the truck, he stood rooted, staring at the inn. He should go back to her, right now. Clear up whatever misunderstanding had upset her.

Turning to the truck door, he ducked when something swooped near his head. "What the—" Each time he attempted to get back in his truck, black creatures flitted close. He waved to drive them off. More and more surged out at him.

"Get away." He swung harder. Glancing up, ice filled his veins. Their tiny faces resembled Sheree's. The same upturned nose, the same red lips, the same beady eyes.

Their screeches echoed through the darkness, oddly sounding like laughter. The creatures swarmed, pressing him toward his back door. Tugging his jacket over his head, he crouched and sprinted inside. Wings beat at the glass after the door closed behind him.

"Get lost!" His yell had zero effect. The creatures flew in a chaotic mass, flitting crazily. The black mass of bodies blocked his view of the inn. Not until he moved away from the door did they disband into the night.

Try as he might to conjure the warmth of Joss's embrace, her beautiful face, the only one who came to mind was Sheree. Frustrated, he went to bed. Each fleeting thought of Joss only brought an angry screech at the window.

Chapter 6

Footsteps on the stairs, and Taz's subsequent whining at the door, convinced Joss to leave her bed. Each day, she awoke and rose at the same time, drowsiness leaving her almost as fast as her eyes opened. Normally, she wouldn't spend the night reliving a man's touch, his skin moving along hers, moving inside her. Her body heat rose at the memory, causing her to push away the blanket. After it faded, cold crept back, and she burrowed into the covers again. More alarming was the fact it had actually happened. He'd given her no warning, no indication he'd thought of her romantically, but when he came into the kitchen, she knew exactly what he had in mind. Only one thing.

How long had he considered it? Not long, she guessed. An inkling, maybe, when he bought the flowers. Beneath the intense desire rising in waves like heat on a summer blacktop and propelling him toward her, she caught a vibe of something else—surprise. As much as her own.

So why did it happen? And why had she let it? Especially after what Aunt Lydia and Gram had revealed about her father? And John? A shiver coursed over her.

Taz sniffed at the door and waited with a look of expectation.

"Be right there, sweetie." After throwing on jeans and a sweater, she shuffled out. No one in the front or dining rooms, so she continued on to the kitchen.

Maybe Kyle had come home after all. Not even a phone call to let her know he wouldn't make it. Of the evening's surprises, her son's absence should have come as the least unforeseen, yet it cut deep. She'd nearly forgotten till now. How embarrassing.

Gram sat at the kitchen island cradling a mug with the string of the tea bag hanging over the side. "Good morning dear. Did you sleep well?" The twinkle in her eye indicated she already knew Joss's night had been a restless one. Hopefully, she didn't suspect the details.

"Yes, how about you? Were you comfortable?"

"Absolutely. The mattress is perfect, not too firm nor too soft."

"Wonderful." She hoped her grandmother wasn't embellishing to boost her spirits. "I better start the coffee. The others should be up soon."

"The inn's progressing nicely. I'm so glad to see you moving on with your life, dear. I worried about you."

"Grieving is a process. It may have taken longer for me, but there's no set standard for how long we mourn." She hated to compare herself to Gram, who'd functioned normally within a year of burying Grandpa. Outwardly, at least.

"Oh, I know. I knew you'd recover fully when you were ready."

"I wish you'd put more faith in me." Her grandmother instilled a strong ethic in Joss since she was a girl to triumph over any challenge.

"It wasn't a question of having faith in you, dear."

The click of heels preceded Lydia's entrance. "What wasn't a question of faith?"

Joss sighed. Now she was outnumbered.

"Morning, you beautiful ladies." Annie's cheer suffused the awkwardness. "No Black Friday shopping today?"

Joss probably should have. She was awake early enough, but Black Friday shopping never appealed to her. Consumerism embodied in mass hysteria, killing family traditions.

"No. I'd hoped to hear from Kyle, but..." She shrugged.

Annie's mouth dropped open. "No word? Did you try his cell?"

"Yes, I left a few voicemails. He'll call when he wants, I suppose."

Lydia raised a penciled brow. Her lips barely moved as she murmured, "He's a bit too much like his father."

Joss held back an argument. She'd never revealed her family quirks to her son.

Annie bustled into action gathering breakfast ingredients. "Thanksgiving was a wonderful success, don't you think?"

Joss held her coffee beneath her chin to absorb the warmth of the steam. Nothing quite so steamy as last night. "Oh, yes." If Annie only knew. "How's Tammy?"

"Fine. She must've sampled too many appetizers, and shouldn't have followed up with three helpings of dinner." Annie wrinkled her nose. "How strange about the snow, huh? The way it came down last night, I would have bet a hundred dollars we'd have inches on the ground. Plowable snow. And today, nothing. Like it never happened."

"Yes, very strange." Many forces conspired, it seemed, to get her alone with Eric. What—or who—she wondered, glancing at Gram and Lydia. Moot questions. She'd learned long ago not to inquire about such things. Tilting her head, Annie's piercing gaze broke Joss's fog.

"You're not very talkative today," Annie said. "I thought you'd be as excited about yesterday as me."

"I am excited." She sure was last night. "I'm burnt out, I guess. Not used to the hubbub yet, after three years alone." Lying didn't come easily to her, and she was sure Annie read her like a bad book.

Gram merely smiled. Oh, no, had she heard the commotion?

Of course not. Her grandmother didn't need to hear. She simply knew. She always knew. In cahoots as usual, the tilt of Lydia's head, the wicked curve of her lips, alerted Joss to the fact both understood, somehow, what had happened.

Annie's forehead creased in concern. "You're not coming down with something, are you?" Emptying pancake ingredients into the mixing bowl, Annie prattled on. "Owning a business where you come in contact with so many people can be a problem. They bring their germs here and sometimes leave them behind to share with you."

"I'm fine. I think I hear some guests. Let me go see if they need anything. I warned them last night how addicting your pancakes are." Anything to get away from the scrutiny of Gram and Lydia.

A mischievous smile lit Annie's face. "Let's hope they're enticing enough people will come back for them."

"Yes." Some addictions, she hoped, weren't contagious.

No more innuendo crept into the conversation. After finishing breakfast, Joss tried Kyle's cell again. His sleepy voice muttered something like, "Hello?" in an agitated tone.

Relief washed over her. "Kyle. Are you all right?"

"Yeah, fine."

Anger tightened her nerves. "Why didn't you call me?"

He groaned. "Sorry Mom. We hit this freak snowstorm on the way home, so crashed at a friend's. Weird, because we usually get snow at State College before here. Then I couldn't find my cell until it rang this morning."

Right, she wouldn't want them driving in snow. "I was worried."

"I wish I could stop over. My ride's leaving today. I'm on his schedule."

Stop over? She wanted to hug him, tell him he'd always have a home with her, even though he'd never stayed at the inn. Their old house was less than twenty minutes away. Maybe she shouldn't have sold it. But then she wouldn't have moved on with her life, either.

"I was hoping to see you." She sighed. "I'm glad nothing's wrong. You'll come for Christmas, though, won't you?"

"Sure." His voice softened. "Gotta go. Love you."

"Love you, too." Saying it aloud released the twisting tangles in her heart. No need to worry.

The inn guests left, and she said goodbye to Lydia and Gram. Despite having Charlie and Annie for company, the house was too big and empty.

* * * *

For days, she tried not to think of Eric. And failed. Thoughts of him flew at her vividly, and surprised her at every turn.

To occupy herself, she dug out the Christmas decorations. Too few to fill the inn, unfortunately. Joss would have to add to the collection next year. The cost of upcoming renovations weighed heavily in the budget, and the work she planned for spring would figure greater than the small amount they'd already accomplished. She'd splurge on a huge tree for the front window.

She found an evergreen grand enough for a passersby to see and be warmed by its cheer. Annie's husband Chet brought it to the inn in his pickup, and helped them erect it in the tree stand.

Two days later, Joss decorated it, first stringing the lights, then hanging the ornaments she'd collected for decades. The glass icicles. The jeweled snowflakes Gram hand-crafted long ago. The small, red glass balls resembling dew-kissed berries when they shone in the light. The glitter and glue and Q-Tip snowflake, pieced together by pudgy small hands so long ago, block letters on the back signed *Love, Kyle.* Her favorite ornament.

Finally, she strung rows of wooden cranberry beads, somewhat sparse on such a large evergreen. Stepping back to admire her work, warmth filled her.

Eric would see it every day as he drove past. Did he put up a tree? Or did he forego decorating his home and have the office staff decorate the practice? She hoped he wouldn't spend Christmas alone. If he came for Christmas dinner… She shuddered. Though she'd relived the night in the kitchen a million times since Thanksgiving, she couldn't let it happen again.

* * * *

First on the morning schedule, a pup's spay. Enough to keep Eric's mind occupied, yet routine enough to allow it to wander. Efforts to steer his mind away from Joss Gibson failed every time. The woman frustrated him.

Worse, thoughts of Sheree grew more distressing by the day. Every time he thought of stopping by to see Joss, Sheree would pop into his head. Offer him a drink, then sit on his lap and offer herself. Each time it happened, he was less startled. Though his brain wanted Joss, his body seemed to want Sheree. He couldn't understand it.

Only at work was Eric in his element. Animals responded to him better than people. A simple touch communicated his intent to help, to heal, to care. Much more effective than words, which lately tripped him up at every turn.

No, he corrected himself. Only with her. The harder he tried, the worse the situation grew. No other female twisted his insides in a tumult.

Karen had allowed his nurturing side to flourish. She never argued, never challenged him. In some ways, it represented an empty aspect of their marriage. In yielding to him, she'd given little consideration to things. Important details. He preferred to discuss issues, air out ideas. Compromise provided equal ground in a relationship.

Turning to the vet assistant, he nearly forgot her name. At the last second, it hit him. "Terry, will you bring the dog to the back?"

"Sure." Bending to gather the pup in her arms, she cooed, "Snuggles, you'll be fine in no time. Your mommy will take you home soon."

Ugh. "Snuggles?"

"Yes, that's his name."

"Are you married?" he blurted. At her wide eyes and gaping mouth, he rushed to cover the awkwardness. Such a stupid thing to bring up, but he knew so little about her. About any of his employees. He'd locked himself inside a prison of grief for too long and it was time to break free. "I mean, you're very good with the clients. The animals. A business conference I went to"—he needn't mention it occurred years ago—"recommended vets get to know their employees' personal history. To make the atmosphere more relaxed." God, he was babbling. He never babbled. She might think he was hitting on her. Or off his rocker.

Splaying her hand beneath the pup's rump, she wiggled her left hand, where a small diamond ringed the third finger. "I'm engaged."

"Good. Congratulations." *Whew. Off the hook.* He flashed a grin.

A confused frown tainted her smile. "Thanks." She carried the dog out.

Get a grip. Keeping up such questioning would land him in a lawsuit for sexual harassment or worse.

Everything was a jumbled mess.

Chapter 7

The weeks before the holidays usually slowed down. Eric looked forward to it, and dreaded it. This year, the practice kept him busy right through December, more people making appointments before going away on holiday, most bringing their animals away with them. The few people who boarded their pets needed shots updated so the kennels would allow the vaccinated animal to stay without fear of infecting others. Eric barely had time between appointments to catch a breath.

Still, he had no excuse not to have called her. He shouldn't have left the situation so awkward between them. Every time he reached for the phone to speak to her, Sheree's voice would sound through his head. *"Call me. I'll cheer you up."* Somehow, he doubted it.

The inn across the street bustled with life, with more guests leaving and arriving on weekends than the place had seen in years. From his bedroom, he could see twinkling inside. A few strings of white lights glowed around the porch. Nothing gaudy. The tree looming through the front windows drew his gaze again and again, until his heart ached. He wanted to be there, sitting by the fire with Joss in his arms, the shadows of the evergreen on the ceiling, the scent of pine filling the room. Her lavender scent intoxicating him.

Why couldn't he work up the nerve to call her? Better yet, go there and see her?

Because she doesn't want you. He didn't need a sledgehammer to knock him over the head. Her reticence, immediately after, had the same effect. But why? Making love to her had been amazing, if too fast. He wanted to make good on his offer so he could hold her all night. She'd only reject him again. The first time humiliated him enough.

That night, when his sister called to remind him of his family obligations, he reluctantly agreed. "I'll be there Christmas Eve."

"And you won't run off the next day?"

"Of course not."

She sniffed. "Well, you usually do."

"I'll stay until the day after. All right?" Maybe when he returned he'd be able to deliver the present wrapped in gold foil, sitting on his dresser.

* * * *

"I've told you everything." Sheree pounded her fists against the steering wheel, wishing she'd remembered her gloves. The freaking heater waited until the coldest day of the year to die. With rent due, she'd have to scrimp on other necessities. One good thing about waitressing at the diner—customers' leftovers. But now she'd have to add more shifts to earn enough to fix the car. Maybe get a second job, except where, in this tiny town? No one needed extra employees. Holy cow, she needed a break, and if they wouldn't give her one, she'd find a way without them.

"I want Eric. Now." The bastards had frustrated her beyond belief. The tantalizing hologram of Eric was the last straw. She didn't want some ghost of him. She wanted the man, in the flesh. Sheree let out a frustrated exhale, and her breath billowed in a cloud.

The dark man's eyes narrowed, but didn't dim their glow. "You're in no position to make demands."

She searched ahead for a spot to pull over her car. *No, don't draw unwanted attention again.* Last time, the officer had let her go with a warning, but she'd had to plead and cry. From now on, she'd beg no one. "This is a waste of time."

He turned his attention out the window. "Hardly. Our arrangement is mutually beneficial."

Funny, his breath made no steam in this cold. "Not so far." Her idea of benefits included Eric. Living in his big, lovely house. Cooking him dinner instead of serving the local geriatrics, cozying up to him at night. Sleeping later than daybreak and not working her buns off until dark.

"You'll see results soon," he said. "I hope we will as well."

She blurted, "It's not my fault she's not doing anything interesting to report."

"Perhaps you're not trying hard enough."

Resisting the urge to mimic him in a mocking tone, she said, "I told you, I've done everything I can."

"It seems unlikely."

She splayed her hands on the steering wheel. "I don't know what you want then."

"You're not making progress on your own. Get help."

She turned to argue, but the jerk had disappeared again.

* * * *

Entering the kitchen, Joss inhaled the delicious mix of apples, thyme, onion and celery wafting from the oven. "The turkey smells wonderful."

"I hope it tastes as good," Annie said, stirring the gravy. "I don't want to give Tom Larsen an excuse to complain."

"I'm not worried about him. I want the girls to enjoy themselves. It's their night to celebrate their victories."

Annie's quick smile erased the sullen mood. "They did so well on the riding circuit, didn't they?"

"Yes." Joss hoped it wouldn't give Tom the incentive to push even harder. His lust for trophies and blue ribbons lent an acrid smell to him. It had grown unbearable recently. The four riders, girls between twelve and fifteen, tended to wrinkle their noses when confronted with his presence, as if they too, smelled it.

Even now, sitting in the front room with their families, the girls gave Tom a wide berth and spoke formally, if at all, to him. Their usual easy camaraderie stiffened around him more each day.

The horses most definitely reacted badly. When Tom grabbed hold of a halter, the horse snorted, nostrils flared, eyes rolled fearfully to watch the trainer. Joss said nothing. Riding lessons grew infrequent during winter, though the girls came out on days the temperatures held above freezing to trot their horses around the ring. The girls posted gracefully in the saddles, and their breath, like the horse's, billowed in the cold air.

When Joss announced dinner, the parents, too, avoided sitting near Tom. When Joss and Annie served the meal, Tom ate ravenous and wild-eyed like a starving animal. With gaping mouths, others watched, at first forgetting to eat their own food.

Afterward, Tom rose to speak. In a booming voice, he glossed over the girls' hard work, cautioning at the same time they could never become complacent if they hoped to ride in the top circuits one day.

A sour look came over a few parents, who mumbled among themselves. Immediately after Tom finished, one father said, "Let's go open presents."

The girls rushed to the tree, where their exchanged gifts waited. Clearing the table, it reminded Joss of when Kyle was a boy, and she and John would watch as he tore off the wrapping paper, each exclamation more enthusiastic than the last.

She hoped her son would make good on his word to visit. She missed him. And she hadn't remembered John in days. Maybe weeks. More often, she'd thought of Eric. Before Kyle arrived, she'd have to put Eric out of her mind, or her son would surely pick up on it. Like her other relatives, he clued in to such things.

Passing through the dining room, she instinctively glanced out the window. She hadn't seen Eric since that night. She'd been so sure he'd come by within days, and her heart leapt against her ribs each time the blue SUV passed along the road, but he always drove by without stopping.

Annie came out of the kitchen. "How's it going?"

"They're nearly done, I think. Why don't you go on home?" Joss hated for her friend to stay late, especially near the holidays.

"Are you sure?"

"Of course. You've done more than enough."

"All right. Chet's been holding off watching a new DVD. It'll be a good movie to watch in bed."

"A guy flick?" She didn't miss having to endure those.

Annie's grin wrinkled her nose. "I'll get back at him with my mushy Christmas movies."

An ache filled Joss. She'd go to bed alone. Again. In a false show of bravado, she smiled. "You'll have to let me borrow a few. The mushy movies, not the macho ones. Taz doesn't mind, so long as I share the popcorn."

Annie gave a sad smile, then hugged her. "I'll see you tomorrow. How many for Christmas Eve dinner?"

"A family of five. Unless Kyle actually puts in an appearance."

Annie touched her wrist. "He will."

Joss's throat constricted, and the "sure" she uttered came out hoarse. To curtail further pity, she dismissed her friend. "Tell Chet hi for me."

By the time the partiers went home, it was nearly ten o'clock. Something about Tom Larsen unnerved Joss. Tonight, the trainer's presence grated her nerves, pricked alert her faculties. She couldn't quite pinpoint why. The trainer's sharp glances seemed to search for something. Taz watched his every move, listening with raised ears. Only when Tom left did the dog sprawl on the floor and close his eyes.

After clearing the last of the dishes, she stared out the kitchen door. Beyond the empty field, the veterinary practice stood in complete darkness, as if an empty shell. An eerie shiver crept over her, and she rubbed her arms.

Weariness drove Joss to bed. Taz jumped up and curled near her feet. She listened, expecting to hear a truck pull up, and hesitated before turning out the light, though she knew Eric wouldn't come. *Where are you?*

* * * *

Too many nights of insomnia. Eric's nerves jangled. He operated with rote motion, actions ingrained in his consciousness. Could people be mentally battered? Unable to think straight. Haunted by visions of himself with Sheree. His head hurt from trying to drive the images from his head and replace them with Joss. He needed days of good, sound sleep, devoid of dreams.

He found himself parked outside Kara's Kafe for the fifth time this week, and it was only Tuesday. What the hell was he doing? His hand reached for the handle to climb out. He willed it to stop.

The sight of Tom Larsen crossing the street toward the diner caught Eric's attention. Tom publicly disapproved of diner fare. Had the same weirdness trapped Tom? Eric crept out of the truck and along the outside of the building. He peered inside in time to see Tom and Sheree slip into the back room.

Anger pumped through Eric. He gripped the edge of the window. No way. He couldn't be jealous of Tom. He didn't care about Sheree. So why did his teeth clench after seeing them together?

* * * *

"Well?" Sheree folded her arms over her chest, shivering. The dark alley provided cover, at least. She should have grabbed a sweater.

Tom shrugged. "The party went fine. Nothing out of the ordinary."

"Dammit." The woman must be hiding something. Somewhere. Why else would The Underworld suspect her of plotting against them? Or whatever the fool demons down there suspected.

"Maybe the ground's too cold now," Tom said. "Didn't you say it was something underground?"

Did he think her stupid? "Are you serious?"

"Yes. She probably can't do anything until spring."

Hmm. They might buy the excuse. Or it might at least buy her some time. "I don't get it."

Tom stiffened. "Are you sure they'll give me a top rated thoroughbred?"

She rubbed her arms. "All I can do is ask."

He frowned. "I always knew there was something strange about the place."

Yeah. Whatever. "I gotta go." She turned for the door.

He grabbed her wrist. "Hey. I want my thoroughbred."

Yanking from his grasp, she glared. Even one minion could be such a pain in the butt. "I said I'll tell them." First she wanted Eric. Then she'd worry about getting Tom his stupid horse.

* * * *

Not even gravy helped the dry turkey. Eric gulped down a few bites and pushed his plate away. Some Christmas. He should have stayed home. Worry furrowed his sister's brow. "I hope you're eating more?"

"My stomach's in a knot." No need to say why. The more he thought about visiting Joss, the more twisted it became.

His mother assessed him. "You're not coming down with something, are you?"

"No, I'm fine."

"You're not fine," his sister said. "You need someone to take care of you."

"Eileen's right," his mother said. "Aren't you seeing anyone yet?"

He'd prepared for the interrogation, knew they corroborated on how to approach the subject. They'd been at it the past year. So why did it throw him off guard this time? His mouth fell open, and he stared at the centerpiece candle. In its flame, there was Joss. Willowy in a white gown, emanating strength of spirit. Reaching for him. Gazing up at him with fiery-bright love. Lips parting as he bent to kiss her.

Eileen's sharp intake of breath snapped him out of it.

Eyes wide, his sister exclaimed, "You *are* seeing someone."

"No." He couldn't claim to be, exactly.

"There's someone you'd like to date, then?" His mother prompted hopefully.

His father harrumphed. "Leave him alone. His private life is not up for public discussion."

"Thanks Dad." One ally, at least.

Peering over his bifocals, he added, "They're right, son. You're overdue."

"It's time," his mother said.

He had no wish to discuss it. "What's for dessert?" He shoved away from the table and went to the kitchen. A bracing breath, and he returned to make a show of eating the pecan pie slice he'd grabbed, though it did nothing to satisfy him.

With the excuse of having to get up for an early flight, he went to bed early. The television blared in the living room, and his mother and sister at the dining room table argued loudly whether a full house beat a flush in playing poker.

He stared at the ceiling. Does Joss know I'm gone? What's she doing right now?

Sheree loomed over him, startling him fully awake. Her pouting red mouth parted, and she licked her lips, writhing above him. *Come to me,*

Eric. I want you. She dragged her finger down his chest, leaving a sizzling trail.

He scrambled out of bed, wiping away the eerie sensation of her phantom touch.

Maybe his mother and sister were right. It was time for him to date. Boiling Springs wasn't exactly a haven of available women. Sheree displayed her interest clear enough. For the life of him, he couldn't imagine what he might have in common with her. *There's only one way to find out.* His subconscious must be sending him signals. A date with Sheree might break whatever spell he'd fallen under.

He settled back on the pillow. Disappointment tainted his relief. Sex had never been as great as it had been with Joss. And he'd been so indescribably delirious with bliss. He should have known it was too good to be true.

* * * *

Finally, Joss drifted into a restless sleep. The dream recurred throughout the night most vividly, the man in the lavender field making love to her with even more passion. In the morning, she awoke in a sweat and showered to wash off its remnants.

Throughout the day, she returned to the front door repeatedly. Except for Annie, no one arrived until late afternoon. The Andrews, three grown siblings and their parents, had sat down to the ham dinner when headlights shone into the kitchen.

Joss went to the door. "Kyle." The familiar rush of joy hit her. Had he grown taller? Thinner? Her arms ached to hug him.

Annie smiled. "I knew he'd be here."

Straining to see, Joss discerned a second figure. "And someone else."

A girl about Kyle's age climbed out of the driver's side, and the two jogged toward the house hunched against the cold.

"Merry Christmas, Mom."

She gathered him into her arms, inhaled his cold, clean scent. "Merry Christmas to you, baby."

He tensed and drew away. *Guess I better not call him that.* He towered over her, wide-shouldered but body still lanky like a boy. So much like John, the same curly, dark hair and smiles too rare. At least he had her eyes.

To Kyle's friend, she said, "Hi." Almond-shaped, dark eyes met Joss's gaze. She had a pleasant, heart-shaped face framed by straight dark hair past her shoulders, a purple streak running down one side, and a tiny diamond pierced her nostril.

"Oh, that's Jana," said Kyle. "Jana, Mom."

The lithe girl flashed a smile. "Nice to meet you."

"You too." No wonder Kyle had been so busy. The looks they shared gave away their relationship.

Kyle pecked Annie's cheek. "Something smells great. Are we too late for dinner?" He glanced hopefully at the pans on the stove.

"Never. There's always food for you." Annie drew out two plates. "Help yourselves."

Kyle and Jana sat at the kitchen island, speaking in low tones. Smiling almost nonstop.

Annie had already filled containers of food for Chet when Kyle brought their empty dishes to the sink.

"You finished quickly."

Kyle focused on washing the dishes. "We have a party to go to."

Joss struggled to hide her disappointment. "You're leaving?"

"We'll be back." Kyle's smile froze. "Jana's spending the night, okay? I mean, you have extra rooms, don't you?"

Smiling through her surprise, Joss said, "You're in luck. We do tonight."

Annie added, "Weekends and holidays have gotten pretty busy. I'll see you tomorrow?"

"It's Christmas, isn't it?" Kyle opened the door and waved.

His friend said, "Nice meeting you. Thanks for dinner."

Joss hovered near the window as they climbed into the car and drove off.

"He came home at least," Annie ventured. "And she seems nice."

"It would be nice if I could spend some time with him." Since he'd decided to attend Penn State, she'd understood their visits would be limited by the two hours' drive. She just hadn't realized how limited. Before she went to bed, she left a note and a room key on the kitchen island.

Long past midnight, footsteps stumbled through the door and continued upstairs. Neither appeared until nearly noon the next day. Joss knew better than to entertain a fantasy of sharing an old-fashioned Christmas morning with her son. She kept her tone casual when he shuffled into the kitchen. "How was the party?"

In a gravelly voice, Kyle said, "Awesome. Any coffee?"

Taz reared on his hind legs and stretched to his full length so Kyle could scratch his neck.

"I just brewed a fresh pot. I have a small turkey in the oven. It'll be ready about four. Are you up to opening gifts?"

His face fell. "I didn't know we were giving presents this year."

"It's nothing extravagant. Don't worry." Gifts were the last thing on Kyle's mind, apparently. Not that she cared. It was enough to have him here. She led him to the front room, and handed him the three wrapped packages. With Taz lying near the tree, it almost seemed like the holiday they used to share.

The hooded sweatshirt, jeans and scarf he acknowledged with shy *thank yous*. After opening the small gift bag holding one hundred in cash, he kissed her cheek. "Sorry I didn't get you anything."

"I don't need anything." At the hollowness of the words, she nearly crumbled, and feared tears would escape. Jana descended the stairs, so she shook off the sadness and stood. "How about if I make French toast?"

The two said yes, so she set to work, grateful for something to occupy her hands, if not her mind. She wished the kitchen door didn't provide a view of the veterinary practice. Each time she passed, she couldn't help peer out to see if the blue SUV had returned. No vehicles sat in the main parking lot.

After feeding the kids, she left them on their own to speak freely.

Mid-afternoon, Lydia called, breathless with excitement. "I had the most fantastic dream. Two dreams, actually."

Joss chuckled. "Merry Christmas, Aunt Lydia."

"Merry Christmas. Are you alone?"

What a strange question. "No, I'm not."

"I knew it." Triumph edged her tone. "Who's with you?"

"Kyle and his friend." Or girlfriend? Kyle hadn't mentioned her before, so Joss wouldn't assume.

"Oh." Her voice fell flat. "I thought sure it would have happened already."

"What would have happened?"

"My dream. Don't you want to hear? You know they always come true."

Maybe her aunt's did. Joss's certainly didn't. "All right."

Lydia's voice deepened. "A man will bring you a gift of luck wrapped in gold, and happiness tied in a bundle that you'll both give away."

"I didn't know either one could be wrapped in such a way." Joss laughed in spite of the strange apprehension shimmering within her. What sort of bundle? And how would they both give it away?

Her aunt continued. "I'm not sure how these fit together. The second dream was the best. Something to do with the lavender field."

"What?" Joss tensed.

"I know you haven't planted it yet. You intend to, don't you?"

"This spring, yes."

"In this field of lavender, you will find the greatest sexual fulfillment you've ever known. This man will be your lifelong lover and friend."

My dream. "Enough. I mean it."

"I'm only telling you my dream, darling. The most sensual dream you can imagine."

She already knew, but couldn't admit it to Lydia. "Didn't Santa bring you anything else?"

Tittering laughter trickled through the phone. "Oh, my dear, you know I don't rely on mythological figures to fulfill my needs. I'm more self-sufficient than that. And so are you."

"If only." Then she wouldn't obsess about the night Eric took her over the moon.

"Chin up, dearest. Soon my dream will be your reality, and oh, do I envy you."

When Kyle came in, Joss jumped at the opportunity. "Here's Kyle. Say Merry Christmas to Aunt Lydia."

Taking the phone, Kyle said, "Merry Christmas, Aunt Lydia. Are you coming for dinner?"

Joss bustled around the kitchen, preparing a full meal, and was glad Kyle and Jana picked up slack in the conversation during dinner. They left soon after, as Joss suspected they might.

"Guess it's just you and me again, Taz."

When Annie called to wish her happy holidays, she invited Joss over for dessert. "I baked your favorite. Chocolate cheesecake."

"Tempting. But no, thanks. Taz and I are going to watch a movie." An image flashed in her mind of her and Eric in bed, Taz and a bowl of popcorn between them. *Stop it.*

"I'll save you a slice. How did everything go today?"

If it hadn't been for Lydia's weird phone call, the day might have been better. She wouldn't confide it to Annie. "The three of us had a nice time."

Tonight would be nicer if her vision came true. No chance of that. Eric was gone and had been avoiding her anyway. Yes, she'd hoped he'd take some time to decide what he really wanted. Apparently, he wanted Sheree. Tom had taken too much pleasure in sharing the fact Eric was dating her. To ignore the sting of his rejection, Joss had put off making a decision about veterinary care for Taz. A reminder postcard had arrived with a few holiday cards. She'd planned to have Eric take over care of her dog, but how awkward would that be?

She filled the popcorn maker and popped in the DVD. "Come on, boy. Let's go watch a movie." Not the holiday celebration she'd hoped for, but it would have to do.

* * * *

Since arriving home two days earlier, he'd spent all his energy fighting the urge to drive into town. It had exhausted him, so he gave in. Gripping the steering wheel, his nerves rattled more than the truck's springs. A parking space opened up near the diner, and he slid the truck in. He dragged himself inside and hoped the struggle would ease. Patrons occupied every last table, so he took a stool at the far end of the counter.

Sheree approached, hips swishing. "What's your pleasure?" she asked in a breathy voice. Normally a dull platinum, her hair reflected an unnatural sheen, like it had been recently lacquered.

Sweat broke out on his forehead. "Tuna pita, please. And iced tea."

Her light brown eyes reflected a strange tinge of orange. "You eat such healthy food."

"Not always. Dinner's a challenge." Right now, breathing seemed a challenge.

Cradling the order pad to her chest, she sighed. "I know. Come to dinner at my place. I'll cook you something hot and delicious." From the gleam in her eye, and the way she bit her fingernail, she might have said *let's have hot, nasty sex*.

His appetite waned. "Oh, no. I couldn't impose."

"I insist. We can't have you eating frozen dinners, even the manly kind." Her lips curled in a way that reminded him of Catwoman. Her eyes, too, appeared more slanted. Maybe she'd undergone plastic surgery recently.

"I don't eat those." Not the point, he knew. Not in the least. Warmth crept up his neck. He worried he might be sick to his stomach. Thankfully, only words spilled out. "Why not let me take you to dinner instead?" He croaked the question, and immediately wished he could take it back.

She pressed her hips against the counter. "Seriously? When, tonight?"

"No," he blurted. Embarrassed, he clarified, "I have appointments tonight. How about Saturday?" He needed time to psych himself up for it.

"Saturday's great. What time?"

No pretense of having to check her calendar? Didn't most females follow standard dating procedure? "Um, seven?"

Leaning toward him accentuated her cleavage. Magnified it. When he tried to look away, his gaze held there as if caught in the dark matter, the black hole between her breasts. His head swirled, and he unwittingly drew closer as if caught in a sci-fi tractor beam.

"Make it six." The sibilance of the word hung in the air like acrid smoke.

"Okay. Six." Did an hour make any difference?

Standing straight, she broke his line of vision, and his head cleared. After a mental shake, he gulped the milk she set before him.

"Your pita will be out in a jif." With a slow wink, she sauntered to the kitchen.

He checked to see if anyone watched. Sheree acted a bit off the wall today. She'd never come on to him like this before.

Though Sheree continued waiting on other customers, he had the distinct impression she kept him in her peripheral vision. Without staring, he tried to pinpoint, exactly, what seemed different about her. The set of her shoulders—squared instead of slouched. The firm tone in her voice, not soft like it used to be. Definitely the hard gleam in her eye. Cold and distant, despite the enthusiasm she'd shown. No, not enthusiasm. Greediness, then victory. As if she'd laid in wait for him, and when he asked her out, she snapped up the chance with the chomp of an alligator.

Reaching for a packet of sugar for the iced tea, Eric drew back his hand. A mercurial glob rolled across the counter toward the arm of the man beside him. Before Eric could think to warn the guy—of what? Stray mercury from the tuna?—it shot up the man's arm, crossed his shoulder, climbed his neck and disappeared inside his ear.

Stifling a gasp, Eric froze. "Are you all right?" Had he seen something inexplicable? Or maybe some play of light had caused the strange illusion.

The man swiped at his ear with his finger, the way people do to wave off an insect. "Sure. How's it going with you?" His pupils dilated to an enormous size, then flashed silver.

Stiffening, Eric leaned away. Something weird was definitely going on, and it had nothing to do with the tuna.

The man's eyes glazed. "Come to think of it, I'm suddenly not well. Sheree, what do I owe you?" He pulled out his wallet and wobbled to a stand.

No wonder such a strange unsettledness crept over Eric. Surreal, like he'd been thrust into a low-budget remake of *The Twilight Zone*. Left and right, no other unusual globules lurked. He wasn't about to take any chances. "I have to go too."

The walls closed in, the door loomed too far away, as if at the other end of a tunnel. His heart rate climbed the stairway to heaven. A clammy sweat greased his palms. The diner took on a carnival atmosphere, people talking too loudly, their conversations drowned out by laughter and flatware clinking against the white dishes. Everything blurred, as if he rode a carousel.

Everything except for Sheree. The sole unmoving thing in the blur, she stared with intense eyes.

Squinting to focus, he pulled out his cell, pretending to check a message. Standing clumsily, he bumped the man sitting on the stool beside him.

"Where are you going?" Sheree spoke in two different voices, an impossibly deep, menacing voice parroting her soprano. His spine literally tingled. The rest of him went numb. "Uh..."

She sidled closer. "You haven't eaten yet. You're not leaving, are you?"

"Yes." He whirled toward the door.

"Wait," ordered the two voices.

Like a puppet whose strings snapped tight, he halted. "What?" he managed to croak.

Her deep voice echoed inside his head. "You haven't paid."

Gulping hard, he drew out his wallet and tossed a twenty on the counter. "Keep the change."

She commanded, "Not so fast."

Panic churned up, and his tongue thickened.

Appearing at his side, she held up an order slip. "Here's my number." Tucking it into his shirt pocket, she peered up at him through slitted eyes. Dagger-hard eyes.

He tittered like a little girl. "Oh, right."

When she sidled away dismissively, the invisible force released him. As he scrambled for the door, the two voices called after him in a sing-song tone. "Call me."

The door closed behind him, and the pressure in his chest eased, but not much. "Like hell."

Chapter 8

Joss whistled for Taz. "Time for your vet visit, boy. Annie, we'll be back in about an hour and a half."

Annie frowned in puzzlement. "Why not take him to Doc Hendricks?"

Joss held up the leash. "He's so gruff."

Taz slunk away.

"What's wrong with you? Let's go."

Instead, he trotted to the bedroom.

Not in the mood to be trifled with, she carried the harness in and secured it around him. "I'd planned to wait until we got there for this. Apparently today it's more than a formality."

Three months had passed since she'd seen Eric. The few times he'd made a stable call, she'd been off on errands and missed his visit.

Good thing. Tom still went out of his way to tell her Eric was dating Sheree. Sheree! Joss had trouble wrapping her head around it. The night of the Halloween party, Eric had avoided the waitress like a rabid animal. Why date her?

Because you pushed him away after Thanksgiving.

Annie still stood in the foyer. "I agree he's not the easiest person to talk to, but his reputation as a vet is wonderful. Did you know he stayed up all night with Mrs. Albright's dog when Mr. Tibbles accidentally ate a can of macadamia nuts?"

"He did?" It shouldn't have surprised her. The way he bent to speak to Taz on his own eye level. The way he handled the horses, firm yet gentle. *The same way he handled you.*

"I trust Archie and Veronica's lives to him," Annie said. "All eighteen of them."

Joss smiled. Archie and Veronica, Annie's cats, lived an enviable life of luxury. "Taz is used to Dr. Marx, aren't you boy?"

The dog lowered his head and whined.

Annie pursed her lips. "I think he's trying to tell you something."

"Too late now." Joss held up the leash. "We're going. Come on."

She led him outside, and lifted him into the car when he wouldn't jump. After she closed the door, he skulked in the seat.

Getting in, she told him, "No treat for you."

The dog continued to fight her throughout the appointment. The vet assistant asked, "Is he sick? He's usually so cooperative."

She shot Taz a warning glance. "He's fine. Just contrary today."

On the ride home, he rested his chin against the half-open window.

When they arrived home, she ushered him through the back door. "I'm disappointed in you, mister. Behave, or else."

Annie wiped her hands on a towel. "I don't think he wanted to go."

"Please."

"You and he have a bond, stronger than my bond with Archie and Veronica." The impassioned plea took her voice up a notch.

Unharnessing Taz, she asked, "Anyone call?"

Tilting her head, Annie frowned. "Are you expecting someone special?"

No one she'd admit to. "I meant, any reservations."

Disappointment erased Annie's grin. "Oh. Yes. Two."

"Seriously?" Good. She needed work to keep her mind off other things.

"One couple for tomorrow night. Another single woman on Saturday."

"Great."

"Hopefully they won't mind the smell." Annie inclined her head toward the field, where the farmer maneuvered the tractor up and down the land beyond the stone bridge, dredging the earth over.

Something caught in Joss's chest. Hope. Nervousness. She needed the ground to prove fertile. If not, it would delay her plan for at least a year.

"It does smell awful." Annie curled her mouth down in disgust.

"It's the manure. It'll fade soon." Half to herself, she added, "I hope. We'll simply have to warn potential customers about the renovations, as we've been doing." She didn't want to turn anyone away, but honestly inform anyone who inquired there would be some unpleasantness throughout the day.

Joss turned away. "It is a bit strong." But to her, it smelled sweet—like the answer to a promise.

Groaning her agreement, Annie sipped her coffee. "You bought the seedlings?"

"Yes. And Jim Turner's working on the new tack room today." Mr. Turner had leapt at the work offer.

"Did Tom Larsen give you any more flack about it?"

"No, he stopped, begrudgingly, when the girls said they liked the idea. Their gear will be right next to the barn, and in a more secure place. The old summer kitchen has so many windows, great for what I need, but the Suttons said thieves broke in last year and stole some saddles. So I don't know what the fuss was about." Except Tom liked to be in control. An obnoxious man, he pushed his riding students hard. More than once, she'd grown angry at the way he yelled at the young girls. He might help them to win top ribbons on the riding circuit, but to Joss, he took the pleasure out of the sport.

"The summer kitchen will make a nice gardening shed," Annie said. "Handy for you."

More than handy. Vital. "Oh, Annie. If this works out the way I want it to…." She couldn't finish for fear of jinxing it.

"It will. Keep the faith."

"Right." Faith hadn't helped after John's diagnosis. In her heart of hearts, she knew the first day he complained of pain that she was already looking at a ghost.

Her heart of hearts—her inner eye, sixth sense, psychic ability. Everyone called it by a different name. Joss only knew it never failed her.

"I have a knack for these things," Annie said. "Everything will turn around for you."

"Yes, I read something similar in my horoscope." Her smile faded at the sight of the vet's SUV slowing along the road.

Annie stood beside her. "Who is it? Doc Hendricks?"

"Looks like him." Her pulse raced thinking of him standing on her doorstep again.

A knock at the door took her breath away.

Oblivious, Annie strolled toward it. Joss couldn't move until Jim Turner, not Eric Hendricks, stood on the threshold asking for her.

Shaking off her silliness, she forced a smile. "I wasn't expecting you until later, after the foundation dried."

"I checked and it's ready as can be. Lucky the weather's cooperating. I'm ready to get started if you are."

"A man after my own heart." From the moment she awoke, Joss set to work and rarely stopped until exhaustion forced her to. Doing so kept loneliness at bay. The real man after her own heart, she tried not to think about.

* * * *

A call from Dr. Avery put an end to Eric's avoidance tactics. After minor surgery, the large-animal vet counted on Eric to fill in. The former racehorse, Maya, split a hoof and required immediate attention. Eric set aside his personal reluctance and grabbed his medical box.

Tom Larsen waited outside the stall with the teenage owner and her mother. The mare nickered nervously when he stepped inside.

Eric spoke in a low, constant voice. "Okay, pretty girl. I'm here to help." Unlike the ass who stood by watching. If he had to guess, Larsen ignored the injury. Eric wouldn't be surprised if the trainer had noticed the crack in the hoof and pushed the girl to keep going. In a few weeks, they'd compete in the first horse show of the season. He could practically smell Larsen's desire to win Best Trainer trophy, like a stud stallion catching the scent of a mare in heat.

Straightening slowly so he didn't spook the mare, he said, "You'll have to confine Maya to her stall."

Tom huffed. "For how long?"

To the girl and her mother, Eric explained, "As long as it takes. If you don't let the hoof heal, you risk the danger of Maya becoming lame."

With an exaggerated slouch, the teen clucked her tongue. "We've been practicing so hard."

Too hard, apparently. Eric left it unspoken. He turned his back to Larsen. "Amy, have you been picking Maya's feet?"

The teen shifted her feet. "Yes, I clean them before I saddle her."

"And you didn't notice the crack?" Impossible. Someone told her to ignore it. And Eric knew who.

"Well…" Amy's gaze flicked to Larsen.

"Amy?" Her mother asked, her expression stern.

The girl mumbled, "I didn't think it would hurt her."

"Did you see it?" Eric finally asked the trainer.

Larsen's chest puffed like a rooster. "It's probably the farrier's fault. He could easily have tightened the shoe too much." Tom strode outside.

Anger rose up at the trainer's evasion, a clearer indication of guilt than denial. Eric followed him out of the stable. "You didn't answer my question."

Standing beside the old summer kitchen, Joss met Eric's gaze, ducked her head and strode in their direction. "What's going on?"

"Nothing." Tom flashed a smile more plastic than a Ken doll's. "A misunderstanding."

Eric bristled. "Hardly. I understand too well."

Eyes blazing, Tom glared. "You don't have a clue. Fix up the hoof and be on your way."

Steeling himself, he struggled to keep a civil voice. "You realize I live down the road, in plain view of the riding ring? I hope I don't see Maya out there before I clear her. And I'll inform Dr. Avery as well." Possibly the authorities, if need be.

"Tell me what's going on," Joss repeated, stepping closer.

Tom's patronizing tone grated against Eric. "It doesn't concern you."

"It absolutely concerns her," Eric argued. "It's her property."

"Tell me now." Joss rested her hands on her hips.

Her insistence surprised Eric. Pride welled in his chest. Why, he had no clue. She listened to Tom's explanation, then turned to Eric. "Do you have another theory about it?"

Her clear gaze cut through his anger.

More relaxed, Eric answered, "The animal's welfare should be the first concern. Not ribbons. Or trophies."

"I agree," Joss said. "You'll abide by the doctor's word, right Amy?"

Tom balled his fists, shifting his stance. "I'm responsible for this stable."

Joss lowered her head as if ready to charge. "Ultimately, I am responsible. I expect you to act professionally. And make sure your methods are well within the law."

The trainer laughed without humor. "What are you saying? I'm doing something illegal?"

"I certainly hope not." Joss set her gaze on him, keeping her tone sweet. "Or I'd have to ask you to take your business elsewhere."

His lip curled. "I may anyway."

Joss stood straighter, as if ready for a fight. Tom easily stood more than a foot taller, so the sight would have been comical, except the occasion allowed no humor.

Through clenched teeth, the trainer growled menacingly.

Joss met his glare with equal ferocity. "You'd better leave."

"Or what," Tom sneered. "You'll call your grandmother?"

Eric turned to Joss. "What's that supposed to mean?"

Tom strode to his truck, revved the engine and took off.

Her features softened when she turned to Eric.

He shifted under the weight of her gaze. "I don't know why he's always trying to prove himself an alpha male."

"He's not an alpha anything." More quietly, she asked, "Will the hoof heal?"

He couldn't look away from her. He wanted to encircle his arms around her. Inhale her scent. Taste her again. "If they allow plenty of rest."

She peered up at him. "And you? How are you?"

Steeling himself, he forced a casual tone. "Fine. Why wouldn't I be?" His mind reeled. Before he knew what he was doing, he jerked away. Even though Joss's comforting presence eased his tense muscles, pressure continued to build in his brain, urging him to leave.

"I have to finish up. I'm late for another, uh…" He walked off, unable to finish the lie, leaving her as confused as himself.

* * * *

Joss planted row after row of lavender in the new field, with the sound of hammering and the electric saw in the background.

Each day, the vet's SUV slowed in passing. From behind the tinted windows, he watched. The day he'd come to treat Maya's hoof, her pulse had raced at the sight of him.

Standing together in their argument with Tom Larsen that day, Eric's presence had strengthened her. Otherwise, she might have run. Something about the trainer seemed off. If he'd claimed not to be himself, she'd have no trouble believing him. Tom's eyes had flickered red with anger, and his voice had held a subtle echo, as if from a deep canyon. Joss had never encountered anything remotely similar, and didn't like it. It set her on edge.

Against all precaution, she'd wanted Eric to stay with her. Despite the rumors of him dating Sheree, Joss detected his strong desire for her—as strong as her own. If he asked her again to take him to her bedroom, she might not have had the strength to say no. But definitely not her style to interfere in a couple's relationship.

The day after Jim Turner pounded the last nail into the new tack room, and hung the steel door, Joss handed four keys to Tom Larsen, taking care not to make further physical contact. Though the trainer appeared normal enough today, her instincts still sharpened around him, wary of what might emerge.

When the dark blue SUV pulled up alongside the barn, her pulse raced so high, she was sure it revved through the ley line as well.

As Eric stepped from behind the wheel, Tom said something to him that Joss barely heard over the rush of blood through her ears.

Eric's gaze crawled over the new structure, and landed on her with the force of lightning. "So it's finished?"

Joss couldn't find her voice.

Begrudgingly, Tom said, "It's the new tack room. Guess we were in the way." Tom's laugh held no humor.

Folding her arms over her chest, Joss braced herself. "As I explained, Tom, this new tack room will be more secure, so the girls won't have to worry about thieves. And they won't muddy their leather boots walking across the yard carrying those heavy saddles."

"Walking is good exercise," the trainer said.

Eric shot a cold glance at Tom.

Despite bristling at his suggestion that prepubescent girls needed to carry heavy saddle gear, she smoothed and sweetened her voice. "Now they can focus their energy on riding. They were excited about the lockers and the saddle stands Mr. Turner built."

The hint of a smile crossed Eric's face, then disappeared. "You're not going to tear down the summer kitchen?"

"No. It's part of the house's charm." And an important part of her plan.

"And history." Eric's insistent tone left no doubt the past ranked high with him.

"Yes. And history." *Even if it's best to bury it sometimes.* The inn's history provided a great deal of charm. Joss had no intention of disparaging it. "Jim will begin restoring it next week, after the girls move their tack." She aimed the last at Tom.

Relief showed in the vet's relaxed shoulders.

Abruptly, Tom stepped between them. "The farrier's coming soon. We should get started."

Did Eric's glance contain something like disappointment? *Don't be stupid. He could care less.* "Let me know if you need anything." With an inward groan, she excused herself and strode toward the house. If he needed anything. Like what? A back rub? A shoulder to cry on? She could have kicked herself.

She couldn't help glancing back, and disappointment pricked when he didn't do the same.

Chapter 9

A strange foreboding haunted Joss for days after the confrontation with Tom. Though outward appearances indicated nothing wrong, he harbored something dark within. Some unnamable threat sent up vibrations of warning.

To ward it off, she went to the kitchen where Annie's humming mixed with the clatter of cookware. Her friend's good nature always buoyed her.

At the stove, Annie stirred a pot of sauce. "The patio's coming along nicely."

"Isn't it beautiful? It will be better than I imagined." Adjoining the dining room, it would overlook part of the back field, already sprouting with rows of green shoots. Amazingly fast. Joss suspected their speedy growth had less to do with her green thumb than the hum of energy below ground.

"Then we'll have more customers than we can handle." Annie's false bravado sounded through her cheerful tone.

Joss wouldn't quash the mood with her doubts. "Absolutely. The painters arrive tomorrow, and then we'll schedule our grand open house. We'll make this work, Annie. I promise."

"I promise too. We're in this together."

"Like always." Not in the same proportion this time. Annie would lose a job if they failed, but Joss would lose everything.

Maybe it was only a case of nerves. Once the patio was in and the rest of the work finished, she could focus on her true goal.

Before she turned in at bedtime, a hushed hum stilled her. A breeze billowed the bedroom curtain and carried the soft sound. Like the whisper of a secret waiting to be told, the music called to her.

A flicker of light against the wall caught Joss's eye, and drew her to the window. Above the field, the flickers concentrated and grew dense. "Could it be…?" Afraid to say the word for fear it would frighten them away, she crept to the patio and stood on the edge, holding her breath. Before John's death, it had been many years—decades, honestly—since she'd seen such a display. She couldn't quite confirm her suspicion from where she stood, so quietly crept outside, across the yard to the stone bridge. Even at a distance, the illuminated shapes were indistinct. She stepped slowly closer.

The glowing figures stilled. Hovering, tiny heads turned in her direction in alarm.

Joss's breath caught in her throat. "Please don't go."

Gram had been right. She'd almost begun to think she'd imagined them at the Halloween party. That perhaps her grandmother's tales had brought figments of her girlish dreams to life in her mind. Or maybe the night of John's death, she'd conjured them. The flickers, resembling a disco ball in the foyer on Halloween, might have been some trick of light, explained by the reflection of mirrors and candles.

Yet, here they were, more glorious than she remembered, undeniable in their being.

She lowered to the ground and sat back on her legs. The glow around the fae brightened, and more gathered around like a cloud of energy, warm and loving and full of life. The swarm spread out, then approached until it surrounded her.

Laughing, she held her open palms skyward. The small figures floated in her aura, feeding it with their nurturing light. Several of the larger ones flickered near her head. Holding very still, Joss instinctively knew they meant to communicate something. The largest alighted at her brow and touched her temple.

A burst of brilliance within her mind erased everything from her sight. Gradually, the light faded to a mist, from which a vision appeared of the lavender field, with the flickering of the fae concentrated above one spot. As if passing through the crowd, the glowing orbs parted to reveal a man and a woman making love. Joss recognized herself, but saw only the man's strong shoulders and arms wrapped around her. His angled head obscured his face as he kissed her neck, collar bone, and breasts.

Her dream. If it came to her as a half-realized vision earlier, now it played in three dimensional Technicolor. As she watched herself and this man make love, every caress, every lick and thrust, pulsed through her. His sensuous moves brought greater fulfillment than she'd ever known. When it was over, she found herself lying back amongst the lavender, filled with shimmering bliss.

Joss opened her eyes. The largest creature hovered right above her. Without words, it intimated this man was her destiny. Her soul mate and true love. On the night she made love to this man in the lavender, her fate would be sealed, and she would share happiness with him for the rest of her life.

If she hadn't believed it before, she did now.

Unable to speak, Joss conveyed her gratitude through her thoughts. Gossamer wings fluttered, and the lights lifted into the sky.

She stood to watch them disappear. This time, she knew they'd be back.

* * * *

Where the hell am I? One moment, Sheree had been talking to the dark man in her apartment—another of his rude interruptions, with zero warning—and the next, she was here. Now she needed to find out where *here* was.

"Cool digs. Kind of dark, though." She longed to run her fingers over the bronze sculptures of dragons, maybe serpents, sitting on either side of the fireplace. Such a tall fireplace, taller than her. How the fire reached such heights, she couldn't guess. But hey, supposedly it was The Underworld, right? Where anything was possible. Yeah, except her getting Eric. She grimaced.

"Don't touch anything." The dark man shook his head in warning. "Lord Plouton will see you in a moment."

"Who?" Was he British or something? She didn't dress to meet royalty, but then again, he'd provided no notice before whisking her away.

He flicked lint off her shoulder. "My employer."

"Why does your boss want to see me?" This couldn't be good.

"Pay attention this time." His nostrils flared as he heaved a sigh. "To discuss the progress of your case."

From his tone, he meant the lack of it. Well, what had they given her so far?

He whispered, "Stand straight. Here he comes."

"Where?" Was there a door in the room? The candles in the wall sconces did little to light it. The corners faded into a black so thick, the darkness itself might have been the wall.

"Shhh." He nodded toward the fireplace.

A figure approached through the midst of the flames and walked out unscathed.

If her contact guy gave her the creeps, this Lord Plouton was downright spooky, like something out of a Halloween flick. Ghoulish, yet somehow classy. His skin was like ebony over gold. Sheer and shiny too. As he scrutinized her, his eyes appeared to blaze brighter beneath his furrowed brows.

She curtsied. "Pleased to meet you, Your Grace."

He threw back his head in laughter. To his employee, he asked, "Is she putting me on?"

The other man shrugged. "I don't think so, sir."

Lord Plouton's ebony eyes fixed on her. "Tell me, Sheree. Are you a woman of your word?"

"Yes." What did he mean, she'd lied? Knight or not, she wouldn't put up with such an accusation.

His smile turned to a scowl. "Then why, after months of waiting, have you not fulfilled our agreement?"

She could say the same thing. "I—"

Lord Plouton strutted like Mick Jagger, zig-zagging closer. "Are you not dating Eric, as we promised?"

Not the way she'd hoped. "Yes, but—"

Halting, he held up a finger, and cut off her air supply. Grabbing her throat, she gagged, so numb she couldn't tell if her feet still touched the ground.

"What's the problem?"

Trying to speak, she only managed a gurgling sound.

"Even with an accomplice, you have failed to give us what we need." The lord continued, a sharpness to his voice. "What you agreed to supply. Am I not correct?"

The edges of the room closed in. With the little strength she had left, she nodded.

Lowering his finger, she gasped, filling her lungs.

Narrowing his eyes, he practically hissed, "Do you need help?"

Still unable to speak, she nodded again.

To the other man, Lord Plouton said, "See to it." He strode back through the fireplace.

In a snap, Sheree appeared in her kitchen. She caught herself before toppling over.

The dark man sat on her kitchen counter, ankles crossed. "You understand this will increase your debt?"

Incredulous, her jaw dropped. "My debt?" He had to be kidding. She owed them nothing.

He clucked his tongue. "Shall I take it up with Lord Plouton again?"

Her blood sizzled with fury. "No." She never wanted to see the guy again.

Jumping off the counter, he alighted on the linoleum floor with no sound. "All right then. Hm, my employer was correct. You do lack a certain something." He snapped his fingers. "There. I've amped up your feminine wiles. You're welcome."

She rolled her eyes. "Uh, thank you?" What the hell for?

"And I'll allow you certain powers. You will use them to get us what we need."

"Powers?" This sounded promising. She'd love to have such control. Instead of people bossing her around, they'd do whatever she wanted. Oh yeah. She could get used to that.

Rolling his eyes, he disappeared.

"I don't understand," she called to the air.

Nothing. It figured. From the beginning, it felt like a setup. She could never give them what they wanted. "I wish I could see what went on at the inn."

Her television sputtered to life.

"What the…" She tromped to the sofa. The picture onscreen flashed from a long-range view of a kitchen to a foyer. It looked familiar. Like… the inn.

Perching on the edge of the sofa, she laughed. "Cool." Now she'd keep an eye on things. If only she could spy on Eric too.

The image flashed white.

"No, wait." Her desperation faded when the title "Coming Attractions" zoomed in, and then Eric appeared onscreen. Trudging into his bedroom, he unbuttoned his shirt and flung it into the laundry basket.

Delighted, Sheree rocked in glee. "Oh yeah. Gimme more, baby."

He did the same with his jeans. In his underwear, he stretched to the floor and began push-ups, his muscles rippling beneath his taut skin.

Leaning closer, she nearly fell off the sofa. "Enough, already. Isn't it time for a shower?" Drool dripped from her mouth when he peeled off his sweaty T-shirt. "Now this is more like it." Maybe even worth a turn in Hell.

* * * *

"Good morning, sweetie. You're in a good mood today." Joss set her coffee mug on the kitchen counter and bent to nuzzle into Taz's long, soft fur, and rubbed his back.

As quickly as he'd jumped up, the dog bounded out the back door and through the yard, across the stone bridge through the lavender field, toward the road.

"Taz, no." She ran after him, but halted at seeing Eric. The man vexed her, as surely as if someone cast a spell over her, and Joss wouldn't put it past Lydia to dabble in the dark arts. No one would be safe then.

Worse, her strong emotional response roiled the energy beneath into an uncontrollable storm. Yet even if she learned to make it yield to her will, rather than react to her every subconscious whim, Eric wouldn't be safe around her. An uncanny notion haunted her of someone watching.

Shielding her eyes from the morning sun, she strolled closer. Strange, she couldn't get a read of his emotions, like a barrier stood between them. One he seemed to struggle against.

"Did you forget something?" Why was he simply standing there, instead of continuing past the inn on his morning run, like usual? Damn, how could anyone look more handsome with rumpled, damp hair? His chest rose and fell with his breaths, heavy from running.

He glanced away. "I don't think so. Why?"

"No reason. You normally don't stop, so I thought…" Or hadn't thought, or she wouldn't have started this conversation. He appeared anxious to continue on.

Sweat dampened his forehead, and his gray T-shirt clung to his contours. His musky scent mixed with lavender in a heady way, and intoxicated her. Lazy tingles traveled through her toes and up her calves.

"Taz ran toward the road." He spoke in panting breaths. "You should teach him to stay away from it so he doesn't get hurt."

She shifted her feet as the tingling sensation coiled inside her thighs. "He wanted to see you, I think. He's such a people person." What was she saying? He'd think her an idiot.

Eric's grin was lopsided. "Your dog is a people person?"

"He's extremely sociable, yes." Too much so. Like now, nuzzling the vet's hand.

The silence grew awkward. If she didn't get away soon, the vibrations would shake not only her, but the very earth.

"I should let you go."

"Yes, I'm sure you're busy." He turned.

She hastened to add, "No, I meant you must be. You're on such a strict schedule."

"Am I?" His surprise sounded genuine.

"Aren't you?" Now she was confused. He ran at the same time every morning. Certainly had appointments all day, either at his office or on farms.

"I guess you're right. Have a good day." The words came out in a mechanical way, as if rehearsed.

Uncertainly, she said, "You too."

He waited for her response before turning with a deep breath, and set off at an even pace.

Taz barked once, his fringed tail waving.

"Come on, sweetie. And no more road for you." And no more interfering in Eric's business for her. He seemed so relieved to get away.

The dog scampered across the field, making Joss laugh.

With a final glance at the retreating figure, Joss strolled through the budding flowers, brushing her palms across their tops. Strange, not even the lavender calmed her lately. A first. Maybe she'd grown immune.

Or maybe whatever bothered her was stronger than the healing properties of the flower.

* * * *

On Friday afternoon, Eric saw the last patient of the day. Seven o'clock, and he had absolutely nothing to do. He cringed at the thought of dinner with Sheree again. Maybe he could claim sickness. Something no one else needed to know about, nothing contagious. Food poisoning.

One date had led to another. Dinner, once a movie, then he'd headed home, after barely being able to kiss her good night. He didn't know why he had agreed to see her in the first place. Every time he said goodbye, he meant it to be the last. Yet he found himself agreeing to see her whenever she suggested. He was a grown man. Maybe he'd lost control of his faculties.

Maybe he did it to take his mind off Joss. Every day, she worked in the field in plain, unavoidable sight. She must have rigged lights outside, too. From his bed, the twinkling damn near kept him up till midnight. He imagined a celebration taking place, a party. She couldn't possibly have a party every night, could she?

How would you know? You know almost nothing about her. The words, clear as if spoken but by an unfamiliar voice, pinged through his loneliness like a pinball gone wild.

Finishing off his Thai takeout in front of the television, he scanned through the channels and settled on an old movie. Next week, he should go out somewhere. Anywhere. No more sitting at home alone. No more dates with women who couldn't hold his interest.

As if from a distance, he saw himself sitting in the chair, legs sprawled out like an old man, an elbow propped against the arm, head cradled in one palm. The lights in the field glimmered more brightly and captured his attention. The tiny orbs climbed higher and swam through the air as if carried on a current. They grew larger. Bobbing along toward him. His mouth dropped open. Damn if it didn't look like they were right outside the window scratching to get in. Watching him. They reminded him of tiny fireworks. Sparklers swirled by invisible hands. Mesmerizing. The movement lulled him, and his jaw went slack. He slumped in the chair, his mind clear, only concentrating on the swirl of lights. When they passed through the window to surround his chair, he abstractly thought it odd, but nothing to become upset about. So beautiful, they were. Friendly.

With a flash and a chorus of screeches, the tiny lights blended into one searing white landscape. It faded to darkness so thick, it roiled with voiceless laughter. A whisper called his name. The familiar face of a woman with platinum blond hair, ruby lips, and almond eyes emerged. Hard eyes, gleaming. From their depths, a laser light pierced his irises, penetrating his brain. More insistently, the voice called, "Eric." Two voices—one sweet, the other deep as an abyss.

He knew those voices. And didn't like them one bit. *Sheree.* "No."

The ruby lips curled at the ends, more a grimace than a smile. "Oh, yes."

A wispy outline of a woman's figure thickened as if with smoke. Hard nipples protruded through her sheer black robe and the lace of a scarlet demi-bra beneath.

He clutched the arms of the chair, the only thing in the room solid and dependable. "What are you doing here?" What had the waitress done to the lights? He wanted to be in their welcoming presence, not her malevolent one.

Floating nearer, Sheree hovered in front of him, her black robe as see-through as her. Her impressive cleavage was at eye level, impossible to ignore. Sucking air through her teeth, she ran her shiny, blood-red nails across her breasts, tugging the bra down to fully expose them. Cupping one in her hand, she ran her thumb across the pebbled hardness of her nipple.

His brain screamed in warning. He couldn't avert his gaze, or command his erection to go flaccid. With a will of its own, it stretched against his jeans, reaching for her.

Arching her back, her sighs and coos and whispers urged him on.

His fingers itched to touch her, to explore every part of her. He clutched the cushion, the effort so great he stifled a whimper.

A low laugh rumbled through her flat abdomen, and inflamed his desire. He wanted nothing more than to ram himself inside her, lose himself in her depths. So deeply, he'd never find the way out.

"Yes," she urged, her fingers tracing his engorged erection, though the zipper of his jeans stood intact.

Bile rose in his throat. "No." His protest faded, swallowed by darkness.

With one hand, she clutched his neck tight. Her sharp nails pricked his skin. With the other, she grasped his balls and squeezed gently, though at the same time tight as a vise. Such intense pleasure, bordering on insanity. Need burned white hot and parched his skin. His mind simultaneously screamed, *no!* while a deeper voice rumbled, *screw her!*

"Yes, do it," her dual voices commanded. She gazed down at him through hooded lids. The gleam in her eyes glowed red as her lipstick.

Fear iced his muscles, rendered them useless for an eternal moment. A hasty, panic-filled moan escaped. He inched lower in the chair, thinking he'd slip out beneath her.

Her knees jammed against his sides. She tightened her hold on his balls. When he cried out, she let out a laugh suitable for graveyards on moonless nights.

She parted the flowing robe. "What's the matter, Eric? You don't like?" Her vagina glowed bright as lava. It sucked at him like a vacuum, one with acid lining its hot metal cylinder.

Baring her canine teeth, she leaned in, so close he gagged at her rancid breath.

"You're going to give me what I need," she hissed.

"What is it?" he choked out, hoping she wouldn't respond.

The deeper voice answered. The voice, he now knew, belonged to the thing dominating her.

"If I can't have your heart…" The orange-red glow in her eyes intensified. "I'm taking your soul."

Then he'd be screwed for eternity. "No." He'd never believed in soul mates, yet he knew damn sure she didn't fit the bill. Fear caused some shrinkage. Before he could slip his erection from her grasp, she clamped on it again. Pain shot through his groin, and the groan escaping him sounded like a dying beast. His energy ebbed. He struggled to keep hold of it. It was like trying to grab a shadow.

Cradling her breast, she touched one metal-hard nipple to his ribs, a flame-heated iron poker that seared deep within. Despite the excruciating pain, it didn't puncture his skin. The burn's deepening path left a trail of carnage, a scar no x-ray would reveal. Invisible to the human eye, its meaning would mystify those schooled in medical arts. No, it had nothing to do with medicine, and everything to do with her threat. She sought his soul, and left her mark on it. A claim ticket for her to retrieve later.

No way could he let her.

Shoving at her shoulders proved useless. When she repeated her maniacal laugh, he twisted his hips and managed to slip lower beneath her. Or it. Whatever. An all-encompassing desire urged him to get away, far, far away.

Another laugh emitted a breath so fiery hot it singed his face. She dug her nails into his neck. The room fell away into blackness. Her legs wrapped behind his, and he couldn't extract himself from her clutches. She clung as they tumbled backward into a void so terrifying, he held back a scream.

Her screeching laughter echoed endlessly.

Then abruptly, it ended.

The tiny lights appeared around them, their soft glow reassuring.

Her grip faltered. She hissed. "Go away."

"No. Help me." They couldn't leave. They'd come to save him.

The sparkling figures flitted between him and Sheree. In an expanding whirlwind, they multiplied.

Now a madwoman, her eyes widened. Her head jerked from side to side as if in agony. Shrieking, she surrendered her hold, and leapt into the void.

Relief swept over him. Then panic. Sheree had been his only anchor. He'd fall to his death unless his downward tumble never ended. Maybe it was to be his personal Hell.

The twinkling figures swirled around him. Wrapped him in their cushion of light. They slowed his fall until he descended featherlike through the black emptiness. He floated down, down into a familiar seat.

His eyes popped open. He was home, in his chair. No one else in sight.

Patting his fully buttoned and zipped clothes, he heaved a breath, part laugh, part exhale of relief. None of it had happened. He must have dreamed it. A crazy, too-real dream, but nonetheless, a dream.

Glancing up, he froze. Immediately outside his window, the orbs hovered. One by one, their steady lights broke away to swarm into the distance. He rushed to the window to watch them bob away toward the field, where they swam through the night like luminous fish.

"If they were here, then what..." He turned and stared at the chair. Nothing in the room was out of place. It hadn't happened. Not really.

Yet it was too realistic to have been a mere dream.

What, then? A premonition?

Rubbing his neck, his fingers ran across slight bumps. He ran to the mirror, expecting to see indentations of fingernails. Blood red fingernails.

No marks on his neck. Of course not. How stupid.

It had been more than a premonition. It had to be a warning.

* * * *

Heaving a sigh, Sheree stretched her limbs to the corners of her satin-sheeted bed and writhed in imagined pleasure. The astral projection of herself worked way better than she'd hoped. Her fingertips had tingled when she'd dragged her nails down Eric's sculpted chest. Oh, he'd looked amazing.

Wait, who wanted imagined pleasure? If she didn't have Eric soon, in the flesh, she'd be raising hell herself. The Mark should make him crazy with desire for her, yet he resisted. Anger propelled her to sit up. Those damn fae. She'd have to plan some revenge against them for interfering. Her blood red nails scraped the smooth sheets, wishing she could rip their little fairy faces off. For now, though, she concentrated on devising a way to speed things up. She wouldn't wait any longer for Eric.

Setting her stiletto'd feet on the floor, she rose graceful as a ghost from the grave and paced. She could definitely get used to this demon stuff. Damn, she liked the way her legs looked like they went on forever in the heels. And the robe, sheer and sexy, swirled so nicely as she stalked back and forth across her puny room. Smiling devilishly, she imagined herself in Eric's rambling home, sprawled across his bed, probably a king size to accommodate his gorgeous length. Sucking air through her teeth, she couldn't wait to pin him down and finally fuck his brains out. She licked her lips and grasped her breasts. If only Eric's hands were caressing her instead....

Okay, enough dreaming. Think! What linked Eric to the boring homebody, Jocelyn Gibson? Hmm, if Sheree were to arrange a mutilation, Eric wouldn't find Joss so pretty. Hell no, the innkeeper wasn't nearly as pretty as Sheree, especially since the Lord of The Underworld and his minion granted her extra pizzazz. *So scratch that.*

Both Eric and Jocelyn were animal lovers. And he paid way too much attention to her dog at the picnic. Clenching a long nail in her teeth, Sheree's mind went into overdrive. Take the dog out of the picture and remove a link between Eric and Joss. *Of course.* The woman would be struck with grief, so weepy she wouldn't be able to think about Eric. At least for awhile.

An inkling of guilt niggled at her. Joss Gibson had already suffered a terrible loss in losing her husband. Would losing her dog send her over the edge? Elation bubbled up. What a great idea. Then the innkeeper would be out of the picture forever.

Whirling toward the mirror, Sheree drew herself tall and statuesque. Damn, she looked fine. Aphrodite had nothing on her. Hands to hips, she struck several poses to admire the various angles of her perfection.

Oh yeah, the plan. Back to work.

Inhaling deeply, she extended her arms, making claws of her hands, and closed her eyes.

Nothing.

Wait, how was she supposed to summon the damn demon anyway? Before, he always appeared whenever he wanted something from her. Fuming, she glared at her reflection. Sure, but when she wanted something, where was he?

A growl grew in her chest, exploding through her throat. In fury, she whirled. Slamming into someone, her growl increased to a shriek. Someone had broken in! Smacking at him in desperation, she darted her gaze from bureau to chair. *Find the cell, dial 911.*

With a sickening crunch, her body petrified. Her muscles useless, her voice gone. Her eyes became stuck in their damn sockets.

The man moved into her line of vision. The demon.

She'd sigh in relief, if she could.

Clad in black, the dark man's smile appeared luminous. "Good. Now we can have a civilized conversation."

Protest welled up within her, unable to escape. Yeah, real funny. Guess his idea of a civilized conversation was one-way. He talked, and she could do nothing except listen.

Maybe he recognized the venomous gleam in her eye.

"Oh, pardon. You'll need the use of your mouth, I suppose." Raising a brow, he scanned her length.

Sure, begrudge her the benefit of speech. *And stop ogling me!*

Poising his finger beside her lips, he warned, "I'm here to discuss your plan, so make it quick."

Yes! Her plan. He'd heard her after all.

He touched her face. Or appeared to. Nothing registered until her mortified skin returned to life. Moving her jaw, her tongue flopped awkwardly when she asked, "How soon can you do it?"

Pursing his lips, he stared coolly. "Is there nothing more to your plan? You haven't worked out any details?" Rolling his eyes, he clucked his tongue.

Details? *Think, quick.* "Send some dark spirits to kill him. They can lead him into the path of a speeding car." Yes, perfect idea. No one could claim it was anything but an accident. "In stormy weather," she blurted more clearly.

He stood for a moment, appraising her. "All right. So shall it be." He turned away.

"Wait."

An argument fell silent when he appraised her. "Oh. Right."

He'd barely raised his hand when her body broke out of its prison. She tumbled forward, and then caught herself. Limbs shaky, she eased onto the bed. One of these days, she'd get even with the jerk. The nerve.

The sweet smell of revenge warmed her. "Soon, you'll be mine, Eric." Whether he liked it or not.

Chapter 10

Joss and Annie stood with Charlie Fulton in the driveway and surveyed his handiwork. The newly applied paint gave the house the appearance of a freshly bloomed flower. The lavender swaying in the field beyond set off the matching lavender paint and complementing violet trim.

The healthy sprouts encouraged Joss—and surprised her. Normally, such vigorous growth took several years to achieve. The energy below the property must nourish everything on its surface. Every tree and bloom had burst with vibrant life well before the rest of the town.

The cheery paint buoyed her spirits. "You did a wonderful job, Charlie."

"Sure is eye-catching, I'll give you that much."

Joss couldn't take credit. The ley line beneath the property held great power, as Gram and Lydia had said. The energies would yield more than prizewinning flowers. Her grandmother had told her those from the netherworld blessed Joss with protection.

Joss couldn't deny the fae appeared more active of late. She'd told herself the lavender drew them, and pushed aside darker doubts.

"The color's perfect for our name," Annie agreed. "Lavender Hill Inn."

"I saw the new sign on the way in," Charlie said. "Very nice."

Joss had to agree. Everything was coming together. "And just in time for our second open house. Without your help, Charlie, we could never have finished."

Ducking his head, Charlie said, "I'm grateful to you for the work."

"I hope you'll come then. Annie's planning a fantastic spread."

Annie chimed in, "And you won't want to miss the debut of Joss's lavender lemonade."

Charlie grinned. "I'm not much of a lemonade drinker, but I'll sample it."

"Careful, it will surprise you." More than surprise. The drink soothed people's souls, clarified their thoughts. If they drank enough, it helped them see what was most important in life.

So said Joss's grandmother. Gram also claimed an affinity for all living things, and it allowed her to read their energies. If anyone suffered pain, her grandmother knew, even if it didn't cry out. Her herbal remedies healed wounds and calmed fright. Even animals responded to the soothing scent of lavender. The horses grazed in the lower fields, more content than ever. The ex-racehorse hadn't bucked a rider since last fall, an accomplishment in itself.

The tingling along Joss's skin began at the same time the vet's blue SUV turned into the driveway. With the windows down, sunglasses shielded Eric's eyes. Not enough that his stare didn't weigh on her. He lifted a hand in a wave and continued to the barn.

"A wave." Annie gasped. "He's warming up." Her smirk punctuated the sarcasm.

More like the opposite. He appeared cooler to Joss every time they met. More distant, and so more difficult for her to read.

Charlie agreed, "No one gets much more out of him. Though the animals here see him often enough." He gave Joss a sideways glance.

Despite the good doctor's ambivalence, the tingle crawled up her spine, and she shifted her feet. "I should get inside. We have so much to do."

A good reminder not to dwell on Eric so much. The Victorian still required a good deal of work. She'd be less anxious if she had a better idea of whether her inn would be a success.

What if no one liked her lavender recipes? Then her whole plan would be shot.

Charlie followed. "I'll be out of your hair, soon as I collect my tools." He called hello to the vet, who walked toward the barn.

Eric turned, his back stiff. "Morning."

To Joss's surprise, he halted. Lately, he'd actively avoided her.

"I see you've been busy again, Charlie," he said.

Something in his voice gave her pause. His husky tone sounded as if he struggled to speak. His hair was normally in disarray, one of his more endearing features. Today it appeared untouched by a comb. Dark circles underlined his eyes.

"Yep," came the handyman's good-natured response. "How's business with you?"

"Busy as always." He sent a sharp glance at Joss, and his pained expression eased, replaced with yearning.

Warmth twisted through her. She wanted to take him by the shoulders and—the image that sprang to mind took her breath away. The kind in steamy novels, where the couple entangled so deeply, no one could tell which appendages belonged to whom.

Pretty much like their last encounter.

No, she must put it out of her head. He obviously had. Sheree boasted to everyone how they spent every weekend together. Each time Joss heard about it, it stung deeper. How sincere he'd been when they'd made love.

Her brain took a sharp detour from romance to reprimand. Until a faint red glow caught her eye. Beneath his shirt, it pulsed like a heartbeat, slightly lower than the real one. Alarm rang in her brain like a bell, but he went about his business as usual.

With a wave, she reminded Charlie to send her a bill and strode to the house.

Within minutes, Eric had finished his business and drove off.

To help put him out of her mind, she waited a few minutes to leave. Distance made no difference. The more she tried to concentrate on her errands in town, the more vivid he sprang back. What was wrong with him? He resembled a torture victim, and moved slowly, as if in pain. At the farmer's market, she clutched the basket, closed her eyes and sent healing thoughts his way. Something blocked them.

Only later, when black clouds blotted out his handsome brooding face, and gusts battered her Beetle on the way home, did Eric finally fall to the back of her mind.

Wind whipped through the trees and sent leaves whirling through the air. Joss strained to see through the stream of rain accumulating on her windshield faster than the wipers could handle. "I don't like this, Taz."

The dog's ears pricked up.

"I know, I usually love thunderstorms." This one held danger. With each flash of lightning, the scent of sulfur came stronger.

Gripping the wheel, she drove fast as she dared. Once she reached Yellow Breeches Road, she forced a long breath. "Almost home, baby." The shadows deepened among the trees to near black, almost a palpable presence. A year ago, she'd have scoffed. No longer.

The solar spotlight above the inn's sign gave only a dim glow, serving as a marker to turn. "Oh damn. I forgot the mail." She stopped the car and hopped out, tugging her hood down against the driving rain. At the mailbox, a blur ran past, black and white bounding through the gray rain.

Fear shot through her. "Taz, no! Come back."

His woofing faded down the road as he disappeared into the blackness.

A swarm of tiny lights swiftly appeared. Flashing in his wake, they followed Taz, urgently waving her on. A signal. *A warning.*

"No, no!" She ran after him, her soles slipping on the wet surface, terror mounting, making every movement like slow motion.

Headlights blazed through the curtain of rain as a car rounded the bend. A sickening thump sounded. Taz yelped, a piercing sound the night carried all too clearly. The car sped past her.

For one eternal moment, the orbs shimmered ahead, then dissolved.

A cold lump hardened in her stomach. Instinct told her they'd tried to save Taz. And failed. "No—Taz! Where are you?"

The storm thickened the night's darkness. Joss ran at a steady pace, searching to the left and right. *Please no. Don't let him be hurt.* A flash of lightning lit his unmoving body to the side of the road.

Panic spurred her faster. "Taz?"

She dropped to her knees beside him. Afraid at first to touch him, she rested her palms lightly on his head and back. Faint shudders came through his soggy fur. Still alive! Glancing up, she gauged the distance to Eric's practice. Only a bit farther. She gathered Taz in her arms and struggled to gain her balance as she stood.

No lights shone in the house, not even on the porch. Lightning lit her path up the rain-slicked steps. Her foot slipped. She righted herself. "Sorry Taz. Please hang on, baby." Cradling him as gently as she could, she supported his leg, hanging grotesquely out of place, his life energy slipping away to a hazy place. Time grew short.

Pressing a finger to the dim glow of the doorbell, she held it there.

Light winked on through the window. A few seconds later, the door burst open.

Eric's drawstring pants hung off his hips as if hastily thrown on. His arms flailed stretching into a T-shirt, revealing a glimpse of his taut stomach. Not quick enough to hide the ember glowing between his ribs.

Gasping, she clutched Taz tighter. It finally hit her. She'd never seen The Mark before, but there it was. On Eric.

It explained his gruff behavior. He needed help. She'd have to ask Gram what to do.

His short hair stuck out from his head, and his blue eyes—lovely even in his stern face—took her in from head to toe. "What are you—"

"Please." This was no time for pleasantries. Questions could wait, even about The Mark. "You have to help."

His gaze went to the dog in her arms as if he didn't notice before. "Bring him in."

For a moment, she hesitated. Sensing his overriding concern for Taz, she trusted her instinct and followed him through the house to the dining room. Soaked through, her jacket dripped on the Mexican tile floor.

"Set him on the table." He switched on the light above it. It cast a harsh glow on Taz as she laid him down.

At his touch, Taz yelped. "The leg's broken." He prodded along the stomach, back and other limbs. With a grunt, he finished the exam and went back to the broken limb.

Straightening, he appeared a primal being, so rough around the edges. Joss quelled the urge to smooth them with her touch, absorb the static of his spirit, as she'd done for John.

"He's suffering a great deal. It's best you put him down." He looked at her, finally, her wet hair plastered to her head, clothes clinging.

His words chilled her blood. "No. You have to save him."

"How old is he? Three?"

"Almost four. Why?"

"Do you want his quality of life diminished so drastically?"

"I can't lose him." She didn't add, *he's all I have left of John.*

"The leg's almost severed. I'd have to amputate."

She'd seen other dogs with three legs. "He can survive the injury, can't he?"

"He can. Would he want to?"

Steeling herself, she said, "You have to try."

With a resigned sigh, he bent to lift Taz. Though his movements were swift, his gentleness surprised her.

She must trust Eric would do everything possible for Taz, trust he wouldn't allow The Mark to influence his actions. She followed him to a side door. He threw it open, then strode into the short breezeway connecting his home to his practice. She let him lead. He reached swiftly for light switches she'd have wasted precious time trying to locate. In the rear section of the building were the cages filled with a few overnight guests. A dog pressed his face against the wire and growled. Hissing, a cat watched with wide amber eyes.

They knew better than she about Eric. How deeply had it infected him?

"All right, settle down." He pushed open another door to a room with a table and instruments.

She shivered. This was where it would happen.

He laid Taz on the table. The dog cried and searched for her.

"I'm here, baby. Don't be afraid." She held his head as Eric prepared a syringe.

"This will knock him out so he won't feel a thing."

"I could stay and help," she offered, "if you need me to."

Registering surprise, his gaze flicked to hers. "No. It's best if you leave."

"I'm not leaving until…" She couldn't finish and bit her lip.

"There's a waiting room through that door." He nodded toward it.

She clutched Taz's neck, touched her cheek to his. "I'll see you soon." Trying not to cry, she kissed the dog's head.

Eric took a step back, and held the table awkwardly. Not quite frowning, but definitely uncomfortable, until she looked up through the tears in her eyes. His rigid demeanor vanished, replaced by sorrowful compassion, like he wanted to take her in his arms. No, she couldn't let him waste any time. She forced herself toward the door and shut it behind her.

The reception area was dark. She'd been there before and headed for the sofa under the window that looked out to his house. She hugged the cat-shaped pillow to her chest and pulled up her knees.

She couldn't lose Taz. Not John and Taz too. It was too much to ask of her. Closing her eyes, she sunk into the cushions, trying to block the image of what Eric must be doing in there. How frightened Taz would be when he awoke without a leg. Confused. In pain.

The patter of rain soothed her. She curled against the curved arm of the sofa.

* * * *

"Joss." A hand warmed her shoulder. Again, more insistently, he repeated, "Joss."

Opening her eyes, she pushed hair from her face. The bright light behind the man standing there obscured his features. The surroundings were unfamiliar. Definitely not home.

"The surgery's over," he said. "Taz survived. For how long, I can't say."

The surgery. Taz. Sitting up, she came eye level with Eric, who crouched beside her. Weariness helped fade his earlier jaggedness. Some interior struggle added to his embattled appearance.

She'd deal with it later. "Can I see him?"

"He's still unconscious. It's best if you let him rest."

Nodding, she held her head. Cold rain pelted against the window. The storm still raged.

"Do you have a ride home?" he asked.

She stopped to think a moment. She'd carried Taz here after finding him on the side of the road, whimpering. Such an awful sight. Sobs shook her shoulders. "Sorry. I keep seeing him, lying there in the mud. In such terrible pain."

Roughness edged his soft voice. "He's strong. He has a good chance."

Panic struck. A good chance? Doctors only said it to cushion the blow. Taz must be dying. "Oh, God." She held a hand to her mouth, unable to stop the tears.

"Hey. It's okay."

His hands at her shoulders surprised her. His strokes along her neck and cheeks were like flames along her skin.

Whispering, "It's okay," he drew her against his chest.

Memories whirled through her head, his warm body against hers. She needed him to hold her, and encircled her arms around his neck, her tears wetting his shirt. His soft murmurs into her shoulder calmed her hiccupping breaths. When he grasped her and held her away, she didn't release him.

Dragging her lips across his cheek, she whispered, "Don't let go." Thoughts flew away in a whirl, like the leaves in a storm.

Stiffening, his hands splayed along her waist.

She nuzzled her cheek against his, fingers entwined in his hair. So soft, she wanted to lose herself in him.

With a ragged breath, his hands moved across her back, his lips along her neck, the spot that drove her wild. When he pressed closer, she relaxed her legs open. His mouth sought hers, and he slid her against him with one quick pull, caressing her thigh.

The power of his primal movements sent a thrill through her, even as her mind argued against it. The Mark flared bright on his skin. Something haunted him, and he desperately needed release.

She needed release too. She didn't want to think, but let his touch carry her to another place where worries didn't matter. Where she only knew their bodies moving together. He tugged away her clothes as she wrestled off his, wanting her skin against his. His urgency heightened her passion. She pushed away his drawstring pants and wrapped her legs around him, needing him inside her.

The storm lashing against the window lent a dreamlike quality. With the crack of lightning, his face flashed in the darkness, alternating pleasure and pain.

Desire blanked out thought, and she moved with his thrusts, meeting each with equal force, power flowing between them, washing over them. His heavy moans reached inside her, and she clutched him closer, wanted him deeper, wanted it not to end. When he finally shuddered and gripped her, The Mark had nearly disappeared.

She still moved against him, needing that final release. His groans and murmurs coaxed her to it. Legs wrapped lazily behind his, she stroked his hair, and nuzzled his neck. She didn't want to lose this wonderful sensation of drifting in space, with nothing but each other. Finally, she stilled, clinging to him.

"Are you all right?" he whispered.

"Yes." She wanted to ask him the same thing, but he probably wouldn't know how to answer.

His caresses became awkward. "We should get you home."

"Right." Sooner than she would have liked. Reluctantly, she dropped her arms, searched for her shirt and pulled it over her head.

After tugging up his pants, he stood, T-shirt already covering his head and with one yank, over his chest. Glancing everywhere except at her, he raked a hand through his hair. The other hand absently went to the spot over his ribs, the glow returning, along with the tortured look in his eyes.

God, what had she done? This only complicated matters. And what about Taz? Would he be in any danger from whatever evil possessed Eric? Worse would be to move him in his weakened condition. She'd have to trust Eric's protectiveness would override whatever haunted him. Tomorrow, she'd ask Gram for advice, and if they could help him.

"I'll give you a ride," he said.

"No, I can walk." Thunder growled across the sky.

"Don't be silly. I'll drive you. I just need, uh, shoes." He rushed through the door.

"All right. Thanks." Dropping her head into her hands, she moaned. Of all the stupid things to do. Stupid but incredible. No fair that the best guy in bed in her life was him.

You weren't in bed.

Even worse, she argued with herself.

The footlights in the breezeway highlighted the contours of his chest as he jogged back. "Ready?"

Rising, she tossed her hair back with a flick of her head. "Yes."

He strode through the dark room, clicked open the lock, and held the door.

Driving rain hit her before she crossed the threshold. She followed him to his SUV, where he opened the door. She scooted inside. When he ran to the driver's side, she wondered why he'd never remarried. Any number of women she knew would snap him up in a hurry if he'd given one iota of encouragement.

After climbing inside, he revved the engine. "Some storm."

"Yes." Already reduced to discussing the weather. Ah well. What did she expect? Flowers? Besides, she'd conveniently forgotten about Sheree. Joss couldn't expect Eric to pretend. Why had she let herself act so weak?

They rode in silence until they reached the inn driveway.

"Is that your car?"

"Yes. I stopped to get the mail and…" She bit back a sob as it hit her again. If she'd only shut the door, Taz couldn't have escaped.

"I'll be right back." He jogged to the driver's side and got in, and then quickly got out again, and returned to his truck. "Must've run out of gas. Here are your keys. I locked it. I'd take care of it now but I'm exhausted."

"You don't have to." She didn't want his pity, or misplaced obligation.

He flinched and shifted into first. He braked again near the house. "I'll let you know how Taz is doing."

"Can't I visit him?" Was he banishing her from the property?

Strain sounded in his tone. "Of course. Come as often as you'd like."

"Tomorrow?" she asked.

"You mean today?"

"What?"

"It's two AM."

Mortified, she stammered, "I had no idea." For some reason, the offense seemed double. He rose early for his practice. Before she could apologize, he said, "Good night."

Gathering her purse, she scrambled out with a quick "good night," then paused to add, "Thanks for everything."

A slight nod of his head might have meant acknowledgement or confusion.

"I meant," she hastily added, "everything you did for Taz. Not…never mind." Before any other embarrassment flew out of her mouth, she ran inside.

What an awful end to an awful night.

Chapter 11

The storm had long passed when Eric stepped inside the waiting room. A tumultuous pulse seemed to roil within. Her tangible essence hung there. That she'd clung to him didn't surprise him. Most people needed comforting in such situations. That she'd asked him not to let go triggered a powerful surge he couldn't hold back. It would have been like holding back a flood with a mesh screen. Despite the insistent stab to his flesh, pushing through the pain brought him to a place of relief. Because of Joss.

Every moment they'd shared came back vividly. He closed his eyes and let it wash over him again. Weariness prompted him to move, finally. After one last check on the dog, he stripped and fell into bed. For a long while, he stared at the ceiling.

After knowing her touch again, he craved more. Every muscle ached for her. Fighting against the pain, acid rose, stinging every pleasant memory away. It began the instant she'd nestled against him. Images of glistening red lips in a scowling face framed by platinum hair misted in his mind, trying to blot out Joss's face. An invisible hard nipple had seared past his ribs. It had almost caused him to push Joss away. Instead, he'd tightened his grip. If he'd rejected Joss, the need for Sheree would have claimed him, and he'd have driven in an instant to be with her. No, Joss's touch excited him even more than before and calmed the wound Sheree had inflicted.

The strain of his pain warring with pleasure caused him to pull away too soon. Aside from Sheree's haunting image, being with Joss was natural. Right. Even driving her home—such a simple act, taken for granted by too many—seemed intimate. Yet the small pleasure, too, was robbed from him. Every wonderful sensation was matched by a piercing sting.

Despite only having a few hours sleep, Eric awoke with renewed vitality. She'd visit today, and he'd see her. It would be worth whatever pain he endured.

* * * *

The morning sun taunted Joss, a painful reminder of the day before. If only she'd kept driving instead of stopping for the mail. She should have paid more attention to the danger in the air. To her own instinct. For too long, she'd dulled her extrasensory perception, and now Taz paid the price.

And what about Eric? She had no clue how to ease The Mark torturing him. Until moving here, everything in the other realm she'd assumed was out of her life forever. Now the very ground roiled beneath the inn.

Glad no customers had checked in, Joss shuffled into the kitchen in her robe.

Annie whooped. "Hey, look what the cat dragged in."

Joss couldn't prevent the well of emotion from bursting forth in a sob.

Rushing over, Annie held her arms. "Oh honey, I was only teasing. What's wrong?"

Trying to control her blubbering did little. "Taz. He was hit by a car yesterday."

Annie gasped. "Oh, no. Is he…"

"No. At least not when I left him." Her lip quivered. "Dr. Hendricks amputated his leg. I don't know how he'll survive without it. He'll hate me." She plopped onto the stool.

"No of course he won't. Taz loves you. He'd do anything for you. I've never seen a more devoted dog."

"He means everything to me. I can't lose him."

"I'm sure he'll be fine. Dr. Hendricks is a great vet."

The sting of Eric's quick goodbye came back fresh. He couldn't dump her off fast enough. Maybe he'd anticipated the danger. "Yes. It's people he's not especially great with."

Clucking her tongue, Annie shifted to one hip, the embodiment of sympathy. "Was he awful to you?"

Awfully amazing. Warmth coursed through her and she rasped a breath, remembering his touch. She busied herself pouring coffee. Enough of that. He clearly wasn't himself. "Actually," she said, concentrating on her cup, "considering I woke him up, hysterical and in tears, he was very gracious." Hearing herself say it was the first she'd recognized the fact. "He worked on Taz for hours." At least three hours, if he brought her home at two. Unless their tryst lasted longer than ten minutes. At the time, it seemed sublime eternal bliss. So much for her oath not to let it happen again.

"Are you okay?" Annie's voice broke through.

"Yes. Why?"

Annie winced. "You're kinda spacey."

"I'm exhausted. I couldn't sleep, worrying about Taz." In between visions of Eric, naked, the way his muscles rippled when he moved, how well they'd moved together. Their bodies fitting together just right. How could she have ignored The Mark and allowed it to happen? She'd wanted to ease his pain, but couldn't deny her own desire. Maybe whatever possessed him had wanted to make love to her, not him at all. The abrupt way he left her...

"I'm impressed Dr. Hendricks worked so long at it."

"What?" Joss froze. Had Annie read something in her expression?

"Everyone says how thorough Doc Hendricks is. Hours seems overly meticulous, even for him. He must like you a lot." Smiling, she bumped her elbow into Joss's side.

"Sometimes I think he doesn't like anyone. Not even himself."

"How long will Taz have to stay there?"

Her lip quivered. "I don't know. There's still a chance...." She couldn't finish. Couldn't think about it now. If he survived, he would need to adapt. Relearn everything. What would happen when he tried to walk? Would he fall? Or learn to compensate?

Annie knit her brows. "You better take it easy today."

"I have to keep busy so I don't have time to think." She shuffled to the shower, and her head cleared a little. After dressing, she closed her bedroom door and dialed Gram.

"Hello, dear."

"Gram, I need your help."

"What's wrong?"

"I've seen someone who bears The Mark."

"Are you certain? Who?"

"Eric. No, I can't be sure. I've never seen it before, but he's acting so strange. Is there anything we can do to help?"

"Yes, but it's going to take some time to gather what I need. In the meantime, stay away from him."

"I can't. Taz..." Her lip quivered, and she steadied herself to relay the accident story. "It's more important that I visit Taz to make sure he's okay."

"Take no chances, dear. Never be alone with him."

A hysterical laugh bubbled up. She cleared her throat to cover it. "Right. Let me know as soon as you have what we need." She'd do whatever it took to make Eric his old self again.

"We'll talk soon, dear. Give my love to Taz."

After she hung up with Gram, Joss forced herself through her rote routine. By midmorning, she couldn't concentrate any longer. "I'm running to the bank and stopping to see Taz on the way back. I might be awhile."

"Give him a kiss for me."

Grabbing a stuffed animal from the dog bed, she hurried out. In a haze, she drove to town, doing her banking on autopilot. Not until she parked in the lot next to the vet's did awareness kick in. In high gear.

Inside, the receptionist asked her to take a seat and called the assistant. Joss fingered the beat-up Sylvester the Cat toy Taz loved to chew on.

A young woman in puppy print scrubs called from a doorway, "Joss Gibson?" Leading her to the back room, her blond ponytail swished side to side. "I'm Terry. Taz is pretty groggy."

Joss tensed, glancing left and right for any sign of Eric. The only other person besides Terry was another woman in scrubs cleaning a cage.

"Here he is." Terry stood to one side of a large cage atop another.

Joss hiccupped a breath. With closed eyes, Taz laid still except for the steady rise and fall of his chest. Stitches stretched across the skin of the amputated leg, making her gasp.

"Can I touch him?"

"Not yet. Don't worry, he'll know you're here." Terry's thin smile did nothing to encourage hope. "I'll be back in awhile."

With a sigh, Joss leaned against the cage. Not even a place to sit. The passageway wouldn't comfortably accommodate a chair and a passerby. She pressed against the cage, wishing she could hold him. If she'd caught him one minute sooner, none of this would have happened. "I'm so sorry, baby," she whispered.

With the twitch of a paw, Taz whimpered softly.

Terry appeared behind her. "Probably having a bad dream."

"Can you put this in with him?"

"Sorry. We can't expose him to any outside germs."

"Right. I should have known better. It's just…he loves this."

The door opened, and she met Eric's gaze. Wide-eyed, like a trapped animal. Unkempt as one, too, he looked like a wild spirit. From his quick wince, he appeared to be in physical pain at the sight of her. Ducking his head, he strode toward her.

Her pulse sped up to a crazy beat. How ridiculous to bring an old stuffed toy, especially one missing its eyes.

A half-smile twisted his lips. "Shouldn't it be a Tasmanian devil?"

Funny he should mention devil. Releasing a breath, she was glad for some excuse to look away. "He's loved it since he was a puppy. It's black and white like him, and smelled like him, so I think he believed it was his brother." *Can you sound any more idiotic?* She turned her attention to the unconscious dog. "How is he?"

His arm brushed hers when he moved past. "About how I expected. Stable enough."

She wanted to fold herself against him, absorb his warmth again. Until a cat in the nearest cage arched its back, bared its fangs, and hissed. The feline knew as well as Joss about The Mark.

To calm the animal, she reached through the wire to scratch its head. "Enough?" How stable was stable enough?

Appearing relieved, Eric shifted away from the cat. "Hopefully enough to fight off any infection."

No need to ask what would happen if Taz weakened. Gulping hard, she stared at the dog, willing him to heal quickly. To her surprise, a vibration of energy pulsed through her. If she didn't know better, she'd have sworn it came from under the ground.

Stiffly, he stepped back. "Well. I have to…"

Forcing a smile, she nodded. "Of course." Had he sensed it?

His expression was unreadable as he studied her, unmoving. "Right. Well." He turned.

"I hope you're not exhausted. It was very kind of you to help."

"It's what I do."

"I barged in late at night. Such an imposition. I…" *should stop talking now.* From his pained expression, she judged her presence more than an imposition. She caused him actual physical discomfort.

"It's fine." He touched the paper he held to his other palm. For a moment, they stood in awkward silence.

"Please don't let me keep you."

"Right." With a curt nod, he stepped back, then whirled away.

"Bye." Sarcasm hung heavy in her soft tone. What did she expect? If he comforted her again, it would multiply the error. And her heartache.

The door opened again, and Terry approached. "How's it going?"

"The same. I better get out of your way." Smiling her thanks, she followed the assistant back to the waiting room. She swore his stare followed her outside. Gravel spun beneath her tires when she pulled onto Yellow Breeches Road.

* * * *

"Doctor? Where are you going?" a woman behind him asked.

"What?" Eric strode from the back with no aim except to get away. As much as he wanted to stand beside Joss, seeing her gave a jolt to his system. Somehow his discomfort eased the closer he drew to her. Her presence acted as a salve to the acid building in his veins.

Unlike last night, Joss brushed him off today. No warmth in her soft voice. Had he expected her to take him in her arms again? If her fleeting glances gave any indication, she wanted him nowhere near.

As soon as he'd left her, the searing pain came back with renewed force.

Terry held out a folder. "Room Five. This way." She jerked her head back.

He considered making an excuse for his preoccupation, then abandoned it. Either explanation would sound like bad fiction. "Thanks."

Following the assistant in the opposite direction, he tensed in passing the entry again, muscles aching to press her against his chest, run his fingers through her silken hair. He'd learned to read Karen's caution signs. Joss's definitely said stay away.

She's upset about the dog. Give her space.

Clinging to her to ease his own discomfort would be too selfish. He couldn't drag her into whatever mess he'd created for himself.

Entering the room, he set the file on the counter. "How's Jackson today?"

The Yorkie growled.

Tsking, Mrs. Ballard shushed the dog. "You're not being polite, Jackson. What's gotten into you?"

Sighing, Eric steeled himself for the long day ahead. He'd love an answer to the same question—what *had* gotten into him?

* * * *

Annie's humming drew Joss into the kitchen. Turning, she switched off the running tap water. "How is he? When can he come home?"

Recounting the brief tale, Joss shared the awkwardness between her and Eric. "It was so strange. Kind of gave me the willies." She wouldn't say the real reason.

Her friend gave a smirk. "Or something else."

"Oh please." *Then what's the tingle in my nerve endings?* Like she'd tapped into some unseen energy force, her blood stream conducting it throughout her body.

"You should invite him to dinner. To thank him."

"That's the worst idea you've ever had." Though Joss imagined it vividly.

"You know you want to."

"To eat together and say nothing more than 'would you like more' or 'how about dessert' or 'oh, look how late it is.'" Joss gave a short laugh. "No thank you." Not until Gram came up with a solution.

"So, you'll loosen him up."

Joss shook her head. "Too much work." Unfortunately, beyond her expertise.

"Men appreciate a good meal. I bet he hasn't eaten a home cooked dinner since Thanksgiving."

"Let his mother cook for him. She must be used to his stony silence."

"You could discuss your mutual love of animals."

"No, Annie. Not happening." Frustration seeped through her tone.

"Honey, you need to have a life. Even if you don't want to date Doc Hendricks, use him for practice."

The notion knocked the breath out of her. *Oh, you have no idea.* "I have a life, thank you." Cutting off her friend's argument, she hastily added, "And who said I want to date? I'm not ready. And honestly, I don't know if I ever want to marry again." Glancing pointedly at Annie, she needed say no more.

More timidly, Annie ventured, "So don't marry him. Just spend some time with him. Ask him to dinner. You know, as a fellow animal lover."

Or just a lover. "A practice date, huh?" She smiled despite herself.

"And to repay him."

"I'm sure I'll be paying him plenty." How much? Money wasn't a consideration when she opted for surgery. Putting Taz down wasn't an option. He deserved a fighting chance. She ignored the small voice that said Eric did too. She'd help him as soon as she knew how.

Annie screwed up her face.

Time to focus on other things. "So, how many for dinner tonight?"

"Counting you?" Annie winced.

Joss's hopes fell. "Please don't say one."

Tentatively, Annie smiled. "Three."

Joss groaned. But business had grown steady as word spread about the inn's delicious offerings. Had to expect an off day, now and then. "Some extra money would come in handy for those vet bills."

Perkily, Annie said, "We haven't established our name yet."

"We need to. Tomorrow's July first, and we haven't even planned for Independence Day." She could barely remember what month it was, let alone the day.

Annie waved. "We can pull off a July fourth event easily. Afterward, let's make one up—Beach Day? Hey, I bet Doc Hendricks looks great in a Speedo."

He looks great in much less. Coyly, Joss said, "If he wants to come, he'll come." Getting him to loosen up was a horse of a different color.

* * * *

How many years since Eric attempted any conversation with a woman? For pleasure? Too many—that much was painfully obvious. He drew a blank when faced with Joss, despite dreaming of her all night. Those dreams provided sanctuary from the nightmares, if temporarily.

The veterinary assistant sidestepped him since their conversation. He purposely kept his distance and any remarks more curt than usual.

Arriving at Mr. Olson's farm, Eric grabbed his bag and strode to the barn where the farmer waited. For once, Eric welcomed the man's supervision of the vet call. The old mare shuffled her feet in the aisle, flinching at his every touch.

"Steady girl." Olson drew down the lead rope to lower the horse's head. "Must be something in the air. The animals are skittish lately."

"Seems to be going around." Wherever he was, at least. Their flight instincts kicked into high gear when they smelled something wrong. Only the horses at Lavender Hill Inn acted somewhat normal.

Alarm filled the farmer's face. "Some kind of virus?"

To quell the man's fears, and any gossip, he forced a chuckle. "No, nothing like that. Probably just restless because of too much pent-up energy."

Olson's only reply was a grunt.

Eric administered the shot quickly and bent to his bag. The man led the horse out to the pasture, then stood at the fence watching.

Joining him, frustration coiled inside Eric. Every facet of his life seemed to be off track. "How do you handle being alone?" he blurted. Embarrassed, he added, "Sorry." He had no right to pry. Ten years Eric's senior, Olson lost his wife a year before Karen died. Occasionally, the man showed up at social events in the company of a woman.

"Probably about as good as you." Olson chuckled. "Not very good."

"You've dated, at least. I can't even approach a woman."

"The first step is to put yourself out there."

He grinned. "If there were only someone worth putting myself out there for."

Olson cast a sideways glance. "If I were younger, I might ask Mrs. Gibson."

Eric stiffened. He never considered other men wanted her. Of course they would.

The farmer continued. "Maybe you should. I've seen the way you look at her. Like you're plenty interested."

"No, I couldn't. I have no time, my days are full with the practice." Olson grunted again.

"I don't even know what to say to a woman. It used to be so easy with Karen." He'd been foolish to think Joss would find him interesting. Someone so vivacious and lovely would be bored with his predictability.

"Someone will come along and it'll come to you naturally."

"Maybe." He hadn't fooled the farmer one bit. Nor himself. The more he'd repressed thoughts of Joss, he found he didn't want to, but now the risk appeared greater than a bruised heart. He couldn't expose her to such danger, even if he had no clue what it was.

Chapter 12

The day dawned gray, the sky low and heavy. As Joss walked the edge of the property, Taz's absence registered keenly. Their morning ritual, she joked to Annie, was to patrol the perimeter. Without him, she was too vulnerable. Taz always walked the boundary exactly, guided by some internal compass. A mystery of the border collie breed. Or maybe the dog followed the flow of energy beneath his padded paws.

Standing at the farthest corner, she imagined the field beyond the house in autumn. The lush purple blooms swaying in the breeze would die down, and her master plan would be in limbo until the next growing season. Would people still come to the inn with no lavender in bloom? No soothing scent in the air? No lemonade? Guests left happy enough, but a passersby came few and far between.

"Have faith," her grandmother's voice whispered through the lavender.

"I know. And by helping others, we help ourselves." Joss hadn't forgotten. *I'm just slow to action and I've wasted too many years.* She was more than ready to help Eric, if she only knew how.

Today, she'd go in to town and collect any business cards or pamphlets from other shops to distribute to the inn's customers. Once people knew how beautiful Boiling Springs was, they'd have more reason to return.

First, she needed to see Taz. And make sure Eric was still okay.

Arlene, the receptionist, greeted her on the way in.

"How's your father?" Last time Joss saw him, his pale complexion and dark-circled eyes left her worried.

"Chemo wears him down, but he's a trooper."

Joss's heart went out to her. "His positive attitude will see him through. And you, too."

The woman's smile beamed gratitude. "Give Taz a kiss for me."

"I will." Joss headed down the hall to the kennels. Seeing Taz lying motionless except for the steady rise and fall of his belly tugged at her heart. Reaching her fingers through the cage, she said, "Hey buddy."

Two people entered, and she snuck a glance, though she already knew by his strong presence who it was. Eric and Terry halted, discussing a patient, and he handed her a folder. Joss looked away when he turned toward her.

The assistant called, "Hi, Mrs. Gibson."

"Hello Terry," she called after the departing girl. Eric's approach seemed hesitant until she said, "Hey."

His shoulders stiffened as he approached. "Hey."

"How's my baby?"

Something like hope shone in his eyes as he stepped beside her, less frazzled than before. He appeared stronger, even though the ember-like glow beneath his shirt remained.

"How's Taz?" she clarified.

"Steadily improving." More softly, he asked, "How are you?"

The question surprised her. "I'm fine. I miss him. The house is so quiet." The echoing silence threatened to engulf her sometimes.

At the click of the door, they both tensed. Terry rummaged through a drawer.

Eric eased away. "He'll be home soon."

The thought both relieved and frightened her. "I better go."

"Already?" he blurted.

Another surprise question. "Yes, we're planning a Fourth of July event. I know you're busy but—"

"I'll be there." His blue eyes held the depth of the sea.

"Good." His promise both relieved and frightened her.

* * * *

According to the schedule, the horse at Lavender Hill Inn was due for a visit. Just thinking of going there intensified the searing pain in his chest. It took most of his energy not to drive to the diner. Sheree waited for him. Her image beckoned him every night, her sultry laughter filled his ears. It sapped his energy and focus to fight it. With the last of his reserves, he'd resist.

If he let whatever infected him take over his life, he'd be lost forever. He must hold on with his last shred of strength. Going through his usual routine was the only way to get through each day.

Blanking his mind, he packed his bag and drove. A whisper drifted through his mind, *"Come to me, now."*

He gripped the steering wheel to prevent turning toward town. With a flick of his hand, he turned up the radio volume and sang along in a loud falsetto: "Hot blooded." A laugh bubbled up. How apropos. His blood heated at the mere thought of Joss.

The whispers grew to a buzz, fading as he steered into the inn driveway. The scent of lavender acted like a balm on his inner wounds. The sight of Joss gathering flowers in the field arrested him until she straightened and glanced over. Discomfort drained away and unlocked his muscles. He didn't need to strain to reach for his bag and walk to the barn. The force that sought to control him had less effect on him here.

Whatever it was about this place, he wished he didn't have to leave. Each night, darkness closed tighter around him. One of these nights, it might swallow him whole.

* * * *

Bringing the cut blossom to her nose, Joss inhaled. Eric disrupted her on so many levels, not even lavender could calm her. His presence sparked a buzz in the atmosphere, alive with his interior struggle, and with her physical reaction to him. Desire percolated up every time he was near.

After gathering the ripe blooms, she hurried to the house. Opening the door, she paused to glance back, and her breath caught again when she met his steely gaze. Her nerves prickled like fire ants crawled across them. With a huff, she stomped her foot on the step to deaden the sensation.

The ringing phone gave her an excuse to run inside. She grabbed the extension in the kitchen.

"Jocelyn," said her grandmother's stern voice.

"Gram. What did you find out?" She stopped herself from adding, *about The Mark*. Annie wasn't in sight, but might be within earshot.

"Trouble's brewing. It concerns your Doctor Hendricks."

Why did everyone keep saying such things? "He's not *my* Doctor Hendricks."

"He's in danger, Jocelyn. You must warn him. Tell him to keep his distance from the waitress at the diner. Sheree."

"Is she planning to marry him?" Intended as a joke, the words backfired, and left a sour taste in her mouth.

"Have you seen him recently?" Gram sounded more serious.

"Yes, he's here now."

"Does he still bear The Mark?"

Glancing out the door, Joss watched him carry his bag into the barn. "Yes."

Gram exhaled, audibly upset. "Then we must move quickly."

Apprehensive, she gripped the phone. "To do what?"

"To save him."

* * * *

Eric moved through the stable on autopilot, not actually having an excuse to be at the inn except he needed the relief. Since he'd awoken—if he'd slept at all—he mulled over possible excuses in his head to avoid the date Sheree had demanded. It no longer mattered whether the strange vision of her held any significance in the real world. Whether she was merely a lonely waitress, or a woman possessed.

The dream disturbed him. Deeply. He'd never be able to relax around Sheree. Be in her company without keeping close guard, watching for signs she'd morph into whatever thing she'd become in his frequent hallucinations.

Inside the barn, the horse backed away with wide eyes, but he was able to coax the mare to cooperate. Maybe the lavender soothed them. Or maybe Joss's presence. Pulling out an oat treat, he approached Maya's stall. The mare shook her mane, and nickered to the horses outside through the barred window. When he slid open the door, she whirled in a one-eighty, her rump passing dangerously close.

"I know," he said softly. "You're tired of being inside."

Holding out the treat, he waited for her rubbery lips to scrape along his palm, then rubbed her forelock. Surprise pricked him at seeing Joss outside the stall.

"Hi." He turned too quickly, and the horse tossed her head with a whinny.

"How's she doing?"

"Fine. Restless from being pent up."

"Good." Joss seemed to study him. "And you?"

Yeah, I'm restless too, he wanted to say. He almost laughed.

She apparently picked up on his odd behavior. Tensing, her gaze cooled. She backed away as he opened the stall door and slipped into the aisle. The horse whirled again, lowering its head and charging forth.

He slid the door shut before it pinched the horse's nose. "She's wound up."

Joss stroked the mare's head. "All the horses are lately."

"They are?" Pretending to be clueless sent a prick of guilt through him.

"They seemed very content early this season, and went through practices smoothly. Then all of a sudden, they became skittish."

"Skittish how?" he asked.

"Throwing their heads, shuffling in the aisle when the girls groom or saddle them. Especially around Tom, for some reason."

Tom would make anyone skittish. Eric held his tongue. "Maybe he changed their feed to a higher protein base. I'll talk to him."

"Good. I've been afraid someone might get hurt. Triple Power threw Abbey the other day."

"Threw her?"

"Yes, he bucked her right off. Luckily she landed free and clear."

Could be a simple explanation. "Maybe something spooked him."

"Or someone."

He didn't have time to ponder her meaning. If he didn't get out of here right now, he knew exactly what would happen. He'd take her in his arms and kiss her. He could guess what would happen next.

Excusing himself, he grabbed his bag and strode to the truck.

"Wait. Eric."

He cringed at the faltering way she said his name. "I have to go."

"Are you sure you're all right?"

Good question. If only he knew how to answer. At the moment, he found it difficult enough not looking her in the eye. "Fine. See you." *Goodbye* was probably a more accurate word, though he wished it didn't have to be. He'd rather tell her *see you* and mean it. Frustration tensed his muscles and he slammed the back of the truck too forcefully.

She followed him to the driver's side door as he climbed in. "You don't seem fine."

"I have to go." Somewhere he didn't look forward to going. Somewhere unpleasant things waited. He shut the door before he could change his mind.

The only way to get it over with was to simply do it. He would tell Sheree, face to face. No date tonight. Or ever again.

Steeling himself, he drove to the diner. It occurred to him it might have been kinder to call instead of confronting her at work. Hell, a few dates didn't mean they were involved. Only a few people sat at tables, and one man at the counter. Not exactly a crowd.

Sheree's head popped up as he entered. Surprise gave way to a wide smile. "Well, hello there. Take a seat. I'll be right with you."

"No, I'm not staying." He stepped to the side and waved her over.

Her smile faded. "What is it?"

He looked away, anywhere except at her. "It's about what we discussed. About going out. I can't. Sorry."

"No." Conviction hardened her voice.

"Pardon?"

Her eyes narrowed. "You and I are dating. I'm making you dinner on Saturday, remember?"

If she didn't remind him of a pathological killer, he might laugh. "What?"

"You promised me. I already bought the food and everything." She seemed to strain to keep her voice under control, the growl underneath echoed as if from a deep cavern. The centers of her eyes flashed red, like the redeye caused by a camera's flash.

Enough was enough. "Sorry. I can't." He backed away and practically ran out the door. Roaring rushed up behind him, like water bursting out of a broken dam, like the breath of a giant opening its mouth to swallow him. He whirled to face it. *Nothing there.* Nothing he could see, anyway. The noise ebbed away into silence and the street returned to normal again.

"What the hell?" A shiver ran through him. He stood there dumbly, unable to process.

A man walked by with his German shepherd. "Hey doc. You all right?"

If one more person asked him that, his skull would crack.

Now he knew how to answer. "Not really." Nor did he have a clue how to fix the situation.

* * * *

Irritation chafed Joss's nerves until bedtime when she opened her window wide to let the scent of lavender waft into her room. Lavender, a balm for the senses. Even sweeter and more potent because of the near-invisible beings tending her field. Hopefully, bringing her luck and protection from ill fortune.

Inhaling its fragrance, she nestled into her pillow. At a hushed sigh outside, she stiffened. Not a human sigh. It emanated from the ground, an echo of a rush of air along an expanse of land.

Soon after, the front door creaked open and shut. Footsteps through the foyer echoed down the hall.

She sat up and listened. A customer? At this hour? The hair on the back of her neck prickled. If only Taz were here to protect her. No, if a burglar broke in, she'd want Taz safe.

Peeking out her door, she waited to catch sight of the late visitor. Soft voices indicated more than one. Female voices.

Not an intruder then. She might have preferred a burglar.

Steadying her breath, she carried her cell down the hall. The silhouettes of two figures loomed near the glass of the front doors. The whisperers bickered with a familiarity that eased her nerves. "Aunt Lydia?"

The two shushed and turned. "Jocelyn," Gram said.

Joss switched on the light. "What are you doing here? Why didn't you call?"

"I called earlier, dear. Don't you remember?"

Right. The warning about Eric. "Not about a midnight visit. Did you find everything we need?"

"I obtained the last ingredient only hours ago. We are here to help him, if you're willing to assist."

"Of course. Even if it involves dancing naked under the moon or chanting forbidden verses." Bad joke, but she had no idea what to expect.

"They're most certainly not forbidden. Ancient, maybe, but—" Gram shrugged. "Jocelyn, I know John used to object to our family and our ways, and I know you lost your identity because of him. Now is the time for you to become the person you were meant to be."

She tried to inject steady force into her words, yet failed. "I'm the same person I've always been." Not true, she knew. The missing elements left a gaping void that cried out to be filled again.

"No, Jocelyn. When you denied your heritage, you forfeited your true self. Now you must reclaim it, if only to help the one you love."

Surprise snapped her straight. "I don't love him." Did she?

Softness filled Gram's eyes. "I'm not here to quibble."

"It's an emergency, Jocelyn," Lydia added with soft urgency. "One threatening everyone, including you."

"I'll do whatever I need to do to help him." The steady gazes of her aunt and grandmother reassured her. In a small voice, she said, "But we can't help him if he doesn't ask for it." If she remembered correctly.

"Of course, darling, but he's about to."

"How do you know?" After all this time, she should know better than to ask.

With a smug smile, her grandmother carried her bag to the kitchen. "He's on his way here now. We have to hurry."

Lydia winked and bustled behind Gram.

Joss had to follow.

In the kitchen, her grandmother stood at the sink filling the kettle. Turning, she peered out the door. "Oh, how marvelous. They're very active tonight. Good thing—we'll need them."

Gram moved to the counter, where she'd already laid out several jars. Some appeared familiar, others not. "What's this for?"

Gram's eyes sparkled. "Tea. It's going to be a long night."

Of that, Joss had no doubt.

Bustling between sink and counter, Gram hummed. "Put on some music, would you, dear?" At Joss's questioning look, her grandmother added, "You know what I like."

All too well. Gram liked it cranked to the highest volume. Joss would keep it low tonight. From the CD player sifted the searing slide guitar of Bonnie Raitt, her gritty voice stripping the last remnants of sleep away. The slow beat wound into her bones, swayed her hips and she crooned the chorus: *That's just love sneakin' up on you.*

An insistent knock stilled her.

Eric.

If only he were here because he wanted to be, not because he needed help.

Either way, she let him in.

Chapter 13

The night air misted on Eric's face, a cold reminder of his desperate plight. He shouldn't be at Joss's door, imposing on her of all people. He needed refuge. Sanctuary and sanity. Relief from the burn deep inside. Sheree, or whatever force consumed her, etched an imprint inside him, a searing brand. Something deep in his flesh throbbed with pain, urged him to find Sheree. Be with her again. Become hers in a wild, primal way.

Earlier tonight the need had grown unbearable. Her acid had spread through his veins, an intoxicating mix of desire and need, his flesh incomplete without pairing with hers. His nerves had stretched taut, veins strained against his skin, threatened to break through unless he went to Sheree. Surrendered to her. Became one with her. Relentlessly, the call had prodded *go to her*. It crawled beneath every inch of his skin so he couldn't stay still. Whatever she'd imprinted inside him wanted her. Wanted to seduce him into wanting her. Somehow he knew in doing so, he'd step over a boundary, and whatever portal he entered, would slam behind him.

He couldn't close his eyes without seeing the hideous twisted features of Sheree, with Kara's Kafe transformed into a hellhole awaiting his return to swallow him into its cavern of flames. Once inside, he'd never return.

The axis of his world was tipping on a precarious tilt. He feared the balance might shift at any time and send him toppling over the brink. Of what, he had no clue. Only that it meant the end of everything he knew to be true.

Tonight it had reached epic proportions. For hours, an internal struggle had raged. It had taken every ounce of his energy to simply stand immobile. Despite his increasing struggle against the terrifying images that haunted him relentlessly, he'd fought the instinct to seek help from

Joss. He couldn't drag her into this madness, or expose her to the lunatic he'd become.

He'd stood at his bedroom window, concentrating on Lavender Hill Inn, though the flickering over the field burned his eyes. Focusing on the inn had provided him some measure of control. Lights in the house had given him unsteady peace. Even a blink had disrupted it. The intensity of the flickering orbs had caused his eyes to water.

He'd closed them for one moment and the burning within him had licked his limbs into movement, had whispered to him, *"Go. Now."* His nerves had jangled inside his limbs. "Sheree." He'd reached atop his dresser and grabbed his car keys. *Yes,* the whisper had said, *"Sheree will bring you relief. She's the only one who can."*

"Sheree." Like every night, she had waited for him. She would take away this haunting madness, give him what he needed.

He'd pounded down the stairs and outside, not bothering to close the door. Fumbling the keys into the ignition, he'd slammed the gas pedal before it was fully in gear, causing the truck to lurch forward with a roar. Pulse at light speed, his sweaty hands had slipped on the steering wheel. A thousand tiny voices had screeched at him in chaotic chorus, *"Go, go, go."*

At the edge of the practice's parking lot, he'd jammed on the brake. Headlights had dazed him, and the voices had stilled for one second. The approaching vehicle had appeared to float along, leaving a glowing mist in its wake. A beautiful trail of soft flowing light. Quiet. Calm.

With his last reserve of strength, he'd yanked the steering wheel in the opposite direction to follow the vehicle. The voices had screamed with renewed intensity, ratcheting up the volume. Like angry bees, they'd swarmed his head, buzzes urging him to seek out Sheree.

"No!" He'd swatted aimlessly, and their attack had increased in number and volume. The truck had fishtailed along the road, and the taillights of the car ahead had drifted around the corner. The lights in the field had grown larger, blinding him, his retinas ready to spontaneously combust.

His front tire had caught a rut, sending the truck up the hill toward the inn. His vision blurry, he'd known enough to brake. The SUV had lurched over the mound, airborne, like a wild mustang desperate to throw off its rider, then had slammed to the ground and halted.

Shielding his head with his forearms, he'd waited, chest heaving. When his breathing quieted, he peered around him. It had seemed quiet enough. No screeching, no insane nagging voices. The soft lights bobbing around the truck still hurt his eyes, if less than before.

Stumbling out of the truck, he hadn't flinched when the lights had glimmered around him. By their glow, he'd dragged himself to the inn's porch, his spirit yearning for relief. Still, he'd hesitated before knocking. How to explain it? She'd think he went crazy. He'd begun to wonder himself.

Now, the door to the inn opened wide, and Joss stood there. Light framed her outline and glinted off the golden strands of hair so she appeared to glow. Her face held no hint of surprise.

"Eric. Come in." She lightly grasped his arm and drew him inside.

He put up no resistance. What a complete idiot he was. "I'm sorry to bother you so late."

"It's fine." Barefoot, she stood gazing up at him, shapely legs bare to her thighs. Her faded T-shirt revealed soft mounds punctuated by protruding centers.

His mind blanked, relieved of everything except the beautiful vision of her. "Joss."

A clank in the kitchen told him they weren't alone.

"Gram and Lydia." She sounded none too happy about it.

"A late night reunion?" Damn, was he intruding on some family emergency? Why else would they be here at this hour?

Her steady gaze unnerved him.

As if steeling herself, she inhaled audibly. "You'd better come with me."

"Do you need help with something?"

She halted and turned. "No. Just the opposite." For a long beat, she met his gaze hard, then led him on.

"What?" Mired in confusion, he stood there until she swung open the kitchen door and waited.

Beyond, her grandmother and aunt bent over the island, intent on their work. Seeing him, they straightened with solemn expressions. The three women emanated an air of expectancy and reserved determination.

His spine iced. They'd known he was coming. How? More importantly, why?

Had Joss not anchored his spirit here, he might have turned and fled.

A breath escaped, part laugh. Fled to where? He had nowhere else to go. Except to *her.*

The elder woman extended her arm. "Come."

The command propelled him forward. Whatever awaited, he would endure it.

Beneath the grandmother's smile lurked something distasteful, revealed by the stiff curve of her lips. "Please sit."

Doing so indicated his acceptance of more than the invitation, and she seemed to relax.

In a softer tone, she asked, "Would you like some tea?"

Uncertain, he glanced at Joss, who nodded encouragement.

The bluesy music unwound his nerves somewhat. Tea couldn't hurt. "Sure."

Set in motion, the three ignored him, huddling and speaking in low tones. When they turned in unison toward him, the motion seemed choreographed. They surrounded him, Joss and Lydia on either side.

Standing opposite, the grandmother set a mug in front of him.

He wrapped his fingers around the cup, but its warmth didn't penetrate deeper than his outer skin. As if his life force was already fading. He feared he was soon to follow.

He ventured, "None of you seem surprised to see me."

The elder woman said sympathetically, "You've suffered through a difficult time. We understand."

Meeting each of their gazes in turn, he held Joss's the longest. "What is going on?"

She searched his eyes. "It's my fault."

"Nonsense," the grandmother said. "They were here long before."

Sorrow filled Joss's face. "No one came to harm because of them."

"I beg to differ." Lydia leaned closer. "Two years ago, a teenager hung himself. Nothing to do with you, and everything to do with them."

"Ronnie Landon?" How did they know about him? The kid fell in with a bad crowd, got involved with drugs.

The grandmother nodded. "And last year, the farmer's wife who was found in the field…"

"Carrie Enders?" Gossip around the office said she'd fallen in love with a trucker who let her into his cab on layovers. He'd refused to take her away, and Carrie went on a bender with a few strange guys. One of the farm hands found her dead in the cornfield. Ed Enders sold the farm, unwilling to plough the land.

Lydia lifted her cup. "They were becoming more active. It was only a matter of time."

Eric's eyes burned. "I'm not following any of this." Had the world gone mad? Or had they concocted this as some elaborate put-on?

"Of course you are," the grandmother said. "You're not allowing yourself to believe the truth."

"You must. You're in grave danger." Lydia touched his arm, tensed and eased away. "Their mark is upon you."

The brand Sheree left inside him. How did she know? "Can you erase it? It's driving me crazy."

"We'll certainly try, dear," said the grandmother.

Lydia added, "It's why we're here."

The knot of tension in his stomach unfurled. They'd help him.

A glance at Joss edged his relief with embarrassment. He'd never exposed himself as a bigger fool to anyone, or made himself so vulnerable. Yet she gazed at him with acceptance.

"Drink," she said, glancing pointedly at his tea.

He lifted the mug to his lips. The hot liquid flowed over his tongue and down his throat with tingling effervescence. Whatever Sheree introduced to his system didn't like it, and the sting shot through him, fighting against the drink. When it reached his stomach, the sensation expanded, flooding him with warring elements. Burn and cool pricked through his veins like needles, sending him to his feet.

Joss grasped his arm, and laid a hand on his stomach. "I have you."

Despite the pain, he exhaled in relief. Never had three words meant more.

* * * *

Joss held tight even though the disruption within him transferred to her. Beneath her hand pricked tiny zings, turbo-charged ants skittering helter-skelter, assaulting her consciousness. A hundred times worse than before. How he'd managed to deflect them, she couldn't guess. Not many people showed such fortitude.

When the disturbance quieted, she glanced at Lydia, who nodded.

"Please, sit," Joss tugged him down.

Lydia pulled on his other side. "You'll need your strength."

"What is happening to me?" He spoke with the weariness of an elderly man, yet his gaze pierced hers with vigor.

Deferring to Gram, Joss drew back. She didn't want to be the one to explain. He'd hold it against her.

Gram refilled his mug. "Drink up."

Through his weariness, his determination blazed. "First tell me what's going on."

Demurely, her grandmother smiled. "You may find it more difficult to swallow than the tea."

Her serene patience seemed to frustrate him further.

"Am I losing my mind?" Desperation edged his voice.

"No, dear," Gram said. "Something much more important."

His lips curled, but he didn't work up a smile. "Don't say my soul."

Sternly, Gram arched her brow. "We can't help you if you don't want it."

"I do, but…" He met each of their gazes in turn, then expelled a sharp breath.

"What does your heart tell you?" Lydia prompted.

His brows furrowed. "My heart?"

"Yes," Joss managed.

His uncertain glance sent a flush of warmth through Joss. Did she have a place in his heart? She hadn't meant to. His whirlwind emotions overwhelmed her, as John's used to, shifting swiftly from bliss to rage. If she'd left any mark within him, he'd captured it forcefully, absorbed it fully.

Finally, he said, "I don't know."

Patting his hand, Gram smiled. "Many of us need time to understand our heart's desires. Unfortunately, you don't have such a luxury. If you'd like us to help you, you must ask."

Skeptical as ever, he asked, "Help how?"

It didn't deter Gram. "It's an arduous process. Trust is imperative."

"As is an open mind," Lydia said.

"Quite literally," Gram added.

He slumped and held a hand to his temple. "I don't have much of a mind left."

An urge came over Joss to rub his shoulders, rest her cheek to his, tell him he'd be fine. She held back when Gram held up a hand in signal for her to wait. He must ask of his own accord, without further coercion.

When he opened his eyes again, he met Gram's steady gaze.

"I'll do whatever it takes to get my life back."

Gram arched her brow in prompting question. His statement fell short of what they needed to begin.

Apparently realizing his mistake, he slowly asked, "Will you help me? Please?"

"Of course." Gram gathered some items.

"It's why we're here," Lydia reminded him.

Creases of worry in his face erased. When he turned to Joss with tenderness in his eyes, she again yearned to enfold him in her embrace. Now was not the time. They had work to do.

Joss hoped she was up to the task ahead. "I'll get the candles. Where are we going?"

Already headed there, Gram said, "The dining room."

Joss inclined her head, inviting Eric to follow. He wasn't going to like it.

* * * *

His muscles shook when he stood, and Eric steadied himself before following them to the dining room. The dining room? Were they going to feed him scones to go with the tea? Some sort of Mad Hatter tea party? Nothing surprised him anymore.

So he thought. By the time he reached the doorway, candles lit every table. The three women waited beside an empty table.

Gram gestured. "Lay down."

A trembling laugh escaped. He withheld an argument. Right about now, he wouldn't mind lying down, even atop a hard wooden table. Zombie-like, he shuffled ahead and eased himself down. Mostly, he was relieved to turn over control of the bizarre situation to these women who moved with the surety of those who were highly skilled and practiced often.

How the women attained such experience, he couldn't muster the strength to ask. Something told him he wouldn't want to know.

The grandmother stood at his head, the aunt on his right. At his left stood Joss—beside his heart. When she reached over to take Lydia's hand, something swept across him, and his heart lifted, strained against his ribs, hungry for her touch.

After the three joined hands, the grandmother leaned over him, her upside down head hovering above his. "You must follow us without question."

"Didn't you want me here, on the table?"

"We don't mean physically," Lydia said. "Open your mind, let it float where it will."

"So long as it floats with us," the elder woman said.

His mind?

"Yes," the grandmother's voice said within his head.

Startled, he glanced up at the woman, then at Joss. All around them, flickering lights bobbed and shimmered. The soft glow of candlelight lent a haze to her beauty. "I'll try."

The grandmother sounded far away. "Don't try. Do. Relax."

Relax, he told himself, and closed his eyes. The three women chanted in low tones, words he couldn't comprehend. Soothing and entrancing. Joss's voice rose clear above the rest. He wanted to reach for her, hold her close. She laid her hand on his chest atop The Mark. Her warmth, different than the burn of Sheree's brand, seeped down and enfolded it.

Barbs pierced upward, making invisible slashes in his skin. Stabbing Joss, too, but after each jab, she steadied herself and chanted louder. Healing waves of energy wore away the sharp points, smoothing the knifelike edges down to mere nubs. Rendering them powerless.

And robbing her of her very life source. Trapped in his head, his struggles against the mummy-like wrapping of their power proved useless. All he could do was direct every beat of his heart to strengthen her, will his lifeblood to reinvigorate her.

Within another room inside his brain, noises erupted, a cacophony of screeches, moans, pleading. The faint image of Sheree beckoned from afar, sorrowful and pathetic. *"I need you,"* she whined, reaching for him.

"Be gone," the grandmother commanded, and Sheree hissed.

Joss repeated the order again and again, more loudly each time until her voice grew raspy.

A grinding moan filled his ears and rattled his bones. He convulsed upward, the imprint bubbling in his blood. Boiling it. Melting his flesh. The anguish erupted in a strangled cry.

Sheree faded to a mere point, then blended into the void.

Sweating, he shuddered. He floated, drifting in nothingness. He should be alarmed, but it was wonderful. Their three glowing figures surrounded him, hands joined, and another layer of light glimmered around them, iridescent bubbles floating soundlessly. Cocooned in their glow, airiness filled his every pore, illuminating most. Some spots remained dark and heavy, his spirit mottled as a leper's flesh.

The grandmother said, "You came to us just in time."

She was right. He couldn't have held on much longer. Here, he had no cares, though myriad questions swarmed through his head. Answers would have to wait. The women somehow shielded him from danger. Their chants grew in fervor, dissipating the darkened areas. Some stubbornly clung, tearing at his cells, burrowing to hide beneath his DNA structure.

At the grandmother's gesturing, the glowing image of Joss approached him. Or his spirit. Whatever people called their disembodied selves. It didn't matter. The closer she drew, the stronger her presence pressed against him, as if they were truly together in the flesh. When she encircled her arms around him, echoes of the trio of voices reverberated deeper, sending even the most belligerent black points scurrying away, their screams fading to nothingness. The process cleansed him, yet stripped him of his last vestige of strength.

Transformed from dark to light, his spirit like a wisp of smoke, able to rise indefinitely except for the ring of force keeping him in place. The women. Their voices now whispers, lulling and cradling him during their descent. The world around him solidified with clarity. When he again opened his eyes, the aunt and grandmother rocked gently, eyes closed. Joss swayed too, watching him.

"It's over." He didn't need to ask. He knew. Except for the tiniest scar, none of the imprint remained. "I'm free."

Sadness washed through Joss's face. She swept it away with a smile. "Yes. You're free."

"For now," Gram added. "You still bear the scar of The Mark, making you vulnerable when they return. Rest now. When you awake, it will only seem a dream."

More like a nightmare. Too exhausted to express his gratitude in words, he smiled and let sleep overtake him.

Chapter 14

The ritual left Joss invigorated rather than weakened. When she'd embraced Eric's disembodied self, she'd also accepted her true spirit. Doing so rewarded her with empowerment. It completed her, healed her disparate selves into one. She'd never again deny that part of herself. Whether she would actively use such power, she couldn't say. Probably not before better understanding it. Certainly not as entertainment, like Aunt Lydia. Possibly to enhance certain aspects of running the inn—some herbs and flowers, such as lavender, positively affected those who ingested them. Definitely if another situation arose where she could use it to protect another.

Especially Eric. He'd been a pawn in this game, but why?

Gram knew, Joss was sure of it.

Her grandmother averted her gaze. "He needs to recover."

Joss moved to one side. "Let's put him in my bed."

Lydia supported his other side. "Lucky you."

She wouldn't fall prey to her aunt's lascivious humor. She'd sleep in Kyle's room, if she could sleep at all. Energy coursed through her veins, filling her with bliss. Physically, she and her aunt shouldn't have had the strength to lift Eric's full weight. Somehow, they carried him with ease.

After lowering him to the bed, Joss lifted his legs and untied his shoes. "Will he be safe?"

"Here, yes. Tonight, he must rest to regain his strength." Gram crept to the hallway.

Joss left the door ajar to listen for him and followed Gram to the kitchen. "And tomorrow?" Some part of her hoped Gram would say he'd have to stay longer.

"We will enlist their aid in protecting him." Her grandmother took the steaming cup Lydia offered.

Joss also accepted the mug her aunt held, and her embrace. Lydia kissed her forehead. "Good work, sweetie."

Gram gazed outside, where illuminated orbs floated around the pane. "Yes, I'm proud of you, Jocelyn. You were wonderful tonight."

Past tense, unfortunately. Guilt now plagued Joss. "I'm not proud. This is my fault, isn't it? None of this would have happened if I hadn't moved here."

"No one can blame you, dear," Gram said. "I'll venture the people here would have succumbed to their false promises."

Lydia sipped her drink. "Your positive influence disturbed their roots. They're trying to frighten you away."

"By threatening Eric." In a strange way, it was perfectly logical. "Won't I make things worse for him?"

"Absolutely not. Your presence will only enhance the protective effect."

"The lavender." Joss remembered the lights above Gram's field when she was a girl.

Gram smiled. "They do love it, you know."

Pointing a glossy nail at Joss, Lydia added, "So will your customers."

Delight filled Gram's face. "Mm, lavender sugar is lovely on cakes."

"Lavender lemonade's so refreshing in summer." Lydia sipped her drink.

"Yes, I'd already planned to use the recipe and many more. Are you sure no one else will be hurt?"

"We can never be sure of anything, only try our best. And we will." After sipping the last of her tea, Gram stretched. "I'm ready for bed."

"Me too." Lydia carried her glass to the sink.

"I'll get those. You two go get settled, relax. It's been quite a day."

Gram beamed. "Exhilarating."

"Mm, yes. The chamomile did the trick too. I'm ready for a nice comfy pillow." Lydia kissed Joss's cheek. "Good night, sweets. Take care of our darling."

"And get some rest," Gram added with a kiss.

"Sleep well." Joss wondered whether she could with Eric in her bed. After washing the mugs, she went to the bedroom. With one hand rested on his stomach, his other arm raised above his head, he slept peacefully.

She eased beside him, the only chance she'd have to observe him at close range in such repose. Even at rest, his life force affected her with a startling impact. The very air came alive with vibrancy. She laid there a long time, studying him. The grandfather clock struck two, and she checked the bedside clock. Two. The right time.

Her last thought before drifting to sleep.

* * * *

Unfamiliar warmth disrupted his slumber. A body curled against his side. Comfortable, but strange. So wonderful, Eric didn't want to open his eyes. Curiosity got the better of him. He slitted one eye open.

Joss.

His eyes popped wide. Definitely Joss, her honey-gold hair glinting in the morning sunlight. He wasn't dreaming. He eased his head up to peer over his shoulder, then rested his head back against the pillow, trying to recall how the hell he came to be here.

Last night, his head spun, some sort of fever battered him. He'd almost gone to Sheree. Instead, he came here, to Joss. And her crazy aunt and grandmother. Somehow, not so crazy. Whatever they'd done had healed him.

Images flashed through his mind of Joss, displaying graceful ferocity and ethereal beauty. Disconnected, the visions confused him except he clearly recalled Joss's unquestioning protection of him. Shielding him from his pain.

Inhaling, she shifted, lids fluttered and her hazel eyes gazed into his.

Awe washed over him again. He couldn't quite reconcile the Joss of yesterday with the vulnerable woman lying beside him. Studying her provided no clue.

Softly, he asked, "Who are you?"

Tensing, she drew away. "What?"

Damn. Leave it to him to fumble something as simple as good morning. Nothing about her was simple, or ordinary. "You stayed last night."

With a wry smile, she sat up. "This is my bed."

"Oh. Right." He rested his head on his hands. "But you stayed with me."

"I came in to check on you. You looked so cozy, I curled up too. I shouldn't have."

Yes. If he argued, she might withdraw, like before. "Are your aunt and grandmother still here?"

"They stayed upstairs." Reading him too well, she added, "You were too weak."

"I am kind of beaten up." Yet she seemed somehow stronger. "How are you?"

"Never better." She stood and put on a robe. "How about some eggs? Or pancakes?"

Hunger rumbled through his stomach. "Both?"

"You have your appetite back." She knotted the belt. "I'll start the coffee."

After she left, he caught an awful scent. Of himself. His T-shirt smelled of sweat. And fear. The morning's normalcy contrasted the bizarro events of the previous day. He couldn't recall exactly what happened, but it seemed another world. No, a very strange dream.

In her bathroom, he found a towel and took a quick shower. He hated to put on the same clothes, so left his shirt off. For now, it would have to do.

Eric followed the smell of food to the kitchen, where Joss and Annie moved around each other efficiently.

Gaze wandering down his length, Annie froze, open-mouthed. "Good morning."

"Hi." Damn. Should have put the shirt on after all. "Excuse my appearance. Joss said to make myself at home." He wouldn't mention he normally slept in the buff.

Joss's eyes twinkled with mischief. "Did I mention Dr. Hendricks stayed the night?"

Annie tilted her head toward Joss. "No, in fact. You did not."

"I might have an oversized shirt to fit you. Let me go look." Joss hurried out.

Annie ogled him. "It explains breakfast. Joss isn't a breakfast eater."

"She's not?" Something to file away, hopefully for future use.

As she returned and tossed him the lilac-colored tee emblazoned with the Lavender Hill Inn logo, Joss shot him an indecipherable look. "Gram and Aunt Lydia are here too."

Hint taken. He struggled into the shirt. A snug fit, but it would have to do for now.

"Did you have a party or something? And didn't invite me?" Annie sounded truly hurt.

"Of course not."

Joss's helpless look, he could decipher. "My truck broke down."

Annie set her hand on her hip. "And you couldn't walk home?"

"No, he came here for help," Joss said.

"Because you're a mechanical expert?" Annie challenged.

"No, because…" Joss extended her hand toward him in a take-it-away gesture.

"I couldn't find my flashlight," he blurted. "And it was too dark to check under the hood. And my head was killing me, so Joss's grandmother gave me some tea...."

Joss nodded. "And he fell asleep."

"Where?" Annie's eyes narrowed.

"What?" Joss asked.

"Where did he fall asleep?" A gotcha expression lurked in Annie's subdued smile.

"Good morning," Lydia sang, entering. Passing him on the way to the coffee, she purred, "Well, hel-*lo*."

"Morning." Now he felt ridiculous wearing Joss's shirt.

Relief sounded clear in Joss's voice. "Aunt Lydia. Did you sleep well?"

After the aunt poured her coffee, Eric prepared himself a cup. The women puttered around, their good-natured banter putting him at ease. When they ate breakfast in the kitchen, the hominess left him with another kind of hunger—to have it every day.

After finishing, he offered to help clean up. They shooed him away.

"You're right," he said. "I should get to work."

Joss turned uneasily to her grandmother, who reassured them both, "You'll be fine. However, I wouldn't eat at the diner."

"Yeah. Probably not a good idea."

"What's wrong with the diner?" Annie asked.

Eric covered quickly. "I must have eaten some bad tuna. My stomach was a mess yesterday."

When Annie turned away with a confused frown, he inclined his head toward the other room. Joss followed, and her relatives trailed along.

"I couldn't leave without saying how grateful I am to each of you."

Lydia smoothed her hair back. "You owe us nothing."

"If I can ever repay you in any way—"

"No," Joss said. "It's not necessary."

Her answer left him more helpless than yesterday. More pathetic. Of course these incredible women didn't need anything from him. If anything, he'd be back groveling for help.

With a nod, he ducked his head and trod to his truck. The engine started on the first turn of the key. With no other reason to stay, he backed onto the road and drove the short stretch to the parking lot of his practice.

* * * *

"It's not over." Gram stood beside Joss outside, watching Eric's truck wind down the driveway.

Joss feared it too. "Is he safe?" She hated to let him leave the inn.

"For now. We'll need to take more aggressive measures to make sure he stays that way."

Oh no. Joss knew the dangers of such measures, to her business at least. Gossip was the most minor, and the worst would be a label befitting the level of paranoia. Not quite *The Amityville Horror*, but enough for people to avoid the inn. It could ruin her community standing, and the inn.

"Are you sure it's necessary?" Eric would never look at her the same. He left in such a hurry today, she wondered if he'd ever come back.

"Don't worry, darling." Lydia walked toward the inn. "Nothing anyone else will notice. But we do need to act quickly."

Gram nodded. "We missed an opportunity to block their activity at Beltane."

May Day. To anyone else, the first of May was an opportunity to celebrate spring. According to Gram, humans could come to harm if they didn't perform the annual ritual to protect crops and herds. Joss laughed to herself. *Wonder if I could convince Annie to bake some Beltane oatmeal cakes?* Enough for all of Boiling Springs? No, probably not.

She hurried to catch up to Gram at the back steps. "Please tell me it's nothing outrageous." In second grade, she'd lost most of her friends after revealing some of her grandmother's secrets during show and tell.

Before going inside, Gram turned long enough to say, "Leave it to us."

Luckily, Annie had blasted the radio and hummed along with the tune. She smiled when they entered. "So, he didn't need to fix the truck after all."

"Who?" It dawned too late. Eric. "Oh, right. He probably just flooded the engine last night."

"So he didn't need to stay." Annie held a finger to her cheek. "Where did he sleep? Only two rooms were used."

Gram busied herself filling the kettle and putting it on the stove.

Heat prickled Joss's neck. How to explain? "He wasn't well so I let him stay in my room." She wouldn't lie and say she'd stayed in Kyle's.

Annie seemed to read Joss's reluctance to answer any more questions. At the timer's ding, she opened the oven door. "Anyone want muffins? I found the most beautiful blueberries at the market yesterday."

Thank you. Joss wanted to hug her, and explain. Maybe someday, when it was a distant memory. "Sounds delicious."

"They would be perfect," Gram said, "for a Fourth of July celebration."

"You're right." In typical Lydia fashion, she gazed up and splayed her fingers. "It would announce to the world that Lavender Hill Inn is open for business."

Pinching the top of the muffin, Joss popped the hot, fruity bit into her mouth. "We've been open for business since last summer."

Gram arched a brow. "Of course, dear, but this would make a definitive statement."

Like her grandmother's pointed glare. Something was up, and Joss wasn't sure she wanted to know.

Annie joined them at the island, munching. "Yep, we're wide open. Didn't you invite them to our event? It'll be exactly what we need to kick off the summer season."

"Exactly. Such a smart girl." Gram beamed at Annie.

Joss knew her grandmother had her own strategy. If not during the Fourth of July, her family would think of some other way to pull off their plan. Hiding in plain sight might be the best answer.

"You always know best, Gram." Joss may not have her grandmother's power, but she possessed magic of another kind, one that suited her in the world she'd created for herself. She could plan a party to beat Hell. With Gram's help, they could do it literally.

* * * *

The steady lineup of patients helped occupy Eric's mind. Not enough to block the vivid memories of the last few days. Like a horror movie on endless replay, the images returned in flashes when he least expected it, akin to an LSD trip. He might be writing in a chart, and Sheree's twisted features loomed on the page. Or he'd step into an exam room, and a hissing, feline face resembled her too.

Mid-afternoon, the flashbacks inexplicably faded. His nerves loosened, no longer bound by fear. Something had changed. Though he couldn't pinpoint what, exactly, he was grateful for it nonetheless. By dusk, the waking nightmare had ended. No Sheree in his head for hours.

Thoughts of Joss still came unbidden for another reason. Visions of her in that dream place, a soft white aura heightening her natural glow. Her presence as he slept hadn't tripped his subconscious to awaken. Too bad. Then he could have remained aware of every moment he laid beside her, and listened to her hushed breaths. After seeing her in all her glory, he might have been too stunned to kiss her. Then again, how could he have resisted? If he could relive the time he'd spent with her, he'd endure the illness and pain all over again.

Outside, the twinkling orbs nestled in branches of trees, surrounding his practice and house. Their presence comforted him, and for the first night in nearly a week, he went to bed knowing he'd rest without fear, though not undisturbed. His dream had seemed so real, and yet surreal.

Joss had appeared nothing short of glorious. Even after he'd awakened, she'd seemed different somehow, but nothing he could pinpoint. Yesterday had blurred the line separating reality and dreams, and all he could say for sure was that he no longer suffered pain. Not a physical sort.

He ached for Joss all night.

Chapter 15

The list was daunting, yet with each item Joss read off, Annie replied, "Check."

After her friend confirmed the final item, Joss scanned the list. "And we didn't miss anything?"

Washing her cup, Annie shook her head. "Nope. We covered everything. It's going to be easy peasy."

Dread numbed her as she paced, glancing at every detail. "Don't jinx it." Or Gram and Aunt Lydia would. She almost looked forward to the event so they'd go home.

Annie feigned a pout. "It's true."

"It makes me nervous not having time for RSVPs." She'd always put stock in going with the flow rather than planning, one reason John would have frowned on her purchase of the inn. This once, she'd like to have an idea of what to expect. Nervousness quelled any notion of what was to come.

"Open houses don't ask for RSVPs. People come and go as they please. A steady stream." Annie's arm mimed the flow in and out, in and out.

"A steady stream," she repeated like a mantra. If it were possible to will every person in town to attend, Joss's fervent chant would bring them. With the exception of the waitress. She could do without a possessed guest, even if it meant two for the price of one.

A thought struck her. Of course. Tom's irritating presence had become grating because he, too, had been affected. Willingly or not, the trainer had been marked, though he appeared not to fight against it. Tom, Sheree—how many others?

With a deep breath, she gave it over to whatever power controlled such things. "No use worrying. We've done everything we can." For now.

"Right." Annie arranged the towel on the oven door. "Exactly why I'm going home, and you're going to bed, so we can be rested and beautiful for tomorrow."

"I don't know about beautiful." Joss chuckled, silently adding *or rested*. Party details would fly into her brain overnight and squawk like crows.

Annie narrowed one eye. "You bought a new outfit, didn't you?"

"Yes." Another expense she regretted, but appearances counted. Especially since she'd be making a first impression on some. And a last on unseen others.

With a definitive nod, Annie grabbed her handbag. "Good. Then we'll knock 'em dead."

Joss repressed a shudder. "Let's hope so." For some, literally.

When a knock sounded at the front door, Joss froze. "No one's booked for tonight, are they?"

"No." Annie appeared as puzzled as Joss.

She hurried to open it, and surprise choked her words.

"Hi, Mom." Kyle shifted his duffle bag.

With a laugh, she hugged him. "Why are you knocking? This is your home now, too."

Stepping inside, he hesitated in the foyer. "I probably should have called."

"No, there's always a room for you here. Sorry it's a mess. We've been so busy getting ready for tomorrow."

Annie squealed. "Ooh, you're here. Now everything's perfect." She rushed, arms open and rocked him.

Her son's gaze rolled across the foyer into the adjoining rooms. "Looks great."

"Your bag's small."

"Yeah, I'm only staying overnight."

"Oh." She forced a smile. Not much time for catching up. Then again, the sooner he left, the sooner he'd be out of harm's way. "Are you hungry? We have plenty of food."

Annie's eyes widened. "I'll make you a plate. You can be our first unbiased taste tester." She beckoned him to the kitchen.

"Unbiased?" Her son laughed. "Is she kidding?"

"Better not argue." Joss linked her arm in his.

Kyle endured Annie's fussing good naturedly, as he always did. His cell phone vibrated many times. Only once he checked the display. Friends? Girlfriends? She hoped he wouldn't settle down too quickly. He had so much passion, yet lacked focus. The right girl would complement him, help him find his way through life.

For now, Joss reveled in the surprise of having him at the inn. One night was too short. Time mattered most when valued. And she treasured having him for however long.

From the foyer, nine chimes sounded.

Kyle chuckled. "Nine? It's eleven. You should have gotten rid of that weird clock."

She wondered if she shouldn't have placed it somewhere less conspicuous. But it was so beautiful, and everyone admired it. Until it struck the wrong hour. "Never. You know your great grandfather hand-carved it."

"I know." Waving in surrender, he carried his plate to the sink. "I'm overdue for some sleep."

With a quick kiss to her cheek, he murmured, "Good night." On his way out, he held a hand to his stomach. "Great food, Annie, as always."

Annie called good night after Kyle, then turned her smile on Joss. "I've stuffed our boy to the gills. Mission accomplished. I better go."

Joss followed her friend to the door and waved as the car pulled away. Two honks of the horn answered, and bolstered her. They had both invested everything in this. It had to work.

The breeze carried a scent of lavender, and she inhaled deeply, hoping its calming attributes would take effect. Below the field, crackles interrupted the usual steady hum of energy. Even the ley line was restless. She walked to the sprawling side patio and stood on its edge. The solar lights lent a homey atmosphere, and she imagined people sitting at the teak tables tomorrow. Overhead, stars shone crisp in the indigo sky, and the Milky Way glowed faint. A good sign.

Shimmering shapes covered the field like a glittering mist. They were extra busy tonight, here and at Eric's. Gram must have spoken to them and enlisted their aid.

"This is going to pay off, John." She'd used every last bit of what he'd left her. Despite the fact the inn sat on a ley line, or the fae returned to her life, he had to approve. For once.

The stars glimmered more brightly for a moment and winked in answer.

* * * *

The sun barely topped the horizon when Eric tied his running shoes, stretched by the back door and then ran at a steady pace down the road. Near the inn, he halted at the house. A light shone in the summer kitchen. Joss must be working, at such an early hour. Her whirlwind energy amazed him. Paralyzed him with its speed and intensity, which swept him up, out of the depths of grief into her light and laughter.

Exactly what he needed.

A memory teased at the back of his mind, something he couldn't quite place. Joss had done more for him, something amazing. Hard as he tried, he couldn't remember what.

The sign outside the inn announced a Fourth of July picnic. Maybe he'd go for awhile. It was an open invitation, after all. He hated being home on a holiday. Alone. He also avoided family picnics.

Besides, he needed another taste of the lavender lemonade. Refreshing and different, it had comforted him last time. In fact, he'd relaxed for the first time in much too long. The rest of the day was a blur, yet seemed to end well. He squinted as if to force a clearer memory, but it eluded him.

He wanted to go, he decided. If only to be near her.

He took off at a run, suddenly lighter.

* * * *

A zephyr of a breeze billowed the sheer white curtain lit with sunshine. Rising, Joss stretched and went to the window. The world had come into bloom. The emerald green grass set off the vivid purple flowers in the field beyond. In the garden leading to the stone bridge, butterflies sipped at the phlox, and hummingbirds dipped their long beaks into the orange buds of the woody trumpet vine climbing the archway. The house's new paint reflected the sun's rays, and she imagined the house practically radiating its welcome atop the hill. Lavender Hill.

Time for her life to come into bloom as well. Happiness buoyed her as she readied.

Annie's exuberance filled the kitchen when she flung open the door. "Today's going to be incredible–the start of a whole new era."

"Morning." Joss smiled at Annie, Gram, and Lydia.

From her perch on the kitchen stool, Lydia's smile froze, and her gaze crawled down Joss's length. "You're not wearing work clothes today, are you?"

Joss chuckled. "No, I'll change before one. I didn't want to wrinkle my good outfit. I'm going to make tea this morning in the summer kitchen, and you know what a klutz I am."

The grandfather clock's five chimes prompted her to check the oven clock. "Nine already." Plenty of time, she told herself, but still hurried outside, waving at Gram's call to let her know if she needed help.

She primped the sprigs of mint and lemon thyme as she watered the rows of plants on the counter. The summer kitchen's wide windows allowed ample sunlight for growing the herbs, essential for the lavender lemonade she intended to be one of the inn's signature offerings. The fresh-grown basil, parsley, thyme, and other herbs, Annie expertly added to the inn's nightly dishes.

After fashioning several large tea balls from lavender, Joss carried one inside and filled a pot with water to begin the first batch. Annie hummed along with the radio, swaying her hips with the soft rock music. Diana Ross's velvet vocalization filled the kitchen. The rhythm coursed through Joss and she let her body move in time. Humming gave way to lyrics, and she raised the spoon to her mouth like a microphone, rolled her shoulders with the beat and sang. The words poured out as if she herself had written them. She'd finally broken out of her shell for the world to see. No more hiding the real Jocelyn Gibson. She couldn't remember the last time she'd been so fulfilled, so happy.

Annie danced to her side and sang into the spoon too. At the end of the song, they doubled with laughter. Joss's hiccupped to a stop when she turned.

In the doorway, Eric Hendricks stood, mouth agape. *Now he thinks I'm plain silly.* Dark circles beneath his eyes spoke of his sleepless night.

"Hi. I didn't hear you come in." Joss smoothed her T-shirt, her palm settling on her fluttering stomach.

With a look of remorse, Annie lowered the radio volume.

"Hello. Sorry." Appearing baffled, he stared. "I didn't mean to interrupt."

The pulsing took up residence in her blood stream and turned electric. "You're not. We're getting ready for our open house."

"Right, the sign caught my eye. I came to check Maya's hoof and decided to stop in."

Making calls on a holiday? Joss kept the question to herself. Her tingling senses argued otherwise.

"Wonderful," Annie gushed. "Our first guest. Offer him some food." She nudged Joss forward.

"Please. Try something." With a nervous laugh, she lifted the nearest tray and held it out.

Hunger in his gaze, he stared at the plate. "I don't want to ruin your work."

"We cooked it for people to eat. Go ahead."

As he reached for a canapé, she noticed his long, thin fingers as they pinched the mushroom cap in a sensuous motion. Beautiful hands with a tantalizing touch. When he brought the button to his mouth, the lightning along her nerve endings zipped through her belly to her hardening nipples. Her own lips parted in anticipation, and she found herself shifting closer, drawn to his earthy smell, like a meadow after a thunderstorm. Exhilarating and calming.

"Excellent." His gaze met hers, fell to her mouth and he swallowed hard.

"You're boiling." A twinkle in her eye, Annie nudged Joss.

"What?" Realizing how close he stood, Joss stepped back and returned the tray to the counter top.

"Your water for the tea." Annie inclined her head to the steaming pot on the stove.

"Oh, right." Joss turned off the burner and dropped the tea ball into the churning water, which then took on a rosy hue.

Eleven chimes sounded, and Eric glanced at his wrist watch. "Eleven already."

"No, it's only...eleven," she said in wonder as she checked the time. The correct time. Again. Stunned, she snapped her mouth closed.

His brows twitched together in confusion. "Right, the clock just chimed."

"But it's never right." Or hadn't been for many years.

"It was the first time I heard it. The Halloween party," he reminded her.

"Oh. Yes." She'd forgotten. Or blocked it from her mind.

Kyle shuffled in, hair ruffled, drawstring pants and a rumpled T-shirt. "Any coffee?"

Thankful for the relief from the awkward moment, Joss bustled into action. "I'll make some. I was concentrating on making the tea and forgot."

Assessing Kyle, Eric's eyes lit with intensity.

On any other man, Joss would have labeled it jealousy. "Dr. Eric Hendricks, this is Kyle. My son."

Eric's head snapped back, as if surprised. "Nice to meet you. I wouldn't have guessed, you look too young to have a son...in college?"

Nodding his greeting, Kyle said, "Yeah. I have to head out soon."

Eric raised a hand in a wave. "I'll get out of your way too. You probably still have a lot to do."

Joss stepped closer. "You'll stay for the open house, won't you? Both of you."

"Course they will." Annie grasped Kyle's shoulder. "They wouldn't disappoint us when we're counting on them."

Kyle mumbled, "Sure."

"Wonderful. It starts at one." Smiling, she turned back to her work.

Of all the powerful forces in the universe, guilt ranked near the top. Not one Joss liked to use. In a pinch, it came through. She was careful not to employ it too often, though. Negative energy only returned the same, and drained her.

"See you at one then." Eric headed for the back entrance.

Annie tapped her chin. "Interesting."

"Who is he?" Kyle poured coffee.

"The local vet."

His expression turned sickly. "He comes to the house?"

To cover her confusion, Joss opened the frozen lemonades. "No. I mean, not for Taz. For the horses boarding here. Dr. Hendricks takes care of them."

Kyle leaned against the counter and watched the blue SUV retreat. "Huh."

The single word conjured John in all his skepticism. Joss wondered, not for the first time, whether Kyle inherited any of her perceptions. "I'll go dress and let the tea cool."

A wry smile tugged up his mouth. "You're making lavender lemonade?"

She forced a cheerful tone. "Yes, and I'm hoping Gram's recipe will become Lavender Hill's draw. Besides Annie's great cooking, of course."

If lavender brought luck, she hoped in her case, it would be true for matters of the heart as well as business.

Chapter 16

Eric downshifted and steered the SUV into the SureMart lot. Normally he shunned this store, believing its chain the downfall of mankind. The need for groceries and to avoid seeing anyone he knew brought him there. If a place existed where he could be anonymous in a crowd, it was this store. Like a microcosm of a big city, it drew all kinds. And was the only local store tactless enough to stay open on a holiday.

Wheeling a mini-cart inside, he aimed it for the food section. Shopping for one usually fooled him into believing he lived efficiently, and was self-sufficient. Today, the single-serving products seemed inadequate. He imagined Joss beside him, lifting a plump peach to her nose. No, she wouldn't shop here. She supported local growers at the farmers market. It had amused him, at first, but grew to appreciate the notion one person could make an impact. He now stopped there for fruit and vegetables, and often lingered in the off chance he'd see her. A few times, he'd run into Annie. If she mentioned it to Joss, at least she'd think about him.

Turning a corner, he should have been in the next aisle over, not the feminine hygiene products. He whirled the cart around and stopped dead, limbs stiff and cold. Sheree bore down on him with the focus of a huntress. When the front of her cart bumped his, she stopped.

"Where have you been hiding?" Her snide tone was irritating, but at least she spoke in only one voice.

"Not hiding. I've been busy." He stepped back.

Keeping pace, she advanced. "Where have you been? I've been waiting and waiting."

Glancing behind him, he despaired at shoppers crowded there. He couldn't make a break for it. "I told you I wouldn't be back."

"You were with someone else. Don't deny it."

"I don't need to deny it. We aren't dating." He said it loud enough for the women nearby, who shot disapproving glances their way.

Sheree hissed, "You were with her. The woman who owns the inn."

Why couldn't she say Joss's name? "I have to go." When he jerked the cart back to steer around her, the corner entangled with the edge of Sheree's cart.

Demolition derby-style, she smashed both carts into the side, and tampons tumbled into his basket. Her eyes gleamed mischievously. "I know what they gave you."

With a nervous chuckle, he asked, "What? I don't know what you mean."

"Oh yes you do. They brewed their special tea for you. Do you know what's in her tea?"

He shrugged. "Herbs. Chamomile or something."

Sheree giggled. Not a girlish titter. No, this was a spine-tingling, shiver-inducing, watch-out-behind-you kind of laugh. "Oh, that's rich. Chamomile. No, it's much trippier than Celestial Seasonings. Their ingredients are illegal."

She'd baited him, but it didn't stop him from asking, "What ingredients?"

Shifting her hips, she smiled, then bent over, her rear protruding. "Did you know, in the Middle Ages, people brewed tea with primrose? They believed it helped them to visit the other world where goblins and fairies lived."

He half-shrugged. "Primrose is a flower."

"A flowering herb," she corrected. "Used to induce symptoms of madness." She said it in a teasing way, as if it were something teenagers might try.

"I don't believe it."

"They took you dancing down the primrose path."

Her sing-song tone sent a chill through him. "No. They wouldn't." Would they? Or could that explain the awful nightmares? But then, whatever he'd ingested, it had helped him. Freed him of the strange urges—for Sheree. He never wanted to suffer those again.

At her breathy laugh, the scar deep in his chest itched to life. Then burned. He could almost smell the stink of flesh. His own.

She leaned closer. "I wouldn't go to the inn's open house. You never know what might upset your stomach."

Dread stilled him. "You're not going, are you?"

"I wouldn't be caught dead there."

He resisted the urge to say *pity*. With one desperate grab, he jerked the cart to dislodge it, causing them to entangle worse than before.

Demurely, Sheree stepped away, her amusement growing in tandem with his frustration and confusion. The racket of metal clashing against metal seemed to echo in the public address system.

Teeth clenched, Eric glared at the curious passersby. "When will they replace these awful carts?"

At his final attempt to free the cart, it tipped, spilling its contents.

The burn in his gut spread. *Get away from her.* He fled the aisle, her taunting call echoing after him, "Cleanup in aisle six."

The resonating hiss reverberated in the PA system and screeched with feedback. Covering his ears, Eric worried his heart might burst out of his chest until he escaped into the light of day. He ran for his truck, slammed the door, and drowned out the noise with the squeal of his tires.

* * * *

At quarter to one, Joss paced between the window and the table.

"Anyone?" Annie called from the kitchen.

"Not yet." What if no one came? Worse, what if something went horribly wrong when they did? "Our grand opening's not starting off so grand."

"They'll come." Her friend's casual tone gave away no anxiety, yet Joss knew by her constant primping and straightening of silver. Annie was trying to convince herself as much as Joss.

Kyle carried his bag in and set it beside the counter.

"Oh honey, not there." Joss didn't trust herself not to spill something on it. "Why not put it in your car?"

"You might want to move your car," Annie said, "so you don't get blocked in."

"By the crowd of vehicles?" he scoffed.

Realization struck Joss. Gram's car was missing. Without a word, she'd left?

Annie waved a spoon. "They'll be here in droves. Before you know it." At the crunch of gravel, she rushed to the door. "See? Here's one now."

Joss smoothed the fabric of her sundress. "I'll greet them."

Stopping in the foyer, she tucked a stray hair back. At footsteps on the stairs, she turned.

Aunt Lydia descended in lavender Capri's, a matching ruffled sleeveless top. Glistening peachy lips bloomed into a smile at seeing Joss, and she struck a pose. "Am I not dressed to kill?"

Don't remind me. "Definitely stunning."

Lydia twirled. "I'm wearing lavender in solidarity."

"It suits you." She had more urgent things to consider. "Did Gram go somewhere?"

"To pick up a few necessities. She'll be back tonight." Lydia rushed to Kyle as he walked in and pecked his cheek. "Such a handsome boy. You devastate the ladies, don't you?"

Kyle smirked. "I try."

"Let's hope the inn is charming too. How does it look?" A scan revealed everything seemed to be in its place.

Lydia squeezed her shoulder. "You've worked wonders in such a short time. Darling, you've always been such a force of nature."

"It runs in the family." Joss peered outside, where a man held open the car door for a woman.

Lydia set a hand on her hip. "Surely you're not worried? Today will be a smashing success."

Had her aunt seen it in the cards? She wouldn't ask. "Let's hope you're right."

"I always am."

Joss couldn't argue. All her life, everything her aunt foretold had come to pass. She sometimes withheld information from her customers, especially bad news. Later, she'd told Joss what she'd seen. The future always caught up with each of them.

When another pickup and a compact car wended down the drive, Joss sighed in relief. "Thank goodness. More people."

Lydia murmured, "Yes, it's others we need to worry about."

She'd deal with it later. Joss plastered on a huge smile and went out to greet them.

By two-thirty, people filled the tables on the patio. Blue morning glories climbed the iron trellis beside the summer kitchen, spilling over the roof. The scene would have been idyllic if Tom didn't scowl at everyone's approach. He stood alone beneath the wide branches of the oak that shaded the yard.

Making the rounds with the pitcher, Joss avoided him, then returned to the food table where Annie doled hot cobs of corn onto a platter.

A man walking across the grass caught her eye. Eric, carrying a red, white and blue bouquet. "He came back," she whispered.

Annie glanced over. "He said he would."

She hadn't meant to say it aloud. To cover, she added, "Yes, but he's so busy. He might have been called away."

"By who? The entire town's practically here."

As Joss took in the crowded patio spilling into the yard, satisfaction warmed her. "Pretty much."

Eric stepped toward her and held out the flowers. "Happy Independence Day."

Much happier now that he'd arrived. "Thank you. They're lovely."

But why so shy? If she read him right, he waited for her to say more, but about what?

He ducked his head. "I don't know what type of flowers they are."

"The beautiful kind." It didn't matter to her, only the fact he'd given them.

Turning pensive, he shifted his feet. "An article said some flowers can be used as medicine or garnish."

What was he getting at? "Of course. It's the premise of Lavender Hill Inn." She led him to the table and poured a glass of lemonade. "Lavender is used as both."

At his skeptical glance, she smiled. "Go on. It will soothe you."

After hesitating, he sipped. "This is very good. I've never tasted anything like your lemonade."

"I hope not. It's an old family recipe."

"Family secret?" He peered down at her, waiting.

One of many. No need for him to know any more than he did already. "Handed down through generations."

Tom stepped beside her. "What's your special ingredient?"

Momentarily startled, she joked, "If I told you, it wouldn't be a secret."

"Hemlock?" Tom asked loudly.

She bristled at the accusation. "Of course not." She didn't expect any battles before nightfall.

"Then what?" Eric asked. "Primrose?"

Stunned, she couldn't answer for a moment. Why was he siding with Tom? "No."

Tom slammed his glass onto the table and boomed, "It should be illegal to add untested herbs to drinks served to the public."

Everyone sitting on the patio or standing on the lawn turned to watch.

Tom turned toward her, his back to the crowd. His eyes glowed red. "You should know better than to dabble in things you don't know about."

So this wasn't about the refreshments. Meeting his gaze, she drew to her full height. "In that case, you needn't worry. I'm well versed in my field. I never dabble." A threat she might not be able to make good on, but she'd do her best.

Clenching his teeth, Tom gave a low hiss and stalked away.

Eric whispered, "Were his eyes glowing?"

She turned to him. "I don't know. Are mine?"

* * * *

What the hell did she mean? Then Eric caught the slant of her brow. She was angry. Probably the primrose comment.

A woman beside him said, "Jocelyn, your lemonade is the best I've ever tasted." He'd concentrated so fully on Joss, he hadn't heard the aunt's approach.

As if she'd waved a magic wand over the patio, everyone went back to their own conversations.

Pointedly, Joss said, "Thank you, Aunt Lydia."

Lydia closed her eyes and lifted her chin. Her eyes popped open. "Oh. Very interesting."

"What?" Suddenly violated, he shifted away.

Lydia's hazel eyes caught the blue of the morning glories, chameleon-like. "How are you?"

"Fine, thanks." Until a minute ago.

Easing away, Lydia peered at him with intensity. "Still, you must be careful. You might suffer a recurrence if you don't take care of yourself."

"I'll keep it in mind." Whatever had sickened him, he doubted it would return, but he couldn't deny the truth in her words.

Joss shushed her aunt. "Not now, please. Can we please try to act normal?" Lifting a tray of cookies, she carried it to the tables.

Joss's retreat left Eric unsettled, as if he were a sailboat caught in the wake of a passing ocean liner. It put him off kilter, and he braced against the tug of her undertow. Was she some sort of herbologist, or was there more to her brew, as Sheree said? He might have found out if Tom hadn't interrupted.

I have to find out. Excusing himself, he followed Joss. "So what is in the drink?"

"Nothing illegal." The hurt in her face took him aback.

"I didn't say there was." He hadn't argued with Tom either. Taking her hand, he led her into the house. "I still need to know."

Anger brightened Joss's lovely eyes and tinged her cheeks red. "How dare you?"

He couldn't let her beauty distract him from the truth. He eased closer and kept his voice low. "What did you give me the other night?"

She glanced down the hall. "Certainly not hemlock."

"Primrose?" he prompted.

"I'm not sure what Gram used. Whatever it was, it worked. Didn't it?" She met his gaze with a defiant glare.

"Maybe it did more than it should have." A love potion? His desire for Joss had only deepened. His fingers itched to touch her skin, to pull her against him, hip to hip.

The slam of the screen door startled them both to turn.

A wild look in her face, Sheree stood on the threshold in a wide-legged stance, as if bracing for a fight.

"What are you doing here?" Joss asked.

The waitress's sly smile widened. "I've come for Eric."

Shit. No way. "No, Sheree."

Sheree hugged the door jamb. "I want you, Eric. Come with me. Now." Joss focused on her. "Leave, Sheree."

Why couldn't she come inside? She writhed in a desperate struggle to enter, yet didn't step over the threshold.

She pointed at Eric. "Not unless you come with me. Now."

"Uh, no." It would take a lot more than primrose to go anywhere with her. She'd never get her claws in him again.

"Oh, yes. Willingly or not. I will have you." She licked her lips. Extending her arm, she pointed a long red nail at him. A spark shot out of its tip.

Heat lit beneath his skin, an ember reignited where The Mark had been. He clutched his chest.

"Stop it." Joss stepped closer to Sheree, then back to him.

Sheree's smile warped. "Stay out of this." She crooked her finger, beckoning him.

Breaking into a sweat, his feet slid toward the door. "No." He exerted force against the forward movement. Still, he shuffled ahead. The burn in his chest intensified. His tongue became a dead weight. He managed, "I don't want you. I want Joss."

Joss caught Eric as he crumpled. "Go away, Sheree."

"No." But the demon waitress moved further back.

Pressure eased on Eric's muscles, and he exhaled in relief.

Joss's grip on him tightened. "I'm warning you for the last time. Go now."

Eric's head swam as he registered the power in Joss's voice. It anchored him.

Sheree emitted a high-pitched noise and clenched her hands. "Eric."

A glow lit Joss as the floor vibrated. Pure white rays emanated from her. She pointed, and the rays shot from her finger. "Now, Sheree. Go."

Outside, a truck's engine revved. "Come on, Sheree," Tom called. "Jump in."

Glancing back as she lowered down the steps, Sheree spat, "You'll be sorry." At another rumble, she ran toward the open passenger door and scrambled inside the moving truck. Her face out the window bore an odd expression of triumph.

Breathless, Eric's vision cleared. No longer lightheaded, he asked, "What just happened?"

Had he imagined it? Joss appeared as surprised as him. The glow around her had faded. She had always appeared more luminous than others, but he knew better now than to attribute it to her skin care products. This was real magic.

* * * *

Damn. What *had* just happened? Joss's emotions carried her away. Or worse, she might have inadvertently summoned the power of the ley lines to do her bidding. Her toes began to tingle when the floor vibrated. Incredible energy had zapped along her legs to her head, borne along by fury and an urgent need to protect Eric.

What if she'd imagined some harm to Sheree? She might have caused real damage.

She couldn't explain to Eric, not without sounding like a lunatic. Energy still vibrated through her body, scattering her thoughts. Flustered, she headed back to the kitchen, calling over her shoulder, "I think I just saved your sorry ass from your girlfriend."

Who seemed strangely pleased Joss had sent her away. What did it mean?

Once through the door, she leaned against the counter to steady herself.

"Hey, what's wrong?" Annie touched her shoulder then jerked her hand away. "Ow. You shocked me hard."

"Did I? How weird." Joss forced a laugh and turned before her friend could figure out exactly how strange.

Narrowing her eyes, Annie assessed her. "Are you okay? You seem, I don't know. Weird is a good description, actually."

The truth might be best. "I had a rush of energy, now I'm kind of shaky."

"Maybe it's early menopause." Annie dragged a stool over. "Sit."

Doing as she was instructed, Joss fanned herself. "I hope not. I've had a few hot flashes recently though." She wouldn't reveal Eric had caused them.

Annie frowned. "I'll get you a drink."

"Jocelyn?" Aunt Lydia's voice echoed from the dining room and she rushed in. "Oh, there you are. What's wrong?"

"Nothing," Joss stressed, rolling her eyes in Annie's direction to quiet her aunt.

Thankfully, Lydia got it. With a discreet nod, she glided to Annie's side. "Would you mind checking the food table, dearest?"

Glancing between the two, Annie said, "Sure." In two seconds, she was gone.

Lydia rushed over. "Did you cause the tremor?"

Great. Her aunt had figured it out. "I think so."

Clasping her hands together, she held them to her lips. "I suspected as much. Do you know what this means?"

"That I'd better be careful what I wish for?" How many times had Gram teased her when she was younger? *Careful what you wish for, you might just get it.* Now she understood.

"Yes, and much more."

"How much more?" Maybe she didn't want to know.

"Your grandmother will return tomorrow. We'll discuss it then."

Quite a bit more, then. "I can't wait." Maybe Gram could tell her how to get rid of it.

Chapter 17

Tom's truck fish-tailed along the driveway and onto Yellow Breeches Road.

Sheree clutched the dash. "Slow down. Are you trying to get us killed?" Just when she was about to get what she'd been waiting for.

Tom laughed. "Do you think we have to fear death now? With them on our side?"

More like they used her and Tom to get what they wanted. Now, Sheree knew something to report. Finally. "Don't bet on it. But I want to see their faces when I tell them what she's done." Even more, she wanted to see Eric in her bed, in the flesh, as she'd seen in the vision they'd dangled before her like a seductive carrot.

A dark figure caught her eye. He stood among the trees to the side of the road. "Pull over! It's him."

When the truck came to a stop, she threw open the door. Did he already know? Ooh, if they tried to get out of giving her Eric, she'd give them what for. Her hands clenched in anticipation of the fight.

The dark man leaned against a tree. "What took you so long?"

Her blood boiled. "We got here as soon as we could. I needed to tell you right away."

He strode deeper into the thicket. "Yes, yes, come along."

Tom appeared as confused as her. She scurried after the man. He knew something. Wait, how could he when he hadn't been there? Only she could provide the details.

A shiver passed over her. Her mother used to say, *the devil's in the details*. If Mama could only see her now, she'd cut a switch for sure. Sheree pulled herself taller. No, the days of locking her in her room were far gone. Sheree had escaped the old nightmare. She could finagle her way out of this one, too.

Right now, she wasn't so sure about following this weirdo much farther. The trees crowded uncomfortably, blocking out the late afternoon sunlight. A strange hush settled over the place. She couldn't see one bird or squirrel. Thick shadows shifted behind the trees in a creepy mist.

She hugged her arms across her spangly red, white, and blue striped T-shirt, then stopped short.

Ahead, the dark man's boss sat by a fire. She could swear the flames danced in a circle, fiery legs kicking and bending gracefully.

The dark man halted and bowed. "Lord Plouton, I bring you Sheree and Tom."

Rising slowly, Lord Plouton snapped his fingers. The flames consolidated into one blaze, ordinary as any campfire. This man wasn't dressed for camping. Beneath his black suit jacket, unbuttoned to reveal washboard abs, his ebony skin had a dull sheen to match the fabric of his suit.

His white teeth flashed in a smile. "Ah, yes. We meet again."

She closed her eyes a moment. When he looked at her, she fell through a seemingly endless abyss. "Hello."

Tom blustered, "We have news, your lordship."

"Do you?" he asked, mockingly. "By all means, I'm waiting with bated breath."

She wasn't about to let Tom steal her thunder. He might've been there, but he didn't see what she saw. "You were right. Jocelyn Gibson used the ley line. Today. I was there."

Yep, caught his attention now.

Peering at her, he asked, "And?"

"She glowed. The ground shook. She forced me to leave."

Raising his hand, Lord Plouton opened his palm as if performing a magic trick. "How?"

Sheree twitched. "Pardon?"

Lord Plouton strolled near. "How, exactly, did she force you?"

Trying to recall, Sheree found the details lacking. "Lightning came out her fingers."

"So she hit you with a lightning bolt?"

"Not exactly." Or had she? It had gone fuzzy in Sheree's head. Mrs. Gibson had stood there and glared. Refused to let Eric leave. *The bitch!*

Plouton circled too close. Wherever he moved beside her, her skin grew so hot it could have blistered.

"Tell me what happened, Sheree."

"I stood on her porch. Something kept me from going inside." Fear. Mrs. Gibson looked like she might try to kick Sheree's ass.

"And?" he snapped.

Recounting the event, Sheree embellished somewhat. The vibration took on the magnitude of an earthquake. The light around Joss intensified to a spotlight. And when Joss pointed at her, definite zig-zagged bolts shot out. If she hadn't left when she did, Joss might have electrocuted her. Finishing the tale, Sheree almost danced, it sounded so juicy-good.

Strolling, Lord Plouton appeared to be in deep thought. He halted. "Are you sure?"

"What do you mean? I was there. Of course I'm sure." She stopped short of demanding Eric, now.

"Get out." Lord Plouton whirled away. Darkness covered him, and he was gone.

"What? No. I gave you what you asked. Now I want Eric."

"Tonight." The dark man's tone sounded too soothing and fake. She didn't like the way he said it. Not one bit.

* * * *

Downing lemonade, Eric wondered how he could remain relaxed even though the woman opposite him at the table droned on about marriage, the one subject he avoided with a passion. Especially when it regarded his own. Yet here he was, almost contributing to the conversation.

"You know how devastating it is to lose the one you love." Lydia glanced back as Joss came outside. "Poor Jocelyn spent twenty three years with John. To tell you the truth, I never believed he was her true soul mate."

The first interesting thing she'd said. "Why?"

"She's an Aquarian. He was a Gemini." Lydia tossed her head, flicking her brassy curls. They caught the dappled sunlight through the leafy canopy overhead.

He voiced what he guessed to be her point. "Ah. It wasn't written in the stars." Whatever the phrase meant.

"Exactly." The aunt tapped the table with her long red and white striped nails. She'd painted each thumbnail blue with a single white star. "When were you born?"

"August." Opening a greeting card sent by his sister, another from his mom, comprised his celebratory activities. Woo-freaking-hoo.

Arching a brow, Lydia said in a knowing tone, "A Leo. What day of the month?"

"The twenty fourth. Why?"

With a whoop, she clapped her hands.

"Is it a good sign?" Obviously, she thought so.

"Leos are notoriously compatible with Aquarians. And to people born on the twenty fourth day of the month, family means more to you than anything. You maintain the harmony and balance within your family."

He kept silent, hoping she'd stop this line of conversation.

She scrutinized him. "What about you? Did you lose your soul mate when Karen died?"

Normally, he'd have excused himself after such a question, and never spoken to the inquirer again. An atmosphere of calm quelled any reaction, so he found himself answering, "I don't know." How did she know Karen's name?

He'd never considered it at any length. He loved Karen with all his heart, and losing her left a gaping hole that had never healed. Joss had replaced Karen in his mind, soothing as the lavender scent wafting through the window.

His honesty provoked a thoughtful *hmm* from the woman.

Joss appeared, brandished the pitcher defensively. "More?"

"Please." Grateful for the interruption, he set down his glass.

She glanced at her aunt and back to him. "How is everything?"

Lydia tapped a nail on the table top. "We were just discussing, dear, how you both lost your spouses."

"I was referring to the food." Shifting her hip, Joss leveled a wary gaze at her aunt. "What, exactly, were you discussing?"

With a flourish of her hand, Lydia waved. "Nothing specific."

Words escaped Eric's mouth. "She said John wasn't your soul mate." Immediately mortified, he straightened, tense and wary of her reaction.

Joss's jaw dropped. "What? How could you say such a thing?"

People nearby turned toward them. The patio shook, and Joss blushed.

Lydia straightened. In a hushed tone, she said, "I merely said your astrological signs were incompatible."

Refilling her aunt's glass, Joss explained brusquely, "Aunt Lydia objected because we married young."

Lydia gave a conspiratorial nod. "She was only nineteen."

"Oh." He nodded discreetly.

"What do you mean, oh? I wasn't..." Joss whispered, "Pregnant."

"Of course, I didn't—"

"I wasn't." Her abruptness snapped his attention back to her. "We loved each other. We wanted to spend the rest of our lives together." She glanced at her aunt. "My family knew he didn't approve of them. And I didn't know…" She blinked back sudden tears. "We thought we'd have more time."

The last thing he'd wanted was to upset her. He understood too well.

"I suppose," she continued, "you were sensible and waited to marry."

"I was twenty six." If only he'd married at a younger age, he would have enjoyed more time with Karen. Maybe things might have turned out differently. Or maybe it would have ended sooner. Whatever powers controlled the universe had a hand in his life and were beyond his control.

"How long were you married?" Joss asked.

"Eleven years."

"No kids?"

Why did she seem disappointed? Did she think he didn't like children? Another confusing aspect about her to ponder.

"We were waiting until both our careers were on a steady track." A nerve pulsed in his jaw. "I thought I'd planned out our lives." A foolish notion.

"None of us can plan for tragedy," she said softly. "I wish I could be young and daring again."

"You've accomplished quite a bit in less than a year. You still have youthful tenacity."

"Jocelyn's talents and skills are extraordinary," Lydia cut in. "No small thanks to our family connections."

Joss glared. "Stop, Aunt Lydia."

A rumble sounded. He scanned the sky. It held only a few wispy clouds. Strange. "Connections?"

"Never mind. My aunt is apparently on a fishing expedition."

Confusion at her response caused him to frown. "I don't follow."

Abruptly, she turned. "I have to see to the other guests."

Mouth agape, whatever argument formed in his head against her leaving came out as a croak. Hadn't they been having a real conversation, finally? Somehow in the space between him and her, its meaning twisted into something different than he'd intended.

Her aunt *tsk'd*. "I don't know why she defends him. John never understood."

Neither did Eric, and something warned him against prying any further, though Lydia wouldn't need much encouragement. "Excuse me."

On the pretense of using the restroom, he wandered inside, hoping to run into Joss. No luck, so he went out again, keeping a wide berth between him and the aunt.

Being in a crowd didn't lessen Eric's loneliness. Surrounding himself with acquaintances didn't fill the void. He wished he could be with someone he loved.

Joss.

* * * *

Eric's groan caught Joss like an invisible tether, though her head still buzzed like angry bees. Why would her aunt discuss such personal matters, with Eric of all people? Lydia hid something more than tarot cards up her sleeve. Discussing her marriage to John had reopened old wounds, the raw pain creeping up on her again.

A dangerous way to be, apparently. It had opened up more than old wounds, judging by the ley lines' rumbling. She'd have to be careful, or she'd scare away her guests.

Her insides tightened as she walked away, as if the tether between them reeled her back. She shook it off. Now was not the time to think of Eric. She had responsibilities. After a glance, she reminded herself again. He watched with a different sort of intensity. It slowed time, stretched to its fullest, filling the moment. It took her breath away.

And her coordination. When she swung her head forward again, her shoulder slammed into a guest.

"I'm so sorry." Joss hurried across the patio. Someone called her name and asked for another drink. Bracing herself with a breath, she forced a smile. "Here you go. Did you have enough to eat? We'll have desserts out soon."

Annie appeared at her side. "How's it going?" Her gaze flicked to where Eric sat, and a knowing look settled on her face.

"Fine." She squared her shoulders.

"Do we need anything?"

"Let's go check." It would give her a chance to clear her head.

"Everyone looks full and happy. Something about your lemonade makes them act drunk, without the sloppy part."

"Good." Then it was doing its job.

Without moving her lips, Annie murmured, "So what's up with him?"

"Him?" She feigned ignorance.

Annie's attempt to say "the vet" came out garbled.

Joss huffed in embarrassment. "Oh I practically bit his head off."

"Why? What happened?"

"Lydia happened." And Joss had tapped into the underground energy without meaning to.

"What did she tell him?"

"She said John and I weren't soul mates." Her whine reminded her of Kyle's, when he was three.

"Oh." Annie busied herself lifting chafing dish lids.

"Don't tell me you think so, too." Joss once loved him with all her heart.

"Well..." Her friend winced, backed toward the door, and opened it.

Joss followed her inside. "Oh, Annie. Never mind, it doesn't matter."

"I know how much you loved him. And I'm sorry you're still hurting. You'll find someone wonderful, though. I know it." Turning playful, she giggled. "Maybe someone here today."

"I'm in no hurry to find anyone. And if you're referring to the man speaking to my aunt, he's too young."

"How young is too young?"

"He can't be much older than forty." Verbalizing it made it almost seem a punishable offense.

Annie laughed. "So?"

"So I'm forty-four." And getting older every day.

Her friend blew raspberries. "Less than five years difference."

"In another ten years, it will seem much worse." A few gray strands already mingled with her golden hair.

"You're a very young forty-four. You're vivacious and beautiful."

Joss waved away the compliment. "Stop."

Annie went on insistently. "Intelligent and energetic. You need a younger man to keep up with you." Annie shrugged. "I'm only pointing out the obvious."

"Please, stop."

Annie's lips twisted to one side, an indicator of her self-restraint. She wanted to argue. "I'm going to push more pie before the fireworks." She arranged slices on a tray and hummed on her way out.

Joss held her fingers to her eyes. She should serve more lemonade. People would want it to go with dessert. *He's out there.* Being near him rattled her to the core. Maybe expanded to shake the ground too. He might have forgotten what happened between them. Joss couldn't.

You're letting your imagination run away with you. Her mother used to repeat the saying nearly every day, probably to counter Gram's influence, who told her to trust the energy flowing through her, leading her in the right direction. Trust her heart.

How? She couldn't trust her heart when she had no idea how to control it.

* * * *

A few guests left. Taz's loneliness reached out to Joss from the veterinary practice down the road. Not wanting her dog to think she abandoned him, she went to Eric who sat on the stone wall at the back of the patio with a glum expression.

"I know your practice is closed today, but could I possibly see Taz? It's the first holiday without him, and I don't want him to think I've forgotten."

Eric rose. "I'll bring you over."

"No, I could let myself in. You should stay."

"I'll take you over, if you promise to excuse my messy truck."

"Why don't I drive? Let me tell Annie first." Joss found Annie refilling a coffee carafe in the kitchen. "Would you mind if I left for a bit? Things have slowed down, and everyone's finished their dessert. I can't let a day pass without seeing my baby."

"I'll handle it. Go on," Annie urged.

"Thanks. I won't stay long." Hurrying outside, she gestured to Eric, who followed.

His long legs jammed his knees against the dashboard. His presence overwhelmed the car, and her. *You're only visiting Taz. He'd have extended the same professional courtesy to anyone.*

Inside the practice, he switched the lights on dim.

She spoke softly to the dog, and his tail flopped.

"He's still sedated and groggy."

"He knows I'm here, and that's what matters."

"Yes. You're here." He stepped behind her. "Do you mind never having a holiday to yourself?"

"No, I love being surrounded by people."

He eased closer. "Sometimes it's nice to be alone."

"Sometimes."

Huskiness edged his soft tone. "Like now."

Her skin prickled at his nearness, so close his breath warmed her hair. His arm brushed hers as he reached to take hold of Taz's cage.

She turned to face him, and there was no mistaking the heat in his gaze.

He whispered her name, and it sounded like an eternal wind, seeping into her soul and creating a whirlwind there. It caught her up, lifted her heart to his. She leaned into him as he pressed his soft, warm lips to hers. She opened to him, wanting whatever he was willing to give, and equally returning what he offered. Hungrily, his tongue probed hers, and he pressed her against the kennel.

Taz lay quietly, but barking and hissing erupted on both sides of his cage.

Eric whirled her around in a dreamlike waltz to an exam room, and lifted her onto the table. His gritty voice rubbed her heart raw. "I want you so much. I can't think of anything else."

"What about..." Joss couldn't bring herself to say Sheree's name. "Your girlfriend."

"No, she's not." Inserting himself between her bare legs, he slid her toward him, pushing her sundress higher, running his hand up her thigh. "I want you, Joss. No one else."

When a small voice in her head warned it was madness, she hushed it. Sanity was overrated, she countered. A little craziness might be exactly what she needed. Laying her palms against his cheeks, she drew him to her in a rush of need. His hands explored her curves and contours, his lips along her skin like a symphony come to life. When he guided himself inside her, they moved with the rhythm of the wind and stars, a storm within a place of eternity.

Light seeped away outside, leaving only the fireflies, blinking like a firestorm in their own revelry. Holding him tight, she breathed in the moment, so beautiful she never wanted to let it go.

His whisper came softly, almost inaudible. "Stay with me tonight."

The words galvanized her back in reality. The event still went on at the inn, and she'd left Annie alone to deal with it. "I have to get back." Gram would be returning soon. Then all hell would break loose.

Resignation thinned his lips before he briefly touched them to hers. He helped her down, and she adjusted her sundress, grateful the travel-friendly fabric didn't easily wrinkle.

"Ready?"

"I think so." Her cognitive function became spotty. Probably because she'd lost several neural connections. Whoever coined the phrase "mind-blowing sex" knew what she and Eric experienced. Regaining her equilibrium would take a great effort. Now, she luxuriated in the lush moment, content to not to think, only feel.

One final check of Taz took her aback. She could swear he was smiling.

Chapter 18

Outside, Eric breathed in the lavender-scented air. Darkness gathered under trees, and the blue of the sky shifted from azure to indigo, the horizon rimmed with orange. Halting to stretch before getting in the car, he wished he could scoop her up in an embrace. She was always rushing off, hurrying here and there. Out of his reach. They'd finally reconnected, and he didn't want to lose the bond again.

The engine revved and the headlights outlined the building in stark relief. No sooner had he plopped into the seat beside her than she drove off, barely braking before turning toward the inn, her intent gaze focused ahead.

When she parked, he hated to let go. "Joss…"

"I have to hurry. It's almost time for the fireworks." She grabbed her purse and climbed out.

Heaving a breath, he followed more slowly. *We just made our own fireworks.*

Joss rushed toward the patio where Annie waited. "How's it going?"

She seemed surprised at Joss's breathy tone. He flashed a smile in greeting, not sure whether he should stay or leave. So it wouldn't appear suspicious, he sat at a nearby table.

A mischievous gleam twinkled in Annie's eyes. "Fine. How's it going with you?"

"Good. Taz is recovering well. Right?" She turned to Eric almost in desperation.

"Yes. He's coming along."

"Sure." Annie sounded anything but sure. "It's nearly dark. Everyone ready for fireworks?"

The two women spoke to one another, but he couldn't make out what they said. Annie cleared some dishes off the serving table and went inside. Joss came to where he stood looking out over the field of flowers, dazzling in the display of flickering lights gathered there. "The fireworks will start any minute."

Eric nodded toward the field. "It's amazing how they flock to the lavender."

"Gram used to say they're fairies. They bring good luck and protection."

He gave a short laugh. "I never used to believe in magic."

Kyle strode outside, then stopped short. "Mom."

At the young man's glare, Eric shifted uncomfortably. "I should get going." Much as he'd like to stay, he couldn't push things. Nor could he kiss her goodnight as he wished. Instead, he touched her arm and nodded goodnight to Kyle.

Heading home, he couldn't deny a certain magic in the atmosphere. Maybe even a bit of luck. A strange thrum filled the air. He cut across the yard, past the stable to the stone bridge. Like metal to a magnet, his steps brought him to the field. Darkness spread across the lavender but the lithe stalks beckoned him on, swaying in a slow waltz with the wind. At the far edge of the grounds, he halted and faced the house.

Solar lights lined the patio, and silhouettes of people moved there. Kids ran in the yard, laughing. Music played softly in the house and floated through the night. He longed to be part of the homey scene.

The place brimmed with life. A year ago, he wouldn't have believed it possible. He crouched and ran a palm across the tops of the blooms, then drew his hand to his nose. The aroma hit him with a rush. Powerful. So soothing, he stretched out among the flowers.

In one year, his personal life had changed drastically too. Finally able to relax completely, a wave of well-being washed over him. Breaths relaxed into a slow rhythm, his muscles unwound. Odd. A beer or two sometimes took the edge off like this, but he didn't like to drink much in case an emergency call came in.

Loud pops and hisses sounded, and kids squealed. Flashes lit the sky for seconds then dissolved. A jet stream of smoke streaked upward and exploded into a blossom of yellow light. People at the inn clapped and cheered, and the show grew in intensity.

After the fireworks display fizzled to a stop, he reluctantly stood and headed home. Several times, he turned back subconsciously to glance at the house, and the silhouettes of people moving under the party lights. He searched for Joss, but gave up after awhile.

Long after the laughter faded and headlights of departing visitors swept through his bedroom like search lights, the scent of lavender drifted through the window. With it, came sleep.

* * * *

The stars twinkled brighter tonight, like the fairy lights in the field. So bright, Joss could almost hear them hum. The sizzle and crackle below ground grew louder. The ley line seemed impatient. Maybe it knew what awaited them all.

"Mom," Kyle repeated, stepping closer.

"Sorry, sweetie. Did you need something?" Clearing the last of the dishes from the patio, Joss breathed in the evening air. Even its lavender scent didn't ease her mind.

"What were you doing with *him*?"

"Checking on Taz." She returned to clearing the tables, hoping to end her son's interrogation.

"It took two of you?"

Assuming a casual tone, she lifted the dishes. "He's the vet, Kyle. Because it's a holiday, I couldn't get in to see Taz without Dr. Hendricks." Eric's formal name came out awkwardly.

Heaving a breath, Kyle stared across the field toward the practice. "Right."

"Honey." She reached for him, but he evaded her touch.

"I'm going out with some friends."

She called as she went inside, "Have a good time." *He's too much like his father.* An exasperated sigh escaped when she set the dishes in the sink.

A pent-up smile widened Annie's eyes as she drifted close. "Soooo. What's new?" Shoulders hunched, she gripped the countertop.

Rinsing the plates and restacking them, Joss averted her gaze, and hopefully, the conversation. "Not much food left. I'm calling today a success."

Annie's teasing tone belied her feigned innocence. "Yes. Very surprising, toward the end, wasn't it?" She nodded slowly, probably to pump for more info.

Bracing for the onslaught of another interrogation, Joss turned. When she opened her mouth to explain, only a choked sound came out. Tonight had not gone as planned, most definitely. And she couldn't decide what to do about it.

Annie grasped Joss's shoulders. "Hey, I think it's wonderful. He looked happy when you guys came back."

"Oh, God." She rubbed her temples. "What gave us away?"

"Well…it's pretty easy to put together. Rumpled clothes. Mussed hair. Goofy grins." Her own grin dissolved. "His. You weren't grinning. Why not?"

"This is crazy. I never intended it to happen before, and certainly never intended it tonight."

"Before?" Annie blinked hard. "It happened before?"

"I didn't tell you because it should have been a one-time thing. The night Taz got hurt, I was so upset about losing him, and he held me, and things got out of hand."

"Right." Hurt evident in her downturned mouth, Annie backed away.

"Annie, please. I'm sorry. I didn't know how to explain it."

"Why do you need to explain it?"

She resisted the urge to melt into her friend's arms. "I don't know. It's…" Words like wonderful and dangerous came to mind, a bad mix.

"Exciting? Fun?" Annie prompted.

"Yes, but also crazy."

"He doesn't seem to think so."

Turning back to the sink, she loaded plates into the dishwasher. "I don't want to get caught up in something doomed to turn into a mess." Or doomed her lover to an early death.

"Because he lives nearby?" Confusion knit Annie's brow.

"And I'm not ready for such a relationship." Every time she was with him, the energy bristled like lightning. No wonder The Underworld had taken notice of him.

Annie handed her the last of the glasses. "Don't worry about it. There's no rush, right? Take your time, and it will come clear."

"You're right. Thanks, hon." After giving her friend a quick hug, she surveyed the kitchen. "You put in a long day. Why don't you sleep in tomorrow?"

Annie brightened. "Because! We already have five dinner reservations for next weekend, and I have so much to plan."

"Five? From customers who were here today?"

Annie's curls bobbed with her enthusiastic nod. "Isn't it great?"

"Yes, fantastic."

"I'll take these inside." Grabbing the dishes, Annie sauntered off humming.

Joss gave one last check of the patio. Beyond the field lit with fireflies, stood Eric's house, visible at the bend in the road. A light winked out in a room upstairs, and the house went dark. Something like gravity pulled at her, urged her to reclaim the bits of herself she'd left there earlier. To complete herself again.

But first, she still had a few things to take care of, like shutting whatever door to Hell had opened. She definitely didn't want any more demons crashing her parties.

* * * *

Aunt Lydia sat at a table in the dining room with Annie, tarot cards spread between them. Both women hunched forward intently.

Her aunt concentrated on the cards. "Mmm."

Annie spoke in a hush. "What is it? What do you see?"

"You have many intriguing aspects."

"Intriguing how?" Eagerness shone in Annie's eyes.

"You're talented, intelligent, an expert chef. Fun to be around." Lydia used her theatrical voice, brimming with drama and intrigue.

Sighing, Joss set the dishes in the sink. "I already told you about Annie's wonderful traits."

Straightening her spine, Lydia sniffed. "The cards reinforced it."

"Anything else?" Annie leaned forward.

Joss rinsed off the plates and stacked them in the dishwasher. Her aunt droned on, describing Annie's virtues, carefully sidestepping any direct predictions. Not because Lydia couldn't nail them. In general, people didn't want to hear what their futures really held. Somehow, it took away the verve of daily life.

After wiping the counters, Joss scanned the extra food stacked in plastic containers. "I hope those won't go to waste."

"I'll take some home," Annie offered. "I give our neighbor Mr. Adams something every week, to make sure he eats once in awhile. Since Edna died, he's skipped some meals."

"Oh, the poor thing. Take the lot of them. Some of this will freeze."

Standing, Annie stretched. "What a great day."

Lydia gathered the cards. "You certainly outdid yourself. The food tasted wonderful."

"Everyone said so," Joss added. "Why don't you go get some rest? I know I'm ready for bed." Though the day's excitement left her wired and eager for more.

It would be a long night.

Her aunt laid out cards and studied them. An eyebrow snaked up. "Well, you have the going to bed part right."

Joss winced. "Aunt Lydia…" She plopped onto a chair, unable to argue any further.

Quickly returning to her seat, Annie leaned her chin on her palm. "Ohhh, I knew it. Tell us more."

With an air of practiced mysticism, Lydia studied the cards laid out before her. "I see great change. And great love awaits. The love of a handsome man who adores you."

With a gasp, Annie smiled. "How exciting."

Joss lurched out of the chair. "It's hooey," she lied to Annie as her thoughts shifted to Eric.

"Accurate hooey," her aunt reminded her.

Joss forced a laugh. "You should be getting home. It's been a long day." But she and her family still had plenty of work to do. She gestured Annie away.

Grabbing her purse, Annie said, "Yes, I'm pooped. Good night." She lingered in the doorway long enough to tease, "The clock has been chiming the right hours."

Lydia's blue eyes focused on Joss. "Remember what your grandmother told you. One day you will fall under a man's spell, and the grandfather clock would tell you it's the right time."

Affecting a stern tone, Joss hoped to deflect her aunt's hopes as much as her own. "I'm going to my room. Alone." She rose.

Lydia's sing-song voice taunted. "Not for long."

"Right. Soon Taz will be home." The cards had only revealed her sleeping with someone she loved. How had Aunt Lydia known about her dream?

Chapter 19

Work held Eric hostage. He needed to see Joss again, but couldn't until he'd visited with every patient. Hours from now.

At the approach of footsteps, he looked up, and his heart flip-flopped in his chest. Walking toward him, the overhead light gave Joss's honey gold hair a glossy sheen. So beautiful, she might have been an angel.

It took him a moment to find his voice. "Good morning."

"Morning. How's Taz?" She smiled at Terry, who passed by.

The assistant walked backward to say, "Doc Hendricks, Mrs. Albright's in three."

Damn. If he kept the woman waiting, he'd never hear the end of it. "Be right there." To Joss, he responded, "Taz is better."

Stepping closer, she asked anxiously, "Can I bring him home then?"

The scent of lavender and vanilla piqued his consciousness. Clutching the file, he fought to maintain a professional façade. "I was about to call you to give you the good news. Taz is ready for release. We'll have to go over a few guidelines first."

Her eyes widened. "Today?"

"Yes." He touched the small of her back and guided her to the kennels.

Laughing, tears sprang to her eyes as the dog lifted his head to sit up. "Hello baby. He does look better."

"You'll need to restrict his movements for a week or two. No running, of course. Take him outside on a leash. He's been up a few times. He's pretty shaky. It will take him awhile to use only three legs. His balance will be off."

"Yes, I understand."

He instructed her on continued care of the amputated limb. "Do you have a blanket in your car?" Before she could answer, he blurted, "He's too heavy for you to lift. I'll drive him over."

"No, you have patients."

Unfortunately. "I'll bring him at lunchtime, then."

"Great."

"I better not keep you any longer from seeing Mrs. Albright. I'll go home and get everything ready. Thank you."

After flashing a nervous smile, she went outside. The hallway seemed to dim, her warmth gone. Out of his reach again.

"Doc? Anything wrong?" Terry asked.

"No." Not for much longer, he hoped.

He tried to rush through the visit with Mrs. Albright and her dog Mr. Tibbles. As usual, the woman's complaints went on and on, taking more than the allotted time for her visit. He'd never been so eager for a lunch break.

Only a few animals occupied the kennel. A tomcat with a ripped ear, a trophy of its last fight. Another cat whose lungs he'd drained of fluid to accommodate the weeping owner, though he'd warned the woman the cat would die of heart failure soon, and urged her to put it down. Against all odds, she'd held out, hoping for a miracle.

In his fifteen years of practice, he'd never experienced a true miracle. Not his decision, though. He did as the owner asked.

And Taz had been a trouper, enduring exams and probes with no whimper of complaint, no growl of warning. He rose and went to the back. Taz thumped his tail in greeting. He unlatched the door and bent to examine the dog's amputation site. Clean pink flesh. Taz had progressed wonderfully. His heart lightened, and he ran his fingers through Taz's fur. "Want to go home? I'll do my best to see you often."

The dog's tongue lapped at his hand, so Eric scratched behind his ear. "Yeah, I know." An irresistible force drew him to Joss, and he had to explore wherever it led.

* * * *

Tiny rumbles shook the floorboards. Joss tried to quell her nervousness, but with Taz coming home and Eric delivering the dog, the two simultaneous events were too much.

True to his word, Eric drove Taz home at quarter to one. Joss took deep breaths before opening the door as he carried the dog inside.

"Oh, wait." She retrieved the dog's bed from her room. He never used it there anyway, so she set it in the alcove next to the reception desk. "I can keep an eye on him out here."

Lowering to the floor, Eric gently set the dog down. When he stood, he eased closer to Joss. "I wanted to ask—"

A high-pitched squeal sounded inside the dining room. Annie rushed in and hugged Joss. "Finally." Bending to the dog, she gently hugged him too. "We missed you so much."

When Taz looked up at her with soulful gaze, Joss tried not to cry. "Isn't it wonderful?"

Annie turned to him. "It was so nice of you to take time away from your practice."

Joss couldn't express her gratitude enough. "Yes, thank you."

The grandfather clock sounded, and Eric frowned. "One already. I have to go. Patient waiting."

So soon? Joss sent a hard glance at the clock. "Oh."

"Call me," he said. "For anything."

"I will." She walked him to the door, wanting to say more, but Annie hovered near the dog. "Thanks again."

A nod, and he trudged to his truck and got in.

Gripping the door jamb, Joss willed herself to not call out.

From the doggie bed, Taz whimpered.

"Do you need to go out, baby?" *Stop focusing on yourself.* Taz needed her.

She slipped the harness under him and fastened it. "Let's see if you need a walk."

On his first attempt, his rear slumped down again.

Joss's heartstrings tugged. "Oh!"

Annie appeared at her side. "He'll be fine. Eventually he'll learn to do these things on his own."

Doubt coursed through her. "I did the right thing, didn't I?"

"Of course. You won't do him any favors by doing everything for him, hon."

"You're right." She lead him slowly out, grateful for Annie's loyal friendship and tough love. Hard to hear, but necessary. She'd stay strong for Taz and help him through.

After limping a few steps, the dog halted and looked up at her. He shivered despite the warm night air.

"Sweetie." Wracked with guilt, she bent, wishing she could help somehow. An image glimmered in her mind. She *could*, just this once.

She waited until the afternoon had passed and Annie had gone home for the evening, then returned to Taz, sleeping by the desk. Holding her hand just above him, she pictured his wound healed, his energy restored. In her head, the dog ran on three legs as fast as he used to on four.

From her palm, a glow steadily increased until light surrounded Taz. The vibrations passed through Joss, stronger and stronger. The dog closed his eyes and shuddered. After a few moments, Taz opened his eyes and stood taller.

Joss withdrew her hand. She wasn't supposed to call on the power, especially not for her personal use, but who could fault her for helping Taz?

Of course, those in The Underworld would. If what Gram said was true, they'd use any excuse to start trouble for Joss's family. "I won't do it anymore," she vowed. Taz licked her hand. "You're welcome, sweetie." She kissed his head and rose. Hugging herself, she headed to the kitchen to make tea.

A few minutes later, the back door opened, and Gram entered on silent footsteps despite her black boots. She wore black pantaloons fastened with a leather belt, and a midnight blue blouse that matched a short cape. On either side of the belt, silver hilts shone.

Swords? Joss's first reaction, besides being grateful Annie had gone home an hour earlier, was to ask whether Gram had auditioned for a local production of *Lord of The Rings*. The notion vanished when Gram faced her in grave seriousness.

"I sense terrible danger."

* * * *

Eric's muscles stressed after repeated push-ups, the veins of his arms bulging from the strain. He lowered to the floor and rolled onto his back to catch his breath. Lying back, he stared at the ceiling. He wanted to go to Joss.

Sleep would elude him tonight. He should have returned to the inn after work to check on Taz. Being near Joss always calmed him, buoyed his spirits. Already, it seemed longer than a day since he'd seen her at the Fourth of July picnic.

He inhaled deeply. The lavender eased his nerves too. Of course, lavender's medicinal properties were well documented. If one could believe herbs actually contained healing properties. He'd scoffed at the Google results: a balm for lovesick hearts, a mood booster, a sleep enhancer, an antiseptic and anti-inflammatory agent. It had intrigued him to learn hospitals used lavender during World War II to disinfect rooms.

But the faerie lore…he had to laugh. Lavender repelled other insects except the fireflies, always hovering near it. More than he'd ever seen in this area before Joss planted the field of lavender.

Tomorrow, he'd go check on Taz and see Joss. Right now, he needed a shower. Peeling away his sweaty T-shirt, he stepped inside the bathroom and twisted the faucet knob. Dropping his shorts, he stood under the shower and let the warmth ease his muscles. Lifting his face into the spray, he turned his head. Water ran in rivulets down the opaque glass shower door. He tensed at seeing the outline of a small hand, smaller than a child's. It faded slowly.

He released a sharp breath. "I'm imagining things."

Like images on photographic paper, small hands appeared randomly, one by one, disappearing as quickly as they came.

"Who's there?" His attempt to sound stern came out in a cracked voice.

A hollow whisper echoed. He couldn't make out the words.

"Get out. Or Jocelyn will make you leave." Why the hell had he said that?

The glass cleared, and a hiss sounded through the steam. Hastily he turned off the water, hesitating before pushing open the door to grab the towel. In the harsh glare of the overhead light, everything appeared to be in place.

He rubbed the steam off the mirror, relieved to see only himself reflected. It had worked. They were gone.

After toweling off, he stood in the doorway to his room and listened. All quiet.

Crossing the floor, he fell atop his bed. Resting his forearm over his eyes, he let his muscles go slack. With a sudden wind that rattled the window pane, an odd sensation prickled the hair on his neck. Another breeze wisped through the room, almost tangible in form. He stilled, listening to the increasing whine. He could barely make it out—*Eric.*

Alarmed, he peered over his arm. The whisper came again, more audible. "Eric."

"Who's there?" Scrambling to his feet, he scanned the room. No one. At least, no one he could see.

In the corner of the room, a shadow shifted. A hand, gray like mist, reached out. *"I miss you. I thought you loved me."* The faint outline of a familiar face emerged from the darkness. Below it, a body took shape, a body he knew every inch of after years of holding it close.

"Karen?" It couldn't be.

"Don't you love me?" Her features grew more distinct with sadness.

"You know I do." He'd always been faithful during their marriage.

"I need you." She extended her arms toward him, beckoning. Her left hand bore no ring.

Despite the strong tug to follow, he held back. "Karen, I need to know if it's the real you."

Softly whimpering, her arms withdrew into the shadows. *"I knew it. You don't love me anymore."*

"Of course I do." Then why was it so difficult to say it now? After all those nights he'd laid in bed, wishing for her to return? Wishing he could have such a moment as this? The years seemed an eternity.

"Then come to me." Her hushed voice echoed through his head.

When the hands reached out to him again, he went to her. Taking her cold hands in his, he stepped into the darkness and, like a revolving door closing around him, it enveloped him.

His whisper evaporated in the night. "I thought I'd never see you again." He touched a hand to her chin and tilted up her head. Horror gripped him.

A crooked smile tainted Sheree's lips. "I'll bet." Her cackling laugh thundered in his ears.

"No." Beneath his skin, his blood burned as if filled with acid, leaching from the spot within his chest. Jerking away, he turned to run back, but found only emptiness. And nothing beneath his feet. He tumbled through black space, his screams echoing.

* * * *

A knock at the front door unnerved Joss. "I'm not expecting any late guests." The clock had just chimed nine.

She grew more anxious at Gram's knowing look and hurried through the foyer.

Standing on the threshold stood her mother. But not the mom who used to putter around the kitchen or drive Joss to the library. An impossibly youthful version. Her blond hair hung in waves to her shoulders, her blue eyes sparkling and clear. The silver hooded cloak was of the thinnest fabric, shimmering as if woven of starlight. The matching gown clung to her thin frame, the picture of elegance. Or fae royalty. Like Gram, her mother wore swords in her belt, sheathed in leather like two smaller knives.

Outside, Lydia, also donned in some crazy medieval-looking garb, bent over the car trunk and drew out weapons. Hopefully, none of them would have to use any.

Speechless, Joss struggled with surprise, happiness, and anger. Why had Mom stayed away so long? Where was she when Joss had needed her most? The more upset she grew, the more the walls shook. Joss gripped the door tighter.

Her mother smiled. "Hello, sweetheart."

Immediately, the quaking settled. Joss was more centered, though no less surprised. "Mom. I can't believe you're here. Come in." Before a spy caught sight of her. Surely her visit heralded something important.

Gliding inside, her mother paused to briefly gather her in her arms, press her lips to Joss's cheek. "It's so good to see you, baby." The light scent of woodland flowers filled the room.

"You, too." It would have been better to have known where she'd hidden all those years. Joss held her tongue.

Overnight bag in hand, Lydia climbed the steps, robes flowing.

Joss waited until her aunt had entered. "Gram's in the kitchen." But they probably already knew she was here.

Lydia set the suitcase on the floor. "We brought you something suitable to wear tonight."

Something told Joss the outfit would be better for Halloween, but she kept the thought to herself.

With a regal nod, her mother took Joss's hand and led her through the dining room, robes flowing in a delicate, diaphanous wave. She released her and pushed open the kitchen door.

Rushing to her, Gram enveloped her in a hug. Lydia stood close, waiting.

The door swung closed, and Joss held back. She couldn't pretend to be entirely happy. She still harbored too many unanswered questions.

When Lydia opened the door again, she waved Joss on. "Get in here. We have a lot to discuss."

"Yes, we do." Tonight, no question would go unanswered.

Returning to Joss's side, her mother linked arms and tugged her inside. "It's been difficult to stay away."

"Then why did you?" Joss couldn't keep the hurt from her voice.

Her mother laid a palm against her cheek. "To keep your true identity secure. It was the only way to keep you safe."

"Because we're related to a goddess?" Why would Joss need protection? Gram went to the blender. "We need margaritas."

Joss sat on a bar stool and propped her head in her hands. "I don't understand any of this."

Sitting beside Joss, her mother took her hand. "We're not a typical family."

"Right. We put the *fun* in dysfunctional." She sighed. "Or we're more seriously disturbed than most others."

Her mom smiled. "If having powers makes us dysfunctional, yes." Turning serious, she added, "You, Jocelyn, are the most important."

"So not true." Compared to her relatives, Joss ranked least important.

"Yes," her mother insisted. "You have proven yourself to be the one who holds the greatest power. The one foretold for centuries. You control the power below."

"No, I don't." The reverse was true. The ley line used Joss as a release. No sooner did its energy come to mind, than it zapped wherever it wanted.

"You haven't yet mastered your skill," her mother said. "The reason I'm here."

"You can teach me? What if something goes wrong?" Then she'd anger those in The Underworld again, and put Eric in danger.

Her mother nodded. "A wise answer. I was sent to warn you against using the power."

"I haven't meant to." Joss wouldn't mention the one instance with Taz. "It just happens." If only she could stop it.

Smoothing back Joss's hair, her mother smiled. "It responds to your will. Your mind and emotions."

Joss huffed. "Great. So I only have to stop thinking and feeling."

Pouring the margaritas from the blender into the salt-rimmed glasses, Gram said, "Not stop, dear. Learn to direct them to the proper place."

"Easier said than done." Joss sighed.

"Try now." Mom crossed her arms and waited.

"How?"

"The ley line reacts to you. If you're upset, energies surge forth. Focus on containing them below."

She blew out a breath. "Okay. I'll think of something that causes a strong reaction in me." *Eric.*

Energies rumbled the floor, shook the appliances. *Oops, shouldn't have thought of him.* An image popped into her head, nuzzling into him in her bed, the bliss of sleeping in his arms. Electricity shot to her core. *Oh no.*

The vibrations rattled the cabinets.

Joss gripped the counter. "Stop."

Slowly, the ley line quieted.

She winced. "Sorry."

"You'll master it soon. You must," her mother said. "Lord Plouton will claim abuse of the treaty otherwise."

"Even if it's a lie?"

Lydia shrugged. "It's his way. He's always twisted the truth to his advantage."

Joss would have to learn, and quick. "I still can't believe we're related to a goddess."

Gram raised her glass. "Here's to Iris, the messenger goddess, connecting humans to the gods."

"Earth to sky," Lydia added. "One reason she's called the Goddess of the Rainbow."

"Or Daughter of Thaumas," her mother said. "The Wondrous One."

"And the West Wind is her boyfriend." To Joss, it still seemed an unlikely fairy tale. "It makes no sense I'm related to someone like her."

Her mother straightened. "It makes perfect sense. Iris also represents new endeavors, and you've proven great skill in that area."

"More likely I share her skill of putting men to sleep." Joss gave a wry laugh.

Lydia swirled her fingernail around the edge of her cup. "Hardly, darling. Especially not Eric Hendricks."

After a sip, Gram set down her glass. "He's always worshipped you."

"No, he was lonely. And so was I. Nothing more to it." Besides his incredible lovemaking skills, but she wasn't about to share that with them.

"You're sure he won't remember anything?" Joss stressed the last word to ensure Gram would get her meaning.

"Only his suffering during the time of The Mark. The rest will seem like terrible dreams."

On a sigh, she said, "Good."

"Tonight," Gram said, "we complete our family reunion."

Joss's mother nodded gravely.

"You don't mean…" A glance at her mother, grandmother, and aunt confirmed her suspicion. "Oh, boy."

Mom reached across the island to take her hand. "I'm afraid I have terrible news. About your Eric Hendricks."

Joss held more tightly. "What?"

"He's trapped," her mother said, "in The Underworld."

Gram laid a hand on her shoulder. "In Tartarus, dear."

"Hell." Lydia stroked her arm.

"No. We saved him from The Mark. How could this happen?"

Her mother shook her head. "All I know is, he's there."

"Is there anything we can do to help him?"

Gram sighed. "We will find out later."

Joss fought to steady herself, and nodded. Later couldn't come soon enough.

Lydia extended her hand. "Come. Let's try on your outfit." When Joss hesitated, her aunt linked arms and led her to the foyer. She released her, lifted the bag, and handed it to her. "I can't wait to see you in this."

The suitcase was surprisingly light in Joss's hold. "You really shouldn't have."

"Nonsense. You're a goddess. You should look like one."

That didn't sound promising, but she flashed a wan smile. "Be right back." Heading to the bedroom, she glanced over her shoulder at her family. Still watching her, smiling.

Did she really want to join the ranks of the Goddess Brigade? She set the bag on the bed and blew out a breath before releasing the two silver latches and lifting the lid.

The clothing within shimmered. Not quite like the fabric of her mother's outfit, but light as gossamer, the color of sea foam. When she lifted the gown and turned it, the blue shifted to green with a soft glimmer reminiscent of moonlight on the sea. Joss suddenly couldn't wait to try it on, and shed her jeans and T-shirt in a hurry, and then stepped into the gown. It fit as if sewn for her. She turned in front of the mirror over her bureau, at a loss for words. It was nothing short of gorgeous.

Next she fastened the wide leather belt around her. It, too, had a sheath, but no sword. *Guess I don't rank as high as I thought.* She didn't blame them for not trusting her with a weapon.

Lastly, she drew out the midnight-blue robe. As lightweight as the gown, and its color likewise shifted with her movements.

Nothing ridiculous about this outfit. With pride in her steps, she approached the front room where her family waited. They turned toward her and their eyes widened.

Oh crap. They're too quiet. "Well?"

Her mother rose and strode to her. "I could not be more proud, Joss. You're amazing."

A hitch in Joss's breath surprised her. She covered the unexpected emotion with a grin. "Not exactly goddess material yet."

Mom nodded with certainty. "Yes, you are. More than I could have hoped."

"Truly, Jocelyn," Gram said.

Lydia affirmed it with a gracious nod.

Before this moment, Joss didn't think she'd be able to say, "I'm ready whenever you are." Now, she meant every word.

Chapter 20

Gram took hold of Joss's hand, her mother grasped the other, and Lydia held on to Gram. The grandfather clock struck twelve.

If ever there was a right time, this better be it. Joss closed her eyes and imagined a place of wondrous beauty and peace. A swirl of colors formed in her mind and expanded to surround them with hues of sky blue, tulip red, sunny gold, and spring green. Lifted by the soft chants of Gram, Mom and Lydia, Joss floated up, weightless. The colors coalesced into a sparkling arch that drew them higher into a mist.

The path to all that was, is, or ever will be, Gram had described it earlier. The only path leading them where they needed to go.

Joy buoyed Joss ever higher, up to the apex of the bridge. From there, she looked down at the landscape below, fields stretching into forests and glens of green. They descended lightly into a circle of grass surrounded by lush gardens.

Music such as Joss had never heard enticed her to find it. "Who's playing such wonderful tunes?"

Gram held her wrist. "The Dryads, in the trees. We have no business with them."

"Can't we go listen for a few minutes?" The music beckoned her almost irresistibly.

"A few minutes here may translate into years at home. We must go now." Gram led the way. "Stay close, and take care. We must show utmost respect. No matter what, don't drink or eat anything."

Joss couldn't remember seeing her grandmother so serious. As she walked beside Mom and Lydia, Joss found it difficult not to stray off the path to investigate. Flowering vines trailed from branches, and behind the veil of petals flitted winged beings, shimmering with the glow of pure energy. They tended the flowers, some with blooms nearly as large as themselves. The gardens ended where the forest began, and Gram reminded them to be careful. "Stay away from the scaled ones."

The air grew murky, and they soon passed a swamp with a thick skin of slimy green. A head with bulging eyes surfaced to peer at them. Joss hurried to keep pace with her grandmother, who moved with purposeful steps toward a lusher portion of the woods. Trees gave way to a large clearing, alive with dancing creatures. Their laughter and conversation stilled at their entrance.

The beauty of the faces surrounding them, staring at them, awed Joss. Every one with flawless creamy skin, glowing with a pure light. Their eyes appeared glistening jewels of crystalline blue, smoky quartz, or pale emerald. Each bowed as the crowd parted. At its center sat a young woman dressed in robes of bright colors, her golden wings in repose. Above her head hovered a ring of shimmering light.

Gram curtsied and gestured behind her back for Joss, Mom, and Lydia to do the same. "Hail, Goddess Iris," she said.

Iris? Her ancestor? Lowering her head, Joss snuck a peek. The goddess's long hair shone like silken onyx, her smile demure as she nodded.

A male flitted in front of them. "Only the purest of heart may continue."

Iris intervened by holding up a hand. "Jocelyn is pure of heart. She's continuing the long tradition of providing a safe haven for our kind in the mortal world by growing the revered triad of oak, ash and thorn. More importantly, lavender, which we have long honored to be the sign of a strong woman. A goddess." Iris nodded in acknowledgement.

Nervous that she'd appear to misrepresent herself, Joss deepened her curtsy. "Please, I'm no goddess."

Iris tempered her correction with a smile. "Every woman is a goddess in her own right, and deserves to be treated as sacred."

Joss couldn't argue with the idea.

Gram straightened. "If you please, Great One…we are in dire need of your assistance. Our town is under attack by agents of The Underworld."

The goddess's smile faded. She went rigid except for her wings expanding with a flash of gold. "Are you certain of this? Take care before you answer." She indicated an ornate jug beside the silver throne. "The penalty is steep."

"Penalty?" Joss couldn't let Gram risk injury.

Iris lifted the jug. "This ewer contains the waters of the River Styx. Are you familiar with the River Styx?"

If Joss remembered her mythology correctly, she was. "The river's a boundary between earth and this realm. It circles The Underworld nine times."

"Though this is no court, I demand the truth from those who visit. Those who do not abide my rules suffer eternal sleep. So I ask again, are you certain?"

Gram bowed. "The fair ones tending my granddaughter's lavender field confirmed it."

Iris set down the jug and floated along, the ribbons on her staff fluttering. "This is indeed distressing news. How many?"

"The fae know of two," Gram said. "More are said to be on the way."

Joss stepped forward. "There's another problem."

The hush falling over the clearing set her on edge. Apparently, she shouldn't have spoken directly to the goddess, relative or not.

"What problem?" Iris's diction was crisp.

She steadied her voice. "They've taken a man prisoner."

"What man? Someone important to you?"

"Yes, goddess." Joss had to save Eric's life. She couldn't bear the thought of him in pain or of losing him.

Iris narrowed her eyes. "If they use a pawn to lure us out, we must ready ourselves for battle. A terrible battle." Iris's colorful robes swirled as she strode, deep in thought.

Halting abruptly, the goddess returned to her throne and coolly appraised Joss. "Why should we lend our assistance? You've denied our very existence most of your life, despite having enjoyed our favor in your youth."

Bowing, Joss mustered courage. "For which I am most grateful. It's true I turned my back on my heritage, and I beg your forgiveness."

"I seek not to pardon you, only to know you will truly honor your heritage. Celebrate it, rather than shamed by it."

Mom's smile lent her courage, and Joss straightened. "For many years, I repressed the gifts bestowed upon me. I have begun to reacquaint myself with them. I cannot promise to use them every day."

"Most do not, yet their respect doesn't falter." Iris leaned closer. "Until you fully embrace and accept your true self, you will find no peace."

For decades, Joss had tried to quell the aching loss of her former self and yearned to revive the girl she used to be, who loved her life, who believed in possibility, and yes, in magic. Iris had slammed the idea home. "I understand. Thank you."

"Don't thank me yet. We have much work to do." Silence increased the tension during their wait. The goddess touched her feet to the ground. "If we are to succeed, we must gather other forces to our aid. But first, you will accompany me," she said to the three.

Gram, Mom and Lydia bowed. Joss blurted, "Where?"

Staff in hand, Iris strode off. "The Underworld, of course."

* * * *

The four women followed the goddess along a rough path ending at the bank of a river. A hooded figure in a filthy cloak waited beside a long boat with a tall, curved bow, holding a lamp in its curl. Upon their approach, he turned. A scraggly beard contrasted with his eyes that appeared to spout fire.

If Iris noticed the stench emanating from the man, she gave no indication, merely bowing. "Charon, we seek an audience with Lord Plouton."

Arching a brow, Charon's eyes blazed brighter. "And my payment?"

From her waist, Iris drew a Golden Bough. "I need no obols as fare. My guests are not dead, and you know I am immortal. Take me to Plouton."

With a low growl, Charon moved aside. Iris stepped inside the boat and sat on an ornately carved wooden chair. Gram gestured for them to follow and took a place on the bench behind. Lydia's seriousness set Joss on edge. She'd never known her aunt not to make light of a situation, except during readings. Here, there seemed little to make light of. Joss settled on a seat behind Gram.

The boatman stood at the helm and pointed forward. Invisible hands moved oars lining the boat's sides.

The world's vivid colors faded to shades of gray and black. From within the darkening curtain surrounding them, yellow eyes stared out hungrily. Joss peered over the vessel's edge. Below the surface slithered indistinguishable forms. The shape of a face materialized, its blank stare haunting. The features solidified, melding into someone familiar. Eric. He opened his mouth, bubbles rising to the surface. "Joss. Help me."

Fear strangled Joss's throat. "Eric." She reached toward him.

Mom grasped her arm before it touched the water. "Never touch the River Styx. Your soul might be cursed to ride this journey forever."

"But Eric—"

Sternly, Gram said, "It's not Eric."

Shuddering, Joss pressed closer between Mom and Gram. Maybe not, but the specter of him probably meant something terrible.

The goddess stared ahead as the boat sped forward into the depths of darkness. The air grew murky, heat laden with unfamiliar scents, not altogether unpleasant. Joss guessed it was part of the initial allure, and wouldn't be so enticing once the gates closed behind in finality.

The boat glided to a stop at a dock. Iris thanked the boatman and climbed ashore. Joss scrambled behind Gram, Mom, and Lydia to keep up with the goddess flying ahead, her golden wings glinting in the lantern she held.

"Say nothing unless spoken to," Iris cautioned.

No need to remind Joss twice. She wanted only to leave.

Outside a heavy iron gate, a three-headed dog growled at their approach.

Iris bowed. "Step aside, Cerberus. We come to speak to Lord Plouton. I'm sure he's expecting us."

With a growl, the dog shuffled aside as the gates creaked open. The goddess glided ahead with surety. Joss's confidence disappeared when the gates clanged shut behind them.

The narrow path led to a tall door gleaming red in the surrounding blackness, magnificent in its intricacy. In it appeared millions of scenes, each one a story in itself. Millions of stories, each ending in disaster. Joss pitied the souls damned for eternity.

At Iris's knock, the door slid open. She strode inside.

Exchanging wary glances, the four followed. Crystal chandeliers lit the ceiling of the long hallway. Nothing like Joss expected. Artwork filled the walls, classic paintings beside contemporary. Sculptures stood sentinel along the gilded walls, exquisite works of alabaster and metal. Was Hell something like rehab? Could its prisoners still use their time creatively?

Iris flew before them, her feet not touching the sleek marble floor.

Ahead, piano keys tinkled, building to a crescendo.

The hallway emptied into a spacious room whose golden walls were lined with books, TV, DVD player. Magazines and newspapers littered a bronze table in front of a sleek black leather sofa.

At a baby grand piano sat a tall, thin man, eerie in his handsomeness. His skin, the color of charred bronze, gleamed in the soft light of the wall sconces as his hands moved across the keys with deft precision. His long black hair shifted across his face as he played.

"Don't listen," Iris murmured. "He plays to weaken you."

Joss tried to block the melody. The notes seeped into her mind, cradling her. Calling her. Her body edged forward unconsciously. It took every part of her being to will it to stop. They waited as he finished playing with flair, fingers arched above the keys until the sound died away.

When he looked up, Joss's blood chilled. His eyes held the fire of millenniums, entrancing and deadly. She forced her gaze away.

Chuckling, he approached. "Iris. It's been too long. Forgive me for being so engrossed in playing. You know how I love music."

Daring a glance, Joss stiffened as Iris tilted her cheek to receive his kiss.

"Yes, I remember," the goddess said. "Your one weakness."

The tale of Orpheus came to mind. Because of his exceptional musical talent, Orpheus was the only person upon whom Plouton, or Hades, bestowed mercy, allowing Orpheus to remove his beloved wife from The Underworld. On one condition. Plouton must have known Orpheus's weakness, knew he wouldn't be able to resist turning around to be sure Hades hadn't deceived him into leaving with anyone but his wife. The deal breaker. The devil always based the last conditions on the other's weaknesses, thereby causing a person's downfall. Joss would keep it in mind, but he must already know Joss's weakness—Eric. The bargaining chip in this crazy game.

"Music and beautiful women have always been my weaknesses, and you grace me with the presence of so many." He smiled at each in turn. "May I offer you some refreshments?"

"We appreciate your generosity," Iris said, "but this isn't a social visit."

All innocence, his face blanked. "It's not?" His gaze traveled to Gram, Mom, and Lydia. When it met Joss's, he smiled. "I don't believe I've had the pleasure."

And you never will. Joss shivered.

He threw his head back and laughed. Wagging his finger, he smiled. "I love feisty women. Of any age." His mischievous gaze scanned across each again. "Please, have a seat."

"We cannot stay long," Iris said. "We came only to ask for your aid."

Holding a hand to his chest, he asked, "My aid? I'm flattered. I don't see how I could possibly assist such forceful women."

Iris widened her stance. "You could call off your peons."

"They act of their own free will, as does everyone. I love the beauty of it all." He tapped a finger to his cheek. "With the exception, apparently, of you, my dear. When will you tire of being handmaiden to Hera? Personal messenger girl to another goddess, when you are a goddess in your own right?" He tilted his head teasingly.

Except for the smallest twitch of an eye, Iris stilled as if turned to stone. He'd obviously hit a nerve, possibly as old as time itself. "I am here on behalf of no one except myself. And my family."

His eyes flashed bright, gaze scorching into Joss's. "All the more interesting, then, isn't it? Of course, your last venture on behalf of family had little impact, sorry to say." He clucked his tongue slowly. Pointedly.

Iris gave a barely perceptible flinch. "This has nothing to do with Demeter, and you know it."

"Thank you for reminding me. I must prepare the palace for my wife's return. Persephone always expects a warm welcome."

Joss wished she could remember whether Persephone returned to Hades willingly or not. Could they enlist her as an ally? Probably not if Persephone cursed her rivals for his affection, first turning Minthe into a mint plant, and transforming the nymph Leuce into a white poplar tree. Joss knew too well the dangers of jealous rages. No, Persephone wouldn't be a reliable accomplice.

"I'm sure your welcomes are exceedingly warm." Iris's voice sounded like silken ice. "Why pursue such a fruitless venture? You know it leads to disaster."

"Ah, but whose?" He steepled his long, bony fingers.

When the goddess straightened to her full height, he held up a hand. "If I called my minions home," he said, "what would I receive in return?"

"Your honor intact."

"Honor," he chuffed, whirling to sit on an immense ebony throne. "I wouldn't know how to behave. Such a grace has no bearing in my dominion." His gaze crawled over Joss. "Suppose I sweetened the pot?" He snapped his fingers, and a servant appeared holding a tray. Taking a canapé off the platter, he said, "Serve our guests, John."

Joss froze as she met the gaunt face of her dead husband, John. A strangled cry arose in her throat.

Iris thrust her staff to block Joss from lunging toward him. "Enough games. If you will not grant our request—"

Examining a morsel, he snapped, "Why should I? You know perfectly well the territory was off limits since the Great War." He waved away John, who pixilated into nothingness.

Despair welled in Joss. Iris glanced back, and something in her face assured her the servant wasn't her husband, only an illusion.

Shifting uncomfortably, he looked pointedly at Joss. "She invaded neutral ground."

Invaded? Joss opened her mouth. Gram's sharp glance silenced her. To speak would be to open up to punishment. Arguing was useless. He appeared pleased the confrontation had begun, and he could pass blame to someone else.

Her tone pleasant, Iris said, "Jocelyn's only intent is to run her business. Not use the ley lines for her own gain."

"Oh really? And the lavender is a coincidence, I suppose? Give me a bit more credit, Iris. I have an eyewitness who swears Jocelyn's used the ley lines for her own benefit. Right, Sheree?"

The waitress shuffled forward as if restrained by chains, though none were visible. Her wide-eyed stare held fear, and her lip trembled. "Yes."

Plouton waved her away. Shadows engulfed her.

"It's obvious you've been amassing your minions to lure me into battle. Why shouldn't I oblige you?" He leaned back, tension blazing in his hard gaze, even when his lean muscles displayed only ease.

"We wish no battle. Please reconsider."

"I am not the one who initiated it. Perhaps you might change your mind if I reminded you what's at stake. Or should I say, who?" Another snap of his fingers brought a vision of Eric bound in chains, his face a mask of pain.

Joss couldn't restrain a gasp. Mom, Lydia, and Gram clutched her arms to steady her, but she jerked free. "Let him go."

"In exchange for what?" He arched a brow. "Yourself, perhaps?"

Gram clamped a hand over Joss's mouth as Iris stepped in front of her. Joss mumbled against her grandmother's fingers.

"Silence." Gram removed her hand, but held up a finger. "Say no more."

Anger coursed through Joss. Who the hell did this guy think he was, playing with others' lives?

"Of course not." Leaning on her staff, Iris laughed. "If you are so weak as to use a pawn, I can only assume your position is worse than I first believed."

His eyes became gleaming crescents. "We shall see who is weak."

Iris set her staff at arm's length. "As you wish." With a bow, she flew back toward the door. Gram and Lydia tugged Joss along.

"Give my best to the family," he called, "especially my mother-in-law, Demeter. Tell her we'd love to have her over." His laughter echoed off the marble floor, mixing with Eric's moans.

"We have to stop them from torturing Eric," Joss whispered through clenched teeth.

Two walls of fire whooshed to life on either side, tongues of flame licking at their heels. The marble cracked, and the floor beneath their feet crumbled away as they hurried on.

"Keep moving no matter what," Iris said.

Sure, easy for her to say. She had wings. Joss grasped hands with Gram and Mom, who held Lydia's. Ahead, the door shut with a resounding clang. Terror seized Joss.

Iris held out her staff, and a hole in the door dissolved long enough for them to pass through. The three-headed dog snarled, lunging toward them. Iris coolly tossed something at the beast. The center head caught it mid-air and gulped it down. The two jaws on either side snapped for the treat. Within moments, Cerberus slumped to a heap.

"What did you give them?" Joss asked.

"I prepared biscuits in advance. A few teaspoons of honey, a sprinkle of wheat, some strong sedatives…works every time."

So homemade remedies were another gift from Iris.

The goddess's golden wings flashed, brightening her colorful robes. "We must act quickly to divert them. Come."

As if Joss had any thought of staying.

Chapter 21

Sharp screams cut the darkness. Eric wanted to ask who was there. Then again, he didn't want to find out. The occasional hiss of fire mingled with cries. The scraping of metal against stone accompanied pleadings for mercy, and built to a prolonged crescendo in which he could only imagine the blade finding its mark. Shadowy shapes moved around him, unrecognizable except for their pain. Their tortured moans bespoke punishment for sins of their own doing.

Whatever sin he'd committed, it must have something to do with Joss. Or maybe Sheree? Were those nightmares a premonition?

He'd never complain of his boring life again if he escaped. And he'd do his best to stay the hell out of here.

Through the gray wasteland, a man with a haunted look shuffled past.

"Hey," Eric called. "Where are we?"

A shriek of laughter came in answer. "If you have to ask, you're in worse trouble than you thought."

Obviously. He wouldn't argue the point. "Tell me the name of this place." Maybe he could get his bearings then.

"In Tartarus, you fool."

"Tartarus?" He'd never heard of it. At least the guy didn't say he was in Hell.

"Aye. The deepest pit in the universe, an abyss as far from the earth as the earth is from Heaven."

Not what he'd hoped to hear. Still, if he'd found his way inside, there must be a way out. Theoretically. "Where's the exit?"

Another cackling laugh. "You're in the realm of Erebus—Total Darkness. There's no escape. Even if you could escape over the bronze fence, you'd become lost in the triple circle of night that surrounds it."

There must be some flaw, somewhere. "For the sake of argument, if I happened to get beyond the triple circle, then what?"

"Then you'd drown in Pyriphlegethon," the man stated matter of factly. "The river of fire and clashing rocks."

Again, didn't sound promising. "Isn't there a way to follow the river out?"

The man's brow furrowed, and he spoke as if to himself. "All rivers flow into Tartarus and out again."

"So theoretically, if I followed a river, it would eventually lead home? To earth?"

The man spat a laugh. "Tisiphone might object."

"Tisiphone?" Eric prompted. Didn't the guy get it? Eric knew none of these people.

"The Erinye who sits in the iron tower guarding the entrance. The entrance," he added, "so strong even the gods couldn't break it."

"Maybe someone could slip past while Tisiphone is sleeping?"

The man leaned close, his harsh whisper hot in Eric's face. "She doesn't sleep." Withdrawing, he stumbled away. "None of us sleep."

"Great." Add sleep deprivation to the list of tortures.

All of this was beyond his comprehension. Too bad, he might not have the chance to learn the truth.

* * * *

The return journey took an eternity. Joss knew the night ahead held incredible peril, but the only way to meet a challenge was to face it head on and push through.

Returning to her golden chair, Iris issued a sharp command. "It is decided. We go tonight."

Creatures of every shape and size surged away on foot or wing, scattering in every direction.

Staff in hand, Iris joined her minions, and more creatures flocked toward them through the skies. "Lead on."

Joss glanced nervously at her mother and then Gram.

Her grandmother's outfit now fit perfectly. Cape fluttering as she turned, Gram's silver hair caught the light. "This way."

Pixies, crones, gnomes, and brownies mingled with Bean-Tighe, Korreds and Twlwwyth Tegs in a massive army led by Gram and Iris. Winds swirled around them, and above them a heavy gust carried a gorgeous man with the face of an angel and a body rivaled only by Michelangelo's sculptures. He swooped down, enveloped Iris in a cloud, and then titters echoed from inside it.

"Not now," Iris said, and the cloud dissipated.

"Zephyrus," Lydia murmured in Joss's ear. "God of the West Wind. Her mate."

"Thanks for the heads up," Joss whispered. "I still have so much to learn."

"Later, dear," Gram said. "After the war."

Her mother nodded.

Strong gusts converged overhead, and three more gorgeous winged men hovered above.

Gram brightened. "Oh good. His brothers are here too."

"His brothers?" Of course. The four winds.

"The North Wind, Boreas, is the most fierce," Mom added. "Quite chilling."

"And quite the temper to match," Gram said. "Notos, the South Wind, can stir up terrible summer storms. Zephyrus and Favonius are known for gentler winds, still useful in battle."

Flying close, Iris looked amazing, her multicolored robes hugging her classic curves, gold wings flashing in the sky. "My father, the Titan Thaumas, will petition his mother, Gaia."

"Mother Earth?" Joss wondered what possible connection Gaia had to the ley line, and what control. "What for?"

"To join in our fight," Iris said.

"Oh. Any other family expected?" Joss meant it as a joke.

"My sisters, The Harpies, owe me their lives. My mother Electra will do what she can, but..." Iris shrugged. "Cloud nymphs can only do so much."

"Of course." More than Joss would be able to do, she feared. And this was her fault.

Summoning the force of her will, she vowed to defend the innocents upon whose heads she brought this mess.

* * * *

Boiling Springs sat in darkness, sporadically lit by the occasional street light, a porch lamp left on here and there, a few electric candles in windows. Its townspeople slept in blissful ignorance of the armies converging upon it. Forces of darkness and light, either vowed to save them from a horrible fate, or to wreak it upon them.

If Joss didn't know better, the opposing faction mixed up their dates. The empty streets echoed with tranquil silence. "Everything's quiet. Maybe they changed their minds."

"Unlikely." Pensive, her mother scanned the shadows. "Better to face them now. We're ready."

Iris's watchful gaze narrowed. "Oh, they are here. Make no mistake." Glancing to either side, she motioned for the troops to fan out.

Dark figures, ranging from tiny to immense, surged right and left. The night teemed with creatures. If the goddess proved right, they'd soon meet with the enemy.

"How do we keep people safe indoors?" Joss couldn't bear to think of anyone stumbling outside into the middle of such a war.

"The blameless won't hear a thing," Mom said. "They'll sleep through it."

"Or think it a bad dream," Iris added.

Joss could relate. Definitely a nightmare to her. "Wait, what do you mean the blameless?" Aside from Sheree and Tom, could others turn against them?

Iris set her amber gaze on Joss. "Those from The Underworld penetrated long ago, and may have touched more lives than we know. Be watchful. Beyond our circle, no one is familiar tonight."

People had been acting strange lately. "And what about the not so innocent?"

Gram's face filled with sadness. "Any person who appears on the street was called to fight against us."

Gram squeezed Joss's wrist and drew out a sword.

Her family never ceased to amaze her. No way would she stand idly by and watch them fight. "Where's mine?"

"Right here." From the folds of her skirt, Mom drew a long blade. Its edge gleamed with a spark of light.

Joss examined its intricate design. "It's magnificent."

"The elven-crafted swords always are." Mom handed it to her.

Joss gripped the handle to acquaint herself with the heft of the weapon. Lightweight, but its razor-like sharpness would ensure quick death. Despite wanting to protect those she loved, Joss hoped she wouldn't have to find out. She inserted it into the sheath hanging from her belt.

Clanging of metal echoed in the night. Iris cried, "It's begun!" Joss's stomach lurched. Though Joss gripped her sword tighter, she wasn't sure she could raise a weapon against one of the townspeople, no matter what. Once they won—if they won—surely those people could revert to their old selves? Reclaim their old lives?

Explosions of light through the streets and in the air revealed the clash of their warriors against The Underworld intruders.

"Claim victory, ladies." Blade extended, Iris slipped from their midst.

Mom touched Joss's shoulder. "Stay close." On silent footsteps, she followed the goddess.

"Yes," Gram said. "Our power's greater together."

Lydia's squared shoulders gave her a no-nonsense appearance. "We're with you, kid." She drew a dagger from a leg strap, and pressed several sharp, cold metal objects into Joss's palm. "These might come in handy."

"Ninja stars?" When did her fortune-telling aunt become a fierce warrior? Joss stowed them in her back pocket. She feared her nerves would loosen her grasp on the sword's hilt, so kept both hands on it and crept behind her relatives. Never again would she criticize them. Family get-togethers would take on a whole new dimension too.

Joss stayed near Lydia and Gram, each clutching lavender, lips moving in a silent prayer or chant. Joss couldn't tell. She'd never learned the old ways. Now, she regretted it.

Scuffles and a deep growl from a dark alley put her on edge. A brilliant glow briefly illuminated a fae fighting a wolf-like animal on its hind legs, its razorlike claws clashing against the fae's sword. Another burst of light revealed a group of pixies flitting around a monstrous creature. No sooner had it gone dark when another soundless explosion emanated from a pixie writhing on the ground.

Joss gasped. Not explosions at all. The bursts of light meant one of their army had been injured.

Desperate to do something besides watch, Joss asked, "How can we help?"

Iris's wings unfurled, the glint of their golden feathers cutting through the black midnight. As she glided upward, the power of their movement blew back Joss's hair. Glancing down, Iris said, "Fill whatever void you can." She hovered a moment, then flew away.

Hopefully, the goddess didn't include graves in the "void" category. A band of creatures drew closer, their grisly features twisted into masks of rage and depravation, claws and blades slashing. Swamp Thing with an attitude.

"What if they attack us?" she asked in a whisper.

"They won't hurt you," Mom murmured.

"Why not me?"

"They'll want you to barter with," Gram said, "if things don't go well."

"What about you?" No way could she let her family sacrifice themselves.

Gram shot a grim glance at Mom and Lydia. "We'll fight, if we must."

This was madness. She had to stop it. "I should surrender." At Gram's glare, she added, "I'll move away from Boiling Springs, if they'll agree to leave us alone."

Mom stepped between them. "You must never surrender."

"It's too late now. Look." Gram pointed.

A crack of lightning revealed a new swarm of minions approaching. Scaled and winged, slithering and flying, hissing and croaking.

A shadow separated from a nearby wall and rushed toward them.

"Gram!" Joss yanked her grandmother behind her and plunged the sword ahead.

* * * *

Erebus. The realm of total darkness. The description couldn't have fit better. Eric couldn't see much of anything in the inky night. The metal shackles weighed heavily on his ankles and wrists, and any movement caused them to dig into his skin. Something cold and slimy slithered across his foot. He jerked back. Sharp pain sliced through him and he cried out, his groans mixing with the unending background noise.

Tartarus? Must be another word for Hell.

If his gut hadn't told him Joss was in danger, worsening every second, he might have been able to stand it.

Escape was his only choice. Maybe he could find a chink in the metal, a lock to pick. Anything to give him leverage. He'd once read of a man breaking his thumbs to free himself from handcuffs. These shackles would call for a bigger sacrifice than thumbs. His fingers worked along the metal edges. No break, no weak point. He pulled against the connecting chain. It jerked to a stop and seemed to pull back.

Hmm, not quite as solid. He traced the chain away from him to its anchor. Odd. Smooth and leathery to the touch. Not warm, yet not cold either. His fingers found a rounded edge where the surface narrowed, like the hind quarters of an animal.

Rumbling echoed, so low at first Eric couldn't identify it. So deep, it sounded more the beginnings of an earthquake than a growl. No mistaking the noise. It was a growl. Of an immense creature. Attached to him.

Every pore of Eric's skin tingled with dread. No! Animals smell fear. Feed off it to their advantage.

Forcing a breath, he tilted his neck side to side. *Relax.* Yeah, sure. No problem. Especially when the growl increased in intensity.

Turn the tables. His mind raced. Some animals backed off if the prey played dead. Others if the prey displayed aggression. How might this thing react?

Something huge slid along the ground, and the creature turned to face him. Eric was almost sure of it. Had it felt the tug of the chain? Had it been sleeping, and had he awakened it? *Shit. Stay calm.*

"Easy. Take it easy." His voice rang clear through the dark.

The resounding silence buoyed his hopes. *It backed down! Already!* He released a sharp breath, half relief, half laugh. He stopped breathing when the creature rose in front of him. Tall as a three-story building, if he judged the angle of its stinky breaths correctly.

He gulped. "Good. We'll take it slow and easy. Okay?"

It released an ear-splitting, screeching roar. Heat and spittle hit Eric's face and chest.

Oh shit. Maybe the situation called for a softer touch. Aggression was overrated. He'd remember the point, if he ever returned home.

"Good, boy," he murmured. "Nice…monster."

Something whooshed toward him. Its speed overhead ruffled his hair. A limb. Probably clawed.

He hurled himself onto the ground. The swipe grazed his back. The massive creature gave another screech, one of surprise. Probably because it missed. It shifted, most likely readying to strike again, with greater ferocity. He had no doubt he'd pissed it off.

The ground shook, and he knew it stepped nearer. Talking to it didn't calm it. Since they'd been chained together, running wouldn't help. Maybe playing dead would work. Stilling himself, he cringed as a giant foot came down beside his leg. The muffled crunch of metal vaguely registered. The chain loosened.

Eric tugged hopefully. When his tug met no resistance, he gave a laugh, but his joy disappeared as quickly. It wouldn't matter if the thing had accidentally freed him. He wouldn't be playing dead for long. He'd *be* dead if it caught him.

The hulking creature swiveled, and its weight slammed his chest, sending Eric across the hard ground. As he slid, rocks slammed into his side and legs. He couldn't stifle the yowls of pain. The animal waited as if listening, its hissing breaths indicating delight. It fed off his pain. *Stay silent.*

A large, clawed hand grabbed his ankle. It tugged him upward and swung him in a circle. Hurtling through the darkness, Eric clamped his jaw shut. And his eyes, expecting he'd soon become a splat mark on some unseen wall or the stony ground. The air rushed around him sickeningly. Sticky webs matted his face and hair. Something screeched as points of a wing impaled his legs, some flying creature felled by the impact. Still, he stifled his cry of anguish.

A deep voice clipped the night. Commanding. The creature went still, swinging Eric suspended from the chain in mid-air. In the thick tones of an unknown language, the voice sounded urgent.

Eric's playmate released him. With an *oomph,* he hit the rocky ground. He braced for the impact of an immense foot, crushing him into eternal silence. Instead, the thing shuffled off in the direction of the voice. Eric steeled himself again, waiting for some final blow. The swish of its tail receded.

Pushing up to a stand, he took a step. Then another. He raised his arms, and the chain slapped against his arm.

He was free! Metal bracelets notwithstanding. "What the hell happened?"

In the darkness, a man said, "Its master called it for other work."

Another assignment? "I guess I'm lucky it found a new job."

"Others are not so lucky. Our numbers may soon increase." The man's tone sounded ominous.

Dread iced his veins. "What do you mean?" Had it left to kill more people?

"The tormentors do their work above ground tonight. In my time here, it's never been so. It does not bode well for any."

His muscles tensed, ready to spring into action. "Above ground? On earth? Where?"

"A village called Boiling Springs, the master said, on the command of Lord Plouton, ruler of The Underworld kingdoms."

"Oh, no." He'd known Joss was in terrible danger. He never would have guessed the extreme extent. "Why Boiling Springs?"

"Why not?" came the weary reply.

Glancing wildly around, Eric strained to see any break in the darkness. Freaking Erebus. "I need to get out of here, go help them."

Cackling laughter filled the air. "So would we wish to be released. Even into Death's final peace."

There must be a way. Instinct told him to follow the creature, and he stumbled in the same direction. He hoped.

Like a blind man, he held his arms out to feel his way through the blackness. He stumbled across the uneven landscape, and his feet often slipped into crevices and met painfully with large rocks. It was impossible to hear the creature's breathing with moans and shrieks from every direction. He forged ahead, hoping he wouldn't accidentally step on its tail and piss it off again.

A flurry of wings whooshed over his head, and he ignored the occasional hiss in his ear. His determination waned only when the noises died away, and he guessed himself alone. Had he entered some untraveled corridor? How long had he been walking? Time in Tartarus was meaningless with every second magnified by awareness. The torture of not wanting to be there, of escape calling and no way to answer.

In despair, he slowed his pace. He could walk forever and not get anywhere because he couldn't see a damn thing. "I don't care if it takes forever. I'm getting the hell out of here." No, the opposite. He was getting out of Hell.

A cold surface smacked up against his chest, abruptly halting him. "What the..." He ran his hands along it—cold as metal. Flat like a wall.

No, a fence. A *bronze* fence. He'd come to the end of Tartarus. His fingers searched for its top but it exceeded his reach. No way to tell by how much. Maybe some chink existed in it, a crack he might slip through. He edged his way along, its smoothness unchanging for miles. The farther he traveled, the more hope waned.

Freedom from the creature came too late and held no value. He was still trapped.

* * * *

Swinging the sword, Joss stepped between Gram and the shadowy attacker. The steely tip sliced into the creature. It bellowed. She swung again, harder, unable to tell where the shadow-being stood in the darkness. A wail, and the dark wraith melted to a puddle.

Gram laid a hand on her arm. "Thank you, Jocelyn."

"Is it gone?" Joss panted.

"That one, yes." Mom raised her weapon over her head.

Joss gaped when it whooshed down beside her. Another dark puddle formed nearby. "How did you..." Never mind. She had to get used to the enemy's tricks.

Mom jerked her head. "And there are plenty more."

Creatures of every kind swarmed through the hamlet of Boiling Springs, ranging in size from hummingbirds to dragons, stretching the length of a town block. Its roads became a carpet of slithering mass. Winged beings perched in tree branches before flying off to clash in mid-air with the enemy.

Iris flew above them. "Retreat to the ley line."

Joss fell back with Mom, Gram, and Lydia closer to Yellow Breeches Road. Tonight, energy emanated with an audible buzz. The ley line's normally tame hum had grown in intensity to a loud background noise. The forces of light and dark battled for its control. It must have been agitated by the tug of war. Joss wasn't sure she wanted to be near the ley line. If it should fall to the wrong side, they would be in greater danger. Then again, if Iris and her army lost, it wouldn't matter where they hid. Disaster would find them.

Right now, things weren't looking so great. Wave after wave of nasty creatures came, their sheer numbers pushing them back.

Iris gestured to an orb. "We need reinforcements. Get word to Zephyrus. To my father. My sisters. Hurry!"

The glowing globe sped toward the stars.

Joss turned to Gram. "Will our allies get here in time?"

"We can only hope."

"What about Eric? Will we be able to rescue him?" She couldn't bear to think of what tortures he might endure in The Underworld.

Her mother said, "They'll try, Jocelyn."

"Not good enough. They have to bring him home."

A rush of charging creatures met a surge of Iris's troops. Atop a black steed came Tom, swinging a sword. A swarm of arrows zinged past. Wide-eyed, Tom halted, then steered the snorting horse down a side street. He lurched forward with a cry, grasping at his back, where a silver ninja star protruded.

Gaping, Joss turned to Lydia.

Her aunt smirked. "I never miss."

"Quickly," Iris said, suddenly hovering above them. "They will soon surround us." She pointed to a trail of illuminated spots on the ground. "Our brethren suffer injuries. Help them if you can." With a whoosh of wings, she shot upward, wielding her staff to knock what looked like the Wizard of Oz flying monkeys out of the sky.

A terrible unease crept over Joss. The glowing spots had to be trails of blood. Fae blood. Still, she allowed herself to be swept along in Gram, Mom, and Lydia's rush. She bumped up against them when they halted.

"What's wrong?" Joss asked.

"I don't know," her mother said. "The trail's gone."

Glancing around, Joss guessed why. "It's a trap."

From the darkness emerged hulking figures, encircling them. Joss grasped Gram and Lydia's hands. "It's him," she whispered.

At the forefront came Lord Plouton, the ruler of The Underworld. Beside him walked a beautiful woman. Apparently someone wanted them to meet head on.

Joss gasped. "Iris." How could she betray them?

"Not Iris," Mom corrected. "Her twin, Arkhe. See, she has no wings."

The demon winked at Arkhe, then turned his attention to Joss. "Well, well, well. I hoped to see you again. Sorry about the circumstances."

"What do you want?" Gram visibly braced.

The fact Plouton had put in a personal appearance spoke volumes. The Lord of The Underworld wouldn't bother himself with trifles. This must be a major deal.

He strolled forward, his voice silken. "Both sides want the same thing, don't we?"

A laugh escaped Mom. "No. We seek peace. And justice."

"Justice. Exactly. Peace—meh. It's overrated."

Words bubbled out without Joss's control. "Look, I knew nothing about the ley line when I bought the inn. Stop this madness. I promise I'll move away. The world will go back to the way it was."

"Will it? Doubtful, sweetheart. Your very presence ensured everything would change."

"I don't understand."

"For millennium, the energies sat dormant. No one disturbed the line. Thus, no one disturbed the treaty with the opposition. Unfortunately, you violated the terms." He sounded delighted at her faux pas.

"I told you, I had no idea about any of this until too late. If I'd known there was a treaty, I would never have come." Or believed it. It was simply too fantastic.

He waved her off. "Hindsight," he said on a sigh.

"So there's nothing I can do?" It couldn't be too late. She wouldn't accept defeat.

He arched a brow. "Do you propose surrendering?"

Straightening, she said without hesitation, "No." Never.

"Then you must accept the consequences." Fire flashed in his eyes and he whirled away.

"Wait." Hope arose when he slowly turned toward her. She spoke swiftly. "This was a terrible misunderstanding. You must stop it before it destroys the town."

A sly smile eased across his lips. "Boiling Springs could use a makeover anyway. Though I admit, I rather like its name."

Joss's lip trembled with anger. "Let my family go. Let Eric go."

His brows twitched in feigned confusion. "Who?"

"Eric. The man you kidnapped."

Plouton shot a questioning glance to a centurion, who murmured something inaudible. "Ah. Him." His smile turned into a scowl. "No."

"Please. I'll do anything."

Mom, Gram, and Lydia clutched at her from either side, each echoing with a hushed "No."

At his arched brow, she shrugged them off and stepped forward. "Tell me what you want me to do."

"Now, that's more like it."

"I wasn't finished. You tell me, and we'll negotiate."

"Jocelyn," Gram said. "Don't be foolish. He'll steal your soul."

She knew. If her soul would buy their safety, and Eric's, she'd consider the deal.

Chapter 22

The bronze wall might be endless for all Eric knew. It sure seemed to be. He walked for what might have been days, driven only by desperation. When even that began to fail him, he slowed, then slumped to his knees. "There's no use."

Somewhere ahead was a dim glow. A mirage? Like a thirsty man in the desert, he probably had imagined the beacon because he so badly wanted something, anything, to lead him out of here.

Nothing to lose by heading for it. Not like he'd planned to do anything else. Struggling to a stand, he shuffled on. The glow brightened and stretched long rays around him. Enveloped in it, he followed along the wall's perimeter. The light reflected off the wall's bronzed surface. It emanated from a tower high atop the wall, large as a castle, its turrets more elaborate than any Disney structure.

His breath hitched when a shadow moved in front of the light. What had the man said earlier? Someone horrible guarded the exit. Eric must be getting near. Frantically, he searched the wall. So strong the gods couldn't penetrate, the man had warned.

Maybe the gods didn't have enough at stake. Eric did. He had to get back to save Joss from whatever maelstrom befell the town.

High above, a voice screeched, "What fool approacheth?"

Shit. No time to make a plan. "Eric Hendricks." Why his name sounded silly and inadequate in answer to the question, he didn't know.

"Go back, or suffer the consequences."

What, eternal damnation? Too late. "Please, I must leave here."

A cackling laugh echoed around him. Obviously the beast didn't understand.

"There's been a mistake. I'm not supposed to be here."

The laughter faded. "All who approach these gates say the same. Go back."

From some well of strength he didn't know he had, Eric said, "No."

Wings unfurled in a great flap, and the guard—what did the man call her? Tisiphone. The Erinye disappeared in a swarm of insects. The buzzing whirlwind swooped down to the ground, and the insects disappeared. Tisiphone stood in front of him.

The worst fear of Eric's life caused his knees to wobble. He gulped hard and steadied himself. No wonder no one tried to escape Tartarus. The thing was indescribably horrible, with immense bat-like wings stretched high. An ancient hag with a dog's face, serpentine hair writhing atop its head. Medusa's sister? Skin blackened, not of pigmentation, but age and charring. Dried blood stained her ragged robes.

The putrid stench turned his stomach. *Talk about foul.* Despite his experience working on animals with infections, he could hardly stand to look at her face. Fluids oozed out of her eyes, nose and mouth. Antiseptic would do her no good.

Her wings folded behind her as she stepped closer. "What did you say, fool?" she commanded.

Gagging, he said, "With all due respect, I said no."

Narrowing her eyes, yellowish fluid dripped out. "Do you know who I am?"

He bowed slightly. "I'm honored to be in the presence of the goddess Tisiphone." Not exactly how he pictured a goddess to look. More like Joss—beautiful, with an innate glow about her. When he returned, he'd tell her. Treat her like one.

His description seemed to appease her. "Yet you persist in your foolishness."

He mustered his courage. "I don't belong here."

Her laughter reminded him of dogs yipping. "Can you come up with nothing more original?"

Desperation and anger surged forth. "It's true."

She sidled closer, inspecting him. "Why should I release you?"

"I was kidnapped. Held hostage."

Leaning close, she crooked her head. "By whom?"

Swallowing to still his nausea, he tried not to breathe. As terrible as she appeared, she smelled worse. "The Lord of The Underworld."

The sound erupting from her resembled a canine's growl. "What would he possibly want from you?"

"From me, nothing. He's starting a war in my hometown. Against the woman I…" The word he almost uttered astonished him.

"Love?" she finished for him, a challenge in her tone.

He brightened. "You know what it's like to be in love?"

She narrowed her eyes, forcing out grayish-green liquid. "Do not trifle with me. You try my patience with your nonsense. Now return from whence you came." Her robes swirled as she turned.

He stood his ground. "I have to get out so I can fight in the war."

She waved away his argument with a clawed limb. "There has been no war for eons."

"There's one now." Obviously no one alerted the Erinye.

Halting, her nostrils twitched. "Where?"

"In Boiling Springs, Pennsylvania. The place they took the creature I was shackled to. He's going to fight. I have to stop them."

Her assessing gaze went to his wrists and ankles, then let out a hiss. "They never tell me anything."

"Please let me go. I have to make sure they don't hurt Joss and her family."

Slime dripped out of her orifices as she stood pondering.

"I'm begging you. Look, I'm a veterinarian. I have ointments to clear up your..." He had to be extremely careful, treading this uncharted territory. "Your wounds."

"I have no injuries. What are you saying? That I'm hideous? Unbearable?"

He gulped. "Of course not. But wouldn't you enjoy using a nice moisturizer or cleansing cream? You'll love what it does for your skin. My patients always do."

She dragged a paw across her putrid cheek. "Do you think me a fool?"

"Never. I merely suggest you treat yourself like the goddess you are." Every female deserved to do the same.

"How would you deliver these wondrous creams and ointments?"

Oh. Good question. "There must be some messenger between worlds. Isn't there? I'll fill a package and leave it on my back doorstep. Yellow Breeches Road in Boiling Springs, Pennsylvania. Mine is the only veterinary practice on the road, so—"

"Silence!" In a blink, a swarm enveloped her and drifted up to the tower. When the cloud of insects alighted on top of the wall, Tisiphone appeared for a moment, then swirled away.

His hopes dashed, Eric debated whether to argue. He could offer nothing to the Erinye. Begging was useless. Glancing back, he knew returning to the inner realm of Tartarus was also useless. He had nowhere to go, so he stood. He'd stand here until he became a pile of bones, a forgotten monument to Joss.

Clicks sounded, then metal grating metal. A low groan emitted from the wall. Beneath the tower, the wall shifted, drawing inside itself.

"Go, Eric Hendricks. And try not to return." A loud cackle filled the air. A strange coin clanged to the ground near his feet. "Keep this amulet as protection in the River Styx."

It took a moment to register. She was opening the gate. Freeing him.

He palmed the coin and took off at a jog, then ran through the parting expanse of bronze.

"I'll send a courier for the package." Her voice echoed after him.

Silence filled the path as the gate ground to a halt. He ran for what seemed like miles. How thick was the wall anyway? Did the gate never end? Or had she tricked him?

The low grate of metal spurred him faster. Trick, hell. She meant to squash him. She was closing the exit, and the light grew dimmer. He couldn't see the end, if one existed. The tunnel narrowed ahead to nothingness. A moment of self-pity slowed his pace. He was so damn hot. And thirsty. A glass of Joss's lavender lemonade would hit the spot. He'd drink a gallon, then kiss her until that thirst was sated too.

Joss. He had to find her. His feet pounded faster. He couldn't even see now where he was going. Still he kept on, certain the gate must be nearer. The air smelled different now. Not better, but different. It must mean he'd drawn closer. With a last push, he surged forth, though it grew darker with every step.

Finally, the last light faded, and blackness surrounded him. His steps no longer echoed off enclosing walls, and space opened up around him. Had he cleared the gate? Chest heaving, he jogged to a stop. Turning back, he held his hands to his knees to catch his breath. Far away, a light shone, narrowing every second until it became a single ray. Then it, too, was snuffed out. The gate was closed.

For better or worse, he'd escaped Tartarus.

Standing straight, he struggled to get his bearings. *No freaking idea.* He wished he'd paid closer attention to the babbling man. Outside the wall of Tartarus—what lay there?

Oh yeah. Three circles of night.

Another long walk. He'd better get started.

* * * *

Screams echoed through the night. Joss clutched her stomach. Beings of light fell to their slaughter. She had to stop this insanity. Now.

Beneath her feet, the ground buzzed and shifted with crackling energy. Aroused by the commotion, no doubt, and by the opposing factions wanting control. An occasional crack, like the sound of lightning underground, left visible splinters on the face of the earth.

Plouton grinned, waiting for her decision. If she didn't offer herself in exchange, all would be for naught. What if she did? She would surely be lost. Would Eric? And her family?

She steadied herself. "If we forge an agreement, will you honor your word?"

His wince betrayed him. "Honor is a term I avoid. My agreements, as you surely must know, are legendary."

"For their trickery," Mom said. "Don't do it, Jocelyn."

When he held up a hand, Mom gagged for air, clutching her throat, panic in her eyes.

Helpless with terror, Joss froze. "Stop it!"

Shrugging, he opened his hand, and Mom gasped. He went on as if nothing happened. "We can come to a satisfactory arrangement, I'm sure."

An amber glow appeared on the horizon, and spread across the sky.

"Who's coming?" Joss asked.

Her fists clenched, Arkhe hissed, "Electra."

A warm breeze twined through Joss's hair and grew stronger. A cooler wind whipped through the trees, shaking loose leaves. Hot winds gusted.

With delight, Joss faced her mother. "Reinforcements." The Four Winds. Iris's mate had arrived and brought his brothers, as they'd hoped. Through the spreading amber skies, the four winged gods approached. More winged beings, their true hearts shining, followed.

The demon lord's eyes narrowed. "No."

"Oh, yes." Joss's smugness disappeared when his minions closed in, grabbing them roughly. "What are you doing?" she demanded, struggling to break free. The ground rumbled with something like a growl.

"Bring them. And remember," Lord Plouton said to Joss, "if you invoke the power below, your beloved will suffer for eternity." A theatrical whirl and he stalked off into the night.

Clawed hands tightened around Joss's arm and dragged her along.

Ahead, Arkhe and Plouton appeared to be arguing. Because the winds grew fierce, Joss heard only snippets. Enough to guess the Lord of The Underworld was none too happy with the goddess or her estranged family.

Plouton shouted over the howling gusts. "You should have warned me this would happen."

"I didn't expect her to call our family to her aid." Arkhe scanned the amber sky like a frightened child. Of course. Electra was her mother too. And wouldn't be pleased with her daughter, Arkhe.

Halting abruptly, Plouton glared. "Who else might join in?"

"I don't know. The Harpies?" Arkhe sounded desperate.

With a groan, he strode off. "Wonderful. I have no patience for those crones."

So, his plan had hit a snag.

As their captors struggled against the gales, Joss shot a hopeful glance at Lydia and Gram. They'd have to stay on the lookout for an opening, anything they could use to their advantage.

Shrieks overhead caused her to cower. Three winged creatures swooped in, vultures with the faces of incredibly gorgeous women. Their long, sharp claws shredded the helmets of Lord Plouton's guards.

The instant the monster's grip loosened, Joss broke away, grabbing Gram's hand, then her mother's, who in turn grasped Lydia's. Over the trembling earth, they scrambled through the melee toward a cloud of glowing figures. Safety.

Joss hoped, anyway. Below, the ley line almost roared with power, lashing wildly like a downed power line. It called and tugged on her psyche, and filled her head with wooziness.

"What do you wish?" came the wordless question.

Did she dare? She'd summoned the power accidentally before. Could she do it again? And would Plouton make good on his threat?

A scan of the destruction below urged her. A glance at Mom, Gram, and Lydia, whose faces held fear and helplessness, convinced her. She had to try.

Closing her eyes, she silently beseeched the ley line to help. To remove the threat of the dark forces, sweep them away to The Underworld where they belonged. To halt any further destruction, no more harm to any. Especially Eric.

The instant she finished the thought, the world shook. Trees swayed, leaves fluttering. The air crackled with electricity.

"The inn. Don't harm the inn. Or Eric's practice." Taz's presence emanated strongly from there. "And bring Eric home safely."

Iris flitted near, her golden wings brightened in the amber glow of the sky. "Quickly," she called over her shoulder and gestured her staff toward them.

When the Harpies swept in, fear overwhelmed Joss. One lifted her, and the others grabbed Mom, Gram, and Lydia before the winds died down. Before her feet left the earth, a strong tremor vibrated up her legs. Ten times stronger than the vibrations beneath the inn.

"What's going on?" Joss cried. The field below grew smaller, dark figures struggling against light. The fighting concentrated in a teeming line, too close to the inn.

Pointing her staff downward, Iris said, "Behold."

To Joss's horror, the ground split with a resounding crack. Lighted figures drifted upward like paper lanterns. Shadowy creatures tumbled into the widening gulf. Exactly as she'd imagined. Among them, she recognized poor Sheree. Riding his demon steed, Tom yanked the reins but couldn't stop in time. They, too, disappeared into the abyss.

"The ley line answered my plea," Joss whispered.

"At Gaia's instruction. Mother Earth recognized your will as pure." Iris nodded. "Thank you, Grandmother Gaia."

Bowing her head, Joss repeated Iris' words. From now on, she would have to be careful how she directed her mind. Immediately after giving thanks, she concentrated on healing thoughts: trees rooting in the nourishing earth, flowers lifting their faces to the sun, buildings sitting sound as they were before. She also repeated her earlier request for Eric's safety, this time asking it of Gaia.

Standing at the crevice's edge, Plouton glowered up at Iris in a useless silent threat. In a puff of charcoal smoke, he disappeared.

"Good riddance." Iris frowned at Arkhe, who met her gaze.

"I am sorry, sister." Arkhe hung her head. An amber light enveloped her. She disappeared as it spun into a whirlwind.

"What will happen to her?" Joss asked.

Iris sighed. "Mother will decide."

Family ties must be hell when they lasted more than a millennium.

The abyss below rumbled, the two sides sealing shut.

To the Harpies, Iris nodded, and they descended to the ground.

Their feet touched the earth, and Joss thanked the winged creatures. To Iris, she curtsied. "We owe you so much. I can never repay you."

Nodding royally, Iris said, "You are family. Your only debt is loyalty."

No problem. "It is yours, always." With a gasp, she remembered. "Eric. Is he safe?"

"I do not know," Iris said. "We will do our best to locate him."

"Thank you." *Please hurry.*

Iris laid her hand atop Joss's. "Remember to always honor the goddess within you."

Might take a little more work. "I will try."

If only her inner goddess could guide her to Eric, and assure her he, too, was safe. She shuddered at remembering Plouton's warning not to invoke the ley line, or Eric would suffer for an eternity.

Oh, what had she done? Though she could never indulge in her desire to be with him, she wanted to ensure his safety.

"Eric," she whispered. "Please come home safe."

* * * *

The waters of the River Styx seeped through Eric's jeans. With the amulet tucked in his pocket, he waded deeper, edging alongside a long gondola roped to a dock. Hooking his leg on the side, Eric hoisted himself up and over. The high backs of the chairs on the vessel allowed him to slip to the back, where darkness hid him.

At approaching footsteps, he stilled. A hooded figure stepped aboard off the dock, rocking the boat. Heart pounding, he forced long, even breaths in and out. If the ferryman discovered him, he might send him back to Tartarus.

The man hung a lantern on the front of the boat. He stood unmoving, as if listening for a few moments, then shoved the vessel away from the dock. Water sloshed its sides, carrying it along the current. The sound lulled Eric into shutting his eyes. The motion soothed his aching muscles into relaxing. Soon, the world faded away.

The end of a wooden staff poked his side.

With a start, he awoke to find he'd been discovered.

"Two obols," the ferryman said.

Drowsy, he tried to clear his head. "What?"

"Your fare." Crazed eyes glared at him from within the hood.

"I'm traveling away from Tartarus, not to it." Eric hoped his reasoning would suffice.

"Ah." The man took a moment to consider. "No matter. The fare is the same. Two obols."

Slowly standing, Eric steadied his stance. "I don't have it." What the hell was an obol anyway? Besides, they'd already returned. What would the man do, take him back? Doubtful, if he had no fare to begin with.

The ferryman's scowl gave way to a wide smile, revealing crooked teeth. "Well then. Off you go."

Thinking himself dismissed, Eric moved to the side. "Thanks. I'm glad you—" A hard shove sent him overboard. He plunged like a rock into the cold river. Righting himself, he broke the surface and gasped. To his surprise, hands grasped his legs, his waist, his ankles, pulling him below again. Down and down and down he sunk, farther than possible. Water churned around him until he couldn't tell which direction was up.

His lungs screamed for air. A voice froze him in place. *"Eric. Please come home safe."* Joss spoke clearly, though he knew it was impossible. She was home in Boiling Springs, nowhere near.

Hearing her so clearly had to mean she was thinking of him. Missing him. The last push he needed. Desperately, he reached toward an amber glow. Invisible hands shoved him toward the light.

Sputtering, he emerged in Yellow Breeches stream. He climbed on the bank and collapsed. Overhead, the sky shone vivid amber, unlike anything he'd ever seen. *No. Can't…be. Too…late.* Exhausted, he couldn't move. Darkness enclosed him.

Sometime later, he awakened to sunlight, the trickle of the stream and the twitter of bird song. *What am I doing outside?* Sitting up, he glanced in every direction. Branches lay near him, the tops of trees sheared off as if by a hurricane-force wind.

What the hell happened? Rolling over, he pushed up to a stand. The destruction stretched toward town. Glancing back, he frowned in confusion. Between his veterinary practice and Lavender Hill Inn, everything appeared pristine. Untouched. The corridor continued beyond for about a quarter mile in each direction.

Must have been a helluva storm. He'd come to do something important. Why couldn't he remember it? And why was he outside? Weird. Why couldn't he think straight? He rubbed his head, aching like the worst hangover ever.

Just get home. Hopefully he could make it there without any notice. He trudged within yards of the entrance to the driveway and stopped.

Across the road, Joss's lime green VW Beetle sat outside the back door. *I need to tell her something.*

"Dr. Hendricks?"

He turned toward the voice and his practice. His assistant stood in the doorway. "Yes, Terry?"

"We've been wondering where you were."

Where had he been? Images flashed through his head of terrible beasts, ghastly figures moving through darkness. Too nightmarish to be real. "What's up?"

"Patients are getting, well, impatient. We're twenty minutes behind."

"Better get started, then." Another glance at the inn showed another car parked beside Joss's. Must have company. He'd go there later to talk to her. After her company left, and after his head cleared.

Something heavy weighed down his pocket. He pulled out a round, cold, metal object. *Where did this come from?* Like everything else that day, he had no recollection of it. He carried it inside to the store room, and without thinking, collected tubes of medicated ointments and creams inside a box. Before folding the top, he slipped the coin inside, and then set the package on the back step.

For a moment, he stared at it, trying to recall who had ordered it. All he knew was someone who needed these items would come for them.

He closed the door and wished all his problems could be solved so easily.

Chapter 23

The inn seemed strangely silent, with an expectant atmosphere, when Joss went inside with her family. Even Taz, who normally greeted them at the door, sat pensively atop the dog bed by the reception desk.

Joss rushed to hold him. "My poor baby. I'm sorry I left you alone." The dog nuzzled his trembling body against her, and she hugged tighter. "It's over now. You're safe."

Her mother crouched beside Joss and stroked the dog's head. "Tonight, we must meet with Iris and Lord Plouton again."

Dread iced her veins. "Why?" Would they punish her for using the ley line?

"To forge a new treaty," Gram said. "One by which all must abide."

"Already? So soon after battle?" Joss hoped never to see the Lord of The Underworld again.

Mom nodded. "The sooner the better."

Attempting a wan smile, Joss said, "Okay then." Easier said than done.

Gram headed toward the hallway stairs. "We'd better rest while we can."

Mom followed. "Three o'clock will come soon enough. Come, Lydia."

"You don't have to ask me twice." Lydia shuffled behind.

Three o'clock. Joss stifled a groan and went to her room. She turned off the light and stretched onto her bed, trying to let the darkness absorb her thoughts. How could she sleep, knowing what lay ahead?

At some point, she must have drifted off. A glimmering light outside the window caused her eyes to flutter open. Glancing at the clock on the night stand, she threw the covers aside.

Three AM. It was time.

On cue, her mother entered the room, followed by Gram and Lydia.

A rainbow stretched from iridescent amber clouds to her window. Floating along the ribbons of color, Iris descended, her great wings billowing. Reaching the sill, she extended her staff. "Come."

Not exactly an invitation. At her mother's serene nod, Joss clambered out the window. What a poor excuse for a goddess. Demi-goddess. Goddess grandchild. Whatever.

Joss's mother, Gram, and Lydia glided out. Apparently they'd done this before. Maybe Joss would grow more graceful at window escapes, though she hoped it wouldn't be a frequent occurrence in her life.

On second thought, she could get used to traveling this way. Iris in the lead, the rainbow lifted them like an escalator into the clouds, then glided down again into a mist.

Alarmed, Joss whispered, "Where are we going?"

Her mother said, "To accommodate Lord Plouton's demand to meet in a neutral zone."

The mist cleared. Darkness crowded close, walling them in. It breathed and moved like a living thing, slithering and hungry as a snake. It left room enough only to walk around a marble-topped table.

This was neutral territory? Joss hated to think what might happen if one of them stepped beyond the border.

Iris took her place at the head of the table in an ornate gilded chair. At the opposite end, the ebony chair sat empty.

Sitting beside her mother, Joss leaned in. "Where is he?"

Her mother smiled. "On his way. Don't worry."

Iris added, "He likes to make an entrance."

From the black void beyond the ebony chair, a hiss grew in intensity. The darkness undulated, then swirled into a huge tunnel. Torches illuminated its sides, showing the approach of Lord Plouton. Head down, his long black coattails fluttered behind him as he strode with purpose into the room and halted. The tunnel sucked itself shut.

Much as she hated to admit, the Prince of Darkness appeared stunning. Again shirtless, she struggled to avert her gaze from his washboard abs. His black hair hung to his shoulders. He gave a bow, and his black eyes focused on Joss.

Her head swam, struggling against the pull of his gaze. The urge to go to him.

Summoning her strength, Joss collected her resolve. *No.*

His brow arched slightly, and he tilted his head in acknowledgement.

Plouton, impressed? Not likely. Her body shook with the effort, and took her last reserve of energy to simply sit without sliding onto the floor in a useless puddle.

"Enough tomfoolery," Iris commanded.

Spreading a hand against his bare chest, Lord Plouton was the image of innocence. "Moi? I never engage in such nonsense."

A glance at Joss confirmed it. No, far from a game. More like a test of her will. Somehow she'd bested him. The knowledge bolstered her spine.

Iris scowled. "May we begin now?"

"Of course. Why else would I be here?" Flipping back his coattails, he sat and assessed the room. "Certainly not for the décor. Or the refreshments." Tsking, he added, "You should make more effort not to be so boring." He winced as if in distaste.

Sounding imposed upon, Iris asked, "Let's get down to business, shall we?"

Mouthing, *boring*, Plouton then shot Joss a dazzling smile. An umbrella drink appeared in front of him, red and frothing. He splayed his hands around it and looked at Joss in silent offering.

He could certainly ooze charm when he wanted. Folding her hands, Joss forced her attention to Iris.

Iris struck her staff three times against the floor. "We are here to forge a new treaty. A binding treaty. A treaty to—"

His hand mimicking a yapping puppet, Lord Plouton shifted. "A treaty. We get it."

Pursing her lips, Iris glared. "Fine." Reaching toward the empty table, her hand closed around a scroll. "We'll be brief. The terms are as follows. We renew our agreement not to sully the ley lines with our use."

He shrugged. "Impossible. Jocelyn lives atop it."

Hearing him utter her name, Joss shivered. What, now I'm on a first name basis with Satan? No thanks.

"True," Iris said, "only to run her business. Not to gain any personal power."

Plouton chuckled. "So she's a saint already? Be serious."

Exhibiting no stress, Iris continued. "Jocelyn knew nothing of the energies below the property when she bought it. She wants only to live there because the inn is there, and Jocelyn's livelihood."

"Such a shame too. You have such potential for"—his gaze ran across her uncomfortably—"more."

Heat flamed in Joss's face. "I want no more."

"Don't be difficult, Lord Plouton. You of all people know she speaks the truth."

"Difficult? Me?" Plouton steepled his hand below his chin. His ebony eyes narrowed, though he exhibited no anger. Joss guessed he probably enjoyed this sort of meeting. Likely, he didn't often socialize with his contemporaries, so it provided an opportunity for him to wield his sharp wits against worthy opponents.

Plouton shot to his feet, studying Joss as he circled her. "You honestly don't know, do you?"

Joss asked her family as much as him. "Know what?"

"The tawdry back story of the longstanding feud."

At Gram's gasp, Joss froze. "Do you mean the grudge against my family?" She'd been so swept away by what Gram revealed about her father and husband's deaths, she hadn't asked enough questions. Now she wished she had.

Still pacing, Plouton's laugh filled the cavernous room. "Yes, the so-called grudge. Let me fill you in."

Iris clutched her staff. "Lord Plouton."

"The girl deserves the truth, doesn't she? Isn't that what you're always preaching?"

"I want to know." Or needed to, so she might anticipate any future attacks.

"Your great-grandmother Eleanor had an illicit affair with Silas. A demon of title in The Underworld. Believing she loved him wholeheartedly, he killed her husband Jonas so they could be together. Eleanor, to his utter heartbreak, rejected him afterward, called him a monster. Silas couldn't accept the loss and began taking his revenge on other women."

"Oh, God. Why didn't you tell me?" Joss asked.

Gram hung her head. "The fae intervened, tasking Eleanor with stopping Silas for good."

"Yes," Plouton hissed. "She lured him back to her side with promises but gave him poison. He died in her arms as she kissed him goodbye and told him how sorry she was, that she never meant to hurt him but couldn't let him destroy any more lives. Silas's family demanded their own revenge. Caught in the middle, what was I, Lord of The Underworld, to do? I had no choice but to begin a war with the fae."

Iris's expression soured. "War should have been your last choice, Lord Plouton."

Plouton *tsk'd*. "Now, Iris, you'll recall that I allowed only a few instances before calling back my demons. I pledged to them I would exact revenge when the time was right. And then Joss commandeered the ley line." He shook his head at her like she was a naughty girl.

"I did not comman—"

"Hush." Plouton appeared instantly in front of her, scowling. "My demons called for me to do my duty. So I did. And now you beg for mercy?"

Joss steeled herself. *Thought it was the other way around.*

The devil laughed. "What a shame you're on the wrong side."

"I'm not." Joss stood taller.

He waved her off. "A pointless argument. At any rate, here I am, caught in the middle yet again. Do I want war? No. But you're a pretty little time bomb living on top of the world's largest energy source. How do I know you're not going to"—he snapped his fingers—"light the fuse again?"

"I swear to you by all that's good."

"Oh, no. I don't give a rat's ass about anything *good*."

Did he want her to swear by something evil? "I give you my word."

"And what else?" He boomed the words.

"I have nothing else."

"Lord Plouton," Iris said. "If you truly have no interest in war, then the treaty will give you an excuse to end the war. You can easily placate the demons' family by tossing some Underworld land titles at them."

He sank to a seat at the table and tilted his head at Iris. "Do you think so, goddess? Truly?"

Iris toyed with her staff. "If you prefer to battle, Lord, you might find the odds against you now." The goddess glanced pointedly at Joss. "You've observed her great power here. Above, you would not wish to witness how the ley line bends to her will at a mere thought."

Joss froze. Did Iris intimidate the Lord of The Underworld by threatening him with Joss's power?

Plouton sighed and plucked invisible lint from his jacket. "All right. So long as Jocelyn doesn't tap into the energies, nor any of your brethren, I and my minions will likewise leave them untouched."

Iris turned to Joss. "Jocelyn, will you abide by this agreement?"

Good question. She wanted to, but could she?

Joss nodded and found her voice. "Yes."

Her mother leaned close. "Speak the words, or they are not binding."

Mustering whatever confidence she could spare, Joss said, "I will not try to use the power of the ley line."

"Bah." Plouton waved. "What are you, a legal expert?"

Confused, Joss hoped the others would provide her guidance. "I don't understand."

The Lord of The Underworld rose menacingly, leaning over the table to glare at her. "Don't add any language to leave a loop hole. Do you expect me to fall for such a ploy? 'Try to.' I can hear the excuses already." He rolled his eyes. In an exaggerated high-pitched tone, he fluttered his fingers. "Oh, I accidentally called upon the power below to make Boiling Springs a thriving metropolis."

Absurd. Angrily, Joss argued, "I wouldn't."

"Don't give me any malarkey. If you so much as use it to make your damn lavender smell sweeter, I'll descend on you with every last bit of brimstone in my realm."

Solemnly, Iris asked Joss, "Can you pledge your full cooperation?"

Each member waited expectantly. Everything rode on her answer.

She had to. She would. "Yes."

The goddess folded her hands on the table top. "Plouton, you will agree to our terms, or forfeit any future claim on the ley line in central Pennsylvania."

His gaze darted between Iris and Gram to Joss. "You cannot bar me from access to it."

"Oh, but I can. You're well aware of it. Jocelyn will forcefully ensure peace if necessary." Iris relaxed in her chair. "If peace is broken, she can invoke her vengeance. How well can your kingdoms withstand such an assault, I wonder?"

Joss dared not blink nor argue. With every force of her will, she silently begged Plouton to agree.

Narrowing his eyes, he stared like a predator stalking its prey. Nostrils flared, his jaw sawed back and forth almost imperceptibly. When Iris returned his stare with equal menace, he grated out, "What are the terms?"

"No harm shall come to Jocelyn Gibson, nor any of her family. Nor any man she loves, or takes as a spouse."

He laughed. "I can't be responsible for what happens to them. People have accidents all the time."

Iris rose with the dignity of royalty. "Let it be written on the Scroll of Eternity. Lord Plouton forfeits any future hold on the ley line beneath Boiling Springs, Pennsylvania."

His nostrils flared. "Fine. I promise, no harm will come to them from me."

"Nor any minion doing your bidding," Iris prompted.

Plouton grumbled in an ancient language, punctuated by what surely must have been curses.

The goddess repeated her demand. "Neither you, nor any of your minions. For the record, Lord Plouton. Now, or forever hold your peace."

"Peace." He spat a laugh. Rising slowly, he placed a hand on his chest theatrically. "I promise I shall cause no harm to Jocelyn Gibson or her loved ones."

Grabbing his leather gloves, Plouton appeared ready to leave. "Fine, we're done here. Oh, except for one last detail."

Uh, oh. Joss's breath caught in her throat.

Sounding bored, he said, "I'm keeping the two village idiots."

A gasp escaped Joss. "Tom and Sheree? Why?"

Lord Plouton grinned. "What they lack in brains, they make up for in greed and self-absorption. My kind of people. Trust me, you wouldn't want them back. They're more than happy where they are."

Could it be true?

At the snap of Plouton's fingers, Sheree and Tom appeared. At least, the two vaguely resembled Tom and Sheree. A more feral version of them. Meeting the gaze of everyone in the room, their toothy, hungry smiles appeared eager to tear into each.

The Lord of The Underworld lazily shifted his hips. "Tell the members of this esteemed court where you would prefer to spend your time. In dreary Boiling Springs, or with me?"

Both pawed at him like trained dogs.

"Don't send us back there," Tom begged.

Sheree fawned. "We want to be with you."

Despair washed over Joss. She'd never before seen lost souls, yet didn't doubt two stood before her now.

Turning to each one around the table, Iris waited for their nods before her sad response. "Agreed."

"Wait." Joss reached for the flowing robes of Iris's sleeve but stopped herself from grabbing the goddess. "What about Eric?"

Plouton examined his nails. "What about him?"

"I'm not leaving until I know he's safe."

"Oh, joy. You're staying?" His perfectly even teeth glinted in the candlelight when he smiled. A cold smile.

Wanting to pummel him, she clenched her hands. "Release him, or the deal's off."

"Sorry. No can do."

"You leave me no choice."

"Everyone has a choice. Isn't that what you said?"

Throwing her own words back at her. "I... You..." Rage stole her ability to speak a full sentence.

"Me and you? That does sound promising. But it's beyond my control."

"Liar!"

A shrug. "Among other things. But not this time."

Oh God, had something happened? "Where is he?"

Plouton yawned. "No clue. I lost track of him after he left the boundaries of Tartarus."

"He's home?" She looked to her family for reassurance, but Gram, Lydia, and Mom appeared just as confused.

"Quite possibly." He leaned over the table, his gaze searing into Joss's. "What prompted this *tete-a-tete*? Has the weakling mortal captured your heart?"

Anger rose up like a specter within Joss. She knew he meant to rattle her, to weaken her, to infect her with his taunt. No way would she comply. "Interesting. So any 'weakling' can escape the inescapable Tartarus? How did he manage such a feat, I wonder?" Maybe her taunt would cause him to reveal the truth, and end her wondering.

His terrible smile cut a swath through her courage. "Bravo. Kudos on the performance, but know this. I will be watching what goes on at your little inn. Keep your pledge not to use the power of the ley line, and I shall keep mine."

Joss nodded. "You have my word." She turned to Gram. "We have to go."

With a wicked smile, Plouton's coat tails whirled as he readied to leave. "All right then. Wish I could say it was nice doing business with you. Ta."

In a blink, the three were gone.

Meeting adjourned. Easier than Joss expected, and with the best possible outcome. The difficult part, she knew, awaited.

Her first task was making sure Eric had returned safely.

* * * *

Joss followed the three women off the end of the rainbow and into the house. Strange, she should be exhausted but wasn't. "Anyone for tea? Or margaritas?"

"No thank you, dear." Mom took hold of Joss's shoulders. "I hate to leave so soon, but I must."

"Already?"

Mom nodded. "Keep training against the ley line. Your mind is your greatest power." She kissed her forehead, then stepped outside and vanished into the night.

Too late, Joss remembered to respond. "I will." Saying goodbye to her mother was bittersweet. Knowing Mom hadn't abandoned her eased the pain. Now that everyone knew Joss's true identity, Mom could cross from the other realm and visit occasionally. Something to look forward to, although she suspected her mother would keep tabs. If only Joss had the same faith in herself that her relatives did.

Gram and Lydia crowded around with sad expressions.

Joss slumped. "You're leaving too?"

"For now." Gram pulled her into an embrace.

Lydia joined the group hug. "We'll see you soon."

"Drive safe." She walked them to the car, and waited until the headlights faded in the distance before going back inside. Her head swirled with everything that had happened. So much to process, and so much yet to learn. *And I still have an inn to run.* The best solution, for now, was getting back to work.

She patted Taz's head. "We'd better get some sleep." To her surprise, the clock read three seventeen. Another puzzle. No sooner did her head hit the pillow than she fell fast asleep.

In the morning, Joss woke refreshed, and readied for the day. After checking email, she reported to Annie that the Boyers inquired about the possibility of holding a surprise fiftieth birthday party at the inn.

Annie whooped. "Great. Ask them what kind of cake. And for how many."

Her thoughts couldn't be further from the party. "About fifty. I'm going to suggest the white cake with lavender sugar. Hopefully, it will convince them to book it here."

Rolling her eyes, Annie chuckled. "Tone down the enthusiasm, will you? The neighbors might complain."

She sighed. "Sorry, sweetie."

"What's wrong?"

"Everything's great." Since she'd ensured the safety of the town. But what about her?

"Maybe not everything."

No reply necessary, she knew. Annie might not wield real magic, but her friend understood the most important things. A sort of mini-superpower in her own right.

Annie brightened. "Hey, I know what we need."

Joss bet. Still, she found her friend's enthusiasm infectious, as always. "What?"

"Another picnic. We don't have to wait until Labor Day. Let's make up our own holiday. Give people a reason to celebrate."

"You're absolutely right. We'll have a Midsummer Festival. Or something." Another picnic would draw people to the inn again.

And Eric too.

Only a few days had passed since the battle. From across the road, his emotions emanated stronger than ever. More tumultuous than ever. Of course, he had to be rattled after escaping the gates of Hell. So she'd stayed away, waiting for him to settle on a more even keel. And herself too.

"You're a genius, Annie."

Her friend waved her off. "Nah. I just hate to see you mope again."

"Was I?"

Annie widened her eyes in a *duh* expression, then her face softened. "Stop worrying. Everything will work out. I feel it in my bones."

Joss smiled. "Your bones have always been right."

* * * *

Reading the chart notations, Eric strolled down the hall of his veterinary practice. The storm a few days ago had toppled trees in nearby fields, yet his home—and the inn—stood perfectly preserved, following a straight line. Like the storm couldn't touch a certain corridor along the earth. Very strange, especially since people said the heaviest outbreak concentrated in town. He tried to recall the thunder claps or howling winds his staff talked about, but he must've slept through it. The sleep-walking incident still disturbed him. He'd never done anything so weird before.

Nor had his memory blanked before. He recalled nothing about the earth rumbling or the constant lightning, nothing about that day. Like he'd been plucked out of his life, then re-deposited to pick up where he'd left off.

Except he couldn't. Yes, he'd returned to work without any problem. One thing remained for him to do, if he could only remember exactly what.

And though he'd completed every examination like a professional, he did so only by fighting the overwhelming urge to abandon his practice and run across the road to the inn. To Joss.

She'd think you were a lunatic. Maybe she wouldn't be far off. He couldn't stop thinking about her. Wanting her.

But how do I approach her?

"Dr. Hendricks?" Terry spoke softly from the doorway.

He turned away from the window. *Caught staring.* "Yes?"

"New patient in room two."

"Thanks."

"Oh, and Annie asked if she could hang a flyer in our window. I didn't think you'd mind."

"What's it for?"

"The inn's having a picnic this weekend. Kind of last minute."

"Oh."

"You don't mind, do you?"

Mind? "Not at all." Not one little bit. Now, he had the perfect excuse to see her.

Chapter 24

Blooms and herbs filled the summer kitchen, one of Joss's favorite places at Lavender Hill. If she could choose a favorite. Each room held its own coziness and warmth. She had no trouble referring to the inn as home, even knowing it sat atop a hotbed of Underworld activity. Since the battle, she'd guarded against errant thoughts that could lead to misuse of the ley line.

Not an easy task. After glimpsing Eric climbing in his truck and driving away, her mind whirled uncontrollably. *He's back. He's safe. Hallelujah!* Why did he avoid her? Didn't he have any wish to see her? Did he hate her for putting him through Hell, literally?

Gathering tea balls, she carried them the short distance down the path to the back screen door where the tangy smell of barbecue drifted through. Clangs and humming sounded inside, Annie standing at the stove, stirring two large pots at once.

Inhaling, Joss smiled. "Smells delicious."

With a grateful glance, Annie said, "Let's hope everyone likes barbecue."

"They'll like anything you cook. Oh, and I found the old croquet set, and lawn tennis." Mostly because she couldn't sit still and kept herself busy with any possible activity.

"It's a perfect day for it," Annie said. "People will love it. This was such a great idea, having an early August picnic."

"And you're sure we have enough of everything?" The notion she'd forgotten something niggled at her more than usual. Worrying about Eric, she found it difficult to concentrate on anything. Hopefully, he'd follow the line of cars to the inn.

Ticking off the items with an oven mitt, Annie seemed to reassure herself. "Sweetie, we have barbecued beef, chicken, pork, and shrimp, and five side dishes. With blueberry cheesecake and lemon cake for dessert, we'll be fine."

Joss chuckled. "Mm, I'm going to have to buy a treadmill soon."

"Or you could go running…" Annie flashed a devious smile.

Depended on the direction. "On second thought, I'll stick with gardening."

"Any idea who's coming today?"

"Hopefully everyone." To quiet the small voice in her head, she bent to retrieve a pot and filled it with tap water.

"Kyle too?" Annie asked.

"No, he's at a friend's. He didn't want to travel this far so close to the start of senior year. Summer classes kept him busy."

Wide-eyed, Annie shook her head. "I can't believe he'll be graduating."

"He hasn't mentioned any job offers yet. If he needs me, I'll be here for him, waiting with open arms."

"You always are." Annie looped her into an embrace. "He'll find his path."

Patting her friend's back, she leaned away. "I'd better go change. People should start arriving soon."

Taz hobbled behind her as she went to her room. He'd taken only two spills since coming home so Joss tried not to coddle him too much.

Quickly changing into her knit sundress, she surveyed her image in the mirror. "Not bad for an old lady, huh Taz?"

The dog tilted its head and whined.

"You're right. It needs a little something." Opening her jewelry box, she drew out the carved shell necklace and bracelet. John's promise to buy her another from an island vendor slowed her hand as she fastened them. Since their journey to The Underworld, the image of John sometimes haunted her. She closed her eyes and clasped the necklace, stilling her mind. When a vision of John's glowing smile appeared, calm replaced her anxiety.

The crunch of tires on the driveway hurried her. "Customers. Let's go." Stepping into her sandals along the way, she entered the kitchen. "Guests are here," she said to Annie on her way to the window. "Oh, isn't he the new trainer? Did they ever find out what happened to Tom Larsen?"

Wiping her hands on a dishcloth, Annie shrugged. "No one seems to know. He and Sheree just…" She snapped her fingers. "Vanished. Like magic."

Not exactly magic. Not the good sort anyway. "This new trainer seems nice." And sometimes the rumor mill came in handy.

Hurrying back to the stove, Annie lifted a pot lid. "He does. The horses seem to like him too."

"Yes." As much as they did Eric. Even Maya, the finicky former race horse, nickered gently on the vet's visits, head lowered, unflinching at his touch. Joss loved to hear him speak to the animals as if they could respond, asking how they were.

When Taz lumbered to the water dish, Annie paused to watch. "He's recovering so fast. It's amazing."

Joss lost her grip on a mug but caught it. "He is." Hopefully no one else would notice how quickly and think it unnatural.

Grinning, Annie pointed an oven mitt at her. "It's because of you."

Unable to hold her false smile, Joss could hardly ask, "What?" Annie couldn't have seen the small indiscretion that day, she'd gone home.

"He loves you so much. He's working extra hard to get well, and your love is helping to heal him."

"Oh." A fluttery laugh escaped. "I guess."

"You know it's true. Love is the most powerful force in the world. It can overcome anything."

"Anything," Joss repeated. Even those in The Underworld. If Lydia or Gram had said the same thing, Joss would have let it breeze past. Annie's words held weight, and they hit her hard. Since they'd healed The Mark and nothing forced Eric away from her, would he believe it too?

With a breezy tone, Joss turned. "I'll greet our guests."

Two more cars pulled in as Joss went outside. "Welcome. I hope you're hungry. We have every kind of barbecue, plus an assortment of desserts."

Mrs. Albright smiled at her husband. "I've heard so much about your wonderful lavender lemonade."

"I hope you enjoy it." Joss pointed them to the patio, where chafing dishes lined the table against the wall. "Please help yourselves to the buffet. We also have lawn games."

In greeting the owners of Quincy, the quarter horse, Joss caught the gleam of another vehicle in the late afternoon sun. Aunt Lydia's car.

"Jocelyn darling." Lydia threw her arms wide, her gait awkward in her tight skirt, her blouse ruffles flouncing in the breeze. "The drive was so tedious. I could use a lovely glass of your special lemonade."

"I'm so happy you could join us." Though she'd be happier if her aunt would give her a heads up now and then. Joss didn't read cards to see the future, and the inn's limited number of rooms could pose a potential problem. "How did you know about the picnic?"

"The universe, darling. It speaks to me all the time, yadda yadda yadda. But on such occasions as this, it supplies useful information." Opening her oversized bag, Lydia made a show of pulling out her wallet. "How much is a ticket?"

She nudged her aunt's offering away. "Why don't you go freshen up? Then maybe you could help us out."

"Why certainly, dearest." Hips swaying, Lydia bustled into the house.

Joss greeted the family who owned Triple Power, and Jim Turner. When her aunt returned, she handed her the tickets. "I need to bring out food. Can you check these next guests?" She nodded to the van winding down the driveway.

Trouper that she was, Lydia took over with panache. Joss filled the stainless steel trays and lit the sterno. Jim asked if Joss hired her aunt as a hostess, making her laugh. "Oh, no. She's only temporary." Though, she somehow appeared at critical times. Joss hoped tonight wasn't one of them.

Returning the empty pans to the kitchen, Joss lingered at the window. Her nerves tingled, usually a sure sign the vet was near, but no blue SUV sat in the driveway.

"Looking for someone?" Annie teased.

"I'm checking to see who's arrived. It's getting to be a nice-sized crowd." She removed the chilled pitcher from the fridge and hurried through the dining room.

A zing shot through her, so she searched the parking lot and driveway. Still no blue SUV. More vehicles arrived, keeping Aunt Lydia busy. *Good. It proves me wrong about—* "Oh!" Bumping into a man's chest, the lemonade sloshed out onto the plate. Held by Eric.

"I'm so sorry. I didn't see you there." Too busy looking for him, she managed to miss him standing right in her path. So close, the air between them filled with crackling energy.

"Ow, you gave me quite a shock." He flicked his hand as a crooked smile lifted his mouth. "And I wanted some lemonade with my food, but not like this." His faded pink polo set off his dark hair and steely gray eyes.

Oh, no. The effort of keeping her energy pent up collapsed in one jolt. Without meaning to, she'd zapped him. Other than a flinch, hardly noticeable, he hadn't reacted. If anything, his eyes burned brighter blue.

"Here, let me take your plate." When she reached for it, the pitcher tilted and a few drops escaped.

He grasped the bottom to straighten it, still holding his dish, as was she. "I never was good at juggling. I'll take the pitcher. You take the plate."

Lost in his gaze, her grip refused to relax. Finally, she laughed. "Sorry. My coordination's off today." Or any day she was around him, it seemed. To ease the awkwardness, she took a tumbler off the table.

"Real glasses?" He reached for it.

His fingers brushing hers swept away her response. "Pardon?"

"I noticed before you don't use disposables."

Why was he asking such impersonal questions? "They're inexpensive Dollar Store glasses. We practice the three Rs whenever possible. Landfills hold enough throwaways without us adding to it." Why was she babbling? Held by his attentive gaze, words spilled forth uncontrollably. "And we're growing our own organic vegetables and herbs. And the lavender, of course. I couldn't make those special recipes without it." The tingle branched through every vein, setting her body abuzz. She ground her toe into the patio to cut off the flow.

She met Aunt Lydia's amused gaze. How foolish she must appear. "Excuse me." *And rude, leaving so abruptly.* "Help yourself to another plate." She rushed inside.

Cocking her head, Annie asked, "What do we need?"

"Oh, well…" She hadn't actually noticed. She didn't want to go back out yet. "I'll come for refills when we need them."

"Okay." Annie blinked in confusion. "Wasn't that why you returned so fast?"

Waving off Annie's worries, Joss busied herself. "I'm nervous. I want today to go well."

"It will. Can I do anything else to help?"

Joss shrugged. "Go have fun? Mingle?"

"Maybe I will for a bit."

By the time Joss went back out, Annie had joined a four-person lawn tennis game. Whacking the birdie over the net, she whooped when the opposite team missed it. "Score," she yelled, her feet in a happy dance. Onlookers cheered.

Joss yelled, "Go, Annie." Glancing at Eric, her laugh faded. The rest of the world fell away as he rose, gaze locked on hers, and strode toward her with a surety that unnerved her. A shiver passed over her, both hot and cold. "Excuse me. I have to check the other guests."

He blocked her path. "Can't it wait a minute?"

"I still have so much to do. And I haven't even taken Taz for a proper walk." The realization hit her. She'd forgotten him. "If I don't walk him on the harness, he just plops down in the shade."

"Where's his harness?" He extended his hand, palm up. "I'll do it."

Her mouth dropped open. "What? No, you're a guest."

"I'm a veterinarian. And a friend who cares about Taz." His arched brow challenged her to disagree.

Her heart sank. *A friend.* After a beat, she said, "All right. It would be a huge help." Taz licked her face when she fastened the harness around him. "Time for a walk, sweetie."

Eric's hand closed around hers, but she slipped from his grasp, leaving the leash in his hold. He held her gaze. "We'll be back." Eric and Taz strolled leisurely to the pasture fence, and two of the horses bent to sniff at the dog.

Joss tried not to check for them too often. Minutes dragged on. The sun slipped low, and guests began to leave. Her heart did a somersault when Taz and Eric were nowhere in sight. She hurried outside. Scanning the yard to the barn found nothing. When she gazed to the field, her heart flip-flopped again.

Eric stood in the lavender field, surrounded by flickering lights. The intermittent glow dappled his figure. Beside him, Taz sat contentedly.

Struggling to understand its meaning, Joss halted in amazement. Rarely did they appear during the day, and they'd never let anyone else so close. Only her, because they knew her family, and knew she wouldn't reveal them to others.

What, she wondered, were they revealing to Eric? Whatever it was, she shouldn't intrude, so slipped back to the patio.

* * * *

Humidity hung in the air, balmy and sweet. Lavender scented, thick and intoxicating. After a long stroll under the leafy canopy of Yellow Breeches Road, Eric steered Taz back toward the inn. As dusk gathered, the dog tugged him toward the field, and now they both stood in wonderment at the glimmering insects around them. Although larger than normal fireflies, Eric couldn't quite make out distinct shapes. Not unusual, he supposed, yet something about these seemed different. They seemed friendly enough. His tension ebbed in their presence. He inhaled the soothing scent. The lavender must be working its magic too. All that remained was confusion. Joss acted aloof, but when she looked at him, he knew she wanted him as much as he wanted her.

At the tug of the leash in his hand, he turned. "Ready to go in?" He walked Taz back to the house, surprised to find the rest of the guests had already left.

Joss held the kitchen door open. "There you are. I was beginning to worry."

"We were getting some exercise." He walked Taz inside.

She reached for the leash. "I appreciate you taking the time."

Stepping closer, he ran his hands along her arms. "I had selfish motives."

"Eric," she whispered, the worry leaving her face as she gazed up at him.

It was the only encouragement he needed. His mouth found hers. Every muscle ached for her, yearned to wrap around her. Clutching his shirt, she returned his kisses. He swept her up into his arms and carried her to the bedroom and lowered her atop the mattress. Like a fever gripped him, he whispered her name. Wherever their bodies touched, it was as if some force pressed them closer, like a magnetic field surrounded them. A cyclone. With he and Joss at the center, the whirlwind crackled like some crazy science exhibit gone awry.

"Oh, no," she whispered, turning her face away, eyes wide with fear. She squeezed them shut. "Stop."

A zap like a lightning strike stung him deeply, more than her rejection. Stunned, he tensed, every cell ready to burst. "What was that?"

"Stop." More forcefully this time, though she didn't seem to be talking to him. Or was she?

"Will you tell me what's wrong?" Frustration roughed his tone.

Holding her hands to her temples, her hair covered her face.

A rumble like low thunder sounded. He could have sworn it was in the room with them. Whatever was happening, it was frightening her. And he didn't like it. "Don't worry, Joss. I won't let it hurt you."

She turned slowly to face him. "It's not me who's in danger, Eric. It's you." She whispered the last.

"I'm still not afraid."

"Please leave. I need some time to—" She hugged herself.

Not wanting to upset her any more than she already was, he backed away one step at a time. "I'm not going far. Or for long."

She gave the slightest of nods.

Every instinct urged him not to go. Whatever had happened tonight didn't matter. Whatever might threaten them in the future didn't matter. He and Joss belonged to each other.

Jaw clenched, he fought the urge to stay, backed away, and stepped outside. "She is mine. Nothing is going to stand between us. Do you hear?" A few months ago, he'd have slapped himself for making such an announcement to the night. Not now. Unnamable things lurked out there. Unseen yet present.

A strange thrum filled the air. Like metal to a magnet, his steps brought him to the field. Running his hand along their blooms, he sat down, unwilling to travel too far from her. Maybe the floral oil had seeped into his bloodstream, because calm infused him. He and Joss would be together. His heart beat with the certainty. Inhaling deeply, he stretched out under the stars crowding the heavens. Such a brilliant night. If he'd stayed home, he'd have missed this view. Missed being here. He imagined Joss beside him. Bending over him. Lying atop him.

He couldn't guess how long he laid there. The headlights of a car wound through the night. *I should probably leave.* Then he'd have to get up, and the field was surprisingly comfortable.

Soft footsteps crossed the stone bridge and approached. "Hello? Who's there?"

Joss. He sat up. "Hi."

Uncertainly, she clasped her hands. "What are you doing?"

Dressed in only knit shorts and a tank top, her skin caught the glow of the moon. Fluttering in the breeze, her blond hair appeared silver. Magical.

"Admiring the view." He laughed. A good, hearty laugh. It shook the last worry from his muscles. "How did you know I was out here?"

She approached with halting steps. "I didn't. I'm not sure what drew me out here."

Oddly enough, he knew. He had. "Did you ever come out here and look at the stars?"

Skeptical, she peered at him. "Have you been drinking?"

He patted the ground. "Come here and sit."

Wariness crossed her face.

"Please? Sit here and look at the stars with me. Then if you still think I've lost it, you can call someone to haul me away."

She stammered, "All right. For a minute." She knelt and sat back against her legs.

"There. Now look up."

She lifted her chin. "Oh, my." Tilting her head, she craned her neck upward.

"You can't get the full effect sitting up. Lie down." He patted the ground next to him.

"No, I don't—"

He tugged at her arm. "Seriously."

When she settled, sublime happiness washed over him. "Am I right?" Her soft intake of breath told him he was. "It *is* incredible."

Lifting to one elbow, he touched her cheek. "You're incredible."

"Eric..."

"Please listen to me. I think about you—about us—every moment of every day." The torment of his soul echoed in his gritty voice.

Her skin glowed pale blue in the moonlight, so lovely he had to taste her. Leaning to kiss her, she tensed. Moonbeams glinted in her eyes. She touched his face, and he hesitated, afraid she'd reject him again.

Instead, her fingers tangled in his hair, and she drew him down. The warmth of her body beneath him washed away his anxiety. His heart beat rapid as a hummingbird's wings, and his heart poured out of his mouth in endearments and wishes and wants. She didn't respond in words. Her hands slid over his back, down his thigh, and he knew. After removing his T-shirt, he laid it on the ground and lifted her atop it. This time, he wouldn't make the same mistake of rushing.

Crouched above her, he nibbled her breast through her tank top. Unencumbered by a bra, her nipples hardened beneath. At her soft gasp, every cord of his muscle hardened in response. He forced himself to move slowly, and dragged the T-shirt higher, kissing every inch of her flawless skin along the way. She lifted her head and he eased the shirt off, his mouth finding hers the instant it reappeared.

Unlike before, she took her time too, lavishing kisses on him. Opening to him, her tongue met his. Their fingers intermingled as they helped remove each other's clothes one by one. His breath warm as the night air on her skin, she wrapped her legs around him, urging him on, meeting his thrusts. Soft murmurs mingling with his. He wanted to imprint every moment in his memory. Her sweat-glistened skin against his, how perfect she was in every way. The way their bodies fit together as if fashioned from opposite molds. Unable to hold back any longer, a guttural growl escaped as he let his desire loose. She clutched him close, matching every movement. She opened to him as no other woman ever had, uninhibited.

When they lay spent and breathless, he rolled away to relieve her of his weight. He stretched his arm out to enfold her, and she snuggled against his chest.

Despite its awkward beginning, a perfect night. "Who needs fireworks with so many fireflies?"

With a gasp, she jerked her head back. "What did you say?"

"The fireflies. There are so many… Hey, what's wrong?"

She stared at him wide-eyed and open-mouthed, like he'd just revealed himself to be a serial killer. "It's you."

He ran his hand up her back. "Of course it's me." Caressing her, he waited for her to explain. "Hey."

She stroked his cheek. "All this time. It was you."

"I don't understand." What was wrong? Hadn't they shared something wonderful? Obviously she had second thoughts, very quickly.

Perfection had a short shelf life.

Chapter 25

Joss blocked the waves of confusion from her mind. Hearing Eric utter those words—the same words in her dream—shook her to the core. The ground rumbled beneath them. *"Stop it. Now."*

The tremors lessened, and she sat up.

Something had beckoned her to the field. A voiceless thought told her *come.*

Oh, she had, all right. In the most exquisite way. Remembering sent a warm flush through her again.

The man in her dream represented her soul mate, or so she'd believed. So she'd hoped, especially after Lydia's premonition. All this time, it had been Eric. So obvious, it had eluded her.

Eric sat up beside her. "You're not going inside, are you?"

She let out a breath. "We need to talk."

"Okay."

He deserved an explanation. How could she explain her predicament? Rubbing her arms did nothing to shake the chill. "You're the man in my dream."

"What?"

She didn't dare look at him. "Since I moved here, I've had a recurring dream."

"About me?"

"No. Yes. I mean, I didn't know he was you until a few minutes ago. You said exactly what the man in my dream says." She closed her eyes and braced herself. "Right after we make love."

"Incredible."

Her eyes flew open. "Don't you mean insane?"

No doubt in his face. Only love. "Of course not. What does it mean?"

Did she dare reveal it? How could she not? "Lydia said the man in my dream is my soul mate."

A lazy smile, and he reached for her. "I'm starting to like your aunt."

"It's dangerous, Eric." He'd think her truly insane if she revealed her family connection. And the risk it posed for him.

"The only danger is to deny it any longer. I can't sleep. I can't eat. All I do is think about you. About us."

"I can't let anything happen to you." Fear stole her voice, and it came out in a whisper. Every shadow might conceal some dark betrayer who'd report to Plouton.

He drew her into his embrace. "I'd never let anything harm you."

"I know." She cupped his face and kissed him. When his strong embrace tightened, a thrill shot through her, and she melted against him. His moans filled her ears, his breath washed over her like a wave, whispering her name like the wind through the trees, shaking her limbs. The tingle in her senses spread through her veins, burning. Eric was the cause and the cure. The only man she wanted. If she had to go through Hell for him, or fight the forces of The Underworld to protect him, then she would.

He breathed against her neck. "Don't send me away."

She held him with all her might. "Never again." Whatever it took to keep him with her, and safe, she'd do it.

* * * *

Sometime before dawn, Eric kissed her goodbye and she curled up on her bed, hugging a pillow. Until morning's first light, she drifted in and out of sleep.

Annie called to say she needed to pick up more coffee and would be a few minutes late. "We have enough to get started this morning. If the overnight people are coffee lovers, though, we'll be in trouble."

"I'll make a pot for them." She should hurry and shower before they rose. Small tasks required much focus, her mind overwhelmed by lingering sensations from last night. Limbs tangled, skin moving against skin, the delicious waves of bliss.

By the time people trickled downstairs, Annie arrived like a whirlwind. "I hope they like pancakes. I'm in the mood to make stacks."

Grateful for the diversion, Joss fed the three couples. Annie's instincts proved correct. Apparently pancakes were an antidote to hangovers, and they left satisfied, if bleary-eyed. Thank goodness her guests were away at a party much of the night, and hopefully heard none of the noises coming from her room.

A few girls who boarded their horses at the inn arrived with their moms, and soon greeted the new trainer. Lesson day. The riders' posts appeared smooth, heels down. The horses' tails fanned behind them as they cantered.

Grabbing the basket, she strolled to the field and began snipping blooms. Soon the lavender would be gone, and the chill of autumn would be upon them. No more fairy lights.

Across the road, a van drove into Eric's practice. What was he doing right now? He hadn't said he'd return tonight, but her heart told her he would. Was she being selfish, to want Eric, knowing he could be targeted for death because of her?

* * * *

Happier than he could remember, Eric went through the motions of daily tasks. Everything about Joss was right. Never before had he experienced such a grounding, life-affirming force. Fate brought her here for him alone. She filled his thoughts throughout the day, and he couldn't bear to be away from her any longer.

"I have to do something," he said, more loudly than he'd intended.

"Pardon?" Terry asked from the doorway.

Hell. "Nothing."

Warily, the assistant turned.

"Terry? How many more appointments today?"

"Three. If no emergency calls, it'll be a short day."

"Thanks." He knew exactly what he'd do.

After seeing Mr. Harrow's bulldog, who needed only an annual checkup, Eric stopped at the front desk. "If you need me, call my cell." He had no intention of staying home alone. The inn was more like home to him anyway.

Rushing through the breezeway, he laughed. Upstairs, he packed an overnight bag, whistling. After tossing it in the truck, he drove less than a mile and turned down the inn's driveway.

Lying outside the summer kitchen, Taz woofed at his approach, and after struggling to a stand, ran as fast as his three legs could carry him.

"Hey, boy. Glad to see you too."

Taz's single bark seemed to ask, *what took you so long?*

Eric laughed. "I'm a slow learner. But I'm here to stay. I hope."

Joss peered out the window, and her mouth formed a surprised O as she opened the door.

It bolstered his good humor. He probably should have called, but why chance another rejection? "Hello."

"Hi."

He silenced any possible argument with a quick kiss. "Have you eaten yet?"

"No—"

"Good. I'm starving. What are you in the mood for?" He whisked her inside the back door.

"The guests went home, so I didn't defrost anything."

"So we're alone?" He couldn't resist tasting her again. If he wasn't careful, he might devour her whole, but he'd rather savor her bit by bit.

Her lilting laugh sounded like angels, and he rocked her in his embrace. "I couldn't stop thinking about you."

"I know, me too."

His stomach grumbled. Loudly.

"Haven't you eaten?" She broke away and opened the fridge. "I could defrost a few steaks in the microwave."

"Those would take a long time to make, wouldn't they?" Precious time lost to cooking when they could be doing much more constructive activities.

She shrugged. "Longer than I'd like."

"I'm famished. Pancakes would be great. I've heard good things about your pancakes."

Her brow arched. "I'm sure you have."

The hint of a smile intrigued him. "I could help."

"All right."

The words had an airiness about them. An openness. And with openness came possibility.

"First, would you go put on some music? The stereo's in the front room."

"Anything for you." Another kiss lingered, too delicious to stop.

Her smile broke the seal. "Go on."

He hurried to the parlor. Pots clattered in the kitchen. He ran his fingers across the books lining the shelves, then the DVDs and CDs. He stopped at Bonnie Raitt. After popping it in the stereo, he practically danced his way back to the kitchen.

She glanced up from mixing the batter, face luminous in a smile. "Love your taste in music."

"One of the best slide guitarists. And the voice of an angel." Not as sweet as Joss's voice.

A nod, and Joss poured the batter atop the griddle. "And a strong female. Practically a goddess."

He stepped behind her and slid his arms around her waist. "Not compared to you."

Beneath his touch, she tensed, but smiled over her shoulder. "Why don't you start the coffee?"

What happened? Had he said something wrong? He wouldn't push it. "Sure."

She sent another stiff smile as he worked beside her. *Did I say something wrong?* Flipping pancakes, she said nothing more so he didn't either. He found the plates and silverware and set them on the counter.

She stacked three fluffy cakes on his plate. "Dinner. Such as it is. Oh wait, syrup." A quick trip to the pantry, and she handed him an unlabeled plastic jug.

As he poured it, the faint scent of lavender wafted up. "Did you make this?"

"It's my lavender syrup."

Picking up the fork and knife, he waited for her to sit before digging in. Savoring the taste, he nodded. "Mmm. The rumors are true."

She froze. "What?"

"Best pancakes I've ever tasted." His mouth closed around the fork, his smile moving as he chewed. When she stared at his mouth, his appetite shifted lower.

"Good." The word came out dreamily. Pink warmed her cheeks, and she smiled. "I'm glad."

"You'd better eat some. You'll need it to keep up your strength." He winked. "For later."

She bit her lip. "Eric…"

Oh no. He didn't like the sound of her tone. "Don't."

She met his gaze warily. "What?"

He grasped her hand, stroked his thumb across hers. Anything to keep the connection strong. "Please don't second-guess this. It's amazing. Don't deny it."

"It is. It's just moving so fast."

"Seems perfect to me." When she hesitated, he heaved a breath. "If you need to slow down, we will. If you want me to go home, point me toward the door. Just don't shut me out." He squeezed her hand. "Please."

A half-hearted smile, and she nodded. After dabbing a napkin to her mouth, she rose. "Annie whipped up some delicious desserts. White chocolate macadamia cookies or peach pie."

He gave a low chuckle. "Just coffee. Too many temptations."

"Black, right?"

"You remembered."

She handed him a full mug. "It's an occupational hazard."

For him, too, but he doubted he could forget anything about her. After she prepared her cup, he followed her to the parlor.

Eric sunk onto the sofa with an exaggerated sigh. He stretched one arm across the back. An unspoken invitation. Setting her cup on the table, she curled into the space he'd opened for her, and nuzzled against his neck.

Linking his arms around her, he pulled her closer. "So, no guests tonight?"

"None."

He closed his eyes and inhaled the sweet scent of her hair. Lavender. It wound through him, loosening muscles that had tightened through the day. Making him drowsy. "Are you as exhausted as I am?"

She stroked his hair. "Probably. Are you thinking we should go to bed early?"

He grinned. "Now works for me."

"You sure you don't want anything else?"

"You, Joss. I want you." Muscles quivering, he held her in his arms, wanting to crush her to him in an endless embrace. He waited for some sign from her.

Searching his face, her thumbs caressed his cheeks. The world inside her eyes held him captive. He'd do anything she asked. Until he knew what she wanted, he could do nothing. He knew she could divine his thoughts through her fingers. They swept along his lips, up his cheeks, over his ears and through his hair. Soft as a feather, her touch enslaved him. She alone held the key to his release, now and ever.

"Don't torture me," he begged.

Her whisper reached inside and tattooed her essence on his heart. With one word, she unlocked a torrent of desire. "Eric." His name carried his own salvation.

Scooping behind her knees, he carried her to the bedroom. Pressing his lips to hers, he laid her on the bed and eased atop her. One taste, and he wanted to devour her. Her scent filled his nostrils and traveled along his bloodstream like a potent, indelible potion.

When she opened herself to him, he was both powerless and pure, powerful and redeemed. Her legs entangled with his, her touch erased any other reality. He knew only her hands guiding him inside her. Her fingers digging into his back, urging him on. Her murmurings like a prayer and a wish, one he wanted to fulfill again and again.

Her body was the universe, the curve of her hips were mountains he scaled to heights greater than he imagined. The hardened rosettes of her nipples sustained and increased his hunger. He ran his hand along the contour of her arched back and ass like a sacred rite, and the mingling of his sweat with hers consecrated and claimed him. Her kiss healed and restored his heart to function again. It belonged to her.

This night, he knew, would leave her fiery brand on his soul. No other woman could satisfy him now.

Where his heart was once cold and dark, her warmth cracked it open and filled it with the brilliance of the suns through eternity. The light exploded in his brain and rained down on them like shimmering shards. Like the fireflies. The sensation so real, he wondered as he lay in her arms, if he'd hallucinated.

Her body melded to his, her breaths came so soft he couldn't tell if she'd fallen asleep.

"Joss?" he whispered.

She tilted her head on his arm, her eyes bright.

Good. He hadn't woken her. He shifted to his side. She looked so lovely, her hair mussed, her cheeks rosy, her lips full and moist after many kisses.

"What's wrong?"

If he spoke, it would come out wrong. He pulled her against him. "Nothing. I wanted to be sure I wasn't dreaming."

He wouldn't resist happiness anymore. He hoped she wouldn't either.

* * * *

Joss struggled against the emotions warring against each other. How she wanted nothing more than to hold him forever. How tortured he'd appeared in Plouton's heavy shackles in The Underworld. A worse fate awaited him here if she allowed this relationship to continue. *What about my fate? My happiness?* Didn't she deserve any?

Eric rubbed her back. "I know you're afraid. I am too. But I want more than this. The question is, what do you want?"

Thoughts spun through her head. *The one thing I can't have.*

"I want to spend every moment with you," he said. "Get to know everything about each other."

Oh, boy. "There's so much you don't know about me."

"Exactly. I want to know everything." Hope lightened his tone.

"No you don't." He deserved to. *Sure, tell him everything.* Her crazy family history would change his mind in a hurry.

Confusion knit his brow. "Of course I do. It's what I've wanted for a long time."

She'd feared his frustration. Instead, an approving calm emanated from him. He was right. He deserved to know. "You won't when you hear the truth."

"Nothing can turn me away from you, Joss. Tell me and I'll show you." The urgency in his soft voice flared inside her.

How could she explain? She didn't know if she could be a soul mate to anyone. Only after months of processing did she come to grips with her true self. Her family heritage. And, treaty aside, the death sentence it could mean for him should Plouton find his own loophole.

She couldn't explain this to Eric. Exasperated, she blurted, "You're too young for me."

He gave an incredulous laugh. "What?"

Embarrassment flushed through her. Remembering Iris, she took strength from the knowledge she was descended from a goddess. Even if she hadn't been, Iris was right—every woman should be treated like one. And act like one.

Mustering her confidence, she steeled herself. "You're too young for me."

He smoothed away a wisp of hair. His soft voice took her aback. "I'm sorry. I thought you were joking. We're practically the same age, aren't we? I think of us as equals. In everything. Why does it bother you?"

"Because." How could it not bother him? He could easily have any twenty-year-old. Yet hearing him say it aloud, she knew it to be true. Age meant nothing to him. And now Joss knew she'd live longer than most women to fulfill her role as guardian of the ley line. She'd very well outlive him. Lose yet another husband. It broke her heart already.

He cupped her face, tilted it up so she'd look at him. "Joss, you saved my life."

Shock took away her breath. "You're not supposed to remember."

He knit his brow. "Of course I remember. You brought me back to life after grief numbed me to everything good in life. We both deserve happiness, and that means being together."

Nothing would convince him. Except, perhaps, the truth. She could avoid it no longer. "I need to tell you something."

A sparkle of eagerness lit his eyes. "All right."

Oh, God. So unfair he should look even more handsome, his hair rumpled. His chest so inviting, she wanted to rest her head against it.

Instead, she gathered the sheet around her. "You won't like it. You'll think I'm crazy."

He chuckled. "Try me."

She took a fortifying breath. How to begin? "My family is...different."

"Don't remind me," he teased.

This wouldn't be easy. "Not like the usual quirks of most families. We have certain connections. Dangerous connections."

Confusion filled his face. "The mafia?"

She wished. It would be easier to explain, at least. "No. I am a descendant of the goddess Iris." There. The truth was out.

His brow furrowed. "Iris? I never heard of her. Is this some sort of sorority thing?"

She spoke in a stern voice. "You're not listening. Because of this family connection, I have the potential for great power. You can think I'm crazy if you want, but I'm not a witch."

"I never thought of you as crazy, or a witch. I never could."

"Do you believe me when I say I'm related to a goddess?"

He shrugged. "I sure won't argue. You've always been a goddess to me. And not because of your Halloween costume."

"You have to take this seriously, Eric. It could put you in real danger. *Mortal* danger. I know you don't remember, but it already has. In fact, I don't know how you survived."

When he pulled her tighter against him, she braced, waiting for the zap of energy. It didn't come. In fact, the opposite—only good vibes pulsed from him. Strong vibes, enveloping her, igniting her pulse.

He smoothed her hair. "Life is full of risks. It wouldn't be worth living if I can't share my life with you."

Her arguments melted away. The sincerity in his eyes, his gentle touch, stripped away the last of her defenses. "I agree, but—"

"Give me a chance. I deserve at least that much, don't I? Don't *we*?"

"I can't risk putting you in such danger."

"It's not your choice to make. It's mine, Joss. And I choose you. What I need to know is, do you want me?"

For a long moment, she gazed into his eyes, full of both hope and desperation.

She had only one response. "Yes." The single word released her from the past and unlocked the future.

* * * *

The next morning, as Eric finished the last of his goat cheese and tomato omelet, Annie tromped into the dining room. At seeing him, she halted, mouth agape. He lowered the newspaper and met her wide-eyed stare.

Finally, she asked, "What are you doing here?"

Carefully setting his cup on the saucer, he fought to maintain a straight face. "Second time today someone asked me. I hope it's not the new slogan for your inn? Because it's not very welcoming."

Annie's hands flew up. "No, I mean, yes, of course you're welcome. Anytime. You just surprised me. Can I get you anything else?"

"Thank you, no."

Dressed in jeans and a T-shirt, Joss entered from the hallway. "Morning, Annie."

Her smile told him everything he needed to know. No more doubts. They could overcome anything now. "I'm going to check on the horses. Excuse me. Have a good day, ladies."

With Annie still gaping, he wouldn't embarrass Joss by kissing her, so winked. The dog trailed behind him on the way out.

"Stay, Taz," she said.

He waited for the dog to totter off the porch. "Exercise is good for him, and I'm only going to the barn. I'll keep an eye on him."

"If you're sure…"

"I am." Sure about everything now. He couldn't repress a grin.

The dog's turn of loyalty surprised him too, in a good way. Most animals took to him easily. Taz displayed a fierce loyalty for Joss, not uncommon in a border collie, he knew, yet the connection appeared deeper. The dog rarely let her out of his sight. When Taz followed him, it was as if the dog was keeping him under watch.

In the stable, he stopped by each stall and spoke to the horses one by one. "You should be outside on such a nice day." Maybe the farrier was due. He'd ask Joss about it.

Whistling outside drew his attention. Taz glanced away, then back at him.

"We better go see." Eric strode to the driveway, where Joss stood by her car. "Do you know why the horses are in on such a nice day?"

She tossed her purse in the car. "No. Why?"

He liked this. Her leaving, him staying. Talking about ordinary everyday details, rather than fighting.

Joss opened the passenger door of her car. "Come on Taz."

"Where are you going?"

"Running some errands." She whistled and pointed inside the vehicle.

Taz looked up at Eric. He patted the dog's head. "He can stay with me. I have to go to the Millers' sheep farm. He'll like it there. Don't worry, I'll bring him home tonight, when I come back."

Glancing from him to the dog in suspicion, as if they'd conspired ahead of time, she asked Taz, "Are you sure?"

His tail wagged, and his open-mouthed pant resembled a smile.

"Traitor dog," she teased and drove off.

"Careful, or we'll both be in the dog house." Eric helped the dog into his truck.

Throughout the day, Taz shadowed him. Eric liked having the dog around, an inquisitive yet noninvasive presence. If he were to get his own dog, he'd want one like Taz. Smart and obedient, Taz only barked whenever necessary and rarely complained. By the time they returned to the inn, Taz lagged behind and flopped onto the floor once inside.

Bending to his side, Joss sighed. "He's exhausted."

"He had a rigorous day. He's probably starved."

"What about you?"

"Now that you mention it…" He whisked her into his embrace. "I'm starving too." He took his fill of the kisses he'd hungered for since this morning.

The grandfather clock's chime played, then struck seven. He glanced at his watch. Seven exactly. Time no longer seemed an endless prison. He wanted all the time the universe could spare. With her.

* * * *

In the morning, Joss was awash in happiness when she awoke in Eric's warm embrace. Still asleep, he nuzzled into her as if they'd spent every night together. Much as she hated to disturb him, they both had work to do.

Kissing him, she whispered, "Morning."

He opened his eyes, smiled lazily, and trailed kisses down her neck. "Good. I'm not dreaming."

She knew exactly what he meant. As realistic as her dream of her soul mate had been, awakening in Eric's arms was so much better. "I don't want you to be late for your appointments."

He whispered teasingly, "I don't have any today."

She eased away to look at him. "Why not?"

"I cleared my schedule so I could spend time with you."

Unable to hide her smile, she asked, "How did you know you'd spend the night?"

Rolling her atop him, he shrugged. "I had faith."

"Faith, huh?" More like determination. She wouldn't argue. Since his return from The Underworld, she could read his emotions too clearly. He'd broken through some internal barrier. She would too.

And she couldn't turn him down when he looked so sexy, biceps rippling as he held her tighter. She touched her lips to his.

"Why don't you call Annie and give her the day off?" he asked between smooches.

After a moment of trepidation, she agreed. "Good idea." If she was going to make this work, better if Annie not be in the middle of any accidental zappings.

She'd do her best to ensure there wouldn't be many. Last night's decision was the first step in taking charge of her life. Already, her existential equilibrium had evened out. Iris would be proud of the way Joss assumed the mantle of control.

And she'd never felt more like a goddess than when in Eric's embrace.

Still, she must make sure of his safety. Gram could provide her with some insights.

She waited until after breakfast, when Eric had taken Taz out for a walk.

On the first ring, Gram answered Joss's call. "Jocelyn? Is everything all right?"

Joss heaved a ragged breath. "That's why I'm calling. I have to make sure it will be."

"You're being a bit cryptic, dear. Can you be more specific?"

"I'm in love with Eric, Gram."

"Sweetheart, tell me something I don't already know."

How could her grandmother possibly have known? No matter, not why she called. "How can I protect him? I can't let any harm come to him." Losing him now, either by breaking up or by more sinister means, might kill her too.

Silence on the other end of the phone frightened Joss. "Gram?" *Please don't say it's not possible!*

"Calm down, sweetheart. Everything will be fine."

Not the time for empty platitudes. She needed proof. "How do you know?"

"Plouton and his ilk are bound by treaty. Plus, your mother and I have taken extra precautions."

Joss didn't like the sound of this. "Such as what?" She couldn't let her family place themselves in danger for her.

"After some rather intense negotiations, your mother's struck a peace treaty with the family who held a grievance against us."

"That's amazing. Will she visit soon?" Joss couldn't wait to hear all about it, and to thank her.

"I believe she will, dear."

"Good. Then I guess I'm the one who has to make our relationship work." A fact she had to face—she bore the responsibility.

"What's wrong?"

Joss gulped. "I'm afraid I'll screw it all up and lose Eric anyway." She watched him out the window, tossing a stick to Taz. Her life had finally blossomed into everything she'd hoped. She wanted to keep it that way.

"No one can ever know for certain, dear, but if you treasure him, you'll find happiness. Of course, not without some hard work and compromise. But as you well know, no success comes without those investments. Your inn is proof positive."

"You're right, Gram. Thank you." Joss would invest her energy in Eric, in their relationship. She couldn't wait to reap the rewards.

Chapter 26

If Eric ever looked forward to Thanksgiving, it was this year. Joss hadn't so much invited him to dinner as expected him. When she talked of plans, they always included him. A weight seemed to have lifted from her. She no longer guarded her words, and more importantly, no longer shut herself away from him. He'd never been so happy in his life.

Nervousness took root on the holiday anyway. As she bustled out of the kitchen, he asked, "Do I need to play it cool around your family?"

Her easy laugh reassured him too. "I think they knew before I did."

"What about Kyle?" He hoped Joss's son would accept him.

Arranging the silver on the table, her hand hesitated. "Kyle's an adult, and I expect him to act like one."

Expectations were sometimes a setup for failure. No reason to discourage her. "Anything you need me to do, you only need to ask."

She paused again, glancing up with a grin. "I may take you up on it. Later."

His apprehension and anxiety dissolved, as if she'd waved a magic wand to erase them. An airiness expanded his heart, sweeping away the weight he'd carried for years, replacing it with warmth.

"It's only fair." These past few weeks, they'd kept each other up late many times. He'd grown used to waking up in her bed, her nakedness against his, so warm and cozy. Almost too used to it. He didn't want to think what it would be like if they were to split up.

Footsteps on the porch dismissed his thoughts. Guests arrived one after another: her grandmother and aunt, the handymen Jim Turner and Charlie Fulton. A couple checked in, and soon after, the wife's parents joined them for dinner.

Mrs. Avery arrived with her dog. "Mrs. Gibson said I shouldn't be home alone today. When Mr. Tibbles was sick and stayed with Doc Hendricks," the matronly woman shot him a glare, "her dog fell in love with mine. But who wouldn't? Go play with your friend." She set the bichon frise on the floor. Its tiny nails tapped the floor on its way to touch noses with Taz. "They're adorable together."

Joss and Annie set the food on the side tables and called everyone to eat.

"I'll eat later with you," Eric said.

"No, grab two seats and I'll join you. After everything's set."

No sooner had he filled a plate and sat down across from Lydia and Gram, the door opened. Kyle wiped his feet on the outdoor rug and came inside, unwinding the scarf from his neck.

Joss and Annie emerged from the kitchen carrying reinforcements of rolls.

Annie spied him first. "Kyle."

Meeting him as he strode toward the dining room, Joss threw her arms around him. "You're just in time. Fill a plate and come sit." She pulled out a chair beside her grandmother.

Gram offered her cheek for Kyle to kiss. "Good thing you didn't get here any later. This turkey smells too good to save any."

"Even for me?" he teased, and kissed Lydia.

"Well, maybe for you." Lydia poked him.

He and Joss spoke good-naturedly, scooping food out of each serving dish. He took his seat, bantering with Lydia.

In sitting, Joss briefly laid a hand on Eric's shoulder. "How is everything?"

"Never tasted a Thanksgiving meal more delicious." He froze at Kyle's stare, midway to bringing another forkful to his mouth.

Her son glanced from him to her, his mouth a tight line.

"Eat," Gram urged. "Or no pie for you."

Stabbing his fork into the meat, he sliced, brought a morsel to his mouth and chewed.

Joss, Gram and Lydia kept the conversation flowing, with Kyle shooting assessing glances at Eric. Shoving back his chair, Kyle stood, and lurched to the serving table.

Flashing a smile, Joss followed. "I better set out dessert and start the coffee."

Approaching her son, she touched his shoulder. A questioning glance and jerk of his head told Eric what he couldn't actually hear. Kyle wanted to know what was going on. Joss leaned closer to murmur something and kissed his cheek. Head bowed, Kyle nodded.

Eric relaxed. It would be okay. Kyle might need time to get used to the idea, but he wouldn't fight their relationship.

After dinner, he helped Joss and Annie clear the table.

Kyle came in the kitchen. "I'm headed out." He turned to Eric. "I guess I'll see you at Christmas?"

"I'll be here," Eric said. *And every Christmas after.*

"Where are you going?" Joss held out her son's scarf.

"Out with friends." Kyle hugged her and yanked open the door.

Eric hoped Kyle would soon adjust to seeing Joss with him. Time, he now knew, was too precious to waste. He and Joss had enough happiness to share.

* * * *

Joss went to the kitchen to prepare the containers for the Second Harvest pickup. Gram bustled in. "Do you mind if I have some tea?"

"You don't need to ask, Gram. Unless you want me to make it for you."

"I'm quite capable of helping myself, thank you." Gram's smile widened. "Kyle will learn to accept Eric."

"Eventually." Joss smiled, towel-drying the dishes in the rack. Something had been bothering her since last summer. "When you said Eric's memories were erased, did you mean his emotional memories too?"

"Are you afraid his commitment to you is somehow linked to last summer?"

"I don't want this to be the result of some misplaced obligation, conscious or subconscious. I have to know he'd want me no matter what."

Gram's face softened. "No one can erase memories of the heart, dear. They stay with us forever. If Eric held you in his heart before, it was his own doing. You needn't worry."

"I need to know it's real." Her heart proved an unreliable navigator through the sometimes murky waters of love.

"Your own heart can guide you. You can see it yourself."

She couldn't deny the brilliance he emanated when near her, how it glowed when they made love, enveloping her in its warmth.

"You're a strong, wonderful woman. You have no need to fear." Gram sipped.

"Right. Because Iris is our ancestor." Every day, she became more and more like a goddess in her own right. Eric's belief enhanced her confidence.

Gram smiled. "You would be strong and wonderful anyway."

"Thanks Gram." Joss embraced her.

The click of heels signaled Lydia's entrance. "What's wrong?"

"Jocelyn needed some assurances about her relationship with Eric."

Joss rolled her eyes. "Gram."

Lydia clucked her tongue. "Why? You two are disgustingly cute."

"No, I have no doubt about him. I just want to be sure I'm ready." The excuse sounded more flimsy each time she said it.

Lydia took a bottle of wine from the fridge and filled a glass. "Don't let him get away."

She had no intention of letting him. "We're taking it slow."

Gram winked at Lydia. "There'll be a wedding this spring."

"No." A wisp of panic iced her skin. Spring would be too soon. "I said we're taking it slow."

"Of course you did." Gram raised her cup. "Don't forget the lavender this time."

A knock on the back door absolved her of the need to respond. A wedding? Would she ever be ready to marry again?

Only time would tell. Not Gram, or Lydia, or the grandfather clock. Joss would know when the time was right.

* * * *

People had stopped staring at them. They still gossiped, Eric knew. Before, it might have bothered him. Now, he could care less. A bubble of happiness insulated him from it. Being near her gave him a sense of satisfaction, excitement, contentment, eagerness. He couldn't wait to wake up so he could see her again.

Jogging downstairs the Saturday after Thanksgiving, he stopped short. Joss stood on a ladder against the side of the house. The sight of her sent a thrill through him. She must be hanging lights. A job he could help with.

He took the stairs two at a time to change out of his running clothes to something more suitable for less strenuous activity. To compromise the loss of his exercise, he ran to her place.

"Hey," he called. "Need some help?"

The smile she flashed warmed him more than his hooded sweatshirt.

"Hey." She climbed down, wrapped her arms around his neck and stood on tiptoe to kiss him. "You're not busy?"

"Believe it or not, no appointments today. Everyone must still be sleeping off their turkey dinner."

"You should take it easy then. You never take time off."

If things continued so well, he hoped to in the coming months. With her. "I'd rather be here with you."

Releasing him, she grinned. "You might be sorry you offered. I plan to go a bit crazy with decorations. I want this year to be extra special."

So did he. "Tell me what you need, and I'll do it."

She fixed him with a stare like she didn't quite recognize him, then spun into action. In less than two hours, the Second Empire Victorian looked like a ceramic Christmas house.

Satisfied, he set his hands on his hips. "What do you think?"

"I love it." Nestling into his side, she gazed up. "Are you tired?"

"No, why?"

She nodded to the center window. "I plan to put the Christmas tree there."

"I could drive you."

"You wouldn't mind?"

He gave her a quick kiss. "I'll go get my truck." And the gift he'd been saving.

In minutes, he returned to pick her up. As he expected, she knew exactly where she wanted to go. It ignited his hope she'd recognize her desire for him. No more doubts.

* * * *

The Christmas tree looked magical. Joss could think of no other word for it. The glass icicles, beaded snowflakes, wooden cranberry beads and the balls she'd collected since Kyle's birth never looked so wonderful. She'd never before splurged on a blue spruce. Or enjoyed decorating the tree so much. Eric took the time to help make sure every ornament was positioned just right.

They stood back to admire it.

"Oh, and I brought you this." He handed her a package wrapped in gold foil, with a gold tulle bow.

She couldn't imagine the gift inside being any more beautiful. "Christmas is weeks away."

"I'll leave it under the tree. We can open it Christmas morning."

Reluctantly, she said, "Okay," but the box emanated a strong presence in the room, hard to ignore. Passing through the foyer later, the gold wrapping paper glinted in the light. Curiosity got the best of her, and she opened it. Inside was a brass cricket for the fireplace. She'd mentioned it to him in passing, said she wanted one to bring her luck. She'd never imagined he'd paid attention, let alone find her one. Especially a year later.

Lydia's words whispered through the night. "A man will bring you a gift of luck. Wrapped in gold, as pure as his heart."

Carefully, she rewrapped it and set it back where he'd left it. If any doubt about Eric lingered, his gift erased it. Leaning against the chair, she watched the play of soft lights against the ceiling.

Bare feet padded up, and Eric slid to the carpet beside her. "Dishes are done. Can I get you anything?"

Laying her palm against his cheek, she knew the luck was not the cricket. It was Eric. "Yes. You."

"You already have me." He turned serious. "I was going to wait to give you this, but…I'm tired of waiting." Out of his pocket, he drew out a small black velvet box.

Her breath escaped her. "What is it?"

"I know you have lots of people who care for you. I want to take care of you. I want to be the one you want to be with. To tell your troubles to. To tell jokes to—it doesn't matter what it is you say. I want to be the one you turn to. I want to take care of you, Joss, as well as you take care of everyone else."

Words choked in her throat.

"I know this seems too sudden. Believe me, it's not. I've been fighting myself since the first time I saw you because I never wanted to need anyone else again. Now I can't imagine life without you. I hope you feel the same way."

"Eric—"

He held up a hand. "I admit I have flaws. Many flaws, but hey, no one's perfect."

"I'm not perfect either." Even goddesses had flaws. Sometimes fatal ones.

"Until I met you, I didn't know how lonely I was. I used to just go through the motions of my life. Then I'd wake up and think, maybe I'll see Joss today, and this incredible lightness would lift up my loneliness and I couldn't wait to start my day because I knew you were out there." He heaved a breath. "It's not enough anymore. I want to wake up and see you before anything else. To hold you sleeping beside me."

"Eric—"

Soft urgency filled his frustrated tone. "Stop arguing with me, Joss."

She grasped his hands. "I'm not."

Confused, he shrugged. "You're not?"

"No. I want the same thing."

"You do?"

Sliding her arms around his neck, she looked into his eyes, steely-gray but sparkling with warmth. "Of course. I love you." She could think of nothing better than taking care of him. Except for taking care of each other.

Chapter 27

As the music started, guests turned in their chairs, shielding their eyes against the sun. Joss strolled through the flower-decorated arch carrying a bouquet of iris and lavender. Sitting with Aunt Lydia, Gram dabbed at her eyes. Just beyond, waiting on the stone bridge, Eric shifted his feet. Nervous—a good sign. Smiling—a better sign.

The lavender had begun to bloom again. So had Joss's life.

With each step she took, the ground hummed in contentment. In her mind, she saw the veins beneath the earth. Like molten gold—flowing, humming, alive. Every plant and tree reached its roots toward the ley line, hungry for the warmth and nourishment. The line sent its power toward her too. It no longer panicked her. She acknowledged its tingling sensation, but let it pass over her rather than absorbing it. She halted next to Eric, comfortable she could fulfill her earlier pledge. And the pledge she was about to make now.

As she recited her vows, her heart soared over the moon. The rest of her might have followed if he hadn't held her hands, grounding her. Promising to keep her. This time, she wanted to be kept. She'd also entwined lavender in her hair. The sacred way to retain female power, Gram said.

Joss didn't need a talisman for that. She would never relinquish herself again. Through both words and actions, Eric had made it plain he would never ask her to.

Rather than struggling against one another, they were of one mind, one heart. When she told Eric she already had everything she could possibly want, he agreed they would ask guests to donate to their favorite charity rather than give gifts.

When Aunt Lydia asked if she wanted a reading of their future, Joss told her no. She already knew it would be wonderful.

Especially when Kyle hugged her before the ceremony, and said, "I'm happy for you." Touching his cheek, the warmth of his spirit vibrated through her palm. His guest might have something to do with it, Joss suspected. The tender way he looked at the girl whose arm linked with his filled her heart with happiness.

The minister declared them married, and Joss smiled up at Eric. A flash of gold shot through the air, and a gust of wind was a warm puff of breath, riffling through her hair, stirring the leaves in the trees, filling her with delight at Zephyrus's salute.

"Look, a rainbow. And it didn't even rain," someone said.

Beyond the lavender field, along the ley line between the inn and Eric's veterinary practice, a vivid rainbow glimmered.

Such a gorgeous gift. "Thanks, Iris."

At the reception, Gram kissed her cheek. "Keep some sprigs of lavender on the bedside table."

Lydia touched her wrist. "And when it's not in season, make lavender potpourri for your bedroom."

"Why?"

Gram and Lydia exchanged mischievous smiles. Gram asked, "Didn't you know?"

Lydia finished her thought. "Lavender's a potent aphrodisiac."

Joss couldn't hold back her own mischievous smile. "I don't foresee us needing it, but I'll keep it in mind."

In the Second Empire of Jocelyn Gibson, she would rule with love.

Meet the Author

Multipublished, award-winning author Cate Masters has made beautiful central Pennsylvania her home, but she'll always be a Jersey girl at heart. When not spending time with her dear hubby, she can be found in her lair, concocting a magical brew of contemporary, historical, and fantasy/paranormal stories with her cat Chairman Maiow and dog Lily as company.

Cate loves hearing from readers! Visit her blog at catemasters.blogspot.com or email her at cate.masters@gmail.com.

www.ingramcontent.com/pod-product-compliance
Lightning Source LLC
Chambersburg PA
CBHW020749250626
47155CB00003B/985